GOG'S REVENGE

GOG'S REVENGE

A Novel by TED DUNCAN

Printed in the United States of America

Packaged by Pleasant Word, a division of WinePress Publishing, PO Box 428, Enumclaw, WA 98022. The views expressed or implied in this work do not necessarily reflect those of Pleasant Word, a division of WinePress Publishing. Ultimate design, content, and editorial accuracy of this work are the responsibilities of the author.

ISBN 1-4141-0150-3
Library of Congress Catalog Card Number: 2004102831

Table of Contents

Preface

Gog's Revenge is the final book in the end times trilogy I started to write more than four years ago. It has been a long and rewarding experience for me, and I trust it has been for my readers as well.

When I first set out to write, I had planned to pen a single book, and that one a rather short doctrinal treatise. I wanted to address what I considered a number of serious misconceptions concerning matters of predictive prophecy commonly held by most Bible scholars. I only consented to put it all in novel form at the urging of my wife Marge. And now that it's finally over, I'm glad I did.

I managed to include my doctrinal reasoning in the form of a series of appendices (you will discover six more in this book, bringing the total to fifteen), but it is the story line that makes it all come alive. Following the action and dialog through the three novels allows the reader to visualize how all those doctrinal truths could actually be played out in the lives of real people in the future.

If you have not already read *A Snowball's Chance* and *Aaron's Rod*, and have no convenient way of doing so, be sure to read the introduction on the next few pages. That way, you will know what has previously taken place before you plunge into an otherwise confusing *Gog's Revenge*.

But if you have read the first two books, you already know that I take a much different approach to the doctrine of future things than do most scholars. I see the coming Tribulation as being a total of only three-and-a-half years long, and I see it as being followed by the Battle of Gog and Magog before the millennial kingdom actually begins. Some of you may still be finding those concepts difficult to accept, but don't abandon your quest. After reading *Gog's Revenge*, I believe you will see how it all fits nicely together, both logically, as well as biblically.

The two previous novels left you dangling on the precipice of cliffhanger endings, and I've received a lot of pressure from many, requesting I clarify the unresolved issues and not leave you in suspense again. Well, rest assured. *Gog's Revenge* leaves no damsels in distress at the end, and no villains in control—but no fair peeking.

Now that my journey has been completed, I want to thank those who helped me along the way: my good wife most of all, for putting up with my larceny, for I stole much time from her. Most of those countless hours I spent writing early in the morning, late in the evening, and on weekends, should have been hers. Also, she proved to be a constant source of insight and motivation whenever I tended to get bogged down or discouraged.

In addition, I must thank all of those, too numerous to name, who proofread my rough drafts, offered valuable corrections and suggestions, and encouraged me to press on. Without their assistance I would still be muddling along, blind to my many gaffs and oversights.

Lastly, I need to thank the good people of Calvary Bible Church who allowed me to pursue this quest. They not only allowed me to fulfill my passion to write, but they enthusiastically encouraged me to do so. In addition, they purchased my books for themselves and others, without which revenue I could not have continued.

And thank you, my readers, for investing all this time with me. I hope our journey together will prove to be as spiritually profitable for you as it has been for me.

Enjoy *Gog's Revenge*, but take your time; there will be no nine additional volumes to follow. This is all there is, so savor whatever richness you find as you explore future pathways with me. And, as before, I urge you to study the appendices carefully; they form the backbone around which the whole novel is assembled. I believe you will find them as enjoyable as they are informative, and may our good Lord bless and enlighten you on your journey.

Introduction

Our story began in *A Snowball's Chance* with Jamal Davis in trouble with the mob because his number-one-ranked UCLA basketball team had won the game he had promised to lose. His brother Marcus had set him up with the gangsters, and now both brothers were obligated to see that the defending national champions lost a designated contest in the future.

Collegiate swimmer Scott Graham and his teammate Tony D'Angelo were in trouble with the law because of the same game. They had lost money they could not repay by betting on the fixed contest, and they had robbed a convenience store to cover their losses. They had gotten away with the money, but several people had been injured in an unexpected confrontation with an off-duty police officer, and an elderly black woman had been killed. The two robbers escaped, but two relentless homicide detectives were hot on their trail.

The store that was robbed belonged to Saul Frieberg, the grandfather of Aaron Muller, a teammate and friend of Scott and Tony; the woman who was killed was Georgia Davis, the grandmother of Jamal and Marcus. The funeral was conducted by Pastor Bobby Davis, the ex-con-turned-preacher son of the deceased. His message about the coming of the Lord and the end of the age intrigued the above-mentioned young men in attendance, resulting in Jamal's dramatic conversion. Afterwards, they all convinced the pastor to lead them in a Bible study to further explain his prophetic views.

During the following five weeks, Tony refused to give in to the intense pressure to receive Christ because he loved his fun and freedom so much. The street-wise Marcus (nicknamed Snowball) agreed with him and resisted the pressure as well. Scott was under deep conviction and wanted to get saved for his own soul's sake, and also to please his sweetheart Candace Mercer, a Christian co-ed who had refused to become romantically involved with him until he became a believer. But he couldn't bring himself to do it because he feared going to prison for his crimes and losing the woman he loved. Aaron, a devout Orthodox Jew, was intrigued with what he was learning, but he couldn't find the faith to accept the Christians' Jesus as his own Messiah.

At the last session, Scott broke down and accepted Christ as his own Savior, and both he and Jamal decided they needed to go to the police and confess their involvement in unlawful activities. However, both Tony and Marcus protested loudly because they didn't want to suffer the consequences of their brothers' actions.

Tony informed the local crime boss of the two's intentions so he would put pressure on them and convince them to change their minds. When some of his goons confronted Marcus and tried to force him to tell them where the Christians were meeting, he refused, and was shot. He called and warned the others, and his father led him to Christ just before he died. Through his tapped phone, the gangsters learned of the believers' location anyway, and sped off to intercept and silence them as well.

In a high-speed car chase that followed, Pastor Bobby, Jamal Davis, and Scott Graham were gunned down; only Aaron Muller escaped injury. At that instant, the Rapture occurred and the stricken men were taken to heaven, and Aaron was converted to become one of God's chosen 144,000 to serve Him during the approaching tribulation period.

Aaron's Rod picked up the narrative at that point.

Tony D'Angelo witnessed the shooting and the vanishing bodies, but he was not converted. Instead, he was deceived by the convincing lies of the antichrist seen on television, and decided to follow the leadership of charismatic Constantine Augustus, the head of the World Federation of Nations.

The newly converted Aaron Muller assembled his family at his grandfather's store and told them they must flee with him if they had any hope of surviving the coming tribulation. His uncle and aunt, Noah and Sheila Frieberg, refused and returned home, but the rest of the family, plus his sweetheart Anna Berger, traveled with him up into the San

Gabriel Mountains, north of the Los Angeles Basin, where they were to take refuge in an abandoned Forest Service cabin.

On the way, Aaron's vehicle became stuck in a snow-filled ditch, and he used a large branch of a cedar tree to pry it out. Later, after securing his family at the cabin, he fashioned the limb into a sturdy shepherd's rod.

After he had led his entire family to a saving knowledge of Christ, the Lord transported Aaron instantly to the Israeli desert where he was joined by the rest of the 144,000. They were all given their instructions, and then most of them were returned to their places of ministry, but Aaron and five others were left behind to assist Joseph and David, the Lord's two chosen witnesses, in the Holy Land.

The young men joined with several of the priests at the temple square in protesting the blasphemous claims of Constantine Augustus who had called fire down from heaven and declared himself to be the Son of God and the Jewish Messiah. In the violence that followed, Aaron assassinated the antichrist and escaped with a large group of faithful Jews to the wilderness retreat of Masada. There, he defended them with his rod against the fiery military attacks thrown at them by the resurrected Constantine.

After securing the safety of those on top of Masada, Aaron and the other five members of the 144,000 were instantly transported back to their respective fields of service. Aaron saw to the needs of his family in the mountains, but he spent most of the following two years serving the Lord's people and combating the devil's hordes in the turbulent Los Angeles area.

Mark Robinson, one of Aaron's friends, and a fellow member of the 144,000, was commissioned to go to Washington D.C. and confront the president of the United States with the gospel. He was able to convert him and his chief of staff to Christ. Through his counsel, they were successful in convincing the USA, Russia, and China to throw off the antichrist's authority over them, and to fight him for their independence.

What followed were two years of intense warfare, famine, pestilence, and death. The antichrist and his forces beat down the rebel nations, but he could not crush them. He put to death millions of believers, but he could not coerce them into receiving his hated mark of the beast. Neither could he gain victory over the Lord's two witnesses in Jerusalem or over his chosen 144,000 scattered throughout the world.

After a little more than two years of tribulation, Aaron's sister convinced her grandfather to join her in contacting her Uncle Noah and

Aunt Sheila and trying to get them to join the rest of the family at their mountain hideout. But Noah and Sheila had sold out to the antichrist and betrayed them to Tony D'Angelo, who had been promoted to the rank of captain in the World Federation Army.

After he had personally executed Saul Frieberg, Tony disguised himself and deceived Rachel into thinking he was a member of the 144,000. She led him to the rest of the family in the mountains where he was welcomed as a friend. Later that night, after the others had gone to sleep, he slipped out and radioed for backup. He led the dozen soldiers who arrived to the top of the ridge in front of the cabin and sent half of them down to apprehend the unsuspecting occupants inside.

Aaron had found out about the capture of his grandfather and sister, and had forced one of the Federation soldiers to tell him what Tony had done to them. He then raced to the cabin site to prevent him from harming his loved ones, but as he abandoned his vehicle and sprinted to the top of the ridge, the cabin disintegrated in a violent explosion.

Aaron dispatched the remaining soldiers who attacked him, but he found no consolation in his victory over them. Convinced that his family had been murdered, and that Tony, the one responsible for their deaths, had escaped, he sat on the hillside, overwhelmed with grief and pain.

Having left out volumes of pertinent details, that's where *Aaron's Rod* left off, and where *Gog's Revenge* begins. Enjoy your read!

CHAPTER ONE

The Deliverance

The night was still and dark in the San Gabriel Mountains high above the Los Angeles Basin. The rain had stopped, but the thick clouds continued to filter out the ambient light from the stars and the half-full moon. Aaron Muller sat in the wet grass on a knoll overlooking the still-smoldering ruins of the mountain cabin that had just been blown to bits.

He had been too late. As desperately as he had tried, he had failed to arrive in time to save the eight people he loved most in the world. He knew his parents and his younger sister, his uncle and aunt and two male cousins, and his sweetheart Anna Berger had all perished in the violent explosion that had demolished the cabin just before he arrived.

Knowing they were all dead, Aaron's heart was breaking with grief as he sobbed, cradling Armageddon's huge head in his lap. The brave dog had been gunned down, sacrificing his own life to save that of his master, and was now unable to offer any comfort to the young man who grieved alone in the dark. Aaron's leg throbbed where he had taken a bullet through his upper thigh, but the ache in his heart pained him far more.

Tony D'Angelo was behind all this, and what made Aaron's suffering even more intense was knowing that he had let him get away. At one time, in what seemed like a former life, he had been Aaron's friend; but now he was the devil's own, a captain in the antichrist's World Federation Army. Tony had executed Aaron's beloved grandfather Saul Frieberg and had beguiled Aaron's sister Rachel into leading him to the mountain cabin where the Frieberg family had been living out the terrible tribulation period that had devastated the entire world.

Aaron knew that Tony had been trying desperately to apprehend him and his family because of the huge reward the antichrist Constantine Augustus had placed on their heads. Aaron had dared to defy the world's Great Caesar, and the despot was determined to make him, and all those close to him, pay dearly for his treason. But why had Tony ordered his men to destroy the cabin, killing Aaron's entire family? It just didn't make any sense. Tony would have needed them alive in order to use them to get to him. With all of them dead, he would have no leverage at all. Instead, he would have an enraged member of God's divinely empowered 144,000 dead set on finding him and taking revenge.

Tony D'Angelo was much too smart and much too self-serving to make that kind of a blunder. No, Aaron thought, Tony would never have intentionally ordered such an assault. What had happened then? Had it been a tragic accident? Or perhaps one of Tony's men had taken matters into his own hands and had acted on his own. That must have been what happened, Aaron concluded as he surveyed his surroundings, but his deduction failed to give him any comfort.

Looking around with his keen night vision, he counted six dead soldiers scattered along the top of the knoll. He had killed five of them, and Armageddon had dispatched the other one, saving his master's life. To his right, Aaron saw the lifeless body of the huge soldier he had felled with a rock from his sling, and beside him lay the M-16 rifle with the attached grenade launcher he had doubtlessly used to fire the high explosives into the cabin. He recognized him as the mobster who had orchestrated the assault on Pastor Bobby's car the night the rapture had taken place. The big thug had killed Aaron's friends, and had tried to kill him too, but God had sealed and protected the newly appointed member of His 144,000, and the evil giant had been powerless to take his life. In fact, Aaron could easily have killed him instead at that time, but he had spared his life and walked away. Now, as he looked at the distorted face of the dead man lying on the ground near him, he desperately wished he had bashed his head in back then. If he had, perhaps his loved ones would still be alive now.

But he knew he couldn't allow himself to dwell on that subject. If he did, he would surely drown in the flood of guilt and self-loathing that was already rising and surging in the back of his mind. He forced himself to think about something else. The big goon was only there because he was following someone else's orders. Tony D'Angelo was the real perpetrator.

Tony had sneaked away during the skirmish, and the one ultimately responsible for the attack had gone unpunished. But even if he had managed to kill Tony too, his loved ones would still be dead. The death of his archenemy would not bring them back. The young prophet was beyond consolation. He moaned uncontrollably as he rocked back and forth in the chilling darkness, mourning his loss.

How was he going to go on? He had suffered unspeakable hardships over the grueling months of the tribulation, and he had not complained. He was one of God's chosen witnesses, and it was all part of his divine calling. He had only one personal desire during those terrible years, and that was to keep his family alive. He looked forward to entering into the coming millennium with them after the tribulation was over, marrying Anna, and enjoying the abundance and blessing of God's kingdom with them for literally hundreds of years to come.[1]

However, that would never happen now. The future held no present promise for him, and he lacked any motivation to continue on. How could he find the strength to sift through the rubble to locate the bodies of his loved ones? Would he even be able to identify them? How would he mark their graves? It was much too painful to think about. But what *was* he going to do? He couldn't just sit in the grass in the dark all night, holding Armageddon's head in his lap.

At last, he decided he would have to force himself to go down the hill and complete the grisly task that awaited him. It would be more difficult in the dark, but he didn't dare wait until morning. Tony was bound to be infuriated about the death of his soldiers, and he was sure to be bringing more of them back up the mountain to finish what he had started. Aaron was not going to let the bodies of his loved ones fall into the hands of that vile young man and his murdering henchmen. He would bury them himself, and then he would prepare a proper reception to greet the evildoers when they returned.

"Aaron! Aaron! Is that you?" a disembodied voice rang out from the ridge on the other side of the cabin.

Aaron jumped to his feet the moment he heard the sound, ready to do battle with whomever his adversary might be. But an instant later, he

---

[1] See Appendix One for a more detailed examination of life during the millennial kingdom.

recognized his cousin's familiar voice. "Yeah!" he called back. "Is that you, Tim?"

"Yeah, and Steve is here too. Don't sling any stones or spears over this way, okay? We're coming over!"

Aaron was overwhelmed with joy and relief on learning his entire family had not been killed. And if Tim and Steve had escaped, then perhaps others had as well. Hope was instantly reborn in his heart, and he called back, "No, I'm coming over there! Stay where you are!"

Aaron could see much better than could his cousins in the near pitch-blackness of the night, and he could run faster; but that was not the reason for his decision. So filled with hope and divine energy was he, that he simply could not see himself remaining still and waiting for them to make their way slowly over to his position.

He left Armageddon's body where it lay and bolted headlong down the hill, leaping fallen logs and stands of brush. He sprinted past the remains of the cabin without hesitating to look around, and tackled the incline of the ridge beyond it without slacking his pace, his wounded leg responding eagerly to the task. He could now see the outlines of the two men standing near the top of the ridge, and nothing was going to prevent him from getting to them.

In less than twenty seconds, Aaron covered the more than one hundred and fifty yards that had separated them. He jumped the last stand of brush in front of Tim and Steve at full speed, and then attempted to stop before slamming into them; but his momentum was too great, and the wet grass too slippery. Unable to stop, he plowed right into Steve, who fell backward, knocking his brother off balance too. All three of them fell like dominoes and landed in a heap in a manzanita bush.

Unhurt and overjoyed, they laughed and cried and hugged one another as they extracted themselves from the tangle of the shrub's stubborn branches. It was Aaron who finally found his voice and spoke.

"Where did you guys come from, and where is everyone else? Please tell me they weren't in the cabin when it exploded!"

"No way, man!" Steve chirped. "We got 'em all out long before that. In fact, it was me 'n' Tim who blew the place!"

"What . . .? How . . .? When . . .?" he stuttered. Finally, he collected his thoughts and blurted out, "Tell me what happened . . . and where is everybody?"

"Okay," Tim replied, hugging his cousin again. "But take it easy, already. Everybody's safe and out of danger. Here, let's take a seat and we'll tell you all about it."

Aaron agreed, and they sat down on the fallen log Tim had pointed out, with Aaron in the middle, and his eager cousins on either side. For the next several minutes, Tim and Steve, frequently interrupting each other, alternated in telling Aaron what had taken place earlier that day.

Tim started out by telling how Rachel and Papa Saul had driven off in the panel truck that morning, explaining that they were going to gather mushrooms in the big meadow a few miles to the east. But they never came back in the afternoon like they said they would. Tim and Steve followed the tire tracks down the lane where they discovered they turned right toward the main highway, rather than left, in the direction of the meadow. They followed the tracks to the highway where they saw them turn west, toward the L.A. area, and to the unknown dangers that awaited them.

The boys didn't know what to do, so they retraced their steps to the cabin and informed the rest of the family of their discovery. Together, they all waited anxiously for their return.

At about eight o'clock, a Jeep drove up the lane and parked in front of the cabin. Rachel got out and hurried inside with the young man who had driven her home. She was crying when she told the family about the ill-fated plan she and her grandfather had put together to contact Uncle Noah and Aunt Sheila; and how they had been captured, Saul beheaded, and her taken prisoner.

She introduced them to Isaac Baruch, the young member of God's 144,000 who had freed her from jail and stolen one of the Federation Jeeps and volunteered to bring her home. He was dressed in shabby clothes and had long hair and a beard like Aaron, and he certainly talked like one of the Lord's witnesses. So, the family welcomed him and thanked him for rescuing Rachel and returning her to them. Isaac even joined in with the family in prayer, mourning the loss of Papa Saul.

But Tim had noticed when he was introduced to Isaac that the latter's hands were as soft and smooth as a baby's behind, unlike Aaron's rough and calloused ones. That raised Tim's suspicions, and he eyed the visitor carefully throughout the evening. He noticed Isaac's description of his ministry, though fluid and enthusiastic, was sorely lacking in specific details. And when he brushed back his hair, there were no little Hebrew letters on his forehead like Aaron had on his. Tim was almost certain that Isaac was a phony, but he had no idea what he was up to. He determined he would find out.

When they all went to bed, Tim pretended to go to sleep, and soon he was breathing heavily like Steve in the twin bed next to him, but he kept his clothes on and remained keenly attuned to what Isaac might be up to downstairs After about thirty minutes, he heard Isaac get up and quietly slip out the door. Tim crept down the stairs and peeked out the window to see him get into the Jeep. The newcomer sat there for a while, and then appeared to be talking to someone on his two-way radio. A few minutes later, he quietly exited the Jeep and walked carefully back down the lane.

Tim waited a couple of minutes, and then he too left the cabin, and he and Armageddon stealthily followed Isaac's trail out to the main highway. There, they could see his outline next to a tree, and the red glow of the cigarette he held to his lips. He appeared to be waiting for others to join him.

Tim whispered for Armageddon to be quiet, and they beat a hasty retreat back to the cabin. He was convinced that this so-called Isaac was an impostor, and that he had called for more bad guys to come and help him attack the Frieberg family. Tim didn't know who he was, or why he might want to harm them, but he wasn't about to wait around to find out.

He reentered the cabin, woke the others up, and told them to get dressed and pack whatever they could carry with them. Fifteen minutes later, they were all dressed and assembled. Tim had them strip all the beds, and they stored the mattresses, pillows, and bedding in the workshop behind the cabin. Then they headed off through the woods on foot in the light rain, carrying as much clothing and personal items as they could stuff into plastic garbage bags.

At that point, Aaron interrupted, "That scumbag who brought Rachel home was Tony D'Angelo. He works for the Federation, and he's out to get us so he can collect the huge reward Constantine Augustus put on our heads. He got away, but if I know him, he'll be back soon with reinforcements.

"But where'd everybody go?" he demanded. "Or are they still out there wandering around in the woods? And how did you blow up the cabin? Are there any more of Tony's men out there somewhere?"

"Whoa, man, not so fast," Tim chided. "I'm getting to that. Just hang on a second, okay?"

"No, let me tell him, Tim," Steve protested.

Tim was eager to go on, but hearing the excitement in his younger brother's voice, he reluctantly agreed, and allowed Steve to continue.

With his youthful enthusiasm and animated gestures, he told how, with Armageddon leading the way, the rest of the family escaped over the ridge to the east of the cabin, leaving the two of them behind. They went back into the cabin and disconnected the gas lines from the stove, refrigerator, and water heater without first closing the valves, thus allowing the cabin to fill with the lethal fumes. They were going to be ready to give a proper welcome to whomever might be paying them a visit.

They went back into the workshop and wrapped rags around the tips of two of their arrows and saturated them with gear oil. Making sure they had a butane lighter that worked, they then took their bows and arrows and climbed to the top of the ridge behind the cabin, sitting down and waiting under the protection of an old poncho.

Their wait was not a long one. In less than an hour, they spotted the outline of a solitary figure coming stealthily over the top of the ridge to the west of the cabin and scouting around before retracing his steps back out of sight. A few minutes later, they counted more than a dozen ghostly figures emerging into view at the top of the ridge. They lost sight of them in the trees and the darkness, but they could hear them talking softly and moving about.

Then they saw the outlines of six of them emerge out of the trees and quietly approach the cabin. Even in the poor night visibility, they could see that they were soldiers, and that they were all carrying weapons. Tim and Steve threw off their poncho and readied their rag-wrapped arrows in their handmade cedar bows, and waited for just the right moment.

Tim, overcome with enthusiasm, interrupted his brother and continued with the narrative.

"We waited until the soldiers had all disappeared into the cabin, and then Steve lit the rags on the ends of our arrows and we took aim at two different windows along the side of the cabin. At my signal, we shot our arrows at the same time, and both of them hit their mark. They smashed through the windows, and by then the place must have been completely full of gas because . . ."

Steve could contain himself no longer, and interrupted his brother, "BOOM! Man, you oughta seen it, Aaron! That cabin went off like a firecracker on the Fourth of July! The sides blew out, the roof caved in, and stuff was blown all over the place! I've never seen anything like it! Those troopers never knew what hit 'em!"

"That's where I came in," said Aaron. "All I could see was the demolished cabin and the hills full of Federation soldiers. I was sure they were the ones who blew it up. They even had a big dude with a grenade launcher. I just knew all you guys were in the cabin when he nuked it. I thought you were all dead. I guess I kinda lost it there for a minute."

"Yeah, I'll say you did," Tim agreed. "We couldn't see from here, but it sounded like a war was going on. What happened over there anyway?"

"Tony snuck away as soon as the action started, but I'm afraid the rest of them are dead. And I would have been too if it hadn't been for Armageddon. Where'd he come from?"

"I dunno," Steve said. "He must have turned around after he got everybody else to the cave, and then came back here to help us. He flashed by us like a bullet right after the shooting started. We heard him yelp. What happened to him, Aaron?"

Aaron choked up and told them, "Armageddon took a couple of bullets that should have been mine, and there was nothing I could do. He died in my arms. That's the second time he saved my life."

The word about the big dog's death hit Tim and Steve hard too. Armageddon had been with them constantly for more than two years; and without his help, it was doubtful they would have survived. He had been their scout and tracker, their guard and defender, and most of all, their friend and companion. Their jubilation turned to sadness with the news of his death, and they could find no words to express their grief.

"We'll bury him tonight," Aaron said, breaking the silence. "But what did you say about a cave, Steve?"

"Oh, yeah," he said, brightening quickly. "You gotta see it, Aaron. It's so cool. Everybody's over there right now. We can take you there whenever you're ready."

"Good! I'm anxious to see everyone, but we've got some things to take care of here before we go."

"Yeah, I know," Tim agreed. "Aaron, why don't you go get Armageddon, and Steve and I will start digging a grave down by the workshop. Okay?"

"Okay. I'll meet you down there in a few minutes."

With that, Aaron moved off swiftly in the darkness, hardly feeling any pain in his injured leg at all. He located Armageddon easily on the opposite hillside, but he left him there momentarily. He looked around and found four pairs of night vision goggles that had fallen from the bodies of the stricken soldiers. The wound in his leg had stopped bleeding, so he removed the sash he had tied around it and used it to secure the goggles around his waist. He was certain the instruments would prove to be invaluable for the family in the months to come when more and more of their activities would need to be conducted under the cover of darkness.

He decided against taking any of the rifles or the grenade launcher. They would be heavy and cumbersome to carry, and Tim and Steve didn't need them for hunting. And besides, he knew the survival of his loved ones would depend upon God's protection and their stealth, not firepower. They would never stand a chance if they went up against Tony's men, no matter how many guns they might have.

Then he returned to Armageddon and knelt beside him to pick him up. It would have been much easier to drag the heavy body down the steep slope on the wet grass, but the thought never entered Aaron's mind. The dog had been his friend, and one did not drag a friend.

He put his hands under the body of the massive animal and lifted its nearly one hundred and fifty pounds up into his strong arms. As he carried it down the slope in the dark, he thought of the words to a song he had heard years before: "He's not heavy, he's my brother." Mud and blood from the dog's body further soiled his clothes, but he was oblivious to it. He was performing a final act of service to honor his friend, and performing it properly was all that mattered to him at the moment.

When he reached the bottom of the hill, he put the goggles in the back of the Jeep and went around to the back of the workshop. There he found Tim and Steve well on their way to having the grave dug. The soft wet soil was yielding readily to the shovels they had taken from the shop, and Aaron noticed how mature their bodies had become over the past twenty-five months. He had brought two slender teenage boys up into these mountains, and they had grown into men. Like Aaron, they both had longer hair and beards. The men of the family had long since worn out their disposable razors, and had given up on shaving altogether; and were a long way from the nearest barber. Steve had just turned eighteen, and Tim was soon to be twenty. They were tall, strong, and amazingly seasoned for men so young. Their hardened muscles had the dirt fairly flying out of the grave. Aaron didn't bother offering to relieve either one of them, and in a few minutes, their task was completed.

They wrapped Armageddon's body in a piece of canvas the boys had taken from the shop, and then laid him gently into the grave. After they had replaced the earth, Aaron prayed and thanked God for giving them such a faithful friend and protector. He had no illusions about seeing his dog in heaven,[2] but he suggested that if the Lord ever did think about

[2] See Appendix Two for a more detailed discussion of the existence of animals in heaven.

allowing an animal into glory, Armageddon would certainly be worthy of His consideration.

With that taken care of, Aaron was anxious to see the rest of his family, and asked where the cave was located.

"Oh, it's about two miles from here," Steve said, pointing off to the northeast. "But it's less than a mile from the highway up there. It would be closer to drive part of the way, especially since we have a lot of stuff to carry."

So it was agreed. Aaron searched for a key in the Jeep, but found none. He hadn't really expected to. Tony was much too self-centered to ever risk letting anyone else take possession of something of his. He had doubtlessly taken the key with him, but that didn't deter Aaron in the slightest. He had acquired many skills in his struggle to survive over the past two years, and hot-wiring cars was one of them. In a matter of a couple of minutes, he had the Jeep running and the top down. While he was busy with the Jeep, Tim and Steve started carrying all the bedding out from the workshop, and together, they laid it across the back seat. Once everything was loaded, Aaron told the boys to get aboard so they could leave.

"Aren't we going to bury the dead soldiers?" Steve asked. "I know they were working for the devil, but they were human beings. Don't you think we ought to afford them that much respect?"

"No, Steve, I don't think so," Aaron replied. "The Federation troops have treated our people with absolute contempt. You wouldn't believe the stories I could tell you of how they've abused the bodies of those they've killed. I've learned to strike back, and I've never really had time to stop and think about burying those bodies I've left behind. And that's pretty much the case here too. Tony could be back up here again any time, and he's bound to bring a small army with him. I don't want him to catch us in a hole in the ground with nothing to defend ourselves with but a shovel. No, I think we'll do like the Bible says and, *'Let the dead bury their own dead.'*[3]

"When they get here, I want them to think that we got off this mountain just as quick as we could. If they think we left the area altogether, maybe they won't search for us too carefully. It looks like it's getting ready to start raining again, and if it does, it will wash away our tracks and scent so they won't be able to track us down. If we hurry, we might still be able to get away and cover our trail completely."

---

[3] Luke 9:60

Aaron got in behind the wheel, and Tim took the seat next to him. Steve climbed on top of the pile of bedding, and they started down the lane. They reached the logging road and turned right toward the main highway. After skirting the bottom of the ridge, they came into the clearing and pulled to a stop beside the armored personnel carrier left there by Tony's men. After the battle on the ridge, Tony had retreated back to the clearing and had escaped in the Humvee, leaving behind the larger vehicle in which he had planned to transport the Frieberg family back to face interrogation and eventual extermination.

They all got out of the Jeep, and while Aaron was hot-wiring the personnel carrier, Tim and Steve transferred the bedding into the back of the larger vehicle. The rain had started in again, and they didn't want it to get wet. During their task, they discovered the night-vision goggles, and each of them eagerly donned a pair. They were delighted with the results and enthusiastically expressed their appreciation to Aaron for his thoughtfulness.

Once loaded, they put the top back up on the Jeep, and Tim drove it down the road toward the highway, followed by Aaron and Steve in the other vehicle. They left the headlights off completely so as not to attract any attention to themselves just in case someone happened to be in their vicinity or in an aircraft overhead. On reaching the main road, Tim turned right and drove about a mile to the east before pulling over to the side and stopping. Aaron pulled in and stopped behind him, and they all got out.

"This is about as close to the cave as we can get on the highway," Steve said. "We might as well unload the stuff here."

Aaron agreed, and the three of them carried all the mattresses and bedding a short distance up the hill and securely wrapped it all in a big plastic tarp they had brought with them from the workshop. Then they covered the tarp with brush and dead leaves. It wasn't a perfect job, but it was fairly well camouflaged, and certainly could not be seen from the road.

"We've got to dump the armored truck," Aaron said, "and stash the Jeep. I'll need it to get back down the mountain."

"I know just the place," Steve responded. "It's just up the road a mile or so. Just follow us."

Steve jumped into the Jeep behind the wheel, and Tim got in beside him, content to let his younger brother drive, even though he wasn't very good at it. He had learned to drive only recently, and that in Papa Saul's panel truck on deserted mountain pathways. Aaron drove the larger vehicle and followed his cousins up the winding road until he pulled to a stop behind them at the edge of a steep precipice. When he got out and looked over the side of the cliff, he agreed with their choice. The drop off was virtually straight down for about two hundred feet, and then ended in a thick stand of tall trees. A tractor-trailer could be dumped over the cliff and into that cover, and it probably couldn't be seen from the highway.

"We can dump the truck here, and then we can stash the Jeep up a trail in the canyon just around the bend up there," Steve said, pointing up the road to the east.

"Okay. Let's do it," Aaron agreed.

Steve pulled the Jeep out of the way, and Aaron backed his vehicle to the other side of the road. He tossed his rod over to Tim and put the transmission into first gear. He opened his door and stomped down on the accelerator, popping the clutch as he did. The big truck lurched forward and accelerated toward the precipice. Just before reaching the edge, he shifted it out of gear, turned the ignition off, and threw his body out the open door. He landed on the graveled shoulder of the road and dug in lest he go over the side with the vehicle. He sat up to watch it sail gracefully through the air, and then to land with a thunderous crash in the trees below.

With the ignition turned off, there was no electrical current to ignite the gasoline from the ruptured tank; hence there was no explosion. The large vehicle crashed and rolled, but it did not burn. After the commotion finally ended, there was little evidence visible from the road that the trees at the base of the cliff contained the remains of a big metal soldier, killed in action.

After concealing the tracks as best they could, the three young men returned to the waiting Jeep, leaving the rain to erase what evidence they had left behind. With Tim driving this time, they continued eastward on the road, around the bend, and back into a narrow canyon. There, Tim drove off the highway to his right as the road made its turn to the left along the side of the hill. Then he drove the Jeep up a barely distinguishable track, which proceeded farther back into the canyon. After about a hundred yards, the track gave out completely, and Tim stopped the vehicle and turned off the ignition.

"This is as far as we go, men," he said. "But at least we are away from the road and out of sight. I don't think anybody's gonna find it here."

"This'll do fine," Aaron concluded. "I'll know right where to find it when I need it. Thanks, fellas.

"Now, where's that cave you were talking about?" he continued, already beginning to walk off in its general direction. "I can't wait to see everybody."

"Don't you want a pair of these goggles, Aaron?' asked Tim. "They work great."

"No thanks. I guess I don't need 'em. I can see fine. But bring them along anyway. Our dads will no doubt find them useful."

So, the three of them started out together in the darkness and the rain, their steps strong and certain, anxious to be reunited with their family, and confident in God's ability to continue to keep them through their dark and uncertain future.

CHAPTER TWO

The Cave

It was after three in the morning when Aaron, Tim, and Steve finally arrived near the entrance to the cave. They were wet and tired, but excited at the prospect of being reunited with their family. The actual entrance could not be seen, being completely obscured by a tall stand of brush. Even with his enhanced vision, Aaron would never have known it was there had not the other two led him to it. But gaining entrance was not going to be easy.

As they approached the stand of brush, a huge dog emerged from its cover and bristled. He was confused and defensive and about to charge them. Tim and Steve quickly removed their goggles and he recognized them, so he didn't attack; but Aaron was a stranger to him, and he wasn't about to let him approach uncontested.

"Easy, Millie," Steve said, reaching out his hand to the ugly creature. "He's a friend."

"What!" Aaron gasped, staring at the beast that was staring back at him. "She looks just like Armageddon. Where'd she come from?"

"You mean *he,* don't you?" corrected Tim. "And he ought to look like Armageddon. He's his son."

"But . . . how . . . I mean . . . where . . . uh," Aaron stammered. Then he collected his thoughts and asked, "How did he get here, and why did you name him something so stupid as Millie?"

"Well, he got here the same way all little puppies do, Aaron," Steve laughed. "You've been out of touch way too long, my friend. And we think his name is perfect. Millie is short for Millennium. We figured with his dad named Armageddon, it was only fitting.

"We'll tell you all about the dog and the cave and everything soon enough," he continued. "But right now, let's get out of the rain and see the rest of the family."

"Good idea," Aaron agreed, reaching out and petting Millie, who warmed up to him immediately, wagging his stubby tail. "Lead the way."

With that encouragement, Tim turned and worked his way between the brush and the solid face of the cliff. He bent down and disappeared through a dark opening in the rock that Aaron hadn't noticed before. Steve and Millie duplicated his maneuver, and Aaron was eager to follow.

As he looked down the narrow tunnel leading into the side of the mountain, he could see an incandescent bulb glowing softly about fifty feet in front of them. His mind told him such a thing was impossible, but his eyes insisted on what they saw. That was just one more question he would add to his already long list. But all those answers would have to wait. Right now, all he wanted to do was to see his loved ones again.

The tunnel was a long one and naturally formed. Consequently, it was rough and irregular, sometimes wide and easily accessible, and other times narrow and difficult to traverse. As they made their way into the side of the mountain, Aaron could see that pick and shovel work had been done in the tunnel to make it easier to pass through. With the added rock and gravel in strategic places, their footing was fairly consistent.

Millie announced their approach as he bounded ahead of them, barking enthusiastically, and expectant voices at the other end echoed back through the narrow corridor.

When the three of them emerged from the tunnel and into a large cavern some seventy-five yards from the entrance, the whole family was waiting for them. A joyous reunion followed, especially between Aaron and his family. It had been nearly a year since they had seen each other, and they were all overcome with emotion as they hugged and kissed one another.

Especially enthusiastic were the embraces between Aaron and Anna, and between him and Rachel. He had thought both of the innocent young women were dead, and he had blamed himself for their demise. Now he was overjoyed to find them both alive and well.

When the emotional reunion subsided a bit, Aaron looked around and was amazed. The cavern was huge, about a hundred feet across, and roughly circular in shape. Its ceiling sloped up cone-like and stalactite-studded to a height of over sixty feet in the center, and its floor was fairly level, with the exception of several outcroppings of rock and stalagmites. Three incandescent bulbs hung suspended from electrical lines attached to the rocky ceiling, illuminating dimly the entire cavern.

"Wow!" He exclaimed. "How did you ever find this place, and how did you get the electricity in here?"

"Oh, no you don't, mister" his mother insisted. "We're not going to answer any of your questions until you tell us everything that's happened to you this past year, and especially what just took place out there tonight."

Everyone else enthusiastically echoed her sentiments, and though Aaron desperately wanted his own questions answered, he reluctantly agreed to relate to them his own experiences in order to later have his hungering curiosity satisfied. They retreated to the living quarters of the cave where various articles of homemade furniture awaited them. When they all had found a place to sit, he began to tell them what had taken place in his life in the previous eleven months.

He summarized a year of struggles, battles, triumphs, and tragedies; leaving out most of the graphic details of his conflicts, and the cruel hardships he had suffered personally. He became much more specific when he got to the events of that night. He told them in detail about his pursuit up the mountain, his battle with Tony's soldiers, of the latter's escape, and of Armageddon's heroic death. He concluded with his reunion with Tim and Steve and what they had done prior to their arrival at the cave.

The family sat spellbound, listening to him recount his exploits, and begged to hear more. His mother insisted on tending to his bullet wound, but Aaron showed her that the bleeding had stopped and it was already well on its way to healing, so he politely refused any treatment. He also refused to talk anymore about himself until they told him what had taken place in their lives during that period of time. That made sense to the rest of them, and they agreed, electing Tim to be their spokesman since he was involved in more of the activities than anyone else.

Delighted to be selected for the task, Tim began to relate what had happened to them over that same period of time. Members of the family interrupted him from time to time when others wanted to add additional information, or when Aaron wanted clarification about something, but eventually he completed his assignment.

He told in general how they had fared over the previous year, hunting, trapping, gardening, gathering, and improvising to meet their collective needs. All in all, they had enjoyed a relatively uneventful existence, with a few notable exceptions. With a little help from a few over-zealous family members, he filled Aaron in on the details.

Shortly after Aaron had left the previous May, Tim had been out in front of the cabin when he saw Armageddon come limping out of the trees with something held in his mouth. Tim dropped what he was doing and ran to his aid. On reaching him, he discovered the dog was bleeding from many deep lacerations, and the small puppy he held by the nap of his neck was equally chewed up.

Tim took the injured puppy from the big dog and took it into the cabin where the ladies treated his many wounds. Armageddon waited patiently until they got around to him. He had been in so many fights, and had been injured so many times, that it didn't seem like that big of a deal to him.

In fact, he seemed anxious to leave again, and kept urging others to follow. It would soon be dark, but Tim was intrigued with what Armageddon might have in mind, so he found Steve and two flashlights, and the three of them started retracing the bloody trail back into the woods.

They hiked slowly a couple of miles to the northeast, to the base of Throop Peak, where Armageddon became tense and animated. He bristled as he moved cautiously between some brush and the face of a cliff. The boys followed and saw him disappear into an opening in the rock face. They turned on their flashlights and saw the tunnel leading deep into the side of the mountain. They followed their dog to the big cavern at the end of the tunnel, and there made their grisly discovery.

They saw several animal carcasses strewn about, and great amounts of blood covering the sandy floor of the cave. Among the dead were a large female dog, three puppies, and a huge male mountain lion. The sole living creature was a single puppy, savagely mauled and barely alive. From what they observed, Tim and Steve were able to recreate in their minds what had taken place there earlier that afternoon.

Apparently Armageddon had come across the big female Rottweiler mix sometime in the past, and the two of them had "fallen in love." They had mated and the female had chosen the cave as her den where she would raise her litter. The puppies appeared to be about six weeks old, and the boys assumed one of them must have wandered out of the cave and attracted the attention of the opportunistic mountain lion. The big cat had evidently followed the puppy back into the cave, and there had done battle with its mother and its siblings, killing most of them.

It was at that point, the boys surmised, Armageddon had showed up and battled it out with the lion, killing the beast and sustaining his own injuries. Finding only two of the puppies alive, he had taken the stronger of the two back to the cabin, and had been insistent on returning for the other one.

Tim and Steve carried the severely injured puppy back with them that evening, arriving at the cabin after dark. Try as they might, they were unable to save the little female. She died before morning, and they buried her little body out back of the workshop. But the male puppy recovered completely, bearing only the ugly scars as a reminder of his brush with death.

Aaron looked down at the big dog curled up at Tim's feet, a year old now and fully grown; and he couldn't get over the uncanny resemblance he bore to his father. He was nearly as big and his coloring was the same. His tail was only a little longer than that of his father's, and he wasn't quite as ugly, but almost. Also his many scars only helped to make the resemblance that much more striking.

It was at this point that Albert entered into the conversation and continued with the narrative. He told how Tim and Steve had taken their father and uncle with them back to the cave the next day to show it to them as a possible retreat site in case they should be forced to vacate the cabin in the future. Albert and Joseph gladly accompanied them. They had become increasingly concerned about the family's vulnerability at the cabin, and had been hunting diligently for a more secure place where they could relocate.

Making themselves torches, they explored the cave thoroughly, and found it to be ideal. It was remote and almost inaccessible. It was spacious and completely protected from the weather. And what made it even more attractive; it had its own water supply. At the very back of the cavern, they discovered a sizable stream of water cascading out of a crevice in the rock ceiling above. It formed a small pool at the base of the wall, and then flowed out another opening and disappeared into the heart of the mountain again.

Albert was sold on the location immediately. He and Joseph took it on as a personal mission, and that summer they worked on it every spare minute they had. After removing and disposing of the carcasses from the cave, they went to work on completing the project they had already begun. The old windmill left stored in the workshop was converted into a waterwheel and mounted under the stream pouring out of the ceiling in the cave. They made the necessary adjustments and connected the waterwheel to the small generator they had brought up the mountain with them, and it worked perfectly. The stream turned the waterwheel, which turned the generator, which in turn, produced the electricity.

The amount of current it generated wasn't much, but it was consistent and cost-free. Powering modern appliances was out of the question, but there was enough electricity to service several light bulbs and a small transistor radio. They strung the wire and turned on the lights, and then got to work on remodeling the cave to accommodate permanent residents.

They enlisted the help of Tim and Steve and together they hauled rock, sand, and gravel, and leveled the floor in the tunnel and the cavern itself as best they could. Then the four of them transported the lumber from the workshop to the cave, where Albert and Joseph constructed a latrine over a huge crevice in a wide spot in the tunnel, a privacy partition in one section of the cave for the women, platforms for beds, and various articles of crude furniture.

It had taken months to complete the work, but by winter, it was ready for them to start moving things over. They gradually transported most of their tools, and a good portion of their kitchen utensils, clothing, and personal items to the new location, but they didn't want to make the permanent move until they had contact with Aaron so they could inform him of their new location. However, the unexpected events earlier that night had forced them to move immediately.

As Aaron listened to the reports of Tim and Albert, and as he looked around their new home, he could not remember when he had felt the presence of God's love and provision so strongly. The Lord had indeed sent His angels to watch over His people. Only hours before, he had been despairing over the loss of everything meaningful in his life, and now, he was overwhelmed with all the Lord had done for him and his family. He was even comforted over Armageddon's death as he looked at his image curled up on the floor in front of him.

It was late, and everyone was tired, so, after a heartfelt time of prayer and thanksgiving, they agreed to try and get some sleep. The next day they would retrieve the bedding they had stashed back by the road and finish setting up their new home. They made do with the limited amount of bedding available, and soon everyone had a place to sleep. They were thankful for the fact that the cave maintained a constant 68-degree, year-round temperature. No one needed more than a single blanket to stay warm. Even so, it was some time before the last person drifted off to sleep. The activities of the night had pumped so much adrenaline into their systems, they found it difficult to relax.

The sun does not rise inside a cave, and incandescent bulbs do not change in their intensity when day breaks. There was no way for the tired occupants of the cave to sense the passing of time. Therefore, it was past ten o'clock before they were up and stirring.

The first thing Aaron did was to ask Anna to give him a complete tour of the facilities. Someone else might have given him a more comprehensive tour, but he really wasn't interested in all the minute details of how the waterwheel worked, or how the electrical lines were run. He wanted to spend some personal time with the woman he loved.

They held hands and leisurely walked about their new home while the other ladies prepared some breakfast. Behind an outcropping of rock on the left side of the cave was the men's quarters, so far with not much more than some sleeping platforms and some rods for hanging clothes. On the right side of the cave, behind some rocks and the privacy partition, was the women's section. It too was Spartan in appearance, but it did have a couple of handmade dressers in addition to what the men had in theirs.

In the center of the cave was a fire pit, constructed more for cooking than for warmth. The smoke from it drifted up into the high ceiling of the cavern and then dissipated into the cracks and crevices as it wound its way eventually through them to the surface. Around the fireplace were situated several articles of homemade furniture. They were not particularly comfortable, but they did provide a place for the family to socialize in their spare time.

At the rear of the cave, a simple kitchen was set up. It was close to the stream and the pool where water could be drawn and dishes washed. In front of the counter was a long table, formed from planks laid across two sawhorses. On either side, were long handmade benches, which would accommodate five persons each; however, one spot would remain unoccupied. Papa Saul's absence was dearly felt by the other nine members of the family.

After breakfast, it was decided that the women would do the dishes and finish hanging clothes and tidying up the place while the men went back to the road and carried all the bedding back to the cave. The rain had ceased, and they wanted to retrieve their belongings before they could be discovered by humans or disturbed by animals.

The hike back to the stashed bedding was uneventful. Millie exhibited some of the puppy that was still in him by bounding about, chasing birds and small animals, and barking with delight. The five men enjoyed the leisurely walk, which gave them a chance to catch up on the details that had been omitted from the conversation the night before.

The walk back wasn't as enjoyable. Not only was it uphill; each of them was fairly well loaded down with mattresses, pillows, sleeping bags, and an assortment of sheets and blankets. With the load divided, no one had to carry that much weight, but it was awkward trying to maneuver their bulky loads through the thick brush and trees. Yet they stuck to it, and by shortly after noon, they had their cargo safely deposited in a pile in the middle of the cave.

Each person took responsibility for putting his own bed together. Everything was divided and soon eight beds had been completed. Unfortunately, they were one mattress short, but Aaron insisted he didn't need one. He wouldn't be staying long, and besides, he had grown used to sleeping on the ground or floor, on a bench or table, or about any horizontal surface he could find. He would be fine with a platform, a few blankets, and a pillow, which he considered to be a luxury.

Later that afternoon, Aaron took Millie, who had developed an immediate attachment to him, and made his way carefully back to the site of the cabin. They stopped on the eastern ridge overlooking the area to check things out. Everything appeared to be as they had left it the night before. Aaron was about to descend the slope with his dog to look things over more closely and retrieve a few more things from the workshop when he heard the sound of diesel engines to the west of them.

He retreated into some cover and told Millie to be quiet. The big dog seemed to understand and proceeded to lie down on his belly in the grass with his head between his front paws.

They waited in silence for a few minutes, and then they saw three large military vehicles pull up the lane and park in front of the demolished cabin. Well over thirty uniformed men exited the trucks and took up defensive positions around the area, each of them carrying an automatic weapon.

Millie shivered with nervous excitement, but he did not move or make a sound. He had been trained by the master guard dog. Aaron could see so much of Armageddon in him. He reached out and stroked his massive head to reassure his new friend.

He looked carefully in an effort to spot Tony D'Angelo, but he never saw him. That was strange. Aaron was sure his arch nemesis would have returned to the scene of the crime to try to take vengeance on the family that had caused him so much frustration and loss.

A young lieutenant seemed to be in charge. He ordered the entire area searched by his men, assisted by two German Shepherds they offloaded on leashes from one of the trucks. The soldiers and their dogs did a thorough job, but the rain had removed the tracks and the scent that the Frieberg family had left behind, and they returned to the vehicles without uncovering any clues.

The lieutenant ordered some of his men to retrieve the bodies of their fallen comrades and to place them in the back of one of the trucks in body bags. He ordered the rest of his men to confiscate anything of value from the workshop, and then to set it on fire. Tony had ordered him not to leave anything behind that cursed family might find useful, just in case they had decided to stay in the area.

With that all accomplished, the troops were loaded back into the vehicles, and the small convoy turned around and lumbered out of sight back toward the main road. Aaron waited and listened to the sound of the vehicles driving up and down the highway to the west of them as the soldiers searched for any sign of the family in that area. Apparently, they found nothing of interest, because Aaron heard the diesel engines finally drone out of earshot to the west of him. The young commander had apparently given up the hunt and had ordered his men back to their base.

With them gone, Aaron and Millennium descended the ridge and looked for anything of value the soldiers had left behind, but they found nothing. At first Aaron regretted that he had not come earlier so he could have retrieved some things from the shop, but on further thought, he was thankful that he had not. The dogs would have surely picked up his scent, and would have tracked him back to the cave. No, although it was regrettable that he was unable to salvage anything from the shop, it was far better that they had all escaped undetected. They could make do without the few tools and supplies he might have collected, but they couldn't very well make do with dozens of enemy soldiers attacking their position.

The fire had reduced the workshop to a few scorched timbers and had pretty well burned itself out, allowing Aaron and Millie to approach it and pay their final respects at Armageddon's grave site and that of his offspring, killed nearly a year before. Millie whimpered, somehow sensing the sacredness of the two mounds of earth raised before him.

Aaron led his dog up the side of the western ridge, and after searching for a short time, found the sling he had discarded the night before. With it secured to his belt, he led his friend back to the cave, leaving the cabin and workshop in ruins. The buildings had served him and his family well over the past two years, but God had moved them on, and he left the site without regret, having no intention of passing that way again.

CHAPTER THREE

The Power Struggle

Aaron stayed two additional days with his family in their new home. His presence was not absolutely required, but he sensed it would be a long time before he would be able to return. The last year of the tribulation was approaching, and it promised to be even worse than those that had already run their course. Aaron wanted to spend some quiet time with his loved ones before he was thrown into the hell on earth that awaited him at the bottom of the mountain.

He spent some of the time with Tim and Steve, showing them how to use the sling, and helping them to make ones of their own. Millie was smart and strong, but not nearly the hunting dog Armageddon had been. The boys would need some additional firepower in their task of providing fresh meat for the family while their canine assistant developed his skills.

Aaron spent some of his time with his father and Albert, especially going over security concerns. They were delighted with his gift to them of the night-vision goggles, and put them to immediate use as they all walked through the labyrinth of tunnels that led from the back of their cave into the heart of Throop Peak. They were able to see fine, aided only by the weak illumination provided by Albert's penlight. Aaron assisted them in establishing an escape route that led to a concealed exit in a remote area about an eighth of a mile to the southeast. He also helped them run an insulated wire out through the entrance of the cave and up the side of the cliff to act as an antenna so they would be able to get good reception on their radio inside the cave.

He spent some time with the four ladies of the family as he helped them plant their garden after the men had spaded up a nearby, secluded piece of ground close to a stream that they had selected. It was a special time of laughter and fellowship for them all.

He also spent some special time with his mother and sister. Miriam Muller just needed her son close to her for a while. Aaron might be a courageous member of God's 144,000 to others, but he was still her only son, and she just needed to hold him and love him once again. Rachel needed him to assure her that Papa Saul's death and the family's brush with disaster was not her fault. Aaron reminded her that the Bible assured them that all things work together for good to those who love God and are called according to His purpose.[4]

But, most of all, he spent time with Anna Berger. They enjoyed long walks, and even longer talks with each other, usually accompanied by Millie who had taken it upon himself to be their chaperone and protector. It was the first time they had been able to really spend any extended time together since the rapture had taken place over two years before.

They pledged their undying love to each other and spoke of their future life together should the Lord permit them both to live into the promised millennium. After Papa Saul's death, gone were any illusions that the entire family was especially sanctified, and that they would all automatically live through the rest of the tribulation.

They kissed on occasion, but neither of them attempted to pursue romance. They knew Aaron's calling would not permit him to establish a romantic relationship as long as he was a member of God's elect 144,000. They were content just to be in each other's presence and to feel the embrace of their shared love. There would be plenty of time for romance and marriage after the hated tribulation had run its course. They just cherished the time they were able to spend together during this brief lull in the storm.

On the evening of the third day, Aaron said his tearful goodbyes to his loved ones, promising them he would do whatever the Lord would allow him to help secure their safety and well being over the coming sixteen months. He didn't know when he would see them again, but he was confident that God would keep His angels standing guard over them in his absence.

---

[4] Romans 8:28

He waved his final farewell at sundown and walked back to the hidden Jeep he and Tim and Steve had concealed by the creek three nights before. He found it just as they had left it, and after firing it up, he drove under the cover of darkness back into the evil city below. Derek Uptain was overjoyed to see his friend and mentor again, and not at all displeased to obtain a new Jeep in place of the pathetic "Town Car" he had loaned to Aaron in his desperate flight to rescue his family earlier that week.

Captain Tony D'Angelo stared in disbelief at the hideous creature staring back at him from the mirror above his sink. He didn't believe he had ever seen a face quite so loathsome. Gone was that impeccable reflection that had greeted him every time he had gazed into that magic mirror on the wall, assuring him that he indeed was still the fairest of them all.

Now, in its place, he saw a face swollen and distorted. Both eyes were blacked and its puffy nose was pushed over to the side. Its open mouth revealed swollen gums and four grotesquely broken teeth in the front. Besides that, there was a huge gash across the nose and left cheek that had taken forty-seven stitches to close.

No way did that wretched face belong to him, Tony tried to convince himself. The self-assured, devilishly handsome athlete had always prided himself in his striking appearance. It had won him favors with men, and oh-so-many favors with the women. He had lost so much since the disappearance of all those millions of people over two years before: his college swimming scholarship, his chance at a national championship and a position on the upcoming Olympic team, and a possible career on TV or in Hollywood. Those were long gone now, but his good looks had remained. If anything, he had become even more handsome as his features had matured.

But the ugly image in the mirror kept mocking him. It presented him with incontrovertible evidence that indeed it was the true reflection of himself. It appeared to stare back at him with the same look of disbelief that Tony had on his own face, but Tony could see the hint of contempt in its eyes, and the barely discernable smirk on its lips.

In rage, he picked up his shaving mug and hurled it savagely at the mocking image in the mirror. The mirror shattered and the image disappeared, but as it did, it spit glass back in Tony's face, disfiguring it even more.

He collapsed in anguish to the bathroom floor, holding a towel to his bleeding face. It was not the pain he found so unbearable; it was the shame. With his body racked in uncontrollable sobs, he could hear that damnable hissing laughter again, coming from somewhere behind the broken mirror.

Oh, how he hated Aaron Muller! He swore he would kill that dirty Jew if it were the last thing he ever did. He had caused him nothing but pain and misery ever since that rainy night back in the alley when all the craziness first began. He had eluded capture time and time again, wounding and killing untold numbers of Tony's men, and getting him into ever-increasing trouble with that tyrant Eli Rothschild. Aaron and his miserable family had just killed twelve more of his men and had eluded capture once again, robbing him of the lavish rewards Constantine had promised the one who could bring them in. But what was infinitely worse, it was he who was responsible for the butchering of his beautiful face.

Yes, the doctors assured him he would look much better in a short period of time. The swelling would go down, the blackness would go away, the nose would be straightened, and the broken teeth would be capped. Even the scars would fade with the passing of time. He would be almost as good as new. But almost was not good enough! He would never be the same! He swore anew that Aaron would pay for what he had done.

And he was faithful to his word. In the months that followed, Tony concentrated most of his considerable resources toward apprehending Aaron Muller. He hounded him day and night. He would never rest until that scum was scraped off the surface of the earth. At the same time, he continued his relentless search for the fugitive's pathetic family. He knew that when he captured them, they would lead him to Aaron. He certainly had ways of making even the most obstinate people talk.

The waning months of the tribulation were ever-increasingly torturous for President Dwight Honaker and Chief of Staff Ben Hiestead. They continued to grow in their Christian faith, and their witness was remarkable under the circumstances, but their world was continuing to fall apart. The insurmountable forces of the antichrist kept hammering away at their ever-shrinking defenses, and the outcome seemed inevitable.

Vice-president Lowell Renslow grew more insubordinate every day. He was insistent that the only hope to save their country and to defeat the forces of the World Federation was to launch a three-pronged attack at the very heart of the beast, wiping out his forces at his headquarters in Jerusalem.

Frankly, the strategy made sense to Honaker and Hiestead too, but they feared from biblical prophecy that any such offensive launched against the Holy Land would end in total destruction and damnation for the attackers.[5]

So, they continued on their chosen path, even though the end seemed hopeless. They met daily with Mark Robertson for prayer and instruction, and they used all the resources available to them within their ever-shrinking borders to assist him and the other members of the 144,000 in carrying out their missions. They continued to resist the forces of evil in their nation, and to support all that remained of what was good and decent. Though it seemed to them that they were losing on every side, greater good was accomplished for God during the tribulation in the USA than in any other country in the world.

In China, Chairman Chong Xu Wu, a short, plump man of forty-seven self-serving years, faced insurmountable obstacles. His nation was collapsing around him. Federation forces, invading from the east and south, had driven his armies farther and farther westward to the point that there was nowhere else to turn. The tribulation had taken a terrible toll on his people. War had greatly depleted his military forces, and famine had ravished his civilian population. What was worse; pestilence, beasts of the earth, and demonic hordes had shown no partiality, and they had destroyed at random whatever came into their paths. His once-proud land had boasted a population of well over a billion people; now there were far less than half that many.

Emperor Constantine Augustus of the World Federation demanded his surrender, but he was unwilling to give in. In the first place, he was too arrogant to admit that he had lost, and to grovel at the feet of that pompous windbag Augustus. Also, and more importantly, he knew that the self-proclaimed Caesar might very well spare his nation if he surrendered, but he was certain that he would not grant clemency to its leader. Chong had rebelled against Constantine after he had pledged him his support, and for his treason, the emperor would never allow him to live.

[5] Zechariah, chapter fourteen

And he was certain it would not be a swift and painless death either. He didn't want to think about the horrible torture that might lie in store for him if he were to surrender.

Chong, like most tyrants seem to be, was selfish and cowardly at heart. He would allow every citizen in his country to die a horrible death before he would be willing to suffer personal pain or loss. No, he would never give up. He continued to live in a measure of luxury and ease while his people perished by the millions all around him. As long as there was the slightest chance of survival, he would stay his course; and there just might be such a chance.

To the west were formidable mountains, and that was perhaps why Augustus had not come at him from that direction. But with no place left for him to go, Chong found it evermore enticing to send his own remaining armies over those mountains and to attack the beast in his own lair. The spirits of his ancestors, with whom he consorted daily, urged him to proceed with his idea. His military advisors agreed, and together they laid plans and gathered resources for just such an invasion as the final months of the tribulation ran their punishing course.

President Gregor Galinikov of the Republic of Russia was optimistic. He was a big man with thick dark hair and bushy eyebrows to match his heavy mustache. Though in his early fifties, he had more strength and stamina than any of his subordinates half his age. Though his forces continued to take heavy losses and his people continued to suffer horribly in the waning months of the tribulation, he could see his plan coming together—or should he say, Odin's plan.

The great Norse God of War had appeared to him when he was but a teenager, and at that time, the god had assured him that he was destined for greatness; someday he would actually rule the entire world. Odin had visited him periodically during the years that followed, giving him counsel when he faced strategic decisions. Of late, the god had been his daily companion.

Gregor's father was a Russian nobleman and a general in the army, but his mother was Norwegian. Galinikov was already fixed as his family name, and his father chose Gregor as his first name, after his famous grandfather; but his mother insisted on his middle name, Odin. She was deeply into spiritism and had experienced several visitations from the

God of War. It was Odin who had informed her of the time when she would bear her only child, and had told her that her newborn son should bear the name of her god.

His mother consistently called him Odin as he was growing up, much to his father's displeasure. The boy preferred that name himself, and only used Gregor when he had to. Finally, to make everyone happy, he began signing everything with his initials, G.O.G. His young friends, ever quick to spot an opportunity to pester, picked up on the obvious, and, just for fun, started calling him Gog. But as often is the case, the name stuck, and except for times when formality or protocol demanded, the highest office in the Russian nation was held by a man named Gog.

His mother had trained him from early childhood in the black arts of spiritism, and it had been she who had first introduced him to Odin. The great Norse God of War was, in truth, none other than a clever demon, capturing and manipulating the youth's impressionable mind; and he was totally taken in by his mutterings and his magic.

Now, at the time when he needed it most, Gog received precious council from Odin every day. It had been his god who confirmed that he should join in with the USA and China in throwing off the yoke of Constantine Augustus, and it was Odin who advised him how to conduct the war. Even though the Russian military had taken heavy losses and had been pushed ever farther to the south, his mentor assured him it was exactly what was supposed to happen.

When the time was right—and it would be shortly—he would be called upon to orchestrate a three-pronged attack on the World Federation headquarters in Jerusalem, and rid the world of Emperor Augustus once and for all. Odin assured him of a great victory, and that the leaders of the other two attacking nations would pose no threat to his resulting claim to the world's throne. The God of War counseled his student not to become impatient. The time was not quite right to launch the invasion, but that time was rapidly approaching.

Constantine Augustus, the great Caesar of the Revived Roman Empire, grew more confident with every passing month. His forces continued to grow in strength, and those of his enemies continued to diminish. He could see the glorious end coming in the near future. His stranglehold on the portion of the world he controlled grew continuingly tighter, and his domain increased every day, while the holdings of his adversaries and their ability to wage war continued to diminish accordingly. By the summer of the fourth year of his administration, he fully expected to have the whole world eating out of the palm of his hand.

Speaking of eating: his people were the only ones who came close to having enough to eat. He controlled areas of the world that were relatively safe, where crops could be harvested unmolested; whereas, the people of his enemies were constantly on the brink of starvation. And as time went on, the difference in available food would become even more disparaging.

In addition, his war machine alone had plenty of fuel. His armies fiercely protected his oil fields and refineries of the Middle East, and they were relentless in their attacks on those of their enemies. The Russians struggled to produce enough fuel for themselves and their Chinese allies, and their reserves were running critically low. The Americans were somewhat better off because of their large oilfields in Oklahoma, Texas, and Mexico; but they too would be running out of fuel if the conflict continued much longer. Victory appeared to be inevitable for the world's Great Caesar.

It was true; he had not been able to destroy the tens of thousands of young Jewish rebels who continued to defy him. But he had become accustomed to their presence. He ordered his troops to avoid direct confrontation with them, since it always ended in their own defeat; but rather to concentrate on eliminating all of their followers, at which task they were becoming increasingly successful. It could not be too long before the hated troublemakers who led them would also be eliminated.

He continued to be frustrated with the two witnesses who defied him in Jerusalem. But he took consolation in the fact that Emperor Marcus Aurelius, his ever-present spirit guide, assured him that he would be able to destroy them and all his enemies in the very near future. He rubbed his hands in gleeful anticipation thinking about that glorious day.

Even that gaggle living on the top of Masada no longer bothered him. They were isolated and totally unable to hinder his work in the rest of the world. He had them surrounded, and no one was permitted to come or go. He was killing obstinate Jews all over the world, and the emperor assured him that when he had destroyed all those who opposed him on the rest of the planet, he would be granted those maggots on Masada as his final prize. He looked forward to squashing them like the vermin they were.

Aurelius had assured him when he first appeared to him that Constantine was no ordinary man; that he had been supernaturally conceived of a virgin, and that Lucifer himself was his father. He was a god-man, and as such, he was destined to rule the world.[6] As he surveyed his expanding universe, he was absolutely convinced of the truth of the emperor's words.

[6] See Appendix Three for a more detailed study of the supernatural conception of the antichrist.

CHAPTER FOUR

The Bowls

While the world's leaders were planning their strategy for universal domination, the world's people were suffering unspeakable torments. The Book of Revelation predicted that four series of judgments would be poured out on the earth during the length of the three-and-a-half-year tribulation, each one more devastating than the one before. And the last series was pouring out its fury during that last punishing year.

Actually, all four series were pummeling the earth at the same time near the end. At the beginning of the tribulation, only the seven seal judgments were unleashed upon the hapless earth dwellers, and they continued to plague mankind until the very end.[7] Later, while the seals were continuing, the seven trumpet judgments joined in and added their devastation.[8] Then, although not described in detail, the seven thunder judgments added their punishments to the already staggering human race.[9] Finally, near the end, the feared bowl judgments emptied their awesome contents,[10] and all four series of judgments hammered the earth until the tribulation period was finally over.

Although some of the judgments were characterized by demonic activity, those imps from hell were not allowed to do anything unless

---

[7] Revelation, chapter six

[8] Revelation, chapters eight and nine

[9] Revelation 10:4

[10] Revelation, chapter sixteen

the Lord directed or allowed them to do so. To clearly demonstrate the fact that God was in absolute control, He used His two witnesses to announce the coming of each new judgment.

David and Joseph were especially called to act as His two witnesses throughout the tribulation period. They were clothed in sackcloth, and lived a John-the-Baptist-type of existence, dwelling in caves in the wilderness and living off the land. They surfaced from time to time to deliver some of the persecuted saints from the hands of Constantine's henchmen, and to prevent such attacks by launching some preemptive strikes of their own. But their main responsibility was to announce the coming of the succession of judgments upon the sons of men for their wickedness and rebellion against God.

Sometimes they would make their pronouncements from the marketplace in Jerusalem. Often they would choose the site of the Western Wall at the base of the temple mount. But usually they would make their messages known from the courtyard of the defiled temple itself. From out of nowhere, it would seem, they would make their appearance, declare the coming of God's judgment, and then disappear into the crowd before Constantine's troops could apprehend them.

Those troops were under strict orders to shoot them on sight, but they were rarely able to see them for more than a few seconds. On the occasions when there was an actual confrontation between the two witnesses and Federation troops, the witnesses always prevailed. Federation guns jammed, their vehicles exploded, walls collapsed, and various other calamities occurred to prevent the armies of the beast from overtaking the witnesses of the Lord.

There were a few occasions when it seemed there was no possible way for Joseph and David to escape the overwhelming numbers of Federation troops surrounding them, but on those occasions, fire actually came out of their mouths to destroy their enemies and to provide a means for them to get away unharmed.[11]

Although the two witnesses had no power in themselves to bring the judgments down upon the earth, the fact that they always announced their coming made them guilty in the eyes of unbelieving mankind.

[11] And if anyone wants to harm them, fire proceeds from their mouth and devours their enemies. And if anyone wants to harm them, he must be killed in this manner. These have power to shut heaven, so that no rain falls in the days of their prophecy; and they have power over waters to turn them to blood, and to strike the earth with all plagues, as often as they desire (Revelation 11:5–6).

Whenever the grievous plagues gripped the earth, its ungodly inhabitants, instead of turning to the Lord in repentance and faith, shook their fists in blasphemy toward God, and turned in hatred toward His witnesses who did His bidding.

During the last year of the tribulation, both God and His witnesses became increasingly unpopular among the followers of the beast because the plagues then began to increase greatly in both their frequency and severity. As their angels revealed to Joseph and David the details of the plagues about to be released upon the earth, they quickly made their public appearance and announced them before the world of men. Sometimes a news correspondent who happened to be in the area captured their messages directly on camera. More often, the messages were relayed by eyewitnesses to members of the press who, in turn, were eager to relay them through their networks to the rest of the world.

It was a chilly November morning when David stood forth suddenly from the crowd standing in long lines to consult with Caesar's image in the temple. He yelled to be heard, and announced that the seven last plagues were about to be unleashed; seven angels would pour out in succession the contents of their bowls containing the ultimate wrath of God. The first of the seven plagues would bring loathsome boils upon those who bore the mark of the beast.

The next day, the angel carrying the first bowl emptied its contents upon the earth, and the winds carried a contagious virus to the far corners of the globe. The pestilence caused people to become infected and to break out in huge, throbbing, oozing boils; the pain and suffering from which caused those stricken to go temporarily out of their minds. Yet, strangely, it attacked only those who had received the mark of the beast. Those who had sold their souls to the devil got a foretaste of the agony that awaited them in hell.[12]

In the Los Angeles area, Aaron Muller continued his ministry, undaunted by the evidence of disease all around him. He and his people were not affected by the pestilence, but virtually everyone else seemed to be. Because of that fact, the saints were actually granted a brief reprieve from the relentless attacks staged against them. Their persecutors were either incapacitated by their loathsome sores, or they were

[12] Then I heard a loud voice from the temple saying to the seven angels, "Go and pour out the bowls of the wrath of God on the earth." So the first went and poured out his bowl upon the earth, and a foul and loathsome sore came upon the men who had the mark of the beast and those who worshiped his image (Revelation 16:1–2).

cowering in sealed rooms in hopes of escaping contamination. In either case, the beleaguered faithful were able to move about unmolested.

They used that precious time to scavenge and barter for food and supplies, to fortify their positions or to find safer places to hide, but especially, they used that window of opportunity to evangelize those poor souls who were still in no man's land.

There were those who had received the devil's mark and were hopelessly lost and beyond conversion. They suffered the outpouring of God's wrath, but at least they were able to escape the horrible persecution spewed out by the antichrist. Then there were those who had received Christ and were eternally saved and were in no need of conversion. Consequently, though they suffered unspeakable torments at the hands of evil men, they escaped the Lord's specific judgments on the ungodly. However, there were still multitudes that had refused the mark of the beast, but had not yet received the gospel message. Those poor souls caught it from both directions. The beast and his underlings persecuted them mercilessly, and they also suffered indirectly from the plagues the Lord poured out on the world of the ungodly.

It was to those people that Aaron and his colleagues went. They found them, cowering, suffering, despairing, and begging for deliverance. Seeing the unspeakable suffering of the ungodly around them, they were ready, at last, to listen to the gospel message that they had avoided before the rapture. It would not only bring salvation to their souls, it would keep them immune from the pestilence God had poured out on the followers of the beast.

As the word began to spread, thousands came crawling out of hiding and began to experience deliverance and hope for the first time in many long and torturous years. More people came to Christ at that time than at any other except during those initial months when the tribulation first began.

Tony D'Angelo knew what was going on in his district, but he was powerless to do anything about it. His superiors screamed at him, and he screamed at his underlings, but to no avail. Nearly all his men were suffering from the horrible boils, and were incapacitated. They did not have the strength to police their territories even if they had wanted to do so. Every one of them would gladly have accepted a death sentence rather that go out in those streets and risk further exposure to that damnable plague.

In spite of all the precautions Tony had taken to protect himself, he too had been infected by the infestation, and his own body was racked with excruciatingly painful and disfiguring sores. He ordered all mirrors removed from his room, as he could not bear to look at his hideous reflection. His appearance had been repulsive to him before, but now it was downright nauseating. He could only languish in his quarters and suffer pitifully, begging whatever gods there might be to make it all go away. There was nothing he was able or willing to do to prevent the lawless evangelism from taking place within his jurisdiction.

The loathsome sores that infested the Los Angeles area attacked the ungodly on every continent in the world. The boils themselves did not actually kill many people—only those already nearly dead from disease or malnutrition—but multitudes died as a result of them nonetheless. They were virtually without hope already, and the excruciating pain of the plague simply pushed them over the edge. They took their own lives in the vain hope of finding some relief.

Although most of the world was devastated by the plague, there was one area where it did not spread. The peoples of the far north were spared it ravages. The infestation occurred during the winter, and the temperatures in those far northern latitudes were too cold for the virus to thrive. But the ungodly in that region were destined to experience yet a different form of suffering.

In February, Joseph stood before the Western Wall in Jerusalem and warned the inhabitants of the northern latitudes that the second bowl of wrath was about to be poured out into their waters. And shortly thereafter, the second angel poured out the contents of his bowl into the oceans of the north. Actually, the contents of that bowl arrived in the form of two mighty asteroids, impacting the Atlantic Ocean off the southern coast of Greenland, and the Pacific near the middle of the Bering Strait. The bodies of the asteroids were composed of a water-soluble material, which dissolved and turned the seas into a sticky liquid, the color and consistency of blood.

The currents swirled and carried the contamination in all directions, turning the waters crimson throughout the northern latitudes. The contamination was not only unsightly; it was deadly poisonous. Every living creature in the northern seas suffocated and died. Their bloated and rotting corpses floated on the surface of the water, further adding to the stench and defilement.[13]

[13] Then the second angel poured out his bowl on the sea, and it became blood as a dead man; and every living creature in the sea died (Revelation 16:3).

Those who derived their living from the sea were devastated. The waters that once teemed with life now brought forth nothing but corruption and death. People who were already struggling to survive now starved by the millions.

The ocean currents carried the vile contamination southeast from Greenland and into northern Europe, devouring Iceland along the way. The North Sea became defiled, and the inhabitants of the British Isles struggled to survive its stranglehold. The red death surged eastward into the Baltic Sea, ravaging the coasts of Scandinavia along the way.

Kenneth Weinman's life in Edinburgh, Scotland became more tenuous with every passing day. As a member of God's 144,000, he was already a marked man with a price on his head, but with the arrival of this new plague, he became the object of even greater harassment. Interestingly, one would think that the plagues of the tribulation would cause unbelievers to repent and cry out to God for mercy, but just the opposite was true. It caused the ungodly to blaspheme His holy name even more, and to vent their wrath on all who served Him.

Great Britain had been a solid ally of the United States of America in the past, but not since it joined the U.S.E. and the World Federation of Nations. It was now firmly in the grasp of Caesar Constantine Augustus, and it devoted all its resources to promoting his causes and defeating his enemies. The Prime Minister was one of Constantine's most devoted followers, and he was especially ruthless toward those Jewish rebels who continued to oppose his lord and master.

Nonetheless, Ken was undaunted. He continued to do what he had to do to survive and to carry out his divine mission. He narrowly escaped death on numerous occasions, eluding his pursuers when he could, and destroying them when he was left with no means of escape. Angels watched over him and delivered him, for which he was eternally grateful; but his converts were not so blessed. Every increase in persecution meant greater numbers of his believing countrymen lost their heads to Constantine's henchmen. Those who survived were those who abandoned the cities and the polluted seacoasts and fled to the mountains, the area where Ken had provided a place of refuge for his own converted family. There, the banished faithful existed, eking out a living in the highlands, as did their Scottish ancestors before them who fled from the wrath of the English kings.

Ivan Feldsin did everything he could to make preparations for when the plague hit St. Petersburg. The news services warned that the approaching red death that killed everything in its path was sweeping eastward through the Baltic Sea and up the Gulf of Finland. Following the leading of the Lord, Ivan and another member of the 144,000 led a band of believers to commandeer two fishing boats under the cover of darkness and they fished through the night. Unseen angels herded the schools of fish into their nets, and the boats' storage compartments were full by 3:00 A.M.

Barely managing to outrun the advancing plague, they ran their heavy boats up the Neva River to the city of Tosno, where they offloaded their precious cargo onto waiting trucks, which they drove inland to a huge silo near the city of Vyritsa. There, Ivan's family and hundreds of other believers gathered to preserve the catch in preparation for the lean weeks to come.

They smoked fish, dried fish, canned fish, and ate fish until both trucks were empty. Nothing went to waste. Their precious stores were divided among them and they retreated back into hiding. Though all would grow weary of eating little other than fish, at least they had food. Thousands of unprepared citizens around them perished when the seas turned to blood and choked the life out of everything living in them.

Driven by hunger, many ate the carcasses of the dead animals floating in the foul waters of the sea; and though they did not die of starvation, they were no better off than those who did. The contaminated meat poisoned all who ate it, and those poor souls died horrible deaths, convulsing and writhing in agony.

Gregor Galinikov hated to see his people dying, not because he actually cared for any of them, but because their deaths depleted the numbers of men Russia could send into battle. When the time was right to invade Israel and destroy Constantine Augustus once and for all, he would need all the men he could get. He distributed what food reserves were available, and prayed to Odin that the plague would pass quickly, and fish would again fill the sea.

Eventually, the plague ended, and after months, life gradually began to return to the waters of the northern latitudes, but not before millions more had suffered and died. The second bowl of wrath had brought great devastation and a warning of what punishment lay ahead for the ungodly, but tragically, they continued on in their evil ways and blasphemed the Lord even more.

The southern hemisphere did not escape the wrath of God. Though spared the devastation of the second bowl, that region of the world was hit hardest by the third plague. David announced its arrival in the late spring, and shortly thereafter, yet another angel emptied the contents of his third bowl into the equatorial rivers.

During the tribulation, the rivers of Asia, Africa, and South America teemed with flesh-eating fish. So many human beings and animals died during those horrible years, their bodies could not possibly be buried. They were simply thrown into the rivers and tributaries, where the piranhas and related fish devoured them. The pollution and contamination was kept down by such a practice, but it also caused the population of those fish to skyrocket. By the end of the third year, the tropical rivers were bloated with an enormous glut of flesh eaters.

Critical mass was reached in June of the fourth year when the swollen rivers became absolutely choked with fish. They had eaten every other living thing in the waters, as well as every dead body that had been thrown into them, and still they were ravenous. It was at that time the angel received his instructions from heaven, and he emptied his bowl into the fated rivers.

Almost instantly, the piranhas turned on each other and began to devour one another. The rivers fairly boiled as the hunger-crazed carnivores turned the waters suddenly into blood.[14]

Although many other rivers were similarly affected, the Amazon was by far the worst. The massive river system is the largest on the planet, draining over half of the South American continent. The mouth of the Amazon is well over a mile wide, and its volume is so vast it pushes fresh water a hundred miles out into the Atlantic Ocean. But on that day, the fresh water instantly turned red from the blood of billions of fish, torn to shreds by one another.

Those who could, avoided the polluted rivers altogether, finding water from the few alternate resources, but tragically, millions of people

[14] Then the third angel poured out his bowl on the rivers and springs of water, and they became blood. And I heard the angel of the waters saying: "You are righteous, O Lord, the One who is and who was and who is to be, because You have judged these things. For they have shed the blood of saints and prophets, and You have given them blood to drink. For it is their due." (Revelation 16:4–6).

were left with no place else to go. They boiled it, they strained it, they filtered it as best they could, but they could not eradicate the bloody contamination from the water. Disease spread rapidly, and the already staggering death toll rose dramatically.

President Gabriel Eichler fumed and raged. Caesar Augustus was counting on Brazil to produce much of the Federation's massive food supply, and after his country was admitted into the inner circle of the ten ruling nations, Eichler was determined not to let his idol down. He had enslaved his own people and forced them into labor camps to work the soil and to produce the food. But now such production had virtually come to a standstill.

Eichler was convinced the despicable Jews were somehow responsible. His grandfather had been an S.S. officer in Hitler's Third Reich before fleeing Germany at the end of World War II and emigrating to Brazil. From him, Eichler had acquired the ruthless ability to traffic in human life, and an unquenchable hatred for the Jews.

He had persecuted and killed them ever since he came to power shortly before the sudden disappearance of millions more than three years earlier, but now it became an obsession with him. He made it the number one priority of his sizable army to hunt down and destroy every Jew in Brazil.

Julio Otero, along with several others of God's 144,000, operated an underground railroad, smuggling fellow Jews and other people of faith out of Rio De Janeiro and other large cities, and into the rain forests upcountry, where they had at least some hope of survival. It was into the vast jungles of the Amazon Basin that Julio had prepared a place of refuge for his own family just before the tribulation began. There, the newcomers came by the multitudes. They could, for a time, live off the land and catch rainwater to drink, hoping against hope that they would be able to continue to elude Eichler's troops for the final three months of the tribulation.

CHAPTER FIVE

The Heat

Toward the end of June, Joseph's angel informed him that the fourth plague was about to begin. In response to the message, Joseph stood on top of the Mount of Olives in front of an unsteady camera, held in the trembling hands of a network crewman, and told the world to prepare to experience a foretaste of the fires of hell, because God was about to turn up the heat.

On the first day of July, the fourth angel poured the contents of his bowl upon the sun, and it responded with massive solar flares unlike anything recorded since the day of its creation, radiating unprecedented heat in all directions. The bombardment from outer space struck the already-languishing earth with the force of a blast furnace. Except in the polar regions, the temperature rarely dipped under one hundred and ten degrees, even at night; and in the heat of the day, it soared over one hundred and thirty in some areas. Power plants were unable to produce enough electricity to meet the overwhelming need. Blackouts were common and huge chunks of real estate were often without power. People were collapsing from heatstroke and dying by the thousands.

The July sun beat down relentlessly and the humidity soared. The city of Houston was sweltering under a heat wave unlike anything in recorded history. President Dwight Honaker suffered from the heat, but not as other men. Actually, he noticed that all the believers seemed to be able to bear it much better than their unsaved counterparts. The ungodly writhed in misery and died like flies. Yet, he found it interesting that none of them seemed to think of repenting of their sins and asking God for mercy. They appeared to be even more wicked and blasphemous, shaking their sweaty fists toward Him in the heavens as they breathed their last.

As horrible as it was in Houston, Honaker was amazed to learn that it was much hotter in other parts of the world, especially in those areas controlled by the antichrist. As he and Ben Hiestead studied the Scriptures Mark Robertson had given to them, they learned that God had foretold those things through the apostle John nearly two thousand years before.[15]

It was clear from what they were experiencing; the end of the tribulation could not be far away. The angel had just poured out the fourth bowl of wrath, and there were only two more to go before the final conflict and the coming of the Lord. That knowledge gave them mixed feelings. On the one hand, they were thrilled to learn that the world's suffering was about to come to an end; never had they been able to imagine such death and destruction. But on the other hand, they feared how the end might come, and how it might affect them personally.

They knew from their study of the book of Daniel, that there would be a final assault by three nations against the antichrist in the Holy Land at the end of the tribulation: one from the north, another from the south, and another from the east.[16] They were convinced that Galinikov's hordes from Russia would be that power invading from the north, and that Chairman Chong's vast armies would soon attack Palestine from the east. But it was the identity of the nation invading from the south that troubled them.

At the present time, there was no nation south of Israel that posed any threat to Constantine Augustus and his Federation headquarters near Jerusalem. South Africa was indeed a powerful nation, but it was also solidly allied with the Great Caesar, being one of the ten privileged nations in his inner circle. Egypt and some of its neighbors had formed a little coalition of

[15] Then the fourth angel poured out his bowl on the sun, and power was given to him to scorch men with fire. And men were scorched with great heat, and they blasphemed the name of God who has power over these plagues; and they did not repent and give Him glory (Revelation 16:8–9).

[16] At the time of the end the king of the South shall attack him; and the king of the North shall come against him like a whirlwind, with chariots, horsemen, and with many ships; and he shall enter the countries, overwhelm them, and pass through. . . . But news from the east and the north shall trouble him; therefore he shall go out with great fury to destroy and annihilate many (Daniel 11:40, 44).

their own to resist some of Constantine's harsher demands, but he had crushed them mercilessly. They posed no present threat to his regime at all.[17] And besides them, there was no other power to the south that could conceivably launch any sort of offensive against the Federation.

Honaker and Hiestead were forced to accept what appeared to be the inevitable: the United States of America was destined to become that third power, attacking the antichrist from the south. Their nation was already allied with the renegade regimes of Russia and China in defiance of Constantine's demand to rule the world. It was entirely conceivable that the U.S. could launch an all out attack against the Federation's meager defenses in North Africa and sweep across the continent and come up against Constantine from the south. But how could that be?

The two men were determined not to order such an invasion. Although it appeared to be a prudent move militarily, and they were getting increasing pressure from Vice-President Lowell Renslow to implement it immediately, they knew it could only end in disaster. Their study of the Bible revealed to them that all those armies that were to come up against Jerusalem in those last days would somehow become the enemies of the returning Christ, and would be mercilessly destroyed by Him. They would not . . . they could not . . . become a party to anything of that sort. But what *were* they going to do?

The United States continued to lose ground to the relentless Federation attacks, and their still-formidable military continued to be depleted with every day they delayed. There was a groundswell of rebellion festering among the ravaged American people. They were demanding that something drastic be done. With the staggering heat, they were unable to work effectively, and their food and fuel reserves continued to erode away. They were not willing to sit by passively and see everything they treasured slowly eaten up and destroyed.

Renslow seemed to be the undeclared catalyst behind the rebellion, but they did not know that for sure. Whatever was causing it, something had to be done, and soon, lest the whole nation erupt into civil war. And the devilish heat was only aggravating the already-volatile situation. They called Mark Robertson and arranged an emergency meeting with him to get his insight and advice on the matter.

---

[17] He shall stretch out his hand against the countries, and the land of Egypt shall not escape. He shall have power over the treasures of gold and silver, and over all the precious things of Egypt; also the Libyans and the Ethiopians shall follow at his heels (Daniel 11:42–43).

The sweat rolled off the head of the vice-president as he met with his top military advisors on the bottom floor of the command post bunker in eastern Houston. Although they were some fifty feet below ground level, the heat was still oppressive. His advisors were suffering too, but not like Lowell Renslow. His body was grossly overweight and out of shape, and he had little tolerance for heat in the first place. His extreme physical discomfort only added to the surly disposition he had brought into the meeting to begin with.

"Gentlemen, we simply have no other choice," he growled at his associates. "The Russians and the Chinese are ready to launch the invasion. I've talked with both of their leaders since our meeting yesterday, and they are not willing to wait much longer. In a couple of months, the weather is going to turn cold, and they won't be able to get their armies through the mountain passes after the snow flies. Besides, they won't have enough food or fuel to launch an invasion if they don't do it soon. Just as soon as this heat wave passes, they're calling for a strike."

"But sir," General Putnam protested, "we have approached the president before on this matter, and he has been unwilling to even consider it. What makes you think he will consent to it now?" He was the army chief of staff, a big man, and ramrod stiff with military discipline.

"Bob, frankly, I doubt that he has changed his mind," Renslow responded. "And neither is he likely to, no matter how desperate our situation becomes here. That's why I called this meeting. These are desperate times, and they call for desperate measures!"

"Just what are you talking about, sir?" the general wanted to know.

"I'm talking about taking the matter into our own hands. The future of our nation depends on it. The Russians and the Chinese can't defeat Augustus and his Federation without our help. And if we don't join in with them, they will be destroyed, and then there won't be anybody to watch our backsides when the Emperor of the World decides to turn all of his guns on us. No, we have to join in the invasion with our allies now, with or without the president's approval."

"But what you're suggesting is treason," Admiral Hightower exclaimed. "How are you prepared to defend such an action?"

"Oscar, we won't have to defend it," he replied to the tall chief of his naval operations. "We're in a state of national emergency here, under martial law. The presidency is nothing more than a carryover from a previous administration. We have no real legislative or justice system to establish or to interpret our laws. Because of the devastations of the times, no elections were held last year when his term expired, so officially, Dwight Honaker has no right to run this country any more than you and I do.

"Besides," Renslow went on, "the president has become more and more out of touch recently. His religious fanaticism has robbed him of his ability to see things as they really are. He is convinced God doesn't want us to join in the invasion against Augustus lest we come under divine condemnation, but we all know that joining in with our allies in that invasion is our only chance to defeat our enemies and to get our country back!"

"You're not talking about a hostile takeover of the government are you, Lowell?" the admiral wanted to know.

"No, nothing so drastic, I'm afraid. I'm suggesting we simply proceed to formulate our plans with the Russians and the Chinese, and then to pursue them. If Honaker and Hiestead want to come onboard, fine, we'll welcome them. If they don't, too bad, we'll proceed without them. True, they have the support of the common people, but they have no real power. We control the military, and whoever has the guns, ultimately has the go-ahead. Do you know what I mean?"

"Yes, sir," Hightower agreed, as did General Putnam and the rest of the military leaders.

So the die was cast. The United States of America would join in with Russia and China in a massive invasion against the heart of the beast in Israel just as soon as weather conditions would permit, with or without the consent of President Honaker.

The meeting was adjourned, and each man left to try to find some measure of relief from the blazing heat. But Vice-President Lowell Renslow stayed behind. Being a bachelor, he had no one to go home to, and as hot as it was in the room, it was still more tolerable than any place else he could think of. Besides, there remained things for him to do and phone calls for him to make. There was much that still needed to be done before he was prepared to put his plan into action.

It was nearly midnight, and Dwight Honaker and Ben Hiestead sat side by side on the sofa in the basement of the provisional capital building in the southern part of Houston. It was cooler down there, and it provided them with more privacy. Their guest, Mark Robertson, sat in a wingback chair across from them. A coffee table separated them, and they each had a Bible opened and spread out on top of it.

"Mark, I think we understand Zechariah, chapter fourteen, pretty well," the president said. "It makes it clear that when the nations go up against Jerusalem to destroy it, the Lord will return and destroy them instead. But we've been going over the last part of chapter nineteen of Revelation, and we can't figure it out. Here, let me read verses nineteen to twenty-one to you, and then maybe you can help explain them to us:

> *And I saw the beast, the kings of the earth, and their armies, gathered together to make war against Him who sat on the horse and against His army. Then the beast was captured, and with him the false prophet who worked signs in his presence, by which he deceived those who received the mark of the beast and those who worshiped his image. These two were cast alive into the lake of fire burning with brimstone. And the rest were killed with the sword which proceeded from the mouth of Him who sat on the horse, and all the birds were filled with their flesh.*

"We understand that the beast and the false prophet must be talking about Constantine Augustus and his cousin Eli Rothschild. Believe me, the day they get their comeuppance can't come soon enough for us. And the rest of the kings and their armies there will be destroyed by the Lord Himself, right? And the part about Him using the sword out of His mouth is just talking figuratively about the power of His word, isn't it?"

"That's right, sir" Mark agreed. "You two have come a long way in your understanding of God's Word."

"Please, Mark, call me Dwight. I think we've come too far together for you to continue to insist on calling me sir, and Mr. President. The more I come to understand about you and the rest of your 144,000, the more I feel like I should be calling *you* sir."

"Okay, Dwight. It still doesn't seem right, but I'll agree to about anything to keep the president of the United States from addressing *me* as sir. Now, what is it about the passage that you need help with?"

"It's the part about the kings of the earth and their armies joining in with the beast to attack the Lord," Ben Hiestead interrupted, answering the question addressed to his boss. "According to what we've been studying in the eleventh chapter of Daniel, the kings of the north, south, and east all seem to be going to Israel to attack the antichrist there; but here in this passage, they all seem to join in with him in attacking the Lord instead. How can that be?"

"That's a good question, Ben," Mark answered, figuring if he was going to call the president by his first name, he couldn't very well address formally someone else who worked for him. "And unfortunately, I'm not sure I have a definitive answer for you."

"Well, give it your best shot," Dwight broke in. "This isn't just a matter of curiosity with us, you know."

"I know. You're being pressured to join in with Russia and China to launch a three-pronged attack against the Federation headquarters in Israel, right?"

"Yeah, but who told you that?" the president asked in surprise. "Only our top military advisors know about those communications."

"Well, remember, you said so yourself. I'm a member of God's 144,000. And we have sources of information that are not exactly of this world, if you know what I mean."

"Yeah, you're right. I almost forgot. So, okay then, what do your angelic sources say would happen if we joined in the attack? We would definitely want to oppose Augustus, but there's no way we would ever think of going against the Lord when He returns. Our nation is being slowly destroyed while we sit here; and attacking at the heart of the beast seems like a good move militarily, but we don't want to do the wrong thing spiritually"

"I know what you mean," Mark replied, "and I do realize the importance of your decision. And, like I said, I don't know exactly how, or why, it's going to happen; but I'm almost certain that those armies that go up against the antichrist will turn and become his allies against the Lord and His people."

"But how can that be?" Ben demanded. "We would never be so foolish. Not now. Not after everything we've come to understand."

"I know, Ben. I don't know everything, but one thing I am sure of is the genuineness of your faith and your commitment to follow the Lord, no matter what it costs."

"Okay then," Dwight injected. "We're back where we started. With our total opposition to Augustus, and our total commitment to Christ; how could we ever switch sides when the chips are down?"

"I don't think you could," Mark answered, "but that's not the only possible scenario, you know. One of two other possibilities could actually take place."

"What do you mean?" the president wanted to know.

"Again," the young prophet said, "I don't know for sure, but this is what I think will happen. I believe the three invading armies will prepare to engage the combined forces of the World Federation in Israel, and then something extraordinary will happen. Maybe the Lord Himself will return, or all the 144,000 will be transported back to Jerusalem all at once, or perhaps all the Jews will join together to rise up against the antichrist; or possibly, all of those things will happen at once. At any rate, it will create a big enough stir that the antichrist will be able to convince the leaders on both sides that the Jews in Jerusalem pose the real problem, and he will be able to convince them to join in with him in attacking them there."

"Now that's the part we're struggling with," Ben interjected, interrupting Mark again. "There's no way Dwight and I would ever fall for such a deal."

"I know, Ben," Mark said reassuringly. "But I don't think either of you will be there."

"How's that?" Dwight asked. "We would never send our young men into a battle of that magnitude and sit home to watch it on TV."

"No, I know you wouldn't," Mark agreed, "but perhaps your armies won't be there either. Remember, God will fulfill His promises with or without your involvement. If you keep your armies home—and I strongly urge you to do just that—then God will raise up another nation to attack Israel from the south. Then none of your troops will be deceived by the beast, and neither will they be destroyed by the Lord at His coming."

"Then that's exactly what we'll do," Dwight said resolutely, "no matter how much pressure Galinikov and Chong, and even Lowell Renslow, try to put on us. That has been our strategy all along, and you've just convinced us to stick with it, no matter what.

"But you said there were two other possibilities," he continued. "What's the other one?"

"I don't know," Mark said, "but it is possible that the Lord will allow you to be removed from power before the invasion occurs, and the nation's new leaders will then lead our troops into battle . . . to their defeat . . . and to everlasting destruction."

"Yeah, I never thought of that," Ben conceded. "And I bet I know just the one who would love to orchestrate the coup too: that weasel Lowell Renslow. He's been insisting that America's only hope of coming out ahead in this conflict is to join Russia and China in their planned attack. And if he could kill us, or otherwise get us out of the way, he could pull it off. Our military leaders are all basically in agreement with him already."

"You're right, Ben," Dwight agreed. "We had better tighten security immediately; not so much for our sakes. We know we're going to heaven, but for the sakes of all those troops he'd lead off to death and damnation. We've simply got to stay alive, and stay in power, if we have any hope of averting the worst disaster in our nation's history."

Just then, there was an urgent banging on the door, and all three men jumped with surprise. "Who is it?" Dwight called out, with more than a little apprehension in his voice.

"Mr. President, it's me, Private Tanner, sir," came the response from the other side of the door. "I'm sorry to disturb you, sir, but I thought you ought to know. There's a gun battle going on east of the city, and it's a really big one, sir."

Recognizing the voice of one of the most trusted members of their security detail, Dwight agreed to let him in, and motioned for Mark to get the door, as he was the one closest to it.

Mark hurried to the door and unlocked it. When he opened it, in rushed the breathless young private, making his way directly to the president, bypassing and completely ignoring Mark in the process.

The president told the ramrod stiff soldier to stand at ease and fill him in on the details. On settling down and catching his breath, the ruddy-faced soldier confirmed in detail what he had blurted out through the door.

"The report I received, Mr. President, is that a detachment of regular soldiers was fired upon by a large congregation of Christians gathered in an eastside church for a political meeting or something. The soldiers returned fire, and than all hell broke loose. Reinforcements have shown up on both sides, and a real firefight has developed. I thought you would want to know, sir."

"Yes, I do. Thank you, Gerald," the president said to the young soldier whom he had personally won to Christ a few weeks before. "Go have them get my car ready. Ben and I'll get over there right now and put a stop to this immediately." Then he continued speaking more to himself than anyone else, "I can't believe this has happened. Why would a bunch of Christians open fire on our own soldiers? There has got to be a big foul up somewhere. We've got to stop it right now before the whole country breaks out into civil war."

Private Tanner was almost to the door, anxious to carry out the orders of his commander-in-chief, when Mark held out his hand to stop him.

"I don't think that would be a good idea, Mr. President," he said firmly. "We have no idea what is really going on out there, and it could be a trap. Your enemies may have staged this whole thing just to draw you out in the open. The last thing our country needs right now is for you and Mr. Hiestead to get yourselves kidnapped or killed. Let me and some of my friends check this out for you. We're sorta bullet-proof, if you know what I mean. We'll put a stop to the shooting and get a full report back here for you first thing in the morning. How does that sound?"

"Maybe you're right," Dwight agreed, seeing the logic in Mark's words. "You and your buddies go put a lid on this thing quick, and then report right back to us here just as soon as you figure out what's behind all of it. Ben and I'll sleep here tonight, so you'll know where to find us. And, Gerald, have them get the car ready anyway. We may need it in the morning."

"Yes, sir," snapped the private as he exited the door. "Good night, Mr. President."

After he had left, Mark stayed long enough to pray with and for his powerful, but vulnerable, friends, and then he too hurried off to fulfill his mission.

Five minutes later, he was in his car speeding east on the Interstate 10 Freeway. He had been able to reach the other three members of God's 144,000 on his cell phone, and two of them were on their way to join him at the site of the firefight. The third was on a special assignment in Galveston, and would not be able to respond. Unlike the 144,000 elsewhere in the world, he and his fellow witnesses in the United States enjoyed not only the absence of persecution from the government, but also the presence of certain privileges and benefits from it. For example, they had the use of a car and a cell phone, luxuries unknown to most citizens of the war torn and impoverished nation. He was grateful for the air conditioner, which was laboring somewhat successfully in its efforts to drive the hot summer night air from the interior of the old Jeep Comanche.

President Honaker knew the 144,000 to be his greatest allies in his battle against evil during the tribulation, and he had done everything he could to assist them in performing their God-given assignments. Unfortunately, there were not very many of them stationed in what remained of the United States. Their presence was more urgently needed in other parts of the world where God's people were suffering horribly at the hands of ungodly men. The Lord had appointed only four in the Houston area, and no more than ten in the rest of the entire country.

Mark felt a sense of foreboding as he neared the exit that would take him to the site of the conflict. He was not at all sure how he and Seth and Jabin would be able to put a stop to the hostilities. Neither did he know how they had started, nor why. There were too many unanswered questions to suit him, but what else could he do? He wasn't about to sit back and allow Dwight and Ben to stumble into whatever awaited him up ahead. At least he and his fellow witnesses had a measure of divine protection around them.

As he sped down the off ramp, he could see a soft red glow in the distance. He couldn't hear the sound of gunfire yet, but he knew it had to be there. The fire beckoned him to hurry. He prayed as he drove that he would be able to get there in time to stop the bloodshed and restore order before chaos and violence spread throughout the city and swept across the nation, destroying what measure of order and justice the president and his staff had been able to maintain during those dark years of tribulation.

CHAPTER SIX

The Coup

The sweltering night was ablaze with gunfire when Mark plowed his Jeep into the parking lot of the City of Hope Community Church on McCarty Street. Part of the church was on fire, as were a couple of buildings across the street. He had to drive over a make-shift barricade, and took several gunshots through his vehicle in the process. The Christians behind the piles of furniture recognized his Comanche and held their fire as he skidded to a stop next to one of the church buses.

Seth and Jabin had arrived before him and beckoned him into the fellowship hall from an open doorway. Mark retrieved his hunting bow and a large quiver of arrows from the back seat, and made a dash for the protection of the brick building.

Once inside, he greeted his friends briefly, but he was much more interested in finding out what was going on out there in the street. Jabin Weisler, a tall good looking young man with blond hair, who had been a farm boy from Nebraska in his previous life, pulled him away from the open door and closed it behind him.

"Mark, I don't know what you've heard," he said, "but it's probably not true. I got here just a few minutes after you called me and Pastor Covington was still alive . . ."

"What? Don't tell me he's been killed!"

"Yeah, I'm afraid so, Mark," Seth Goodman added. He was a stocky, dark-haired Texas boy who had been an all-American wrestler at Baylor before the rapture. "He died right after I got here. They shot him through an open window while he was leading a prayer meeting in the sanctuary at about nine-thirty."

"But I heard the church people opened fire on the soldiers first," Mark interjected.

"No way, man!" Seth boomed. "Pastor Covington swore all they were doing was prayin'. The goons outside surrounded the building and then opened fire without any warning whatsoever. If the people here hadn't had guns with them, they would have all been killed just like he was."

"But nearly everybody here was packing." Jabin added. "These days it's almost mandatory, with all the wild animals and hoodlums stalking the streets. After the shooting started, a bunch more Christians showed up, and we were able to drive the enemy off the church property and across the street; but they're still out there, and more of them are showing up all the time."

"Have they made any demands or told you what they want?"

"Not a word, as far as I know. It seems what they really want to do is to kill every Christian in the area. We've lost about twenty people already; mostly men, but some women and children too."

"Well, then," Mark said tersely, "I think it's time for us to put a stop to it right now. You guys got your weapons?"

"Sure. My bow and arrows are right over there," Jabin said, pointing toward the articles leaning against the opposite wall."

"Me too," Seth added. "I got my sling right here on my belt, and this pouch is full of ball bearings. "We're ready when you are."

"Then let's do it!" Mark said, slipping his quiver strap over his head, picking up his bow, and heading for the door.

He opened the door and ran toward the front of the church, notching an arrow as he ran. Seth was right behind him, with Jabin following close behind.

When the three approached the barricade, they spread out and jumped the pile of pews and chairs with ease, positioning themselves in the middle of the street. They ignored the bullets zinging past their bodies and began to single out their targets.

Mark pulled back the string on his ninety-pound-draw recurved hunting bow and aimed at the outline of a soldier crouched beside a military vehicle. He released the string, and an instant later, the soldier collapsed in agony. A moment later, Jabin and Seth also released their missiles, and two more soldiers crumpled to the pavement.

For the next ten minutes, they stood their ground, firing one shot after another, and hitting their targets virtually every time. Meanwhile, they incurred some injuries themselves. A bullet grazed Mark's head, stunning him and knocking him momentarily off his feet. Seth took a slug through his right shoulder, but he continued to sling his steel balls with his dominant left hand. Jabin was hit in the buttocks with a round, but it went clean through, and it never even slowed him down.

The commanding officer of the attacking unit called for a cease-fire, and ordered his men to pull back. More than thirty of his troops lay dead, dying, or wounded as a result of the counter-attack staged by the three strange young men in the middle of the street, and he was not willing to lose any more. He had heard of the supernatural powers of God's chosen 144,000, and now he had seen them in action. He decided quickly that he needed no further demonstration of it.

When the firing had ceased, and the enemy soldiers had pulled back, Mark wiped the blood from the left side of his head and asked his friends if they were okay.

"Yeah, I'm alright," Seth said, rubbing his injured shoulder. "I don't think the bullet hit a bone or anything vital. Everything seems to be working okay."

"I'll be fine," Jabin answered. "The slug went clean through, but I know what they mean now when they talk about something being a pain in the butt."

They all laughed. They had just witnessed the death of many of the people they loved, they had each taken the lives of close to a dozen enemy soldiers, and they had nearly been killed themselves, and yet, they laughed. It was partly due to the silly remark Jabin had made, and partly because of the victory they had just achieved, but mostly, it was of necessity. For if they had not laughed, they most certainly would have wept. The emotional pressure had built up inside them to the breaking point, and it simply had to be vented one way or the other.

But the urgency of their situation soon dispelled their levity, and they became deadly serious again. Mark figured that even though the troops had pulled back temporarily, they had not gone away entirely. He was sure they would return, and next time they would bring with them much heavier firepower. The three of them needed to get their people out of harm's way, and they needed to do it quickly.

City of Hope was a large church, and it had a fleet of six buses. On inspecting them, they found that two of them refused to start at all, and a third one coughed and protested badly when they fired it up. But the other three seemed to be in good running order. They had all taken some gunshots during the battle, but fortunately, none of the tires or other vital parts had been hit.

It was decided quickly that the people would be loaded onto the three buses and that the three witnesses would drive them out of town before another attack could be launched against them. They knew of a large Christian compound about a hundred miles northeast of Houston that was well supplied and fortified. They would take them there where they would be safe, at least temporarily.

Sadly, there was no time for anyone to go home and retrieve any personal items, or even to care for their fallen comrades. Some two hundred disheveled believers were crowded onto the three buses, and the three battle-initiated members of the 144,000 drove them away into the sweltering night, praying that the tired engines in their vehicles would not overheat and fail them before they reached their destination.

Mark decided not to call Dwight on his cell phone since it was after two in the morning, and he and Ben would be trying to get some much-needed sleep. There was nothing they could do at the moment anyway. Mark determined he would deliver his passengers to their destination and then he and Seth and Jabin would return to assist the president in restoring order and getting to the bottom of the bloodbath that had just taken place. He would place the call when they got back into town at about sunup.

Dwight Honaker was rattled out of a troubled sleep by the ringing of the red emergency telephone across the room. It took him a moment to collect his thoughts and to realize where he was. He rolled off the couch on which he had been sleeping and walked quickly to the desk on the opposite side of the room. Ben Hiestead was also off his couch and headed in that direction as well. They reached the phone at the same time, but it was Dwight who picked it up and identified himself.

A staff person apologized for the early intrusion, but he informed him that the person on the line was the vice-president, and that he was insisting it was an emergency and was demanding that the call be put through.

Dwight excused the operator, looking at his watch to discover that it was not yet five-thirty in the morning, and told him he would accept the call.

"Mr. President, Renslow here," came the urgent response as soon as Dwight had identified himself on the phone. "I'm out at the scene of the firefight. Believe me, it's a mess. Have you heard from anyone about it yet?"

"No, not yet. I sent Mark Robertson and some others out there last night and I'm expecting to hear from them at any time. I'm surprised he hasn't called yet."

"I'm afraid I've got some bad news for you, sir," came Renslow's response. "Those religious nuts out at that church went crazy last night. They not only opened fire on one of our patrols, but they kept on increasing in numbers and firepower, and they rejected any offer for a ceasefire. Our troops had no choice but to return fire, and when your men got there and tried to break it up, those nuts still refused to put down their weapons. I'm afraid those guys were caught in the middle of a firefight, and all of them were gunned down. Two are nearly dead, and Mark is shot up real bad. We got them inside a building and are taking care of them as best we can, but Mark keeps asking for you. He says he's afraid he's not going to make it, and you're the only one he'll talk to. Whaddya want me to do, sir?"

"Oh, no! I can't believe it, Lowell! Can they be moved to a hospital?"

"I don't think so. We're pinned down pretty good here. It would be tough getting an ambulance in here right now. Besides, I'm not sure they'd make it if we were to move 'em. We got some medics here, and they're doing about everything for them the folks at the hospital could do. I'm afraid you're going to have to come here if you want to talk to them."

"Of course, we'll be right there," Dwight said. "I've got my car waiting for me. Just take care of those boys. Ben and I will be there just as fast as we can. Thanks for letting me know, Lowell."

"Sure thing, Boss. I already told your driver how to get here. See you in a few."

Dwight heard a click, and the line went dead. He hung up the phone and told Ben what he had just heard as they put their shoes on and headed for the door. They had slept in their clothes, so there was nothing to delay their departure.

When they walked out the door, they were greeted with a blast of hot air that nearly took their breath away. The sun had not yet risen, it was the coolest hour of the day, and yet the temperature was still near the hundred and ten mark. They hurried to the curb under the protection of several armed guards, where Gerald Tanner opened the back door of the waiting limousine for them.

"Good morning, gentlemen," he said cheerfully. "I'll be your driver this morning. The A/C is working, and it should be a pleasant trip . . . at least until we get where we're going, that is."

"Thank you, Gerald," Dwight responded. "I'm glad you're our driver. I feel safe in your hands . . . as safe as anyone can be these days."

Ben got in first and slid across the seat, followed closely by Dwight, and they settled in for the escorted ride out to the site of the perplexing gun battle that was supposedly still going on.

As the young soldier closed the door and was going around to take his place behind the wheel, Dwight couldn't help but wonder what was really going on. The reports had been clear, but they just didn't make any sense. There was no way he could conceive of a group of God-fearing Christians launching an unprovoked attack on an army patrol. Then, for them not to respond to the appeal of members of God's 144,000 was inexplicable to him. Also, how could all three of His chosen ones be cut down in battle? Weren't they supposed to be divinely protected or something?

No, it just didn't make any sense. He was anxious to get out there and find out for himself. His heart was filled with concern for Mark Robertson, the young man who was solely responsible, humanly speaking, for the eternal salvation of both himself and his best friend. For all he knew, the boy lay dying in a pool of his own blood even at that moment. The president urged his driver to hurry.

Mark Robertson drove the old church bus aggressively as he merged into the early morning traffic at the eastern outskirts of Houston. Seth and Jabin sat in seats on opposite sides of the aisle behind him. They had been up all night, but they experienced no sense of fatigue. Their senses were keenly alert, and their hearts were anxious to reach their destination.

They had been trying to use their cell phones for the past hour, but none of them had been able to get a signal. The tower must have been down again. That had happened frequently during the course of the hostilities of the tribulation. Underlings of the great Emperor Augustus had managed to freeze all satellite communications, and the U.S. government had been forced to depend on land-based towers for wireless communication, which had often proven to be less than dependable.

Mark was determined to get to the capitol building before the president and Ben Hiestead left to go anywhere. He was certain that foul play was afoot. Someone had definitely planned that unprovoked attack on the prayer meeting, and Mark was sure it was not for the sole purpose of killing Christians. The attack had taken all the present members of the 144,000 away from the city, leaving the capital and its president completely without divine protection. Mark didn't like the queasy feeling he felt in his stomach when he thought about that fact.

It was daylight, but the sun had not yet risen when he pulled the laboring bus off the freeway and headed down the street toward the provisional capitol building. Mark had turned off the air conditioner and even turned on the heater to help cool the engine, but the needle was still pegged on the H, and steam could be seen coming out from under the hood. Mark prayed he would be able to coax another mile or two out of it before it gave up the ghost entirely.

He drove over a slight rise and saw the capitol building in the distance in front of him. He could see the black limo parked in front of it with armed guards positioned around it and a couple of military vehicles idling nearby. He breathed a sigh of relief. It was clear that the president had not left yet, but it looked like preparations were made to facilitate his immediate departure. Mark stepped down on the accelerator and tried to generate a little more speed out of the exhausted bus.

Just then, he saw two men exit the building and approach the limo. A uniformed soldier saluted and opened the door for them. That had to be Dwight and Ben. If he hurried, he would be able to stop them before they got away. But he couldn't afford to be in too big of a hurry. If he were to go tearing up there in an unidentified bus that looked like it was about to explode all by itself, the security personnel would undoubtedly shoot him down long before he could get close enough to signal the president.

The decision was taken out of his hands. The stricken bus lurched, coughed, died, and began coasting to a long-overdue stop. Mark steered it over to the curb and mercifully parked his tortured steed. He grabbed his weapons and leapt from the open door, followed closely by Jabin and Seth. They would have to run the last two hundred yards on foot.

As they sprinted down the middle of the street, they saw the soldier round the front of the car and get in the driver's door. He would undoubtedly be pulling away in a matter of seconds. They forced themselves to increase their already world-class pace.

Guards spotted their approach and failed to recognize them. They interpreted the sprinting trio as a threat against their president and shouted a warning for them to stop, which was out of the question. The three had to stop the president's car from leaving, and they could not do that from a hundred yards away, so they ignored the threats and continued their blistering pace.

The guards opened fire and, for the second time in less than six hours, dozens of bullets began whizzing past them. They ignored them, trusting God's angels to deflect the lethal projectiles away from their defenseless bodies.

Alerted by the sound of the gunfire, Dwight and Ben turned around in the seat and looked through the bulletproof glass of the back window and saw the young men sprinting toward them. They recognized them immediately and Ben jumped out the door to order the guards to cease their firing. Dwight raised his hand and waved to them through the glass. Then it happened.

The presidential limousine exploded into a huge fireball. The vehicle itself was flung some ten feet into the air and disintegrated into hundreds of severed parts. The two occupants of the car were killed instantly, as was the man standing at the rear door, whose pulverized body was hurled a hundred feet across the street and against the side of a governmental office building. Three others were killed, and the flying debris wounded many more. In an instant, not only were many innocent human lives lost, but the life of the United States and its hope of surviving the coming holocaust were tragically and permanently shattered.

Mark Robertson and his friends, who were just approaching the car, were blown backward by the blast. They were thrown to the pavement, and though unhurt physically, they were devastated emotionally and spiritually. They rolled over and looked in horror at the burning wreckage of what remained of the presidential limousine. They cried out in agony and tore their garments in woeful lamentation. They, the chosen members of the famed 144,000 had failed to fulfill their mission. The president and his closest advisor were dead, and the headless nation they once led would soon writhe in its own death throes. The horrible destiny that now awaited the USA was painfully branded into the minds of the three witnesses, even as the burning vehicle before them scorched the boiling pavement beneath it.

CHAPTER SEVEN

The New Deal

Lowell Renslow couldn't have been more pleased. His plan had worked better than he had dared to hope. He had ordered the attack on the church on the east side of the city in order to get those blasted Jewish magicians out of the way. He didn't understand their strange mannerisms or their confusing message of doom and gloom, but he was sure he didn't want to mess with them. They had powers that defied explanation, and they had ways of sensing danger before it ever materialized. Several times before, he had attempted to get that weakling Honaker out of the way, only to have those strange bodyguards thwart his efforts—but not this time.

Renslow's informants, who constantly monitored their activities, had confirmed that one of the four weirdoes was in Galveston, and that the other three had gone to the aid of the besieged churchgoers. Sure enough, they had delivered the Christians from danger, just like they always seemed to do; and they had spirited them away to some distant place of refuge, just as he had thought they would. Their absence had left the president and Hiestead without their protection for many hours.

Yes, his little ruse had cost the lives of about fifty soldiers and nearly that many innocent civilians, but he considered it a small price to pay for the advantage it had bought him. With those troublemakers out of the way, he was free to put his plan into action.

He ordered men loyal to him to sabotage the president's limousine by placing plastic explosives under its hood. Two mechanics and three guards had to be killed in order to accomplish the task, but again, it was considered acceptable collateral damage. Then he ordered others of his men to shut down the communication towers so those prophets, or whatever they were, would not be able to call their president to warn him in time to thwart the plan. After that, he phoned the president personally to convince him to go to the aid of his fallen friends at the site of the gun battle. The booby-trapped limo would be waiting for him and that stooge Hiestead when they responded to the rescue.

Renslow insisted that he be given the remote controlled detonation switch personally. He wanted the honor of eliminating his enemies himself. He had tried in vain to convince them to call for an attack on the Federation headquarters in Israel, but they had refused to even consider it. If the United States was going to survive, they had to be removed. He didn't consider himself to be a violent man, but in this case, he would make an exception. He concluded that the taking of a few more lives was an acceptable sacrifice in order to secure the ultimate survival of his country.

He had positioned himself across the street from the provisional capitol building, and upstairs in a government office building. There, he was far enough away to insure his secrecy and protection; but at the same time, he was close enough to guarantee the effective operation of the detonating device.

When he saw Honaker and Hiestead emerge from the capitol building and get into the car, he readied himself behind the open window, sweat pouring from his brow, and his fingers trembling at the toggle switch of the device he held in his fleshy hands. It was then he saw what was to be an unexpected blessing.

To his left, his peripheral vision picked up the images of figures rapidly approaching the presidential limousine. He looked, and immediately identified the three young Jewish prophets sprinting down the street with weapons in their hands. Soldiers near the president's car yelled a warning, and then opened fire, but the running men failed to alter their course.

The treasonous vice-president saw the rear door open and Hiestead step out with an urgent look on his face. The latter was about to yell for a ceasefire because he and Honaker had doubtlessly recognized the three men and didn't want them to be hurt. Renslow could not allow that to happen. If the three were allowed to speak to the president, then all the efforts of the past seven hours would have been in vain. But a fortuitous opportunity had presented itself, and Renslow was determined to take full advantage of it.

He flipped the detonator switch just as Hiestead raised his hand and opened his mouth to yell at his security guards to put down their weapons. But Ben never got the words out, because the thunderous explosion instantly ended his life and blasted his dismembered body across the street and smashed it into the side of the very office building in which Renslow had positioned himself. The limousine was thrown into the air, blown into multiple pieces by the massive explosion, and its occupants were virtually disintegrated in the same instant. But the vice-president was denied the privilege of seeing the carnage he had created. The blast was far greater than he had anticipated. The force of the explosion threw his substantial body back from the window and landed him on his back in the middle of the small room, peppering him with pieces of glass from the shattered windows.

Fortunately for him, he sustained only a few superficial cuts, but he was badly shaken. His vision was temporarily distorted, and a loud ringing muffled his hearing. He struggled to his feet and managed to get to the window in time to discern the blurred images of the three Jew boys kneeling in the middle of the street. There they were, perfect stooges just waiting to be fingered.

He leaned out the window and screamed to the injured and confused guards below who were cowering behind vehicles and other solid objects, "You men, this is Vice-president Lowell Renslow! Those three terrorists down there just assassinated the president! Don't let them get away!"

Mark Robertson could not believe his eyes and ears. He saw the fat frame of his adversary leaning out the window with his pudgy finger pointing at him and his friends, and he heard his lying tongue accusing them of the unthinkable, but still, he could not fully comprehend the enormity of his situation.

However, he didn't have time to sort it all out in his mind. Bullets from a dozen rifles started slicing the air around him and his companions. Given the green light by the treasonous Renslow, the soldiers had rallied to the occasion and opened fire on the three presumed terrorists, determined to make them pay for their treacherous act against the president they had served and respected.

Mark sprang to his feet, as did Seth and Jabin, and the three of them sprinted to their right and down a narrow alleyway, narrowly escaping the hail of fiery projectiles discharged by the hundreds in their direction. Only because of the supernatural intervention of their angels did they avoid certain injury or death.

But where were they to go? They were on foot, and though they could most certainly outrun anyone in pursuit of them, they definitely could not outrun the vehicles that were already beginning to give chase. The entire contingency of troops assigned to the capitol building would soon be upon them. Continuing to flee would be ultimately futile. There was no place to run, and no place to hide.

Suddenly, Mark had an idea. "Quick," he yelled, "to the back door of the capitol!"

Seth and Jabin had no idea what Mark had in mind, but having no ideas of their own on how to elude their pursuers, they readily complied with his directive. The three of them rounded the corner and headed to the back of the high-rise office complex that had been converted into the provisional U.S. capitol building.

Before they could get near the rear entrance, two guards opened fire. But a ball bearing from Seth's sling, and an arrow from Jabin's bow soon sent them writhing to the concrete. The three witnesses burst through the rear door and overpowered three additional guards with their bare hands.

"Up the stairs!" Mark shouted. "We gotta make it to the chopper on the roof!"

His friends were quick to respond. They too had known about the presence of the helicopter, permanently housed on the roof of the building to provide the president with an immediate means of escape in case the capitol were to come under direct attack. They themselves hadn't thought about trying to commandeer it, but they readily agreed with Mark that it was their best, perhaps their only, chance of making a getaway.

As they bounded up the stairs, Jabin asked, "How do you know the chopper's ready to go, and if there's somebody there to fly it?"

"I don't," Mark admitted, "but I believe it'll be okay. I'm almost sure it was the Lord who put the thought in my mind."

"I sure hope so!" shouted Seth. "Cause if you're wrong, we'll be trapped for sure. Those troops are hot on our trail, and there's no way down. If we don't catch that helicopter, we're dead ducks unless the Lord beams us up Himself."

"Yeah, I know!" Mark agreed, looking over his shoulder at the soldiers mounting the stairs behind them, three floors below. "Just keep on climbin' and keep on prayin'!"

And climb they did. Taking three steps at a time, they fairly flew up the stairs, leaving the already-exhausted soldiers far behind. But they were not concerned about the troops in the stairwell. It was those who would be riding up in the elevator that had them concerned. They had to reach the twenty-fourth floor before the elevators did or all hope would be lost.

Their strength never wavered, and their pace never slackened. They seemed to be borne up those flights of stairs on angels' wings. They burst through the doors, and onto the roof mere seconds before the telltale ding signaled the arrival of the first elevator.

The two security guards patrolling the roof had been warned over their radios that an assault by terrorists was underway and they were to be on red alert. They opened fire as soon as they identified the three men in civilian clothes, but their aim was careless. Two arrows from the bows of Mark and Jabin, though not lethal, rendered them incapable of continuing the fight. They collapsed in pain onto the tarred surface of the rooftop.

Grabbing the discarded rifle of one of the fallen guards, Mark jammed it through the two handles of the doors to prevent them from being opened. No sooner had he done so than soldiers rammed into it from the other side. The rifle held momentarily, but it would not do so for long. The frustrated troops on the other side began firing into the doors to dislodge the obstacle, or to cut it in half, whichever came first. At any rate, their barricade would not hold for long, and Mark knew it. He frantically looked around for Keith Thompson and called his name.

"Is that you, Mark?" came a shaky voice from the general direction of the helicopter.

"Yeah, where are you man?"

"Over here. What's going on?" came the reply as a redheaded young Marine stepped tentatively out from behind one of the cooling towers where he had been hiding.

Mark was delighted to see the handsome young man. He was the pilot designated to fly this specially modified Black Hawk, which was officially designated Marine Two. A larger helicopter, Marine One, was used by the president for longer trips, but it was too big to land safely on top of the provisional White House, so it was housed at the nearby NASA facilities.

Mark had met the pilot many times when he had accompanied the president and his advisors on special flights. In fact, on one of those flights, he had won the young Marine to Christ while they waited together in the aircraft while Honaker and Renslow had been in a lengthy meeting with some of their military generals near the western front.

"Fire her up, Keith!" Mark yelled. "We gotta get outta here! I'll tell you all about it once we're airborne!"

The pilot didn't hesitate. He had trusted his eternal soul into the hands of his Savior at the direction of Mark Robertson, and he wasn't about to question his instructions now. He jumped into the cockpit and cranked the powerful engine until it thundered to life. As the blades began to turn and pick up speed, the three witnesses scampered aboard.

They were none too early, because they had no sooner entered the aircraft than the pulverized rifle holding the doors on the building gave way completely and more than a dozen armed soldiers burst through them onto the rooftop and opened fire.

Mark had just slammed shut the door to the helicopter when its bulletproof glass was riddled with an irregular pattern of shallow craters dug out by frustrated bullets that had thereby been denied entry. As Keith pulled back on the stick and the aircraft lifted off into the morning sky, hundreds more of the fiery projectiles peppered its glass and metal exterior, only to fall back to the rooftop, flattened and spent. The big modified Black Hawk was heavier and less maneuverable than the typical model, but its extra armament was designed to save the lives of its occupants even under heavy direct attack, and it had proven itself trustworthy.

As the aircraft lifted out of range, and the pinging sound of rounds striking its surface finally subsided and ceased altogether, everyone onboard breathed a little easier.

"Head northeast, Keith!" Mark yelled to be heard over the sound of the engine and the pulsating rotor blades.

"Roger that!" the young pilot yelled back as he swung the nose of the chopper off in the general direction of the rising summer sun.

Mark wanted to get the helicopter to the sanctuary where he and Seth and Jabin had taken their refugees earlier, but he knew he dared not attempt to fly there directly. Renslow would no doubt be ordering fighter jets launched immediately with orders to shoot them down on sight. They had to find a safe place to land before the faster jets would have a chance to locate and overtake them. As soon as they had cleared the city and were out over open country, he began looking for a place to set her down.

Over a particularly dense stand of trees in a remote area, he spotted a small clearing and directed Keith to head for it. Once near the ground, he urged the pilot to ease the aircraft under the canopy of a huge cottonwood tree at the edge of the clearing. The pilot inched the craft as close to the tree as he could, making sure the rotors didn't strike its massive trunk. Then he set her down and turned off the engine.

No one onboard said anything as the sounds of the noisy aircraft subsided and finally ceased altogether. They all sat there in silence listening for the sounds of approaching fighter jets sent out in pursuit of them. Their own craft was completely hidden under the dense foliage of the cottonwood and would be virtually invisible to a high-speed jet traveling above them at several hundred miles per hour. The only question that remained was whether or not they had been able to make their descent before they were spotted by those behind them, bent on shooting them out of the sky.

After about three minutes of uninterrupted silence, Jabin said, "I think we made it, boys."

"Yeah," agreed Seth, "I don't hear a thing."

Just then, Mark held up his index finger and signaled for everyone's attention, and then pointed back toward the southwest. Faintly at first, and then growing in volume, could be heard the sound of approaching aircraft. In less than thirty seconds, the sound became almost deafening, and then the jets thundered across the clearing, seemingly just above the tops of the trees. Through the windows, the occupants of the helicopter could see the boughs of their cottonwood tree being whipped about by the turbulence in the air created by the force of the heavy jets slicing through it.

In a few seconds, as quickly as it had risen, the noise subsided, and Jabin whispered, "Whew, that was close. I wonder if they saw us."

"I don't think so," Mark whispered back. Then he thought for a moment and burst out laughing. "What are we whispering for? Are we afraid they're gonna hear us?"

That seemed to break the tension, and everyone had a good laugh. They were reminded again of the fact that people are prone to say and do some of the most outrageous things when under great stress.

Still, they sat there pretty much motionless for several more minutes, straining to see or hear anything that might indicate that their location had been identified, and that the attack fighters would be returning to fulfill their mission. But nothing was either seen or heard, and finally they all breathed a sigh of relief.

Only then did they feel confident to talk freely and begin to move about. They all climbed out of the helicopter and sat in the shade as Mark explained to Keith what had taken place back in Houston and why they had been forced to make such an outlandish escape. The young man sat in astonishment as he heard of the assassination of his president and the charade staged by Renslow to put the blame on the godliest men he had ever met. He asked what the three of them planned to do next, and where they wanted him to take them.

"Nowhere, I'm afraid," Mark answered. "As much as I would prefer riding in that big chopper, it's much too dangerous to be flying anywhere in it right now. We all need to sit right here until dark, and only then will it be safe for any of us to move around. Unless I miss my guess, those jets up there will be combing the skies for us the rest of the day.

"After dark," he continued, "you take the helicopter on over to that Christian compound on that big lake west of Livingston. I think they call it Goshen. You know, it's the place we visited last month with the president and Ben Hiestead. It's where we took those busloads of Christians last night. Explain to Pastor Walker when you get there what has happened, and I'm sure he will let you stay with them. Cover the chopper so it can't be seen from the air. We need to hang on to it, cause I'm sure it'll come in handy in the future."

"Okay, sure, I can do that. But what about you guys?" the young pilot wanted to know. "What are you gonna do?"

"We're gonna walk back to the city as soon as it gets dark and cools off a little bit. I've got a feeling Renslow will be turning his dogs loose on all the believers back there, and they'll need all the help we can give them. But right now, we're gonna stay here in the shade and try to get some sleep. We'll need to recoup our strength to meet the challenges I'm sure will be waiting for us there."

That seemed to satisfy Keith, and he reluctantly accepted his assignment. He would much rather have stayed with the three witnesses and done battle with their enemies, utilizing the two fifty- caliber machine guns mounted at either side door, and the Hellfire missiles slung on the underside of his armored craft, but he bowed to Mark's wisdom. One gunship would not stand much of a chance anyway against the forces Renslow would most certainly throw up against them if he were to locate them.

The four of them spent the rest of the day in the shade of the big cottonwood tree, resting and preparing for the challenges that lay ahead. The heat was oppressive, but the three members of the 144,000 slept nonetheless. They had been under such stress ever since the tribulation began, and had been afforded so little time to rest, they had learned to grab sleep whenever and wherever the opportunity afforded itself, regardless of the circumstances.

Such was not the case for young Keith Thompson. Try as he would, he could not sleep in the sweltering heat. After dozing off and on for a miserable hour, he spent most of his day checking out his aircraft and doing what he could to repair the minor damage the barrage of bullets had done to its exterior. When he was satisfied that she was back in top running condition, he sat in a pool of his own perspiration and waited for his colleagues to wake up.

It was good that they had not tried to travel, for several times that morning; aircraft flew low over their position, doubtlessly on reconnaissance missions to locate them.

In the afternoon, the clouds built up and brought some relief, but it was the major thunderstorm they generated that really did the trick. The lightning flashed, thunder boomed, and dark clouds dumped a deluge of cooling rain that dropped the temperature below a hundred degrees for the first time in weeks. The four young men stood in the middle of the clearing during the entire storm, letting the pouring rain cool their sweaty bodies. Their upturned faces welcomed the heavy caress of the rain, and their open mouths drank in the refreshing liquid. Afterwards, they joined in prayer and gave thanks to God for His goodness and watch care over them.

In addition to the four men, the refreshing storm brought other creatures out in the open to enjoy its coolness. Mark and Jabin each were able to take a rabbit with their arrows, and they all enjoyed a hearty meal together just before the sun went down.

Shortly after dark, the three witnesses said goodbye to Keith and set out cross-country back toward Houston. Revived by the combination of sleep, rain, and food, they were prepared to walk and jog through the night to get back to the city so they would be there to lend assistance to the beleaguered Christians, now so much in need of their help.

Following their instructions, Keith waited until after midnight before he lifted off and made his way to the relative safety of Goshen Compound off to the northeast. Flying high and without any running lights at all, he was able to make it there undetected by any of Renslow's people. Wary watchmen at the compound shot at him as he made his approach, but as soon as his aircraft was identified as the president's helicopter, they were ordered to hold their fire, and he was allowed to set it down in the middle of the square.

Pastor Jack Walker, a balding man in his late fifties with a slightly haggard look about him, welcomed their unexpected guest. He sat up with him late into the early morning, listening as Keith filled him in on all that had taken place during the previous twenty-four hours. He was grieved to learn the fate of those assassinated, and of the attack ordered by Renslow against the three members of God's 144,000.

In the morning after breakfast, a major prayer meeting was held on behalf of the Christians in Houston and elsewhere in the United States. It appeared believers could no longer expect the freedom from persecution they had enjoyed under the administration of President Dwight Honaker. Now, as elsewhere in the world, it seemed God's people would begin to suffer dearly for their faith.

Self-appointed President Lowell Renslow sat in the conference room of the capitol building with his military advisors, going over their proposed strategy to deal with Honaker's assassination and how they were going to govern their nation in his absence. The attack had taken place only the day before, but already much progress had been made in consolidating the new administration. Only two of the men present knew of Renslow's staging of the coup, and they had been sworn to silence. The rest of them accepted his explanation that the unstable Christian community had opened fire on government troops, and that three of their fanatical leaders had blown up the president's limousine, killing him and Ben Heistead and several of his security personnel.

Like Emperor Nero of Rome in the first century, Renslow had found a scapegoat to blame for his actions. Nero had reportedly wanted to clear out the residents from a particularly distasteful slum area in the city in order to allow him to build beautiful structures there in honor of himself. So, he ordered his own men to set the fire, which was even more destructive than he had planned, killing thousands of his citizens, and destroying a huge section of his city. But it accomplished his purpose, and it gave him an excuse to persecute the hated Christians living there at the time. He was able to kill two birds with one stone. He got rid of the slums with the fire, and he was able to lash out against the Christians whom he blamed for starting it.

Similarly, Renslow had been able to rid himself of that coward Honaker, and to promote himself to the role of president, for which he was sure he was much better suited. At the same time, he was able to shift the blame to the Christian community, which had always been a pain in the butt, as far as he was concerned. They were always fasting and praying and encouraging Honaker to seek God's will and to follow what the Bible says. Renslow was convinced that it had been just that sort of stupid advice that had prevented the president from actually taking charge of things and doing what was best for the nation.

Well, that was all going to change now. With Honaker and Hiestead out of the way and himself firmly established in command of the United States, he would lead America out of the stalemate it had been in for more than three years, and he would return it to the greatness it had known before this mess had all begun.

The first thing he had done was to get on the phone with the leaders of Russia and China, and to assure them that the United States was under new leadership now, and that it was fully committed to join in with its allies in a three-pronged assault upon the lair of the beast in the heart of Israel. Galinikov and Chong had been delighted to hear the news, and already plans were being hastily thrown together to coordinate the timing and the logistics of the massive invasion.

Yet, they had to be careful. Their activities were constantly being monitored by Augustus' underlings, and they didn't want to tip their hand prematurely. Once the invasion was launched, their intentions would become painfully obvious to the Great Caesar, but they didn't want him to know what they were about to do until they were actually in the process of doing it. Therefore, the mustering of their troops and the readying of their ships and planes had to be done gradually and secretly, lest Constantine get wind of their intentions and take drastic measures to smash their offensive before it could even get underway.

Hence, Renslow and his men were deliberate in laying out their plans, in no hurry to plunge into action. They all knew there was nothing they could really do so long as the blistering heat continued. The international war machine had virtually ground to a halt anyway, except for a few missiles launched from time to time. No troops could be deployed, no heavy equipment could be moved, and no ships could effectively sail when men around the world were struggling simply to move and breathe. Nevertheless, they were determined to be ready when that time came.

And surely it would. There were already indications that the weather patterns were beginning to change. The thunderstorms of the previous day had cooled things off for the first time in weeks. True, it was still terribly hot, but not as bad as before. They were all optimistic that perhaps soon, the terrible plague would finally run its course.

In the meantime, it gave them time to decide what to do about those troublesome Christians. They had already identified them as the ones who had fired on government troops and had assassinated the president. But they could not actually launch a military offensive against them just yet because, in the first place, it was still too blasted hot. And besides, they had no way of identifying most of them. Honaker had stubbornly refused to have them all sent to concentration camps like Renslow had suggested, or even to be registered, like he had insisted. So, for the present, the Christians were scattered among the general population and very difficult to single out.

But that was all about to change too. Renslow and his brain trust were ready to issue an official proclamation forbidding any Christian assembly for any purpose. Any congregation discovered gathered anywhere was subject to immediate arrest and imprisonment. Anyone offering resistance would be shot. Furthermore, anyone seen preaching, praying, reading the Bible, or anything else religious, was subject to the same treatment. In addition, all able-bodied men were commanded to enlist in the military immediately. Anyone refusing to do so for religious reasons would be thrown into prison as well.

It was Renslow himself who insisted that they require all Christians be registered with their local police departments. He decided that Hitler had a good policy in Germany prior to World War II when he required all Jews to display large Stars of David sewn onto the outside of their clothing. In like fashion, Renslow now would make it mandatory for all Christians to display large crosses in the same way. Once he had them all identified, it would make it easy for his troops to round them up and put them in concentration camps. From there, he could systematically eliminate them.

He was convinced that the world would have been better off without the Jews back in the twentieth century, and he was even more convinced that the world would be better off without the Christians now in the twenty-first century. Hitler had made only one critical mistake: he had lost the war. Lowell Renslow had no such intention. Once he and his comrades in Russia and China had rid the world of Constantine Augustus and his minions, he would restore America to its former glory. Only this time, it would be free from the troublesome, and sometimes crippling, influence of those stupid Christians. And if his alliance did happen to lose the war, then he and the other rebel leaders would all be dead, and their nations would cease to exist anyway. So, they really had nothing to lose.

Renslow felt good about the decisions he and his advisors had made. As they adjourned in the late afternoon and walked out of the building to be driven to their respective homes, they were greeted with a pleasant surprise that added confirmation to his sentiments. Instead of the customary blast of broiling air, they were met with temperatures at least forty degrees cooler. There was even a refreshing breeze blowing in from the gulf.

"The heat has broken at last!" he exulted out loud. To himself he added, "Now we can get down to the business of cleaning up the mess Honaker has gotten us into." Though not a religious man, and determined never to become one, he rather liked the idea of thinking of himself as becoming the savior of the world.

CHAPTER EIGHT

The Emergence

God willed the massive storms on the sun to cease, which had been bombarding the earth with such enormous amounts of energy. Almost immediately, the temperature began to return to normal around the globe. People began to emerge from the rocks and caves, and from the holes they had dug for themselves to escape the heat; life on earth, which had nearly ground to a halt, began to show some signs of recovery. The rains returned, and the farmers went back to their fields. Factories reopened, and laborers went back to their jobs. The undeclared ceasefires were terminated, and the display of human depravity resumed its hellish pace. Military machines ratcheted up their relentless pursuit of destroying their enemies, and the wicked and powerful continued their determined persecution and elimination of the weak and defenseless.

Constantine Augustus emerged from his own bunker-like fortress several levels deep in the bowels of the World Federation headquarters building outside Jerusalem. He emerged lean and hungry—not in his body, but in his psyche. He had a world to conquer, and he had been driven frantic by weeks of forced inactivity. He walked about outside in the ninety-degree temperature and almost felt a chill. The scorching heat must have devastated his enemies and left them especially vulnerable, he thought. Before they had a chance to recover, he would deal them a deathblow. He would strike, as it were, while the iron was hot.

He ordered all his military leaders to launch massive attacks on every front, and not to relent until they had pushed on to ultimate victory.

It all sounded so simple. After all, it was exactly what Emperor Marcus Aurelius had counseled him to do while the two of them were buried together during those scorching weeks in the heart of that Judean hillside. But what he had not taken into consideration was the fact that his own forces had been equally depleted by the prolonged heat wave.

For fear lest they face their master's wrath, his commanders dutifully launched their attacks, but ill equipped and ill prepared, they failed to accomplish their objectives. They inflicted relatively little damage on their enemies, and sustained heavy losses themselves. For the first time since the tribulation had begun, the Great Caesar and his World Federation showed signs of vulnerability. As his weakened military machine was forced to pull back, he ranted and raved, he cursed and he screamed, and he had several of his incompetent generals put to death. How dare they fail to carry out his orders!

He continued to remain in absolute control over most of the world, but he also continued to remain frustrated in his obsession to command the rest of it. The painful fact that his coveted prize persisted in eluding him ate relentlessly at him. Although no one around him yet suspected it, and it was certainly something that had not entered his own mind, he was becoming quite insane.

The newly formed triumvirate, made up of President Lowell Renslow of the United States of America, President Gregor Odin Galinikov of the Republic of Russia, and Chairman Chong Xu Wu of the People's Republic of China, emerged triumphant from the devastating heat of the fourth summer of the tribulation. At Renslow's insistence, they had prepared their forces in advance to throw off the massive assault the U.S. president was sure Augustus would throw at them just as soon as the weather would permit. And they had been successful in their efforts. Their defenses had turned back the onslaught, and they had more than held their own. The three were more encouraged than they had ever been since the madness had begun nearly three-and-a-half years before.

Secretly, they began to prepare for an offensive of their own. By night, troops were transferred: the Russians to the south, the Chinese to the west, and the Americans to the Gulf of Mexico. While the Russians and the Chinese were loading everything on trucks and trains, the Americans were filling their ships with war machines and men of war. The three heads of state were determined to be ready when the right opportunity presented itself.

However, they were not at all sure how that might occur. Constantine's World Federation still held all the important cards. The three rebel nations were still badly out manned and out gunned. A frontal attack on the lair of the beast would be suicidal without some special advantage. But Renslow was confident that just such an advantage would somehow soon materialize, and he and his allies would be ready for it when it did.

In order to be prepared to mobilize immediately, whenever the time was right, he decided to clean up the threat the Christians represented. He would make his public declaration, exposing their assassination of Honaker and Hiestead, and their plot to overthrow the government. He would insist that they be identified and detained. He assured himself they would soon be rounded up and exterminated.

Mark and Jabin and Seth were informed by their angels of Renslow's nefarious plans. They contacted the other members of the 144,000 ministering in the Texas area and got them to pass the word quickly throughout the Christian community not to be fooled by the new president's efforts to identify and register all believers. They anticipated correctly that such a maneuver would be nothing more than a precursor to more treacherous deeds to follow. A simple cross, sewn on the sleeve of a garment, might seem innocuous enough, but they were sure that it would soon lead to future concentration of Christians, and eventually, to their mass elimination.

Furthermore, the witnesses warned all believers who had been serving in the military to abandon their posts. The military was now under the command of a diabolical killer, and he would soon be directing his forces to carry out the dirty business of the devil himself. They further instructed all believers not to stay in their homes, nor to return to their places of employment, but rather to gather together some bare necessities and to flee to places of refuge being prepared for them. Existing Christian compounds were being enlarged to accommodate more residents, and many new ones were being established. They were all in remote locations, where they could be more easily fortified and defended, and where the people could grow their own food.

Such compounds, of course, could not hold out against an all-out attack by the combined strength of the U.S. military, but they would not have to. Mark knew that Renslow's desire all along had been to join Russia and China in a massive three-pronged attack on the World Federation forces in Israel. And now that he was in power, there was nothing to prevent him from pursuing that plan. Therefore, Mark was sure the president would need to send every available man to the front. He could not afford to assign many of his diminishing forces to the task of locating and eliminating a few pesky religious fanatics holed up in the hills and canyons. If the believers stayed in the cities and identified themselves, Mark knew the local police and National Guard troops would be able to apprehend them and lock them away, but if they were far enough out in the country, they would be relatively safe, at least for the time being.

So, the exodus started, slowly and hardly perceptible at first, but it soon grew in numbers and intensity. In a matter of days, tens of thousands of Christians were seen streaming out of the populated areas. However, Renslow was not about to sit back and ignore the ever-increasing number of Christians endeavoring to leave. He ordered whatever troops were in the area to detour, detain, imprison, or shoot (depending on their degree of resistance) any fugitives they encountered trying to escape to the countryside.

Consequently, day and night, Mark and his companions assisted the beleaguered Christians as they made their way out of the cities and towns in the Houston area. They led the way for them, they provided sustenance for their journeys, and they fought off the assailants that tried to impede their progress. But the relatively few members of the 144,000 could not be with all the people all the time. Some of the groups of unescorted fugitives were detained and captured, others were ambushed and slaughtered. Something more substantive had to be done to assist them.

Mark and Seth and Jabin decided to take the extent of their involvement in aiding those escaping to a higher level. They led a large group of frightened saints overland to Goshen Compound on the western shore of Livingston Lake where they had sent Keith with the president's helicopter. After informing Pastor Jack what was going on, and helping their charges to get settled in, they joined in with Keith to assist the remaining fugitives in their flight to freedom. The young Marine was eager to offer the use of himself and his helicopter in the war against evil. He had felt bored and useless sitting around the compound while others served, and risked their lives.

Their first mission was to launch a brazen attack on a remote military supply station south of San Antonio. Keith piloted the craft, while Jabin sat in the co-pilot's seat where he could launch the Hellfire missiles at his command. Mark and Seth each manned a fifty-caliber machine gun mounted at each of the open side doors. The four of them flew the helicopter straight into the base at the end of the day with their missiles firing and their guns blazing. After landing, Mark held off the few brave soldiers, who had not already been neutralized or scattered, while the other three loaded the chopper to the gills with additional missiles and ammunition. They made their escape unscathed and, under cover of darkness, they arrived back at Goshen with a full complement of weaponry.

For the next several days, they wreaked havoc on Renslow's troops whenever they intercepted them attacking any of the caravans of Christians fleeing the cities. With missiles streaking and machine guns blazing, the Black Hawk would sweep out of the sky and obliterate the attacking forces before the enemy hardly realized they were under attack. Then they would disappear into the clouds or the terrain before any retaliatory aircraft could be summoned to dispatch them.

Fortunately, most of the State of Texas was situated on top of a huge oil field, and the U.S. had only recently begun to experience a fuel shortage. Goshen compound had an underground storage tank that was over half full, and from it, the young marauders were able to draw enough fuel to keep their thirsty Black Hawk in the air.

Renslow was, of course, furious, and he ordered the helicopter shot down immediately, but he was soon introduced to the frustration that Constantine Augustus had been experiencing for nearly three-and-a-half years. It just wasn't that easy to kill members of God's 144,000.

Seth's accuracy with the Hellfire missiles was uncanny. Every time he punched a missile away from his aircraft, it seemed destined to find its way to its intended target. And Mark and Jabin were just as deadly with their machine guns. Seth had fired only a .22 rifle and a shotgun before, and Mark had never shot a firearm of any sort, but after a couple of minutes of instructions from Keith, they took to it like seasoned veterans. They stood in the open doorways of their Black Hawk, with their big guns rattling in rhythm, and shell casings clattering by the hundreds around their feet; and woe be to anyone who might find himself in their sights.

Yet, those who shot at them seemed to have lost all sense of aim and accuracy. Thousands of rounds were fired in their direction, from both the air and the ground, but few of them managed to strike the helicopter at all, and none of them was able to do any real damage. At the end of every mission, the four would go over their craft carefully, only to find, to their continued amazement, that she was as sound as ever . . . a few more dents and pock marks, but essentially undamaged.

Keith had always been a good pilot. Otherwise, he would never have been selected to command the president's helicopter, but now he flew like no man had ever flown before. At top speed, he took his craft under bridges, through forests, and between high-rise buildings with pinpoint precision. The tips of his rotor blades came within mere inches of hundreds of solid objects, yet he struck none of them. Even his divinely appointed passengers continued to be impressed.

Such was not the case with those who pursued him,. Seasoned pilots tried to close in on him to get a killing shot, and they would inevitably fail to duplicate his maneuvers. One after the other, they flew their machines into abutments, trees, and buildings, until others began to decline to give chase. What none of them knew was that they really didn't have a chance, for that single helicopter, with its crew of only four men, was surrounded by hundreds of holy angels. They beat back the demons from hell, as well as the men in uniform that sought to snatch it out of the sky. Those on board were literally borne aloft on angels' wings, and as long as they were God's men, doing God's will, they were absolutely invincible.[18]

After four days of sustaining heavy losses, and failing to stop the stream of people leaving the cities, and failing, as well, to inflict any apparent damage at all on the helicopter that protected them, Renslow reluctantly gave the order to cease all further operations. He could have ordered his planes to bomb all the locations known to house the Christian refugees and inflict heavy damage on that way, but he didn't want to expend his precious resources on such non-strategic targets; nor did he want to run the risk of starting a civil war by ordering such a massive and unprovoked attack on so large a number of defenseless Americans.

After all, he convinced himself, those foolish people were not heavily armed, and they posed no real threat, either to the general population, or to national security. He would monitor their whereabouts, and after he had vanquished his foes elsewhere, he would return and deal with that rabble, and with that helicopter crew that insisted on shielding them.

The three witnesses regretted the destruction of property they had caused, and especially the human suffering and loss of life, but they realized they had played a major role in preserving the lives of countless numbers of God's people. Although they found the use of modern weap-

[18] For He shall give His angels charge over you, to keep you in all your ways. In their hands they shall bear you up, lest you dash your foot against a stone. You shall tread upon the lion and the cobra, the young lion and the serpent you shall trample underfoot (Psalm 91:11–13).

onry extremely effective, they realized that God had not called them to conduct mechanized warfare against the evil armies of the world. They were chosen for other things, and they were content to get back to their slings, and bows and arrows.

Because of their involvement, only mere hundreds of believers had lost their lives in their struggle to flee from the wrath of an evil man and those who served him, while tens of thousands were escorted to safety. Those people were all tired and hungry, and some of them were injured, but they were finally among brethren who loved them and would care for them, and, at least for now, they were safe.

What Mark, Seth, and Jabin were doing in Texas, other members of the 144,000 were doing in other parts of what remained of the United States (although not in so dramatic a fashion). Evil men were now promoted to positions of authority, and they were ordered to eradicate the Christian element from their territories. In places where believers had never been persecuted before, they were singled out for eventual extermination because Renslow had judged them guilty of assassinating President Honaker and attempting to overthrow the nation's government. So, his underlings poured out their wrath upon the innocent offspring of Renslow's real enemy, Jehovah God. To have any hope of surviving, believers had to flee into the wilderness. There was no guarantee of safety in the remote places to which they fled, but there was virtually no chance at all should they stay in the centers of population.

If they could, Christians tried to make it to high mountainous regions. There, the terrain was rougher and more inaccessible to those pursuing them, and they could find better hiding places and materials with which to build shelters. The high elevations also provided them with ample precipitation for drinking water, and the alpine forests offered them a variety of food sources.

A great number of believers, however, were unable to travel the long distances to remote mountains, so they took refuge in dense forests, deep canyons, and even arid deserts. They obviously faced greater challenges in locating adequate food, water, and shelter, but they simply had no other choices. Many did not survive the arduous hardships they faced, but with the mutual support of fellow Christians, the presence of members of the 144,000, and considerable angelic assistance, the majority of them did manage to survive those last torturous weeks of the tribulation.

When the heat broke on the west coast, as elsewhere in other parts of the world, the emerging Christian population actually faced few new challenges. With the exception of the relatively small area remaining under the control of the United States, believers had been running and hiding ever since the tribulation had begun. Los Angeles had been the western regional center for all of Constantine Augustus' operations for well over three years, and the believers there had been subject to unbelievable pressure for that entire period of time. Most of those who had not already been apprehended and put to death had already fled to safer places years before. And those who stayed behind were a tough bunch. They had armed themselves and gone underground. Adopting guerrilla warfare tactics, they conducted covert operations against their enemies. They were constantly on the move, and they survived by raiding and plundering Federation installations.

Derek Uptain led one of those guerilla bands of believers, and he had decided that the gestures of loving his enemies and turning the other cheek belonged to another age. He and his men had seen countless numbers of innocent Christians brutalized, maimed, and slaughtered, and they vowed to strike back. They hit and ran, destroyed and dodged, and otherwise did everything they could to make the lives of those Federation stooges as miserable and frustrated as possible. And the one providing him with constant encouragement, information, and protection was none other than the one who had rescued him and led him to Christ in the first place: Aaron Muller.

Aaron had gone through quite a transformation in the nearly three-and-a-half years since the rapture of the church. He had always been serious minded and strong, but in a passive sort of way. He had never been aggressive or violent before the rapture—the lone exception being when he and Mark Robertson had blown up the Dome of the Rock four years before. Other than that unique experience, he had always been rather quiet and reserved . . . but no more.

Now, his weathered face was set with determination, and his powerful muscles rippled beneath his ragged clothing. His movements were cat-like and deadly when he stalked his prey. He never killed just for the sake of killing, but he did not hesitate to take the lives of those killing or plotting to kill his brethren. The whistle of his sling spelled doom for any enemy within a hundred yards, and the explosive power of his rod felled his attackers by the hundreds. The souls of Old Testament heroes seemed to be rekindled in the body of this formerly soft-spoken college athlete. Through him, David felled the giant Goliath once again and led the Israelites unto glorious victory.[19] And through him, Samson wielded the jawbone of an ass once more and slew his thousand Philistines.[20] And Aaron's rod became Shamgar's ox goad, and with it, the ancient judge of Israel dispatched again his six hundred Philistine warriors.[21]

For the first years of the tribulation, Aaron had committed himself to preaching the gospel to those left behind after the rapture, and then to trying to defend the ones who believed from Constantine's henchmen who set about persecuting and murdering them. He had also spent countless days assisting his beleaguered converts in escaping to remote locations where they had a better chance of survival. Those early years had been consumed with spiritual harvesting, and then with trying desperately to protect the fruit of his labors. But now things were different.

After the final ingathering of saints during the plague of the boils, the lines had become clearly drawn. The gospel had been preached to virtually every lost soul in the Southland, and those who were going to be saved had already been saved; and those who were not had already been hardened in their unbelief. Also, the Federation troops had captured and killed about all the new believers they were going to be able to eliminate; the rest had either fled the area or had joined up with one of the bands of armed resistance. The role of the 144,000 had turned from the defensive to the offensive. The forces of evil had wreaked terrible havoc on the innocent people of God for far too long; now it was time for payback.

Aaron led Derek and his ragtag army in daring raids nearly every night, inflicting punishing injury into the very center of the Federation's operations. In addition to neutralizing great numbers of his military personnel, they cut lines of communication, they blew up munitions depots, and they put out of commission countless military vehicles and irreplaceable pieces of equipment and machinery.

When Constantine heard of all the damage his nemesis in Los Angeles was causing, he exploded at Eli Rothschild and demanded some-

[19] 1 Samuel 17:48–52
[20] Judges 15:14–16
[21] Judges 3:31

one put a stop to the young rebel once and for all. Eli, in turn, screamed at Myron Spangler, the head of the World Federation's operations on the American West Coast. Then Spangler turned up the heat on his second in command, Major Tony D'Angelo.

It was ironic how the latter two came to be working together at the top of Constantine's organization in the Los Angeles area. In another life, they had been on opposite sides of the law: Spangler, the tough homicide detective, pursuing two young robbery and murder suspects; and D'Angelo, the cocky college athlete, maneuvering skillfully to keep from being caught. Yet after the rapture, the whole world had turned upside down, and the two survivor-types managed to climb to the top of the only game left in town, that of Constantine Augustus.

During the brief war that followed the rapture, many key authority figures in Los Angeles either perished in the hostilities, or they fled the area when it became clear that the cause was lost. But both Spangler and D'Angelo saw the handwriting on the wall and switched sides early in the conflict, lending valuable assistance to the invading Federation forces. They were rewarded for their contributions by being welcomed into the newly forming leadership team that would administer operations in the Southland for the World Federation. And since both of them had lost their partners, they joined forces and became the most unlikely of bedfellows.

Tony's partner-in-crime, Scott Graham, had been gunned down the night of the rapture, leaving Tony alone. And strangely enough, Spangler's partner, Detective Theo Farley, had been killed by the blast of a bomb he set off while he was trying to defuse it. It had been dropped during the brief Battle of Los Angeles back at the beginning of the tribulation, and some boys, playing in a vacant lot, reported finding it. Spangler hadn't tried very hard to talk his co-worker out of tackling the job, even though he thought he was stupid for trying it; and Farley, ever the optimist, was sure he could handle it. His clumsiness cost Spangler a good partner.

Paul Apparicio, the local crime boss, had been appointed to head up the local leadership in Los Angeles, under the supervision of Eli Rothschild himself. But when the hoodlum was killed in a shootout with some of those religious fanatics nearly two years later, Spangler, who had proven himself both ruthless and efficient, was selected to take his place. And when he rose to the leadership position, he took his equally ruthless new partner along with him. Now, recently promoted Major Tony D'Angelo sat across the desk from him in his large office at the top of the Federation's high-rise Los Angeles headquarters.

"Tony, we gotta do something about that Muller character!" he complained. "Rothschild will have my head if we don't hand that punk over to Augustus soon. He screamed at me for thirty minutes this morning, and I couldn't give him the answers he wanted. Why can't we catch this guy?"

"I don't know. Believe me, I've tried. He's sorta charmed, or something. He's weaseled out of every trap I've set for him since this whole mess first began. I knew he was really different even back then, but now, he's almost god-like. I don't know if we'll ever be able to take him down."

"That's not good enough!" Spangler yelled, slamming his fist down on the desk. "Rothschild's not gonna accept that for an answer, and you can bet that Great Caesar he works for ain't going to either. There's gotta be a way to bring in people close to him, and then use them to get to him."

"Remember, we already tried that boss," Tony replied, absently fingering the ugly scar running across his nose and cheek. "I almost had him too. I had the whole nest of 'em trapped in that cabin up in the mountains, but somebody blew it up . . . with my men in it. Then Muller showed up and killed the rest of my men, and I barely escaped with my life. I have this beauty mark here to remind me of that night."

"Well, what happened to them . . . his family, I mean?

"I don't have a clue. They weren't in the cabin, I know. I sent men back up there the next day, and there wasn't a sign of them. They just seem to have dropped off the end of the earth. I've had people looking for them ever since, but there hasn't been a clue. My men insist they've all left the area entirely, but I have my doubts. I think there're still up there in those mountains somewhere, but I don't know where to begin to look."

"Isn't there anybody else close to him?" Tony's commander wanted to know.

"Yeah, that rabble he runs with. But they're as impossible to catch as he is. Whatever power he has, he seems to be able to transfer it to them as well. All I do is lose men and machines when I go after any of them."

"Well, there has to be somebody else," Spangler protested.

"Okay, yeah, there are," Tony remembered, "but I don't think they'll do us any good. He has an uncle and aunt here in the city, but they work for us. I got them to betray Muller twice before. He's not likely to come to their aid if we put any pressure on them now."

"Oh, don't be so sure, Tony. Those religious types don't think like you and me. A dude crosses us, and he's gone. But those guys don't see it that way. You know, they're all full of love and forgiveness and stuff. I betcha if we hauled his relatives in and started torturing them, he'd come runnin' to their rescue."

"I don't know about that. They've been in our camp since the very beginning. He's not likely to risk his life for relatives who've been sleepin' with the enemy, if you know what I mean."

"There you go again," Spangler countered. "You're thinking like us. They could be boiling your own mama in oil, and you wouldn't lift a finger to help her if she'd crossed you before. Neither would I. But I'm telling you, those guys don't think like us. That's probably their only weakness."

"Yeah, now that I think about it, maybe you're right," Tony conceded.

"Now you're talking, kid. You bring those two down to headquarters here, and we'll put the screws to 'em. We'll broadcast the whole thing out over TV and radio and . . . mark my word . . . that ole avenging angel out there will come flyin' to their defense."

"You got it, boss. It just might work. Besides, it's about the only option we got. If we don't bring Muller in soon, old Eli will have both our heads."

Aaron Muller worked his way up the ridges and canyons of the San Gabriel Mountains under the cover of a moonless night. His enhanced night vision allowed him to see well enough to pick his way even though he purposefully stayed away from any of the established trails. It had been several months since he had visited his family and, even though it was dangerous, he was determined to learn of their welfare. The oppressive heat had been so intense, and it had lasted so long, he was anxious to see how they had weathered it.

Things had quieted down somewhat in the valley below. It always concerned him when that happened. It usually meant that his enemies were preparing to launch yet another one of their violent offensives. He wondered what they were up to this time. However, in the meantime, it gave him the opportunity to slip away and see to his family. Derek and his men were safely hidden deep in the catacombs of the Los Angeles sewer system getting some much needed rest, so he felt relatively confident in his present venture.

It was nearly ten o'clock when he approached the entrance of the cave where he had last left his loved ones in the spring. He was met by an enthusiastic Millennium, who jumped about with glee and insisted on standing on his hind legs with his forepaws on Aaron's shoulders so he could give his long-absent friend a proper greeting with his slathering tongue.

He was not quite as big, not quite as ugly, and not quite as rowdy as Armageddon, but other than that, he was the spitting image of his sire . . . or perhaps one should say, "The slobbering image."

Aaron was playfully trying to hold off the big dog's advances when he was tackled from behind by an almost as enthusiastic Tim and Steve. They had heard the commotion from inside the cave and had come to investigate.

The three of them tumbled and wrestled on the ground, two against one, trying to gain the mastery over the other, but their efforts were in vain because Millie insisted on being squarely in the middle of them. Their playful struggles alerted the others in the cave, and soon the whole family had gathered round to watch the free-for-all. It was the first time any of them had laughed or played in a very long time.

It was Joseph who called a halt to the happy occasion and insisted they all go back inside the cave. It simply wasn't safe to be outside for long, even at night, especially with carryings-on so raucous and noisy.

Once back in their living quarters, the family was able to greet Aaron more appropriately. He was relieved and happy to find that they all appeared strong and healthy, especially Anna. Her soft brown hair glowed, and her hazel eyes danced in the firelight. Her lovely presence reminded him just how much he loved her and how much he had missed her. After a much-needed shower and a change of clothes, Aaron welcomed her to sit beside him as he consumed the good food they set before him. She remained by his side throughout the late hours of the night as the entire family sat up, taking turns telling him how they had managed since last he had seen them.

The Frieberg family had fared better than most of the other hapless earth dwellers during those scorching weeks that summer. Their high mountain location offered them some relief from the heat, but it was their cave that protected them most. Deep within the heart of the mountain, they had been able to escape most of the effects of the sun's sustained assault on the planet. The temperature rose inside, but it never reached the point where its occupants suffered more than moderate discomfort.

They had extra reserves of food, so they did not go hungry. The stifling heat had destroyed their vegetable garden, and it had dried up the natural berries as well, so they had no fresh produce. They had to ration things out carefully, but did manage to have enough to eat. If they had to face the winter with their food supplies so depleted, they would be in serious jeopardy indeed, but Aaron assured them that the tribulation was soon to be over, and that was one thing they would not have to be concerned about.

Tim and Steve had enjoyed success hunting during those hot weeks of drought. If they had gone out during the daylight hours, it would have been totally pointless, as virtually all living beings sought refuge during those punishing hours; but equipped with the night-vision goggles, they were well rewarded after dark. They positioned themselves near the few remaining water holes, and selected their prizes as they came to drink. So, they had plenty of meat to eat, but precious little to go with it.

The main concern for the family had been the diminishing supply of water inside the cave. Normally, the subterranean stream flowed steadily year round, but during the drought, it slowed to a mere trickle, and finally stopped altogether. They found themselves out of fresh water and electricity. They made candles out of animal tallow, and with the use of the night vision goggles, they managed to get around in the near total darkness.

Fortunately, that was just before the heat broke and the thunderstorms brought an abundance of rain. They had the foresight to collect extra water in an assortment of vessels before the stream dried up, so they never actually went thirsty. And the rains had come just in time. At present, the stream was flowing as heartily as it had before, bringing plenty of life-giving water and churning out an abundance of light-giving electricity from the little generator. Life had returned pretty much to normal for the little mountain community.

Aaron rejoiced with them over God's continuing watch care over them, and he assured them that their struggles were soon to be over. Yet, he also assured them that things were almost certainly going to get much worse before they got any better. They were going to have to be extremely careful for the next several weeks.

More and more people had moved up into these mountains to escape the heat and to search for food and water, and many of them could not be trusted. He told the family to remain inside the cave throughout the day, and venture out only at night, and then only to hunt and gather and take care of any necessary business. There was a hefty reward out for anyone who might lead the authorities to any member of the Frieberg family, and the mountains were undoubtedly full of nosey opportunists who would love to cash in on it.

Everyone insisted on hearing what Aaron had been doing during those last several months, but he told them very little. Most of it was much too horrible to share anyway, and his exploits had been so astounding that there was no way he could relate most of it without sounding arrogant and boastful. So he just told them in general of his ongoing struggles against the forces of evil, and of some of his more believable tragedies and triumphs.

Before they all went to bed, Aaron told his family that he would probably not see them again before the final Battle of Armageddon and the Lord's return. He didn't know for sure when all that would happen, but according to his calculations, three-and-a-half years would expire within the next six weeks. They needed to stay tuned to their little radio and follow world events as closely as possible. Prayerfully, all the horrible end times events would take place elsewhere while they were safely tucked inside their sturdy mountain sanctuary.

Long after everyone else had gone off to bed, Aaron sat up by the fire with Anna at his side and Millie dozing at his feet. It was a precious time, a heavenly respite in the midst of a terrible storm. They had come through so much thus far; they were cautiously beginning to believe that they both might actually live to see the end of the nightmare they had been going through for nearly three-and-a-half years. They even dared to speak softly of what their lives might be like together during the coming glorious kingdom of their Messiah. Aaron knew he must leave again the following night, and he had no idea what horrors either one of them would face in the coming weeks, but for right then, they had their hopes and dreams; and most importantly, they had each other.

CHAPTER NINE

The Darkness

At the beginning of August, Joseph and David walked together down the busy Ben Yihudi shopping district in western Jerusalem. The Federation soldiers were powerless to stop them as they announced the arrival of the fifth plague in the final series of bowl judgments. They warned the inhabitants of Israel and its surrounding nations to prepare for the coming darkness; darkness like they had never witnessed before; darkness so intense and so powerful that it could kill those it engulfed.

In the middle of the following night, the fifth angel poured out his bowl into the heart of the area controlled by the antichrist, and the darkness spread like a thick blanket across the land. The effects of it were evidenced in some degree around the entire world.

Tony D'Angelo had his driver pull their vehicle over to the curb and stop. Manny Russo was quick to comply. He had been a driver for Paul Apparicio's underworld operation for years prior to the rapture, and he was used to following orders without question. But that part of his life had ceased to exist. Apparicio was now dead, as was his Lieutenant Sal LaMata, both killed by religious fanatics who opposed them and the Federation they served. The mousy little man didn't care. All he wanted to do was to follow instructions, get his paycheck, and be left alone.

It didn't even bother him that Tony D'Angelo was now his boss. Of course, he remembered that rainy night years ago when he drove the pursuit vehicle while Gino Mantelli gunned down those hapless occupants in that miserable old Ford Taurus. D'Angelo had been an unwilling, sniveling, cowardly occupant in his car back then, intimidated and manipulated by LaMata and Mantelli. But that was then, and this was now. The others had by now either been killed or demoted, and D'Angelo had risen to the top. So be it. As long as all Manny had to do was drive the car, he didn't much care who gave the orders.

He and his present boss were in a long black Federation limousine, and they were on important Federation business, but it would just have to wait. Both he and his back seat passenger had become aware of a change in conditions that demanded their immediate attention.

Tony had called Noah Frieberg that morning and informed him that Commander Spangler had decided to hold a special luncheon and press conference at noon to honor Noah and Sheila and their company for their splendid contributions to the World Federation's operations in the Western United States. Tony was to pick them up at 11:30 and escort them to the Towers Hotel for the gala affair. In reality, the Friebergs were unknowingly to be delivered to the adjacent Federation headquarters building to be tortured brutally before the all-seeing eyes of television cameras from all the major networks. But that was before the darkness fell.

It was eleven o'clock in the morning on a bright August day, when the sky suddenly started turning dark. Tony lowered his tinted window and looked up into a cloudless sky that was rapidly growing dark. After Manny had pulled the limo over to the curb, Tony opened his rear door and stepped out onto the sidewalk where he joined dozens of other people who were gazing up into the gathering gloom.

He could see the sun clearly, high overhead, and he didn't need to squint to look at it. There it was, a big red ball in the sky, growing noticeably dimmer even as he looked at it. No portion of it was being occluded, as in an eclipse. Inexplicably, the perfect circle in the sky continued to grow redder and dimmer in the middle of the day. Tony shivered as he looked at the bewildering phenomenon, partially because it was so mind-boggling, but mostly because of the sudden chill that gripped the air.

After several minutes, the sun appeared barely visible in the muted sky and some of the brighter stars were becoming visible against the darkened background. Tony feared that the vanishing light would disappear entirely, leaving them in total darkness, but that was not to be.

Just when the light approximated that of late twilight, the darkening effect appeared to stop. He could still see, but it was not easy. The photocell-equipped streetlights engaged and gradually grew in intensity until they were glowing merrily in the noonday darkness; and drivers, almost as automatically, started turning on their headlights.

Tony climbed back inside the limo and tried to use its phone to reach Spangler back at headquarters to see what he wanted him to do, but all the circuits were understandably jammed. In light of the weirdest thing he had ever seen, he wasn't at all sure that his boss would want him to proceed with his mission, so he decided to return to headquarters and talk it over with him. The bewildered Manny was eager to comply with his directive. The less time he spent driving in this crazy darkness, the better he would like it.

It seemed everyone was driving with much more caution than usual, as though they were expecting something even more bizarre to happen at any moment. Therefore, it took them longer to arrive at headquarters than it should have, but Tony was in no hurry. The delay gave him time to try to sort things out in his mind. He had a lot of questions for which he needed answers. Was this darkness worldwide, or was it just a local phenomenon? Where had it come from, and how long was it going to last? How would it affect the status of the international balance of power? And most importantly, how would it affect him personally and his ability to survive and prosper?

He was able to arrive at answers for none of those questions, and the newscasters on the radio were of no help whatsoever; they were as much in the dark as he was. When he arrived at headquarters, it was like the proverbial beehive. People were dashing about and yelling at one another. Executives were loudly demanding their underlings produce things for them immediately; and they, in turn, were vocally insistent that such demands were impossible; and no one appeared either pleased or under control.

Tony took the elevator to the top floor and reminded himself that he could at least be thankful that Federation engineers had been able to keep the power on consistently after countless blackouts during the worst of the recent heat wave. Climbing those stairs in hundred-degree-plus weather had not been his idea of a good time.

He knocked on the door and entered Spangler's office in one continuous motion as had become his pattern. "Hey, Boss, what's going on out there?" he wanted to know.

Spangler swore. "I don't have a clue!" he confessed. "The experts have never seen anything like it. There's no eclipse of the sun, no debris in the air, no disturbance in outer space, no nothin'. It just seems the sun has decided to nearly shut down. The lights have come on, and the heaters too. What a mess! A couple weeks ago we were burning up in the worst summer heat wave in the history of the world, and now it looks like we're gonna be freezing our butts off on a cold winter night at noon in August! What's next . . . the whole stinking planet blowing itself to bits?"

"I don't know. At this point, nothing would surprise me. But I figure it's got to be like all the other weird things that have been going on over the past three or four years. None of it makes any sense, but at least they don't last forever. If we just stick this thing out for a few weeks, then whoever, or whatever, is out there will turn the lights back on again. Is this just a local thing, or is it going on elsewhere?"

"All over the world, as far as anybody knows. But what's really weird is that it may be worse in the Middle East. It's dark over there now, so they can't tell for sure, but it's never been this dark before. According to the reports coming in from headquarters in Jerusalem, there's absolutely no light at all; not from the moon; not from the stars; not from nothin'."

"How can that be?"

"I don't know, but that's what they're sayin'. If there're no manmade lights on anywhere, then it's darker than a stack of black cats in a coalmine. And what's even scarier is they say the darkness is so thick it sorta swallows up the light that is there. A powerful searchlight will only shine out a few feet before it's snuffed out. They can't drive any vehicles at all, because even the high beams won't cut through the soup more than a foot or two. I don't know what to make of it."

"Well, it shouldn't be too bad. When the sun comes up over there, it will probably get as light as it is here right now." Then, after thinking for a moment, he added, "But that also means it will probably get just as dark here in a few hours when the sun goes down . . . and cold too, I imagine. It already feels like wintertime out there, and it's in the middle of the day."

"I know," agreed Spangler. "We better get prepared for the worst. It would be just like those fanatics to hit us right here at headquarters when we can't see them coming."

"Oh, that reminds me," Tony butted in. "I was on the way to pick up the Friebergs when the lights went out. Do you want me to go ahead and go get them?"

"No, not now. Things are way too confusing still. We can deal with them later when everything settles down. Give them a call when you can get an open line and explain that the luncheon has been postponed because of the darkness, and we will get in touch with them soon to let them know when it has been rescheduled."

"Okay, but let's not wait too long. Neither one of us is going to be able to face Rothschild or Augustus until we're able to hand Muller over to them, and it looks like the Friebergs are our only way to get to him."

"Yeah, I know. Just give us a few more days to make sure everything is secure around here, and then we'll bring 'em in and light 'em up. When we threaten to make human torches out of his relatives, Muller will come crawling to us out of whatever dark corner he's hiding in."

At about 5:30 A.M., it should have started getting somewhat light in Jerusalem, but it did not. Even by eight o'clock, it was every bit as dark as it had been at midnight. The temperature did drop significantly, but not drastically. The cold was not the problem; it was the awful darkness itself.

True, the rest of the world was affected by the darkness too, but not like in the realm of the beast. There was no way to scientifically explain it, but there was absolute darkness in one part of the world, and only partial darkness in the rest of it. Even at night elsewhere, the stars shone dimly in the heavens, and the crescent moon glowed blood red as it punctuated the early night sky. But within hundreds of miles of Jerusalem, it was pitch black at midday.

And it wasn't like any darkness ever experienced on the planet before. Not only was it totally black, there was an evil presence accompanying it. It snuffed out whatever light it came in contact with, and it inflicted excruciating pain on those it enshrouded. The darkness itself seemed to be alive. It stung and bit at human flesh, and drove its victims mad with pain. No one dared be outside in it. The only way to escape its venom was to stay locked inside a sturdy building with all the doors and windows closed and barred, and by generating light from hundreds of sources to fight back the gloom. Even then, virtually everyone became infested to one degree or another with the boil-like sores the creeping darkness raised on any exposed skin.

Life in the realm of the Great Caesar Augustus came to a standstill. He and his people were forced to stay locked inside their bunkers. They became extremely vulnerable to their enemies, but there was nothing they could do. They spent their miserable days cursing Jehovah God and blaspheming His name, and shaking their angry fists toward the ebony skies.[22]

The darkness that was a loathsome bane to the kingdom of the beast became an unexpected boon to the rest of the world. Outside the Middle East and most of Europe, the darkness was not overwhelming, neither was it painful. Life was hampered, but not stifled. One could see to get around well enough during the daylight hours, and even at night, travel and work were possible with the aid of manmade lights from various sources.

President Lowell Renslow saw the darkness as just the advantage he had been waiting for. When he learned of the conditions in the Middle East, he clapped his fleshy hands with glee. Now he would be unmolested as he loaded his war machine into his ships and set sail for Africa. His allies would also be free to begin moving their mighty armies overland to the very edges of the realm of the beast. When the darkness lifted, and he was sure it that it would before too long, Augustus would come crawling out of his hole only to find the combined forces of three great nations literally camped on his doorstep.

Renslow was quick to get in contact with both Galinikov and Chong, and was pleased to discover that his allies had already begun moving their forces in the direction of Israel. By their combined estimations, within two weeks they would all have their units in place, ready to move into Israel just as soon as whatever forces were out there decided to roll back the darkness.

He wasted no time. He met with his military advisors and shared his daring scheme with them. Any believers had long since left their ranks, so he had little difficulty convincing the infidels who remained to endorse his plans. Within two days, his vast naval fleet was underway, carrying in the bellies of his many ships the men and machines that would finally turn back the tide of tyranny and oppression that spewed out of the mouth of the beast himself.

---

[22] Then the fifth angel poured out his bowl on the throne of the beast, and his kingdom became full of darkness; and they gnawed their tongues because of the pain. They blasphemed the God of heaven because of their pains and their sores, and did not repent of their deeds (Revelation 16:10–11).

Renslow insisted on accompanying his troops, and sailed in the flagship, the USS John Paul Jones, a floating city of an aircraft carrier, some 1100 feet from stem to stern, and standing over twenty stories in height. The mighty craft set the pace, and the armada followed enthusiastically along, traveling at a speed of nearly 30 knots, out of the Caribbean Sea and directly towards the coast of North Africa.

He encountered no opposition along the way. The bulk of the Federation Navy was deployed in two major arenas, halfway around the world from each other. The larger contingent was deployed in and around the Mediterranean Sea to protect the heart of Constantine's empire. The bulk of his remaining ships were stationed on either side of the Pacific Ocean to combat the forces of all three of his enemies that lined that great body of water. What ships he had in the eastern Atlantic were no match for the mighty flotilla that steamed its way toward the smothering darkness to the east.

Tony D'Angelo hurried down the hall, gulping down the last of his coffee as he went. Myron Spangler's voice had been insistent on the intercom; something major was in the works, and he was needed in his boss's office immediately.

"What's up, boss?" he asked as he pushed the door open without knocking.

"Have a seat Tony," Spangler replied, motioning to a chair across from his desk. "I just heard from Jerusalem, and it looks like it's all about to hit the fan over there."

Obliging him, Tony sat down and leaned forward in his chair. "What's going down?" he inquired.

"Federation spies have confirmed that a massive invasion is moving toward the Middle East from three different directions: the Russians from the north, the Chinese from the east, and the Americans from the west. They'll probably deploy their forces just outside the Killer Dark [as they had come to call the area of pitch blackness that had settled over most of the U.S.E. and the Middle East]. Then, when the conditions change, they'll be positioned to launch an immediate attack against the Federation in Israel."

"Wow! Do you think they can pull it off?" Tony wanted to know.

"No, I don't think so, not on their best day; but Augustus doesn't want to take any chances. With that Killer Dark still sitting in his lap, he can't do much of anything over there to prepare to meet the invasion. He'll have to scramble like crazy just as soon as it lifts. That's why he's calling every available man and machine he's got to get over there and help him."

"Whaddya mean?" Tony asked, genuinely caught off guard.

"Just what I said. There's no need to keep planes or ships or guns stationed anyplace else in the world when all the strength of his enemies is being concentrated in Palestine. If the Rooskies, the Chinks, and the Yanks are able to cut off the head of the beast in Israel, then the body will die in the rest the world, and Augustus knows it. I'm shipping out tonight, and I'm ordered to take most of our troops with me."

"What?" Tony gasped. "Who's gonna take care of things around here? There's a lot of crazies out there who would love to destroy everything we've worked so hard to set up."

"You are," Spangler said. "That's why I called you in here. I got older and more experienced people than you, but nobody's better able to handle the job. As of right now, you're the new commander of the Federation forces in the whole western region."

"Really!" Tony blurted out. "You think I can handle it, Chief?"

"Yeah, you're a smart cookie. You and that Graham kid covered your tracks really well after you screwed up that robbery a few years back. We knew you were guilty, but we could never pin a thing on you. You employ the same kind of savvy you used to outsmart Farley and me, and you won't have any trouble handling the riffraff that's out there now."

"But you said you were taking almost everybody with you. How am I gonna run things around here without any help?"

"Oh don't worry about that. I'll leave you plenty of firepower to handle the locals. You're just not gonna need all the ships and planes and tanks and troopers anymore. We're not fighting a war on the other side of the Rockies now. The other side has all packed up and shipped out for the Holy Land already. That's why we gotta ship all our stuff over there too so we can be ready for 'em when the fog lifts."

"But you can't be taking them into that Killer Dark are you?"

"No way, man. It'd be suicide to go into that dark hole. Our ships will have to sail all the way around Cape Horn because the U.S. blew up the Panama Canal, so it'll take us a long time to get over there. But when we do, we'll engage the American fleet waiting off the coast of Africa. If the Killer Dark is still hanging around, we will have them trapped between it and us. But if it's lifted, and they've already launched their invasion, we'll take in after them, and we'll overtake 'em in the desert. Either way, we'll stop 'em before they ever get to Israel."

"What about our bombers and transports?" Tony wanted to know.

"They'll be loaded to the gills, and after refueling in Canada, they'll fly to our bases in England and Scandinavia; as close as they can get and still stay out of the dead zone. Then once the lights come back on, they'll be ready to fly into Israel to support Augustus."

"That's gonna be some war! It sounds like everybody in the world will be squaring off when the fog lifts over there. I can't say I'm sorry I'm gonna miss it."

"Well, I don't wanna miss it," Spangler boasted. "It's about time we got rid of those rebel states once and for all. Constantine Augustus is the best thing that ever happened to this world. If it hadn't been for those renegades who deserted him, we would all be living in the lap of luxury right now. Don't get me wrong, I'm an American, and proud of it, but Honaker was a fool. He and Galinikov and that Chairman Chong character are the ones who caused all the hell we've been going through for the past three-and-a-half years. I'm glad he's finally dead, but that idiot Renslow is no better. I understand he's the one who talked the other two into attacking our headquarters in Israel. The sooner we get rid of them all, the better off we're gonna be."

"But are you sure we will win this war? It sounds like the enemy will have a lot of firepower over there."

"Sure we're gonna win. We've been beating those renegades down to a nubbin for the past several years. They don't have much left to fight with. While everyone's stumbling around in the dark over there, we will be amassing the combined military strength of over two hundred nations, and when the lights come back on, we'll be ready to go in and kick their butts once and for all."

"Yeah, I guess you're right. What do you want me to concentrate on while you're gone?"

"Well, keep the peace, of course. Don't let those guerilla bands get the upper hand. But you know how to do that. I've never seen anybody so ruthless as you. And to think, you were a clean-cut college kid a couple of years ago. As they say, 'You've come a long way, baby.'"

"Yeah, I guess so. But those days seem like a hundred years ago now: no more college, no more swimming, no more pretty face. My parents are both dead, and I have no idea where the rest of my family is. Things like that tend to change a guy, you know?"

"Tell me about it! I used to be the dutiful cop: the defender of truth, justice, and the American way; and now look at me. I'm the biggest crook in the Southland. My family and friends are all gone. I even let my own partner go off and get himself blown up . . . the dumb schmuck. Oh well, when this is all over, maybe things can get back somewhat to normal. Maybe we'll hang out together then, and be pals," Spangler added sarcastically.

"Yeah, right," Tony agreed with equal sarcasm. He genuinely disliked Spangler, he always had, and he was sure he always would. But the older man had been there when he needed a road to the top, so he had linked up with him. But he knew neither one of them had ever genuinely cared for the other. If Spangler caught a bullet over in the Middle East and never came back, it wouldn't bother Tony in the slightest.

"What about the Friebergs?" Tony threw in. "We still haven't decided what to do with them."

"That's up to you, kid. You're in charge now. But if I was you, I'd go after them, and snag that Muller character in the process. I got a feeling this thing over in Israel isn't gonna last too long, and I can't think of a better way to get in good with the conquering Caesar Augustus than to deliver his arch-enemy over to him in chains when it's all over."

"Just what I was thinking, Boss. I'll get right on it."

"Forget that boss business. You're the boss now, kiddo."

"Yeah, I guess you're right. Well, good luck over there in Israel. Maybe we'll see you when you get back."

"Thanks. Maybe we will."

And with that, Myron Spangler picked up his briefcase and walked out the door, without shaking hands, or even saying goodbye.

CHAPTER TEN

The Exchange

Aaron Muller walked alone in the dark, minding carefully where he put his feet. The darkness was intense, and even with his enhanced vision, it was difficult to see where he was going. He descended the steep slopes of the San Gabriel Mountains for what he feared would be the last time before the Battle of Armageddon. He prayed for his family's safety as he walked.

He had stayed several days longer than he had intended on account of the unexpected onslaught of darkness. The day it happened, he had planned to leave after sunset, but when it got dark at noon instead of at eight o'clock; it made him change his plans.

He stayed to make sure his family would be able to cope with the sudden changes. He was relieved to see that the light was not entirely removed, and even at night, Tim and Steve could still hunt with the aid of their night vision goggles. And the drop in temperature was not extreme. The forty-five degree temperature was actually a welcome relief after the many weeks where the mercury in the thermometer never dipped below the hundred-degree mark.

At night, he took a long walk, exploring the immediate vicinity, to see if he could locate any squatters who had moved into the area that could pose a security risk. He was relieved to find no one near their cave site, but he did discover a camp of some rather seedy looking characters about a mile to the south of them, and another suspicious party that had moved into the ruins of the bombed-out cabin the family had vacated over a year before.

He could easily have killed them all to avoid any possible threat they might pose toward his loved ones, and disposed of their bodies, but the thought never entered his mind. He did, however, consider driving them from the area with his rod and his sling, but he decided against it. Those displaced drifters might very well figure out who their attacker had been, and report the incident to the authorities to collect the bounty placed on his head. That would surely bring the bloodhounds sniffing about, and his family would be in serious jeopardy.

So, he decided to do nothing at all. He would leave them alone, but he would monitor their activities secretly to make sure they posed no real threat. For the next two days, he checked on them often, and was convinced that neither of the groups was aware of the family's presence in the area, nor did they appear to be looking for them. They were just two groups of unfortunate people, displaced, and simply trying to survive.

One night, Aaron went hunting with Tim and Steve, and he took a nice buck deer with a stone from his sling at a distance neither of his cousins would have attempted. Game had become extremely scarce, and that which was still around had become understandably wary. The boys were thrilled with the amazing shot, but he was not trying to show off. He wanted to leave them with enough food so they wouldn't have to venture out of the cave at all for the next several days. With the cold temperatures, the meat would last them a good long while.

He was not comfortable with the relatively close proximity of the local riffraff, and he was sure things were going to get worse before the end finally came. He instructed his family to leave the cave only when absolutely necessary, and then only after taking the utmost precautions.

So, on the fourth night, after saying goodbye to his family and their faithful Millennium, and a tearful farewell with Anna, he was headed back down the mountain. He had listened to the radio with his loved ones and had learned of the massive pullout of the military from the area, and of the universal gathering of armies around the Middle East. The Bible prophecy he had learned was all coming true. The end could not be far away.[23]

What could he expect to find now in the valley? With the military pulling out, would chaos and anarchy reign? He hated the tyranny and persecution imposed by the Federation troops, but at least, they pre-

[23] But when you see Jerusalem surrounded by armies, then know that its desolation is near (Luke 21:20).

vented the wholesale slaughter and destruction that occurs when desperate people are left without restraints. He picked up his pace. He felt his people needed him, and he wanted to be there for them.

Tony D'Angelo smiled as he sat in the plush chair that had once belonged to Myron Spangler, and before him, to Paul Apparicio. But they were both gone, and the Western Commander's office of the World Federation of Nations now belonged to him. Before the rapture, he had entertained plans of achieving greatness by the time he was twenty-five, but nothing like this. His hopes back then of becoming an Olympic champion, followed by a lucrative career as a professional swimmer, and then maybe even a movie contract or something, paled in comparison to the success he now enjoyed. Literally thousands of people called him boss, and jumped when he gave them commands.

Even as he sat there, he had dispatched Gino Mantelli, his newly appointed second-in-command, to go pick up the unsuspecting Frieberg couple and bring them back to his headquarters building. Now that the two weeks of darkness were beginning to show signs of lifting, it was time to take care of some unfinished business.

Noah and Sheila were expecting to be the special guests at a gala luncheon, followed by a press conference, in which they would be honored for their years of faithful service to the Federation. Little did they know that instead of to the lavish Towers Hotel, they would be taken to the nearby Federation headquarters building to be interrogated and tortured, but not for anything they had done or failed to do. They were simply to be used as bait to spring the trap on Aaron Muller once and for all.

Tony had indeed summoned television crews from all the major networks to be present in the reception area downstairs when the Friebergs were brought in, but it would not be for the purpose of broadcasting the celebration held in their honor. It would be to send forth the images of their painful torture to lure Muller out of hiding and to compel him to come to their rescue.

The intercom interrupted his thoughts, and his pretty secretary informed him that the limousine transporting the Friebergs had just pulled up in front of their building. Tony thanked her and bolted out of his chair and headed for the elevators. This was one celebration he did not want to miss.

He descended rapidly to the first floor, and stepped out of the elevator to see a middle-aged couple, surrounded by guards in the middle of the reception area, all dressed up, with apparently no meaningful place to go.

Noah and Sheila Frieberg looked confused and frightened. They had expected to be honored and rewarded for their devoted service to the World Federation's cause, but their present surroundings were strange and intimidating. There was neither dinner nor dignitaries present. Instead they found themselves in a sterile government building, surrounded by armed guards. Even the charming and handsome escort who had picked them up earlier, now glared at them with dispassionate contempt.

Noah recognized Tony as the latter approached, and he angrily insisted on an explanation.

"Shut up!" Tony growled. "After all we've done for you, is this the way you repay us?"

"What are you talking about?" Noah demanded. "We've done everything you've ever asked of us. What's this all about?"

"Don't get cute with me." Tony warned. "We know all about your dealings with the resistance forces here in the city, and your allegiance with your nephew Aaron Muller."

"No way! I haven't even talked with him since he smuggled the rest of the family outta here years ago, except that one time, and that was to set him up so your men could take him out. I even went along with you last year and helped you capture my father and my niece. I remained loyal to you even when you had my dad executed. I made Aaron my enemy when I sold him and my family out. He probably hates me for what I did. There's no way he would trust me, or team up with me now."

"That's not what our sources tell us," Tony shot back. "It seems you have been secretly supplying his guerillas with food and clothing, and feeding him information about our troop placements and maneuvers."

"What! That's crazy!" For one thing, I don't know anything about your troop placements or maneuvers; and secondly, I would never give away perfectly good materials to a bunch of riff-raff when I could sell them to you and make a profit."

"That's enough!" Tony yelled, punching Noah squarely in the face, sending him to the floor. Sheila screamed, and he slapped her hard in the mouth, sending her into shocked and terrified silence. "Gag 'em, and strap 'em, Gino!"

Gino Mantelli was quick to comply. He had been a hit man for the mob for years, and inflicting suffering and death on hapless stooges had become commonplace to him. Besides, he had grown to fear and respect

Commander D'Angelo more than any of his former bosses. He remembered back a few years when he had been working for Sal LaMata and had gunned down those snitches in the alley. Back then, Tony D'Angelo had been a whimpering, spineless college punk; but all that had changed. The former pretty boy had become a ruthless and hardened despot, with the looks to match. He had killed more people in the past three-and-a-half years than Gino had killed in his lifetime. The former gangster didn't even want to think about crossing his new boss.

Gino motioned to his subordinates, and they quickly slapped duct tape across the mouths of both the Friebergs and forcefully escorted them to the south side of the reception area where others were removing a portable partition. Concealed behind the sight barrier were two sturdy wooden chairs, arranged side-by-side. They were, in fact, electric chairs, which had been used, along with others like them, to eliminate enemies of the Federation. On seeing them, both Noah and Sheila panicked and tried vainly to free themselves.

Gino's men slammed them down in the chairs and strapped their wrists and ankles securely, attaching, at the same time, electrodes to their calves and tightening metal caps to the tops of their heads. Heavy leather straps were cinched across their chests to hold them firmly in place. Their eyes were wild with panic, but they were powerless to resist. They were at the mercy of the young commander whose steely eyes revealed no signs of mercy whatsoever.

The television crews, which had been sealed off in an adjoining room, were allowed to enter, and they wasted no time in setting up their equipment in front of the two alleged traitors, strapped helplessly before them in the grisly torture chairs. Over the past few years, they had filmed so many abominable things that they had become completely desensitized. Tony stepped in front of the cameras, with the Friebergs clearly seen on either side behind him. The cameras began to roll, and Tony looked sternly into them as he began his prepared speech.

"Ladies and gentlemen, citizens of the World Federation of Nations, it grieves me to bring this into your living rooms, and into your places of recreation and pleasure. As you know, we have done everything we can to provide a safe and healthy environment for all of our citizens, but we have been opposed by evil guerilla forces that have brought violence and bloodshed into our streets. We have tried to reason with them, but we have found them to be incorrigible. We have been left with no choice but to protect ourselves against them, and to eliminate by force the threat they represent.

"You all know that it is a capital offense to be found guilty of aiding and abetting our terrorist enemies, yet from time to time, we have those who ignore our warnings and defy our laws. We have two of those traitors here before you even now."

Tony paused in his delivery to allow the cameras to zoom in on the terror-stricken faces of the two captives who fought vainly to protest through the heavy duct tape, and to establish their innocence.

"You see here Noah and Sheila Frieberg," Tony continued, "who have betrayed our trust. We have employed them, catered to them, made them rich beyond their wildest dreams, and yet they have repaid us by collaborating with our enemies. Through their chain of department stores, they have funneled vast supplies to the terrorist camps, and have leaked secret information to them concerning the whereabouts and strength of our own forces. What's more, they have shielded from us the most incriminating evidence of all. They are close relatives of the guerilla leader himself. Aaron Muller, the most wanted criminal on the west coast, is their nephew.

"Proving the old adage that, 'Blood is thicker than water,' these dogs have bitten the hands that feed them, and they have remained loyal to their evil nephew, and to his family terrorist cell he protects somewhere in hiding.

"My purpose in displaying the consequences of their actions now before you is two-fold. First, I want to make an example of them. We make every effort to display leniency and tolerance, but treason is one thing we simply cannot tolerate. Those of you out there who may be considering rebellious or treasonous acts need to pay close attention to the repercussions such actions would bring you. Secondly, we want to use this occasion to strike a blow at the heart of their terrorist organization. Their trial by fire will lead us ultimately to the evildoers who have compromised and corrupted them.

"Currents of electricity will be sporadically run through their bodies until they divulge the whereabouts of Aaron Muller and his family of terrorists, or when Muller turns himself into the authorities. The lives of these two here will be spared only when we have their nephew in custody. Should they refuse to cooperate, and should Muller be too cowardly to exchange his life for theirs, they will be dead in about five hours. But those will be five of the most excruciatingly painful hours imaginable. It pains me to do this, but we can simply tolerate no longer the death and destruction perpetrated by Muller and his guerilla hordes."

With that, Tony nodded to a technician who was monitoring dials on an instrument board, and to Gino Mantelli, standing next to the captives. Gino reached over and ripped the tape from the mouths of Noah and Sheila an instant before the technician flipped a switch on the control panel, sending a powerful current of electricity through the bodies of the helpless victims.

Their bodies instantly convulsed, their muscles went into uncontrollable spasms, and their involuntary screams filled the air. The current was powerful, but it was not lethal. It produced excruciating pain, but it did not bring on a merciful death. The current was carefully controlled so as not to render them unconscious. For two solid minutes, they writhed in unspeakable torment before another nod from Tony prompted the technician to flip the switch to off again.

The Friebergs collapsed limply, but their screams continued unabated. It took several seconds before their sensory receptors could convince their tortured brains that the source of their pain had disappeared. The smell of scorched hair wafted out from under their metal skullcaps, and Sheila's broken fingernails lay strewn atop the chair arms to which her wrists were shackled. After their screaming stopped, they were able only to mumble incoherently about their ignorance and their innocence. Tony used this opportunity to hammer his point home.

"These traitors continue to claim their innocence, and they continue to profess that they don't know of the whereabouts of either Aaron Muller or his terrorist family. I don't believe them. They have proven themselves to be both liars as well as traitors, and a few more sessions of electrical purification should loosen their tongues. But in the unlikely event that they really don't know where their relatives are, there remains only one means by which their lives can be spared."

Then Tony leaned into the closest camera and spoke as though directly to an unseen viewer, "Aaron Muller, I know you're watching. What you've just seen is only the beginning. This will continue every five minutes until we get what we want. If your uncle and aunt know where you are, they'll tell us soon enough; but if perchance they don't, then you're the only one who can save them.

"Are you man enough to come in and give yourself up in order to spare their lives, or will you prove yourself to be the coward you have always been in the past? Will you run and hide like you usually do, or will you sit there and watch your relatives fry until their brains turn to jelly? Or could it be that you will play the man and turn yourself in? You are the mastermind and ringleader of the terrorists, and you deserve the punishment they are receiving because you deceived and corrupted them.

"What is it going to be, Aaron? Noah may last the full five hours; he looks pretty strong, but I don't think Aunt Sheila can last more than three. Are you willing to let their deaths be on your shoulders? I swear to you, if you give yourself up, we will consider their present suffering sufficient penalty for their crimes, and we will let them go free. Also, I promise you, you will be given a fair trial; and whatever happens, you will not be tortured. We are *not* animals, but we *will do* whatever we have to do to put down terrorism in our midst. It's up to you! You can find me right here at the Federation headquarters on Figueroa. Every hour you delay is another hour of unspeakable torment for your loved ones!"

That said; he nodded again to the technician who flipped the switch on the control panel, sending the murderous current pulsating through the helpless bodies of Noah and Sheila Frieberg once again. Their pitiful wails filled the reception area, and were relayed, via television, to countless locations throughout the Southland.

Aaron stared at the television screen in horror and disbelief. His heart told him what he was seeing could not be true, but his eyes insisted his mind accept the messages they were sending to his brain. As soon as the special news bulletin had first been announced, Derek Uptain called him in from the garage area of their old warehouse hideaway where he had been working on one of their vehicles. He came in, and with about a dozen other members of their resistance group, he watched as the screen portrayed in graphic detail what was going on at the Federation headquarters building downtown.

"I can't take anymore of this!" Aaron cried as he reached out and turned off the TV set he and his friends had lifted in their last raid on a Federation outpost in Santa Monica. "I knew Tony had sold out to the devil, but I never imagined he would resort to anything so unthinkable. I've got to get over there right away. I'm taking the old Mercury, okay, Derek?"

"No way, man!" came Derek's desperate reply. "It's a trap, and you know it, Aaron."

"I know, but I can't sit by and let this happen. My aunt and uncle don't know where I am, or where the rest of the family is either. Tony will torture them to death and they're powerless to do anything about it. I can't let it happen."

"Why not?" his friend wanted to know. "Good people die all the time . . . or hadn't you noticed? And besides, they aren't so good anyway. They sold you and your family out twice if I remember right. Your grandfather is dead, thanks to them. I'd say they're gettin' just what they deserve. Let's forget we ever saw what was on the TV. We have lots more important things to worry about."

"I can't do that, and you know it, Derek."

"Well, what *are* you gonna do? Storm in there, kill a bunch of bad guys, tear the place apart, and set your aunt and uncle free? Is that what you have in mind?"

"No," Aaron sighed. "I wish it were that simple, but it's not. They have them strapped into those chairs, with those electrodes attached to their bodies. The moment I show up and start anything, all they have to do is turn a dial and throw a switch, and my relatives will be dead instantly. No, I'm afraid this is one rescue I won't be able to pull off."

"What!" Derek said in dismay. "Don't tell me you're actually planning on giving yourself up, are you?"

"Yes, my friend, that is exactly what I'm going to do. I know I'll be walking into a trap, but I could never live with myself knowing I sat back and let my own aunt and uncle be tortured to death."

"But you're supernaturally sealed or something, right? D'Angelo and his thugs can't actually kill you, can they?"

"I don't know, Derek. All I really know for sure is that all of us 144,000 were sealed to serve the Lord during the tribulation, but it's almost over now. I don't remember anybody promising us that we would actually live clear through into the millennium. It may be that we can be killed like any other man once the final conflict comes. I'm afraid my prospects over the next few weeks are a bit uncertain."

"But aren't your relatives doomed anyway? If they've received the mark of the beast, there's really nothing you can do for them, is there?"

"But, I don't know for sure if they received it. The fact that they are being tortured by Federation men makes me believe maybe they aren't completely in the beast's camp after all. As long as there's the slightest chance to save their lives, and perhaps to save their souls, then I feel I must give them that chance. Now, get out of my way. Every minute I spend talking here with you is another minute they're being tortured."

Derek sensed he was not going to be able to talk his friend out of going in and giving himself up, and he wasn't physically strong enough to stop him, but he refused to give up. He argued with Aaron as he followed him out the door, he protested strongly as his friend got in the old Mercury coupe and fired it up, and he yelled objections as he watched him drive out into the street and disappear around the corner. Only then, did Derek give up. He sat down heavily on the curb and placed his head in his hands. He began to weep unashamedly, and he prayed as he had never prayed before.

Twenty minutes later, Aaron pulled up and stopped in front of the Federation Building on Figueroa Street. The soldiers stationed there must have been put on alert because the instant he stepped out of the car, a hundred automatic rifles were aimed at his heart. They must also have been instructed to take him alive because no one actually pulled the trigger. He was instantly surrounded and searched for weapons, but none was found. He had left his rod and sling with Derek. He was escorted into the reception area at gunpoint, but no one dared to actually lay a hand on him. They remembered all too well what had happened to others who had tried to assault him.

Tony had been notified the moment Aaron had arrived out front, so he was expecting his special guest. The television crews were dismissed, frustrated that they would not be allowed to film the conclusion of the drama. Tony was anxious to get at Aaron, but He didn't want the public to witness what he had in mind for him. He was also still leery of him, having witnessed up close the supernatural powers he possessed, thus he approached him with caution.

"Well, Aaron, we meet again, at last," he said with a false air of cordiality, but he was careful not to get too close to him, nor to extend his hand.

"Yes, Tony," Aaron responded flatly, "and you know why I'm here, so let's dispense with the formalities. Let my aunt and uncle go free, and you can do with me as you choose."

Aaron looked over at his relatives, slumped back in their chairs, their muscles twitching involuntarily, their mouths slack and drooling, and their vacant eyes rolled back in their heads. They had suffered intolerable torment already, but hopefully, no permanent damage had yet been done. Aaron's heart went out to them in spite of the disloyalty they had shown toward him and his family. He was convinced he was doing the right thing by exchanging his life for theirs.

"Not so fast, my friend," Tony cautioned. "I've seen some of the tricks you have up your sleeve, so before we set them free, I'm going to have to insist you let us fit you with some jewelry we've prepared especially for you."

As he said that, he motioned to Gino Mantelli who came forward carrying a set of sophisticated restraints. They consisted of a pair of handcuffs and a matching set of ankle shackles, which were joined together by heavy chains that were channeled through brackets fastened into a heavy leather belt. Once secured in such a restraint, a prisoner would be powerless to do anything more than shuffle slowly from one holding area to another.

Aaron looked at the apparatus and realized it could well represent the end of his precious freedom, and the termination of all his earthly hopes and dreams. It could lead to mocking humiliation, unimaginable suffering, and a slow and excruciating death; but he felt he had no choice but to accept it if he wanted to preserve any hope of rescuing his loved ones and offering them a final opportunity for forgiveness of sins and the promise of eternal life. He closed his fists and extended his forearms in a gesture of surrender, ready to accept the handcuffs and the rest of the hardware that went with them.

Gino was quick to slap the handcuffs on Aaron's wrists, and then he went to work securing his ankles in the shackles and making sure everything was properly chained and belted together. Only after he had double-checked his work and was confident that his captive was thoroughly incapacitated did he rise and sneer at him. How well he remembered that rainy night in the alley when he had tried repeatedly to kill him, but to no avail. He was confident that things would turn out differently this time.

"All done, boss," Gino announced confidently." "He's all yours."

"Thanks, Gino," Tony replied. "Now you can take care of those two over there."

"No!" Aaron protested loudly. "You swore you would let them go if I gave myself up. I've done what you required; now keep your end of the bargain."

"Foolish man you are, Aaron," Tony sneered. "You always were such a Boy Scout. I promised to let them go, and go they shall: straight into hell, that is! Go ahead, Gino. Send them on their way!"

"You got it, boss," Gino said, pulling his pistol from its holster and walking toward the two semi-conscious forms strapped into their wooden torture chairs.

"NOOOOO!" Aaron screamed as he tried in vain to shuffle after Gino and prevent him from carrying out his orders. But his restraints hobbled him, he tripped and fell headlong, barely able to break his fall with his shackled hands before he landed in a heap on the tiled floor. He looked up in time only to witness the unthinkable.

Gino methodically walked up to Noah Frieberg, put the muzzle of his pistol to the other man's temple, and pulled the trigger. The blast instantly ended Noah's life, blowing out a large portion of the opposite side of his skull. The loud noise startled Sheila into complete consciousness, and she started to protest and beg for her life. But her words never came forth. Another slug, placed squarely in the center of her forehead, silenced her forever.

Aaron moaned and wept unashamedly. He lay on the floor, unable and unwilling even to rise to his feet. His mother's older brother and his wife had just been blown into eternity with no hope of salvation, and he had been powerless to do anything to prevent it. His pain and sorrow were more than he could bear.

But he had no time to mourn their deaths. Gino yanked him roughly to his feet and placed him in front of Tony D'Angelo once again.

"And now, my friend," Tony said slowly, savoring every word, "it's time for you to join them. But before you go, there's a formality we need to attend to. Emperor Augustus doesn't want you killed, so I'll give you one chance to escape death, at least for a while. Tell me where your miserable family is, and I promise you I will send you to meet Caesar in Israel alive."

"Do your worst, you pathetic piece of vomit!" Aaron managed to get out through his sobs. "Your word is as worthless as you are. I would never surrender my family to you under any circumstances!"

"I didn't think so," Tony said glibly. "But I needed to give you the option. That way, I'll have an excuse for killing you myself. I'll just tell Augustus you died as a result of our efforts to get you to divulge the whereabouts of your family. He'll be disappointed, but he'll understand that we were just carrying out his instructions.

"Oh, and by the way: we *will* find your family, it's only a matter of time. Only this time, you won't be around to save them. I can't wait to turn that wretched bunch over to the Great Caesar for him to play with. And, of course, I have some playing-around plans of my own with your sweet baby sister Rachel . . . and maybe with your girlfriend too. Anna's her name isn't it?"

"You poor dumb slob," Aaron said with contempt. "You still don't get it, do you? You still think you're in control, don't you? You can't touch my family without God's permission. You can't even kill me now unless He allows it. And suppose you are able to kill us all; you still can't hurt us. We will simply go to be with our Savior, which is far better anyway. But you, you stupid fool, no matter what you do, you've got a one-way ticket to hell."

"Oh, yeah!" yelled Tony angrily. "We'll see who's the fool here. You sound just like your miserable old grandfather. He sounded pretty tough too . . . that is . . . just before I cut off his ugly head. I deserved to be the one to kill that old fool for the way he talked to me in his stupid old store the night of the robbery, and especially for the way he cursed me just before he died. Yet I deserve to be the one to kill you even more.

"Sure, Augustus wants to be the one to end your wretched life, but all you did to him was kill him, and a bunch of his people. Then he got raised back to life again, and he's as good as new, but look at me. You killed me too, buddy boy, and I'll never be the same. See this crooked nose? You killed it! See these phony teeth? You killed them! And take a look at this pretty scar here. Ain't it a beaut? You killed my face, and with it, you killed my former life! And now I'm gonna kill you, mister hotshot prophet, or whatever you are! May you rest in hell!"

By this time, Tony was totally engulfed in rage. He reached over and pulled Gino's pistol out of its holster and pointed it squarely at Aaron's heart. "You dodged a bullet last time that was aimed at your heart!" he screamed. "Let's see if you can dodge this one!"

Aaron closed his eyes and resigned himself into the care of his loving heavenly Father. He was fully prepared to be ushered into His presence.

Tony pulled the trigger, and he was almost surprised when it fired properly. The 9-mm slug tore from the barrel of the pistol at a speed in excess of a thousand feet-per-second. It sped straight toward Aaron's heart, but instead, it passed unencumbered through the air and smashed into the wall on the opposite side of the room. The heavy restraints fell, and clattered noisily on the floor, but the body they had shackled wasn't there. Aaron Muller had simply disappeared before their very eyes.

Tony screamed and dropped his weapon. His men gasped in disbelief, not able to comprehend what they had just witnessed. They had all seen the impossible, but it was Tony alone who heard the inaudible: the all too familiar sound of that insidious laughter hissing in his ears.

CHAPTER ELEVEN

The Dawning

Aaron Muller winced as he heard the sound of the gunshot, and fully expected to experience that familiar feeling of the bullet smashing into his chest, but he did not. "Perhaps you only feel those shots that don't kill you," he thought to himself. "So this is what it's like to die: no pain, or any sensation at all. If I had known it was this easy, maybe I wouldn't have fought so hard to stay alive for so long."

He opened his eyes, expecting to see the Lord, or at least some saints or angels, but he saw none of them. In fact, he saw absolutely nothing at all. "That's funny," he thought. "Heaven is supposed to be a place of dazzling light, not pitch darkness. What's going on around here, anyway?"

"Excuse me, Aaron, I don't mean to interrupt your thoughts, but I thought I should explain where you are, and what just happened." It was the familiar voice of his angel Eliezer.

"Thank you all the same, but I already know what just happened. I just got shot in the chest, and I'm dead. But what I *don't* understand is why it's so dark. Isn't there supposed to be at least a tunnel of light, or something?"

Eliezer laughed. "No Aaron, you didn't get shot, and you're not dead. You would have been both, had I left you there, but I decided it would be best if I brought you home before that happened. You're in Israel. Others are waiting for you. Come, I will take you to them."

"Wait a minute," Aaron said, suddenly beginning to figure things out. "You snatched me outta there, right?

"Yes, as you might say, I beamed you up. The Lord plans to bring all His 144,000 home soon. I just hurried things up a bit in your case. It seemed like the prudent thing to do, under the circumstances."

"I'll say. I'd have been a goner for sure if you hadn't showed up. Thanks for saving my skin again. I've kept you pretty busy lately, haven't I?"

"Yes, as you would say, I have really needed to stay on my toes over the past three-and-a-half years. That was a very brave and selfless thing you did back there, Aaron. But it was also a careless and needless one."

"How come? They were my aunt and uncle. I had to do whatever I could to try to rescue them. Why didn't you step in in time to save them too? That would have been easy for you to do."

"I'm sorry, but they were not my responsibility. You are. And at any rate, it has been too late for them for years. They chose to receive the mark of the beast at the very beginning of the tribulation. I believe you were aware of that fact, weren't you?"

"Yeah, I guess so, but I didn't want to believe it. I just couldn't bring myself to give up on them."

"You did well, Aaron. Your willingness to sacrifice your life for theirs is duly noted. Thankfully, their eternal destiny is not in your hands, anyway; nor in mine, for that matter. The Lord Himself sees to all such matters, and ultimately, He does all things well. Now, if you are quite ready, let us be on our way."

Aaron felt a strong hand take hold of his and begin leading him through the intense darkness. "Where are you taking me?" he asked. "And why is it so blasted dark?"

"I shall lead you to a gathering of some of your friends. It is but a short distance. And the darkness is a result of the fifth bowl of God's wrath, poured out on the seat of the beast. The darkness that is only partial in the rest of the world is absolute here because of the magnitude of the sin of the devil's spawn who rules over this land. But be of good cheer, it is about to be lifted. Watch your step. We are going to descend steeply and to the right."

Aaron held on tightly to Eliezer's hand as he walked gingerly down a steep and rocky decline. Then he followed his heavenly protector and guide to the right and through what seemed like a hallway. The sound of their footsteps echoed off the walls around them.

Just then, they rounded a corner to the left and, suddenly, Aaron could see a dim light up ahead. He could make out the figures of four men huddled around a small fire. He turned to tell Eliezer of his discovery, and that he could probably make it the rest of the way on his own, but he was startled to discover that the angel had vanished. He felt only emptiness in his hand where once there had been the strong grip of his heavenly guide.[24]

"Wow!" Aaron gasped in amazement. "That guy is spooky. He sure doesn't waste any words on greetings or salutations." Still in dismay, he called out to him, "Thanks, Eliezer! But don't go too far away; I got a feeling I'm gonna need your assistance a whole lot more before this nightmare is finally over!"

One of those seated around the fire heard Aaron's voice, and rose to his feet. He cocked a spear in his right hand and called out, "Halt! Identify yourself, or feel the weight of my spear!"

Aaron recognized the voice of David Rosen, one of the two Israeli soldiers who had led the exodus to Masada at the very beginning of the tribulation. He had not had any contact with him for nearly three-and-a-half years, but his voice was unmistakable.

"It's me, Aaron Muller. I just got transported here from Los Angeles. Don't shoot. I'm unarmed, and I'm coming in."

"Aaron! Is that really you?" came back David's voice. "Come on in here by the fire and get warm, and let us get a look at you."

His eyes beginning to become more accustomed to the dim light, Aaron realized he was in an underground tunnel. He made his way along the uneven surface, and soon joined the others around the fire.

"It is you!" David exulted as he threw his strong arms around Aaron's shoulders. "Welcome home, old friend!"

"Indeed! It's good to see you again." This time it was the voice of Joseph Roth. The taller of the two witnesses hugged Aaron tightly as soon as David released him.

"Aye, laddie," said the big Scotsman Ken Weinman, "come herrre, und give me a hug too. It hus been suuch a loong time, my frrriend."

The fourth man around the fire patiently waited his turn, and then gave Aaron the biggest hug of all. There was no mistaking the huge size and strong grip of the massive Russian Ivan Feldsin.

"Man, it's good to see all you guys," Aaron said at last. "Where are we, and where is everyone else?"

---

[24] When they were past the first and the second guard posts, they came to the iron gate that leads to the city, which opened to them of its own accord; and they went out and went down one street, and immediately the angel departed from him (Acts 12:10).

"We're in one of the many tunnels that honeycomb the area beneath the City of Jerusalem. Most of the believers in the city are farther back in the caverns there," explained Joseph, pointing over his right shoulder. "The Lord plans to bring all of His 144,000 back here soon, but you three are the first to arrive. Ken and Ivan got here less than an hour ago, and now you have come as well. David and I, of course, have been right here throughout the entire tribulation. It's good to have some old friends drop in."

"Drop in is right," Aaron agreed. "I'll never get used to the Lord's mode of instant transportation. Were you guys in a tight spot when you got beamed up? Boy, I sure was."

"Aboot as tight as a guillotine, laddie," Ken said. "I was strapped in und aboot to lose me head when me angel decides to shew up. Und mighty nice of him too, it was."

"Galinikov himself had me backed up against a wall, facing a firing squad, when I got caught away," added Ivan. "I tell you, that man is the devil's own. I actually saw the blasts from the rifles, but Samuel snatched me away before the bullets ever got to me. I thought I was a dead man for sure."

Aaron told them briefly what had happened to him as well, and they all stopped and thanked the Lord in prayer for His amazing watch care over them.

After spending some wonderful time together sharing some of the many trials and triumphs they had all experienced, Joseph suggested they all try to get some sleep. It was going on midnight, local time, and he had been informed from the Lord that the next day would require all the strength and stamina they could muster.

As Aaron stretched out on the rough floor of the catacombs beneath the streets of Jerusalem, he thanked the Lord again for His divine deliverance, and he committed himself anew to serving Him with every fiber of his being. Before he drifted off to sleep, he prayed for God's continued protection over his loved ones back in another cave on the other side of the world. As the end drew ever closer, he was keenly aware of the fact that if his family were going to survive, it was going to be by virtue of the providential intervention of the One who held the universe in the palm of His hand.

In the morning, they were awakened by a strange phenomenon. Light could be seen filtering down from the entrance of the cave. Light had not been seen in Israel in more than two weeks, and yet, there it was, dim but unmistakable.

Aaron sat up and rubbed his eyes. Their fire had long since gone out, but he could see much better than he could before with the aid of its light. He could make out the definition of the walls of the natural tunnel they were in as he followed its pathway with his eyes up towards its entrance. He stood to his feet, as did his companions, and they started walking toward the source of the light together.

"Eliezer told me last night that the darkness was about to end, but I didn't realize it would be so soon," Aaron said. "Let's go check it out."

"Yes, let's do," agreed Joseph, "but be careful. Remember, we haven't seen sunlight in a long time. It could be pretty painful to our eyes until we get accustomed to it."

He needn't have bothered warning his friends. They had already begun to experience what he was concerned about. While they were still well back from the entrance of the cave, the light began hurting their eyes. They were squinting and shielding their eyes from its glare long before they actually stepped out into the direct sunlight.

They stopped about fifty feet inside the entrance and waited for their eyes to become accustomed to the light before they ventured farther. While standing there, squinting, Aaron noticed his rod leaning up against the rock wall of the cave. And draped over the top of it was his sling. He walked over and picked them up and relished the familiar feel of their texture in his hands.

"Thank you, Eliezer," he said to his heavenly guardian, whom he could not see, but whose presence he could sense. "I appreciate you remembering to bring my carry-on items on our flight over last night."

Ken also found his sling, and Ivan his spear. None of the three had been in possession of their weapons when they had been transported, but their angels had seen to it that they had not been left behind. The three warriors had become so accustomed to the feel of their weapons that they felt nervous and unclothed whenever they did not have them with them. Happy now, they were ready to venture forth to face whatever the returned light might reveal to them.

President Lowell Renslow stood on the bridge of the mammoth aircraft carrier, the S.S. John Paul Jones. He was excited and filled with anticipation now that the darkness had finally lifted. Admiral Oscar Hightower, a tall slender man in his early fifties, was giving orders to his crew, preparing to get underway. His huge armada had been sitting off the coast of Eastern Africa for more than twenty-four hours, just outside the outer extremities of the Killer Dark. They had gone as far as they dared, and had been left with no choice but to wait until the light came back.

Now the early morning fog had lifted, and the sun's bright rays dispelled any residue of darkness the plague had left behind. The sky was clear, the sea was calm, and it was a great day for sailing.

Renslow complimented himself for his military genius. By running at flank speed, their massive task force would be within striking distance of Israel within twenty-four hours. The plan he and Admiral Hightower and Army General Bob Putnam had agreed upon was to steam around Somalia, at the eastern-most point of Africa, and to sail up the Red Sea, taking the eastern fork at the Sinai Peninsula, and continuing up the Gulf of Aqaba. They would set anchor off the southern coast of Israel near the modern city of Elat. From there, they would be less than one hundred and twenty-five miles from Jerusalem. It would put them within easy range for their aircraft, and not too long a march, even for their foot soldiers. What made the plan especially sweet was the fact that Constantine Augustus would be virtually unprepared to resist the invasion.

Of course, Augustus had known the Americans were launching an invasion from the west, and he had bolstered his defenses to meet it head-on. But he had stationed them in the wrong places. He had pulled most of his navel vessels into the Mediterranean Sea to protect his west coast, making it virtually a Federation lake. Renslow knew it would be suicidal to try to sail through the Straits of Gibraltar and battle his way through the vastly superior Federation fleet barricading the Mediterranean.

His other logical option was to invade the coast of Morocco, and then to march overland across North Africa, through Egypt and north to Israel through the Sinai wilderness. To cut off just such an attack, Augustus had stationed the bulk of his southern forces across Morocco, Algeria, and Libya. Again, Renslow knew it would be foolhardy to attempt such an invasion. He could never expect his troops to battle their way against such overwhelming odds, over two thousand miles of the most punishing desert in the world, in the hottest part of the summer, especially being separated so far from their supply lines.

So, Renslow had decided to attack in neither of those logical theaters. He made it look as though he was going to launch an invasion in Morocco, but at the last moment, he ordered his fleet to sail southward around the Cape of Good Hope and up the eastern coast of Africa. And just as he made his decisive turn, he sent bombers from his carriers over the top of the Killer Dark, which lay like a loathsome blanket over the northern portion of the continent. Their orders were to take out the Suez Canal. Though the pilots could not see through the opaque blackness, their sophisticated infrared bombsights were able to identify the stranded vessels in the canal, and their payloads found their targets.

With the Suez Canal destroyed, the Federation ships could not sail through it and cut off the American fleet in the Red Sea when the darkness lifted. Until such a time, they could go nowhere, being thoroughly trapped in the folds of the painful blackness. When it did finally dissipate, they could attempt to follow Renslow's trail around Africa, but it would take them nearly a week to circumnavigate the continent, and by then, it would be too late.

Such was not the case with the vast fleet of ships that had arrived from the Eastern Pacific. After sailing around the tip of South America, it had arrived at the western coast of Africa, and was outside the perimeter of the Killer Dark. Constantine had ordered the fleet to pursue the Americans around the Cape of Good Hope and destroy them before they had a chance to launch an invasion against him in Israel. So Renslow had known it was a race against time. The darkness simply had to lift before the Federation fleet overtook him from behind.

The only other sizable force Renslow had to worry about was the large Federation fleet of ships stationed in the Western Pacific. And indeed, as soon as the Great Caesar had realized what the Americans were attempting to do, he had ordered his captains to sail west to cut them off at the Red Sea. However, the Russian and Chinese navies engaged the Federation forces in the south China Sea, and held them up long enough to prevent more than a handful of ships from having any hope at all of getting there in time to intercept the Americans.

Yes, Renslow had thought it through very well. He had known he was taking a gamble, but it was a chance he was willing to take. The Federation ships in the Mediterranean Sea could not navigate so long as the Killer Dark enshrouded them. So, for as long as the darkness prevailed, he needn't worry about them. His only concern was with their two Pacific fleets. If the darkness prevailed long enough, the one steaming in from the west would surely overtake him. Furthermore, the superior firepower of their fleet to the east would allow them to eventually break through the Russian-Chinese barricade and intercept him before he could slip through the Red Sea. Consequently, his wait over the past twenty-four hours had been an anxious one.

But the darkness had been dispelled, and his own fleet was already getting underway. In addition, Renslow's sources informed him that the Federation fleet to the west was still on the other side of the African continent, and the one to the east was still bottled up in Asia. He could expect to be free of any sizable resistance for at least four or five days, and that should give him plenty of time.

Renslow rubbed his fleshy hands together with glee. Things were working out better than he had hoped. He silently thanked whatever gods there might be for his good fortune. His armada was now under a full head of steam. He welcomed the stiff breeze in his round face. He fully expected to be off the southern coast of Israel by first light the next day. Now, if the Chinese and the Russians had been equally successful, they could all expect to strike a three-pronged killer attack into the very heart of the beast within the next few days.

Chairman Chong Xu Wu walked out of his executive command headquarters, which was actually a converted supply trailer pulled behind a military vehicle, and greeted the morning light with immense enthusiasm. He was dressed in a spotless military uniform, complete with insignia, braid, and medals, in spite of the fact that he had never spent a day in actual military service. He was soft, weak, out of condition, and resembled a seasoned soldier in no way at all; but he enjoyed playing the part.

His vast army had been forced to remain encamped in the inhospitable Tigris-Euphrates valley in Iraq for the past three days because of the impenetrable darkness that had loomed before them to the west. Their progress had been swift and brutal up to that point, devouring everything before them along the ancient Silk Road and across the plains of Iran, but the Killer Dark was something that even his hardened troops dared not enter.

But now the darkness had dissipated, and Chong could see all the way across to the Euphrates River, several miles to the west of him, and even beyond. Now that the light had returned, there remained only two barriers between him and that beast Constantine Augustus in Israel.

The first barrier was the Euphrates River itself. The fleeing Federation forces had blown every bridge spanning the vast river along its entire length. Following the sweltering heat in July, massive summer storms had dropped record amounts of rainfall in the high mountains to the north, which had caused the river to rise to unprecedented heights. There was simply no apparent way to get across its surging torrents.

His armies would be able to assemble pontoon bridges, given enough time, but they were slow and difficult to assemble. Even then, they were simply not capable of handling the kind of traffic necessary to transport his massive war machine across to the other side in an acceptable period of time. Besides that, the considerable Federation forces were massed on the other side of the river, and they would contest the construction of any such bridges with all the firepower they had at their disposal.

Those Federation forces represented the other barrier standing in the way of a victorious Chinese assault on Augustus in Israel. The Great Caesar had ordered every soldier, tank, and artillery piece in the area to the western shores of the Euphrates to form a last line of defense. After the Chinese had taken Baghdad on the Tigris, he had designated the rebuilt City of Babylon at the Euphrates as his center of operations. Spreading out from Babylon to the north and south were hundreds of thousands of Federation troops ready to give their life's blood to keep the Chinese from crossing that river.

And crossing that river is exactly what Chairman Chong was determined to do. His ancestors, the spirits with whom he consulted regularly, insisted on it. Besides, he had come much too far to turn back now. He had nearly exhausted the very last of his resources in reaching his present position, and he could not sustain a forced march back to China even if he wanted to. In addition to that, his allies were depending on him. If they had any hope of defeating the combined Federation forces in Israel, they would need all three of their armies there in full strength. He simply had to cross that river; there was no other alternative.

Yet how to cross it was quite another question. Chong walked quickly to the executive mess tent to get some breakfast. After that, he would meet with the vassal kings of the nations that had joined in with him in his westward march, and with his closest military advisors. Together, they would confer and put together their strategy. There surely had to be a way to cross the Euphrates, and they would not rest until they had discovered it.

President Gregor Odin Galinikov languished in his bed, his body racked in pain and burning up with fever as he looked out his window at the bright sunlight. He swore bitterly and cursed his bad luck. Unlike Chairman Chong, Gog was a powerful man. He was tall and strong, and he had always enjoyed excellent health. He was a career soldier, and he had prepared long for this, the greatest battle in the history of the world. He had no intention of missing it.

But what was he going to do? He had contracted some bacteria or virus as his armies marched southward under the cover of the worldwide darkness, and he had become progressively weaker as the days wore on. Now he lay helpless in a hospital bed in Ankara, Turkey, which nation his forces had conquered and now occupied. Medications were in short supply, and what little they had given him had not helped him in the slightest, He had hoped that he would heal during the many days his Russian armies were forced to delay their advance on Israel because of the Killer Dark that extended all the way up through Syria and into the southern regions of Turkey, but that was not to be. The darkness was now gone, but his illness was worse than ever. He tried vainly to get out of bed, but fell back in sweaty exhaustion. He swore again.

He was now forced to order his armies to attack so they could coordinate their strike with that of the Americans and the Chinese, but he himself would not be able to go with them. He hated the very thought of lying in that bed, hooked up to tubes and monitors, and forced to use a bedpan while his troops went forth to war without him.

He turned to his commanding officer, General Alexi Borzov, who was seated in a chair next to his bed. The general was a tall, slender man, in his late fifties, with a big shock of gray hair and a thick mustache to match.

"Alexi, old friend," Gog said weakly, "it appears you will have to lead our armies to victory without me this time."

"Yes, Gog, it seems so," the general replied, feeling comfortable in using his president's nickname since they were in the room alone at the time. "But you will be joining us soon. You look much better this morning," he lied.

"Yes, soon. But be gone with you now. We must strike quickly before Constantine Augustus has time to dig his troops out from the darkness and prepare to meet us at full strength."

"Of course. It shall be done, my captain," the older man said, rising and saluting smartly.

After Borzov left, Gog conversed with Odin, the Norse God of War, for a time. He complained to his mentor and asked him why he had not kept him well so he too could march triumphantly into battle. But Odin, who had become his constant companion, assured him that everything was going according to his divinely orchestrated plan, and that he needn't worry about this brief delay. He would have his chance to lead his armies to glorious victory in the very near future.

That seemed to satisfy the Russian president for the time being, and he rolled over and soon drifted back into a drug-induced sleep.

Caesar Constantine Augustus was busy, but not frantic. He had been in a state of sheer panic when the Killer Dark had first fallen on his domain only, and not over the rest of the world. His military had been paralyzed by the lethal blackout while his enemies had been allowed to muster their forces and virtually surround him. But his spirit guide, the Emperor Marcus Aurelius, had assured him that everything was well under control.

The emperor told him that the great god Lucifer had allowed the darkness to fall especially thick over the U.S.E. and the World Federation controlled Israel in order to seduce his enemies into attacking him there so he could destroy them once and for all. He instructed him as well not to go out and meet the enemy armies as they approached his borders. He was to resist them at a distance with what forces he currently had in place, but he was to keep the main body of his war machine right in the heart of Israel where they could be fresh and rested, well dug in, and readily supplied, while his enemies would be exhausted and depleted from their long and arduous trek to get there.

That reasoning had seemed logical to Constantine, and besides, who was he to argue with a spiritual emissary sent directly from Lucifer himself. So he had waited impatiently for the Killer Dark to lift. There was nothing much he could have done but wait. He knew his enemies could not actually penetrate into his realm on account of the same darkness that prevented him from taking any defensive action.

But now the darkness was gone. Constantine stood on a fourth-floor balcony of the Federation headquarters building and breathed in the fresh morning air, and bathed in the bright sunlight, which he had not seen for more than two weeks. He was talking with his cousin Eli Rothschild, who, in turn, was on the phone with Federation commanders all over Europe and the Middle East.

Following Marcus Aurelius' instructions, Constantine ordered his fighters and bombers to attack the American fleet in the Gulf of Aqaba and the Russian fleet steaming down from the Black Sea. It was imperative that he knock out their aircraft carriers in order to keep their planes from attacking his installations on the ground.

Secondly, he ordered all the Federation forces he had stationed in Europe and North Africa to be transported immediately to the western shores of Israel. He wanted every available soldier under his command in place in Israel by the time the first wave of invaders crossed his borders.

Thirdly, he ordered reinforcements sent to the eastern front. By all means the Chinese had to be held at the Euphrates River. They had no planes or ships, but they had a huge army of over five million men. They must not be allowed to join the American and Russian armies in the invasion. Constantine was confident that his military prowess would be able to handle the attacks from the north and south, but he insisted the Chinese be detained in Iraq until it was over. Then, with all his remaining firepower, he would be able to dispatch their isolated forces at the Euphrates.

The Great Caesar paced back and forth. He was filled with anxious anticipation. After all these years of frustration and delay, finally, he was on the verge of realizing his dreams of world dominion. The warfare would be fierce, and the casualties would be enormous, but that was of no concern to him. In a matter of a few days, a week or two at most, he would at last be the undisputed ruler of the entire world.

CHAPTER TWELVE

The Regathering

The five witnesses walked swiftly along the goat path that took them down the narrow wadi leading east of Jerusalem. It was mid-morning, and already the city was in an uproar. After more than two weeks of paralyzing darkness, the inhabitants of the area were in desperate need of procuring food, water, medicines, and various other necessities. Such commodities were in short supply, and rioting had broken out in several sectors.

Fortunately, the rains had finally returned following the scorching heat of July, and water was obtainable by those who were determined to find it. Also, large grain storage facilities were opened and the hungry were able to obtain at least enough to keep them alive. Emergency care facilities were opened, and medicines were being distributed to some of the most needy, but the little that was being done was woefully inadequate. Vast numbers went with their needs unmet. And what aid that was available was limited exclusively to those who were able to display the mark either on their right hand or their forehead. Those without the mark had learned from long experience not to expect anything but abuse and death at the hands of the World Federation.

And even those who had sworn allegiance to the beast were sorely neglected. Meeting the needs of suffering people was not high on the priority list of the Great Caesar Constantine Augustus. There was a war about to erupt, and preparing for it was the only thing he was truly concerned about. Wave after wave of ships offloaded their cargoes of men and machines all up and down the coastline between Tel Aviv and Haifa. Throughout the land, planes, tanks, heavy artillery, and support vehicles were being readied for the coming conflict. Soldiers and civilians alike were keenly aware of the urgency of the hour. The certainty of approaching suffering and death was in the very air they breathed.

Why then, at that time of urgency, were the five men, chosen and ordained of God, leaving the city where their presence was needed most? That was the question Aaron posed to Joseph as he followed him down the winding path.

"Our departure is but a temporary one, Aaron," Joseph assured his friend, "and my angel has informed me that we will not be going far. In fact, unless I'm mistaken, that small valley up ahead is our intended destination."

He pointed toward an unusual feature in the landscape ahead of them. The narrow wadi they were in was joined by another one from the south, and where they joined, the canyon walls widened and flattened out, forming a natural bowl-shaped hollow before the combined stream beds dropped off sharply into the Dead Sea plain farther to the east.

"Oh, I had hoped we would be going farther," Ivan said, disappointment registering in his voice. "I had imagined we might uncover that Humvee we used before, and maybe take a trip down to Masada. I would love to see those good people again."

"So would I," agreed David. "My family is there, and I haven't seen them in nearly three-and-a-half years. But the Lord has beckoned us out here, not to pursue our personal interests, but to prepare us for His work that lies before us. Besides, we stashed the Humvee off the Jericho road many miles north of here. I'm afraid we can go only as far as we are prepared to walk."

"Yes, that is true," confirmed Joseph. "But don't worry, we are almost there now, and our climb back to the city will take us no more than a couple of hours. The Lord has called us out here, away from the prying eyes of the Federation, to welcome our brethren home. Let us hasten to meet them."

Joseph picked up his pace, and the others followed his lead. In less than five minutes, the five of them were standing in the dry creek bottom in the midst of the wide depression where the two wadis joined. Then it happened.

Suddenly, there was a sound, like that of distant thunder, followed by a flash of brilliant light. Then there was only hushed stillness.

Aaron's eyes took a moment to adjust from the flash of startling light, but almost immediately, he was aware of the presence of tens of thousands of men surrounding them. The entire hollow was filled with the 144,000 faithful, instantly recalled and returned from their places of ministry all over the world.

"Wow!" Aaron breathed. "I don't think I will ever get used to this. I've been beamed back and forth a few times now, but this is the first time I've ever witnessed it happening to others. That had to be the most awesome thing I've ever seen in my life!"

Ivan and Ken voiced their agreement. They too were nearly overwhelmed by what they had just witnessed. But Joseph and David accepted it matter-of-factly, almost as though it had been an everyday occurrence for them. Indeed, they had witnessed it before, and the Lord had prepared them in advance for this present regathering of his chosen ones, so it was not nearly as startling an experience to them as it was to the other three.

But to the newly arrived 144,000, it was mind-boggling. They had been suddenly uprooted from their various places of ministry all over the world, and deposited instantly back into the Judean wilderness in the same incredible way as they had been transported nearly three-and-a-half years earlier. It was several seconds before any of them spoke. They just stood there in stunned silence for a moment, trying to comprehend what had just taken place.

Then, almost simultaneously, they began to talk and laugh and hug one another. There was the beginning of a huge reunion that would have quickly spread throughout the entire area, and would have taken countless hours to complete, but Joseph called a halt to it shortly after it began. He put two fingers into his mouth and generated a whistle so shrill and so loud that it brought the entire gathering almost instantly to silence.

"Welcome, my brothers!" he shouted to be heard. "The time is at hand. Our Lord has called you all home to prepare for the great conflict. The armies of the world will soon descend upon the land of your forefathers, and His chosen ones in and around Jerusalem will need your protection. You are to spend the next few hours here resting in the shade of the clouds the Lord has provided. You can use that time to repair and to replenish your weapons, as you will soon be in need of them. Later we will walk back to Jerusalem and take the Mount of Olives after nightfall."

That seemed to satisfy the regathered multitude. They had become accustomed to accepting immediate changes in their schedules as the Lord had redirected their paths over the past several years. They all soon found a place to sit and began visiting quietly with those around them. As well, they set to work sharpening their swords and spears, attaching arrowheads and fletching to slender shafts, and collecting suitable stones for their slings. They would be ready when their Master had need of them.

Aaron looked around and found it hard to believe that he was looking at the same group of young men that he had first seen nearly three-and-a-half years earlier in a similar setting farther south in the Negev. Then, he had seen a congregation of ruddy college students and young businessmen, for the most part, well dressed and clean-shaven. Now he looked around at a gathering of weathered and seasoned soldiers with shaggy hair and beards, dressed in tattered clothing and worn sandals. They all looked as though they had lost about twenty pounds each through their ordeal, and had aged a good ten years. Aaron also noticed they had a look of experience and confidence about them, and hardened muscles flexed on their sturdy frames as they moved effortlessly about.

Aaron couldn't help but smile as he thought how he and the fellow members of God's chosen 144,000 had more than achieved that "leaner and meaner" look that Coach Englehart had tried to sculpt into the bodies of the members of his swim team at Cal State Long Beach through those long and grueling practices in what seemed like a former lifetime. They had achieved a degree of strength and stamina far beyond what Coach Englehart had ever dreamed for his team. Their bodies were like finely tuned weapons, with virtually no body fat at all. But he, or any other coach in the country, would have been fired immediately had he tried to force them to submit to the kind of lifestyle that had produced such bodies—a lifestyle each of them had readily accepted in order to serve in the army of the King of kings.

After selecting some choice sling stones to fill his partly empty pouch, Aaron chose a spot to sit near Joseph and David. There were some things that had been on his mind that he needed to clarify with them if he could.

"Joseph," he said, when his friend was not engaged in conversation with anyone else. "From everything that's happening, it appears that the Battle of Armageddon could take place in a matter of just a few days, and the Lord could be returning very soon."

"Your observations are correct, my friend. The end of the 'Time of Jacob's Trouble'[25] is at hand."

"But I don't see how that could be," Aaron protested. "The Bible indicates the tribulation will be forty-two months long.[26] That's three-and-a-half years on anybody's calendar, right?"

"Yes, that's right."

"Well, correct me if I'm wrong here, but I remember distinctly when the rapture took place, and when Constantine Augustus defiled the temple to start the tribulation.[27] That was about the end of the first week in March, nearly three-and-a half years ago . . . but not quite. It's just the middle of August now. It will be more than three weeks before we get to the end of a full three-and-a-half-year period. How can the end come in just a few more days?"

At that point, David, who was sitting next to Joseph, entered the conversation. "Your calculations are correct, but you have overlooked one important fact, my friend."

"What's that?"

"You have been calculating the time based on three-and-a-half solar years, not lunar ones. There are 365 days in a solar year, but only 360 in a lunar one: twelve months of thirty days each. That same passage you referred to in Revelation 11:2 that gave the duration of the tribulation as forty-two months also spells out the exact number of days it will last. In the next verse it says, *"And I will give power to my two witnesses, and they will prophesy one thousand two hundred and sixty days, clothed in sackcloth."*

"How is it you have that verse memorized?" Aaron asked. "Have you committed the whole Bible to memory?"

"No, by no means," David admitted. "But that particular verse has special meaning for Joseph and me. You see, God has selected the two of us to be those two witnesses. And our 1260 days have just about expired."

---

[25] Alas! For that day is great, so that none is like it; and it is the time of Jacob's trouble, but he shall be saved out of it (Jeremiah 30:7).

[26] But leave out the court which is outside the temple, and do not measure it, for it has been given to the Gentiles. And they will tread the holy city underfoot for forty-two months (Revelation 11:2).

[27] Therefore when you see the abomination of desolation, spoken of by Daniel the prophet, standing in the holy place . . . then let those who are in Judea flee to the mountains. . . . For then there will be great tribulation, such as has not been since the beginning of the world until this time, no, nor ever shall be (Matthew 24:15–16, 21).

"Sure, now I see what you mean. Forty-two months of thirty days each would be exactly 1260 days, but three-and-a-half solar years would be something like 1277 days. So, instead of the three weeks I was planning on, the end will come seventeen days sooner, or in just a matter of a few days from now. And it's a good thing it will. The way all the armies of the world are coming together here, and the kind of firepower they're packing, I don't see how much of anything could survive an all out military onslaught for three full weeks."[28]

"Yes, it is all in the Master's hands," Joseph concluded. "Everything is coming together just as His Word said it would. Now we must return to Jerusalem to prepare for the end of our journey."

"I remember reading about what's going to happen to you," Aaron said. "Isn't there some way to avoid it? Surely you can't be looking forward to that sort of a destiny; especially after all you've already been through."

"No," Joseph admitted, "I cannot say I relish what is in store for us, but we must commit it into the Lord's hands. Like our Savior did in the Garden of Gethsemane, we have prayed that this fate might pass from us, but ultimately, it must be as God wills, not as we might desire."[29]

With that, Joseph ended the conversation and stood to his feet, and David did likewise. Together they summoned their comrades to prepare for their divinely appointed mission. This time, it was David who called for a meeting of twelve representatives, one chosen from each of the tribes of Israel. These men would then lead their respective armies of 12,000 men into the battle that was soon to take place in and around Jerusalem.

Such a task could have taken seemingly forever to accomplish, seeing that the men of each tribe did not know the other members, and they would have had great difficulty in singling them out and assembling them all together. But the Lord had prepared them already for the task. When they had been transported earlier, all the members of each tribe had been placed in the same area in the hollow valley, so they didn't have to look beyond their immediate surroundings to find their

[28] For then there will be great tribulation, such as has not been since the beginning of the world until this time, no, nor ever shall be. And unless those days were shortened, no flesh would be saved; but for the elect's sake those days will be shortened (Matthew 24:21–22).

[29] He went a little farther and fell on His face, and prayed, saying, "O My Father, if it is possible, let this cup pass from Me; nevertheless, not as I will, but as You will" (Matthew 26:39).

fellow tribesmen. Besides that, He placed in their hearts and minds the name of the man whom He had already selected to lead the various tribes into battle.

Ken Weinman insisted Aaron Muller represent the tribe of Benjamin, and the other men from that tribe voiced their approval. Though having no particular desire to command other men, Aaron accepted their acclamation and consented to be their leader. And just as easily, the other eleven men were chosen from the other tribes.

Ten minutes later Aaron found himself meeting with thirteen other men beneath a tamarisk tree in the center of the hollow valley, surrounded by the scores of thousands of God's chosen army. Besides Joseph and David, he knew Ivan Feldsin, chosen to represent the tribe of Joseph; Mark Robertson, the tribe of Gad; Julio Otero, the tribe of Reuben; and Rico Sandia, the tribe of Judah. He had not yet met Mark's friends: Seth Goodman from the tribe of Issachar, and Jabin Weisler from the tribe of Zebulun. Besides them, there were five other men representing the remaining five tribes.

After everyone had been introduced, David set about explaining the strategy they would employ in capturing the Mount of Olives. Jerusalem proper was much too large, and much too heavily fortified for them to attempt a complete takeover of the entire area, so they would concentrate on the Mount of Olives to the east of the city, from which they would be able to stage future strikes into the heart of Constantine's forces to the west.

Each of the twelve commanders was to lead his army of 12,000 away from their present location in separate directions, ultimately bringing them into various positions surrounding the Mount of Olives just before sundown. Then, at the blast from a ram's horn, they were to converge upon the mountain from all directions, taking it just after dark. The darkness would confuse and frustrate the enemy troops, but it should pose no problem for the 144,000. The moon was nearly full, which would help considerably, and coupled with their divinely enhanced night vision, they would be able to see quite well.

Aaron was to lead his 12,000 around to the left, and attack the Mount of Olives from the southwest, coming up through the Kidron Valley. He was thankful for that assignment because he was somewhat familiar with that part of the Jerusalem area. He and Mark Robertson had fled down through that valley after they had blown up the Dome of the Rock some four years before, and he had been among those who had fled down through that same valley after the antichrist had defiled the temple nine months later. He would be attacking from the opposite direction, and uphill, which was not to his liking, but his familiarity with the area made him feel a little better about his prospects for success.

When it boiled right down to it, the only chance for success any of them had lay squarely with the Lord, anyway. An army equipped with swords and spears and staves, even one 144,000 strong, would have no chance of dislodging an equally large army equipped with the latest in military weaponry. God would have to rout the enemy and drive them out just as He did for Joshua and the children of Israel some 3500 years before. And that was exactly what David and Joseph were counting on.

They had left the enemy with a narrow avenue of escape. Aaron would lead his troops in from the southwest, and Mark would be bringing his in from the northwest, but no one would be attacking out of the City of Jerusalem itself, directly to the west of the Mount of Olives. David's plan was to take the mountain by surprise and to overwhelm the enemy troops so completely that they would flee in sheer panic down the west slope and into the city, leaving the Mount of Olives completely in the hands of the 144,000.

It was a good strategy, and God willing, it would work as planned. But there were two more things for them to consider. David informed the twelve that there would be little or no food or water for them or their troops for the next several days. The scorching heat and the paralyzing darkness had dried up all the springs and had depleted most of the food reserves they had stored away. What little was left had been given to the huddled masses, hiding from the wrath of the antichrist in the caves beneath the city. The 144,000 would have to draw strength from what they had already eaten and drunk, and to trust God for supernatural enablement during the grueling days ahead.[30]

The last thing he had to share with them was even more sobering. For the past three-and-a-half years, the 144,000 had been divinely sealed and protected. They had been hounded, wounded, and tortured, but not one of them had been killed. But David's angel had informed him that the divine protection was about to come to an end. For whatever time remained of their allotted forty-two months of service, they would be as other men. In the battles that remained to be fought, like other

[30] And the angel of the Lord came back the second time, and touched him, and said, "Arise and eat, because the journey is too great for you." So he arose, and ate and drank; and he went in the strength of that food forty days and forty nights as far as Horeb, the mountain of God (1 Kings 19:7–8).

men, they could be killed. Undoubtedly, at the hands of the antichrist and his minions, the lives of many of them would come to a violent end.

It took some time for the reality of that last message to sink in. All twelve had privately come to believe that they were destined to live through the entire tribulation period and into the glorious millennial kingdom that would follow. But, they realized that they had never been promised such a thing. They had been sealed forever, and that seal could never be broken, but that seal only secured their souls; it did not necessarily secure the preservation of their bodies. The thought of the possibility of imminent death was a hard one to swallow.

It was Rico who spoke up first. "Okay, the way I got it figured, whichever way it works out, we win. If we don't get killed . . . we win . . . and we get to go into the millennium with our loved ones. If we do get killed . . . we win again . . . and we get to go be with the Lord and come back with Him when He returns. And then our bodies will be raised and we'll be even better than before.[31] So, whatever happens, we win. What's so hard about that?"

That brought a laugh from everyone, and the tension was broken. They had all signed on for the duration, and they weren't about to let the threat of death detour them from their objective of serving the Lord until it was over. That being understood and accepted by all, David led them in a time of prayer and commitment, and then sent them off to lead their fellow tribesmen into battle.

The large congregation rallied immediately and began to fall in behind the twelve commanders, who were already making their way out of the hollow valley in various directions. Soon David and Joseph found themselves alone in the bottom of the ravine as they watched the last of the 144,000 disappear over the ridge to the west of them.

Joseph looked at David and said, "Well, my old friend, we have done all the Lord has asked of us so far. The rest is in His hands, and those of His 144,000. Are you ready to face our final responsibility?"

David swallowed hard and nodded his head. "Yes," he said, "let's be on our way. We don't want to keep Constantine waiting."

---

[31] And I saw thrones, and they sat on them, and judgment was committed to them. Then I saw the souls of those who had been beheaded for their witness to Jesus and for the word of God, who had not worshipped the beast or his image, and had not received his mark on their foreheads or on their hands. And they lived and reigned with Christ for a thousand years (Revelation 20:4).

They turned and began making their way steadily up the narrow path that led back to Jerusalem. They were in no hurry. There was still plenty of daylight left, and they wanted to relish every moment of it. Life had not been easy for them over the past three-and-a-half years (wandering in sackcloth, and facing hostilities and persecutions every single day), but at least it had been life. What they were about to face now would put an end to all that abruptly.

As they topped the hill and approached the city, they could hear the sound of multiple explosions far to the west of them. What they did not know was that while they had been with the 144,000 in the valley below, massive sea battles had been going on in three other distant areas. Planes from aircraft carriers and land bases had been engaging one another all day.

American aircraft took off from their carriers in the Gulf of Aqaba and joined forces with the Russian planes from their carriers in the Black Sea, and together, they struck at the heart of the Federation carriers in the Mediterranean Sea, and at their land bases in Israel itself. In response, Federation planes struck back at the invading aircraft, and followed them home and attacked their carriers with all the firepower they could muster.

By the end of the day, the results were devastating. Each side had effectively neutralized the other. A total of ten aircraft carriers had been sunk, and at least that many more had been rendered inoperable. Virtually all the aircraft on both sides had either been shot down or disabled to the point that they were unavailable for future missions.

The air war was effectively over in one day. Tanks, artillery pieces, and personnel carriers were rattling toward the heart of Israel from both the north and the south, and Federation forces were being beefed up to meet them when they arrived, but there would be effectively no air support for either side. The coming war was destined to be fought in the trenches, and the potential loss of life was staggering.[32]

Joseph and David approached the City of Jerusalem from the south late in the afternoon. Federation lookouts spotted them as they came, but they did not fire on them. It was apparent that the two were unarmed and posed no apparent threat. The guards called for reinforcements, and watched them approach.

The two entered the Old City from the Dung Gate on the south wall. By this time, there was a small army waiting to surround them

[32] At the time of the end the king of the South shall attack him; and the king of the North shall come against him like a whirlwind, with chariots, horseman, and with many ships; and he shall enter the countries, overwhelm them, and pass through (Daniel 11:40).

and to escort them to their final destination. They made no communication with the soldiers, but made their way to the courtyard just to the west of the Western Wall, the last remaining structure from Herod's temple of the first century. Often called the Wailing Wall, that edifice had represented the holiest site for the Jewish people for over nineteen hundred years, and in all actuality, it still did. The antichrist had defiled their beautiful new temple before it was ever dedicated, and no faithful Jew would so much as approach it thereafter. So, directly in front of the massive wall, David and Joseph stopped and waited for their nemesis to arrive.

Constantine Augustus, of course, had been notified as soon as the two witnesses had been identified. He had hated them, hounded them, feared them, and respected them for over three years, but he had never actually been close to them before. And he wasn't real sure he wanted to at this time either.

The two troublemakers had demonstrated supernatural powers, and no one had been able to resist them. There was no counting the number of his men they had killed, nor the suffering they had inflicted through the plagues they unleashed upon his people. No one he had sent, and nothing he had done, had been able to stop them.

Now, here they were, unarmed and waiting patiently for him in front of that cursed Wailing Wall. At a distance, he looked at them through powerful binoculars, and they appeared harmless enough, but still he didn't trust them. They didn't actually need weapons in order to inflict suffering and death. They had been known to shoot fire from their mouths, and to cut men down with nothing more than words spoken from their lips.[33]

Constantine called for a sniper rifle, and soon one was placed in his hands. He crouched behind a low stone wall and rested the rifle on the top of it. He was shaking noticeably as he sighted through the powerful telescopic sight, and he had to stop to wipe the sweat out of his eyes. The sniper who owned the rifle offered to take the shot for him, but Constantine cursed him and ordered him removed from the premises. This was one shot he had long anticipated, and was not going to pass it off to anyone else.

---

[33] "And I will give power to my two witnesses, and they will prophesy one thousand two hundred and sixty days, clothed in sackcloth . . ." And if anyone wants to harm them, fire proceeds from their mouth and devours their enemies. And if anyone wants to harm them, he must be killed in this manner (Revelation 11:3,5).

He returned to his shooting position and sighted again through the scope. He selected the taller of the two witnesses because he made a bigger target, and because he usually appeared to be the spokesman of the two. He placed the crosshairs directly over the center of the man's chest, took a breath and held it, and then slowly squeezed the trigger.

Constantine was rocked backward, partially by the recoil of the rifle, but mostly by surprise. He had not actually expected the rifle to fire. No one else had ever been able to get a killing shot off at either one of the loathsome rebels before. He looked up in disbelief in time to see the man clutch his chest and collapse to the stone pavement some two hundred yards away.

The Great Caesar whooped and jumped up and down for joy. His men congratulated him on his skillful aim and patted him on the back. He called for his driver to take him down to the scene of the shooting. He insisted on *doing* the next one up close and personal.

David knelt beside his fallen comrade and cradled his head in his arms. Joseph looked at him and smiled. He struggled and spoke softly, "I'll see you on the other side, my friend." Then, he looked upward, his eyes focused on things unseen, and rapture filled his face. He exhaled, his expression froze, and he was gone.

Just then, Constantine's Humvee screeched to a halt, and the newly emboldened Caesar strode up to the two. He pulled his pistol from his holster and pointed it at David's head and commanded him to rise and face him.

Not intimidated in the least, David continued to kneel by his friend and bid him farewell. But knowing he would be joining him soon, he did not prolong his goodbyes. Paying no attention to Constantine's threats, he rose to his feet slowly, and turned and faced his enemy.

"So, we meet at last!" Constantine snarled. "I knew I would beat you in the end. What do you have to say for yourself now, before I put a bullet between your eyes?"

"You fool!" David said sternly. "You have power over us now only because our God has willed it so. Your doom is sure, and it is coming soon. You think you have this coming war won before it even begins because you have the Chinese stopped at the Euphrates River. Well, my Lord has informed me that His sixth bowl of judgment is about to be unleashed, and He will dry up that river, and your enemies will cross it and descend upon you in great multitudes. You will have more troubles than you ever imagined.

"However, your defeat will not come at the hands of the Chinese, or the Russians, or the Americans. They will frustrate and humble you, but your everlasting destruction will come at the hand of the Lord Himself unless you are converted. As His appointed witness, I command you to humble yourself and repent and call upon Him for mercy, that He may spare your miserable life."

"No way! You're the fool if you think I would ever humble myself before your imposter God Jehovah. Absolute victory is within my grasp, and my ability to take your worthless life is proof of my superiority over you, and of the supremacy of my god over yours. I reject your pathetic offer of clemency. What do you think of that?"

"It is as I expected, I knew you would not accept God's summons to repentance, but I was required to offer it to you. Now, it gives me great pleasure to condemn your retched soul to the unquenchable fires of hell. Do your worst, you devil's spawn; I have no fear of you. Your bullets send me only to my God!"

Constantine cursed bitterly and spat on the pavement. "We'll see who goes to hell, you filthy impostor." He raised his pistol and fired it directly into David's face. Again and again, he fired his weapon as his enemy crumpled to the smooth stones beneath him. Then, he stood over the bodies of the two fallen witnesses, and fired into them alternately until his magazine was exhausted. Even then, he did not stop. He continued to pull the trigger, clicking off one empty round after another.

His eyes were aflame with hatred, and his lips were curled back in a hideous snarl. His insane laughter echoed off the ancient wall in front of him, and his body shook with maniacal tremors.

Finally, he came to himself and lowered his weapon. He looked with smug satisfaction on the work of his hands. The two bodies beneath him lay in twisted heaps, blood flowing freely from their multiple wounds. His hated enemies were actually dead at his feet. And it had been so easy! They had been powerless before his superior strength. Surely this was a sign of his invincibility. Who could stand against him now?

Eli Rothschild had just arrived, and witnessed the final shooting. He congratulated his cousin and his master, "Well done, oh Great One! These two are but the first among millions who will follow. Soon all your enemies shall lie dead at your feet. How do you want us to dispose of these bodies? Shall we burn them, bury them, or feed them to the dogs?"

"None of the above!" said Constantine sternly. "Leave them where they lie. Post a guard around them so none of the rabble that follow them will be able to take the bodies away. I want them to rot in full view of everyone. Have TV cameras over here, and broadcast images of their blackened and bloated bodies all over the world. I want all to see what happens to those who dare to defy the king of kings."

And so it was. Constantine and Eli got into their waiting vehicles and had their drivers take them back to Constantine's penthouse where they would celebrate their current victory, and make plans for even more glorious ones to follow.

The sun slowly sank below the horizon in the distant Mediterranean Sea, and darkness began to settle over the Holy City. Joseph and David were escorted by their angels into the presence of their waiting Messiah to receive His commendation for their brave and faithful service, but their vacated bodies stiffened in the evening breeze.[34] The gruesome process of decomposition had already begun, and over the next several days, it would transform their once handsome frames into hideous mounds of putrefaction before the eyes of the watching world.[35]

[34] So it was that the beggar died, and was carried by the angels to Abraham's bosom. The rich man also died and was buried (Luke 16:22).

[35] When they finish their testimony, the beast that ascends out of the bottomless pit will make war against them, overcome them, and kill them. And their dead bodies will lie in the street of the great city which spiritually is called Sodom and Egypt, where also our Lord was crucified (Revelation 11:7–8).

CHAPTER THIRTEEN

The Sixth Bowl

The Angel Mahaliel sped toward the River Euphrates with a heavy bowl in his hands. It was filled with the wrath of God, and the angel was determined to pour it out as he had been instructed. Legions of demons had attempted to overpower him and prevent him from completing his mission, but Michael and the armies of heaven came to his aid and beat back the dark forces and escorted him through their devastated ranks.[36]

It was just after sundown when Mahaliel arrived at his appointed destination. He hovered momentarily over the swollen waters of the surging river some sixty miles north of Babylon. Receiving his final confirmation from the Lord, he tipped his bowl and poured its contents into the darkened waters.

Suddenly, there was a violent earthquake, and the earth rose up in the middle of the river, blocking the flow of its water. At the same time, a great fissure opened to the east through the desert, allowing the torrents to be diverted through its gorge. The mighty waters of the Euphrates made an abrupt left turn and surged eastward through the Iraqi sands to

[36] Then he said to me. "Do not fear, Daniel, for from the first day that you set your heart to understand, and to humble yourself before your God, your words were heard; and I have come because of your words. But the prince of the kingdom of Persia withstood me twenty-one days; and behold, Michael, one of the chief princes, came to help me, for I was left alone there with the kings of Persia." (Daniel 10:12–13).

the Tigris River, some thirty miles away. The liquid juggernaut plunged into the bed of the already swollen Tigris, and their combined waters immediately overflowed its banks.

Great destruction was done by the rampaging floodwaters of the two rivers downstream. Whole communities were washed away in a moment, and countless lives were lost. Thousands of those who had escaped the onslaught of the Chinese armies now had their lives swept away by the thundering torrents.

But back at what had been the Euphrates River, the waters, cut off from the flow from upstream, began to dissipate rapidly. The empty riverbed began to emerge where, only moments before, the mighty river had surged. The dry bed began to follow the retreating waters, and it would be only a matter of hours before the channel separating the Chinese and the Federation forces would be totally devoid of water.

The battle for the Mount of Olives was a brief, but intense, one. Shortly after darkness fell, the twelve commanders each led their armies of 12,000 men up the slopes of the low mountain in a surprise attack. The Federation troops were taken totally by surprise; but one could hardly blame them. The vast army of the 144,000 had arrived secretly, and completely undetected by Constantine's vast intelligence network. Hosts of angels had accompanied the advancing forces, and they prepared the way for them by causing the Federation sentries to be oblivious to their actions. Thus, they were able to move undetected under the very noses of the lookouts. Besides, there were several other matters that had distracted the unsuspecting soldiers.

All day, they had been following the reports of the massive air and sea battles that had been taking place between their forces and those of the Americans and the Russians. Instead of the decisive victory they had been led to expect, they learned that the day had ended in a stalemate, with virtually all the aircraft carriers and the airplanes of all the combatants being put out of commission. That meant that the war would continue, and that it would soon be coming to them. They were engrossed in conversation as to how such a vast conflict would turn out.

On the brighter side, the word had quickly spread in their midst about the wonderful victory their Caesar had achieved over his archenemies. The bodies of those two evil prophets lay dead in the streets of

Jerusalem, and their images were being broadcast around the world. Peoples everywhere were rejoicing and celebrating. Those who had brought so much suffering and death on others were at last dead themselves. The Federation soldiers on the Mount of Olives drank toasts and congratulated one another on what seemed to be a sure indication that their side was winning, and that the war would soon be over.

But on a more sobering note, their commanders had spread the word that some ominous news was coming out of Iraq. It appeared that a massive earthquake or something had taken place over there and had diverted the flow of the Euphrates River, and that its waters were drying up. This caused the soldiers great concern because it could well mean that they would soon be deployed to that area to hold back the advance of the Chinese armies who would now be able to cross the river and proceed in their march toward Israel. The last thing any of them wanted to think about was a forced march out into the deserts of Iraq in the heat of mid-August to face millions of hostile Chinese bent on killing them.

Thus, with all those things on the minds of the Federation soldiers, it was no wonder that they were not aware of their own immediate danger. While they thought and talked about other things, the armies of the 144,000 moved, under cover of darkness, to positions nearly completely surrounding them.

On the signal of a series of blasts from the traditional rams' horns, and a corporate battle cry, the hardened soldiers of the Lord stormed up the hill and quickly overran the Federation positions. Arrows, spears, and sling stones filled the air, and enemy troops fell victim to their accurate trajectories. They returned fire, but they were clearly outmatched, and quickly overrun. In close-in fighting, their rifles and bayonets were no match for the swords and rods of the 144,000. They abandoned their posts, and many of them dropped their weapons as they fled in sheer panic.

Down off the western slope of the ancient mountain they fled, stumbling and falling as they went. Down the historic Palm Sunday Road they ran by the thousands in a desperate attempt to escape the wrath of this army from hell that had appeared out of nowhere. They feared that their assailants were far more than mere mortals, so fast and strong and deadly had they been in their assault.

In less than an hour, the Mount of Olives was firmly in the hands of the 144,000. In the light of the nearly full moon, they secured their positions, and cared for their dead and wounded. Only thirty-seven of their number had been killed, but it was still a sobering confirmation to the rest of them that they were no longer invulnerable. Aaron had Ivan fired up a bulldozer, left behind by the fleeing Federation troops, and excavate a mass grave for their comrades. He had him make it much bigger than their immediate needs required because he was sure they would soon be in need of the additional space. Many more of their number would surely fall in the days that lay ahead before the return of their Lord.

He ordered the bodies covered with tarps only. He was convinced the Lord would soon return and raise them back to life, and just in case He chose to simply resuscitate them like Lazarus of old, rather than to gloriously transform them; it would be an easy matter for them to come forth from under a tarp, but it would be a difficult task indeed for their mortal bodies to rise from under tons of earth.[37]

Aaron called a meeting of the twelve commanders at ten o'clock in the lobby of the Inter-Continental Hotel near the top of the mountain. It overlooked the Kidron Valley and Eastern Jerusalem, with its temple mount. The commander of the Federation troops had used the hotel as his headquarters before he had abandoned it in panic, and Aaron quickly agreed with his choice of locations, and took it over.

The other eleven commanders naturally looked to Aaron for leadership, and since Joseph and David were absent, he accepted the responsibility. He had no ambition to exercise authority over others, but he recognized that God had gifted him with special powers and wisdom, and he knew he must use them for His glory.

He surveyed the other commanders and was relieved to see that they had all survived the battle, and that, other than a few superficial wounds, none had been seriously injured. He asked each of them to give a report as to the conditions in their respective areas of responsibility and was pleased to learn that everything had been secured. Their assault had been swift and brutal; they had taken neither wounded nor prisoners. He ordered the thousands of enemy dead to be bulldozed into a ravine and covered as quickly as possible.

Aaron had sent Ken Weinman and three other men as spies into Jerusalem shortly after the battle was over and the enemy had fled. He

[37] Now when He had said these things, He cried with a loud voice, "Lazarus, come forth!" And he who had died came out bound hand and foot with grave clothes, and his face was wrapped with a cloth. Jesus said to them, "Loose him, and let him go." (John 11:43–44).

had ordered them to bring back information as to the strength and locations of the Federation forces stationed there, and to gather any information they could concerning the whereabouts of Joseph and David. He had an ominous feeling about their welfare as he waited for the spies to return. He was almost certain that they had fallen victim to foul play; there was no other apparent explanation for their absence.

As he talked with the other commanders, the four spies entered breathlessly, winded after their sprint across the Kidron Valley and up the steep slopes of the Mount of Olives. They greeted their brothers in the name of the Lord, and Ken gave his report.

He told them that the Federation troops literally covered the entire Jerusalem area. There were hundreds of thousands already there, with more arriving every hour. It was apparent that Constantine was preparing to defend the heart of his empire with as much force as it required. Ken also reported that the information they had gathered indicated the whole nation was likewise teeming with Federation forces, with ships all up and down the coast offloading men and machines on an around-the-clock basis. He estimated that the emperor had as many as fifteen million men in uniform there to defend his interests.

Then Ken choked up and struggled to say, "But the worrst parrt of the matterr is thut David und Joseph arrr lyin' dead in the strreets, all shot to pieces by thut murrderin' Augustus. Und what's even worrse is thut he wull not allow them to be burrried. We've got to go und brring 'em back, lads. The enemy is overr therre makin' sporrt arround their dead bodies."

"No, Ken," said Aaron softly. "We must allow them to stay where they are. It has all happened exactly as the Bible said it would. They must lie there for three-and-a-half days before the Lord will raise them up and call them home.[38] And besides, they're not there anyway. As soon as they died, they went home to be with the Lord in heaven. It's only their shells out there in the streets. They're actually far better off than we are, my friend."

"Aye, now I rremember. But I still dunna like to think of 'em lyin' out therre like that. The sooner the Lard cuums back, the better it'll be far the likes of oll of us."

"Amen, brother!" Aaron heartily agreed. "The next few days will be horrible ones indeed, but the time is short, and I can almost hear the

[38] Then those from the peoples, tribes, tongues, and nations will see their dead bodies three-and-a-half days, and not allow their dead bodies to be put into graves. (Revelation 11:9).

sound of the armies in heaven preparing to return with our blessed Lord. It is our job to contend in His behalf until He comes."

On the banks of the Euphrates River, Chairman Chong could not believe his eyes. The midnight darkness made it difficult to see clearly, but the evidence was still undeniable; the waters of the swollen river were beginning to recede. That cursed river that had caused him so much frustration and delay was in the unmistakable process of retreating.

His communications officer had informed him that the Americans and Russians had been involved in a massive air and sea war with Federation forces the day before, and at the same time, their armies were marching toward Israel. It had been imperative that China coordinate its attack from the east to coincide with theirs from the south and north. But they simply had not been able to cross the stubborn river.

Chong's engineers had tried desperately to construct pontoon bridges across the waters, only to be beaten back, time and time again, by Federation tank and mortar fire. He had been forced to pull his troops back from the water's edge lest his losses become too overwhelming.

At midnight, he had planned to send them forth again under the cover of darkness, hoping against hope they would be able to construct the bridges before dawn so he could get a landing force secure on the opposite bank. But the moon was nearly full, and there were no clouds in the starry sky. The Federation forces had anticipated his actions and they were positioned to repel any such attempt to cross the river. They had ample light to detect the presence of the Chinese forces, and to direct their deadly fire into their midst.

The chairman had been about to give the order to send them nonetheless; tens of thousands of his men to almost certain death in the swirling dark waters in the slim hope that some of them would be able to make it across. But now, he decided to postpone the assault. He would watch and wait. If the waters continued to recede at their present rate, the riverbed would be dry before dawn, and he could send his entire army across it at one time and overwhelm the Federation defenders.[39]

[39] Then the sixth angel poured out his bowl on the great river Euphrates, and its water was dried up, so that the way of the kings from the east might be prepared (Revelation 16:12).

The sun had not yet made its appearance over the top of the mountains to the east. Nonetheless, Constantine Augustus was up and dressed and pacing the floor. Eli Rothschild was with him in his penthouse suite atop the New Millennium Hotel in Western Jerusalem. From their vantage point, they could see the top of the Mount of Olives in the distance, but they experienced no joy in seeing the first rays of sun emerge above its heights.

Constantine swore as he was forced to deal with the fact that during the night, a ragtag army of misfits, wielding ancient weapons, had vanquished his forces there, and had taken control of that strategic location. The Mount of Olives was higher in elevation than the city of Jerusalem, and an army controlling it would have a tremendous tactical advantage over troops attacking it from the city below and to the west.

"I don't care how many men we lose," he stormed, "you order a counterattack. We must retake that mountain. Do I make myself clear, Eli?"

"Yes, oh Great One. It shall be done. They have no guns, no tanks, no mortars, no artillery of any sort. We should overrun them in no time at all, your Excellency."

"I wouldn't be so sure of that, Eli. I don't know how they got here, but unless I miss my guess, that army is made up of all those thousands of Jewish rebels who have been plaguing us all over the world. We weren't able to kill any of them before, and I don't suppose it will be an easy matter now."

"Yes, oh Great Caesar, but things have changed. You were able to kill their two leaders easily yesterday. Their decaying bodies lie in the streets of the city even now. And besides, our troops that survived the battle last night reported killing many of their attackers. If they were protected from death before, you have broken that spell, and you can destroy them just as you have destroyed all your other enemies."

"Yes, you're right. I shall destroy them, but it will not be easy. Though some of them have been killed, they die hard. There is no reason in the world that they should have been able to take that mountain last night, but they did. Though they don't have any modern weapons, they do have some magic up their sleeves. Don't forget what has happened every time we've tried to wipe out that rats' nest on top of Masada. We must be prepared for a massive battle, and we must be prepared to suffer terrible casualties, but we must retake that mountain. Do you understand me?"

Oh, yes, Master," Eli pledged. "It shall be done. We still have some time before the Russians and the Americans get here, so we can concentrate all our firepower on the Mount of Olives. We will throw everything we have at them. The mountain will be ours before noon, my king."

"Good! See that it happens," Constantine said resolutely. "We need to get that mess cleaned up as soon as possible because we have more important matters to attend to. The Americans and the Russians are headed this way and we must be prepared to meet them with overwhelming force. Besides that, the news out of Iraq is not good. That Jewish rebel told me, just before I killed him, that the River Euphrates would be dried up to allow the Chinese to get across and attack us here. I don't know how he knew, but it appears to be happening. Our reports tell us the waters are receding. If that river dries up and the Chinese get across, I don't think our forces there will be able to stop them. I don't know how many they have in their army, but our reports tells us it numbers into the millions."

Just then, a voice came over the intercom announcing breaking news. No one dared actually deliver a message in person to the emperor any longer. The word of his throwing just such a messenger over the guardrail to his death had circulated throughout his staff, and none of them was willing to risk being a participant in a repeat performance.

"Yes, what is it?" Constantine snapped, obviously annoyed.

"Oh, Great Caesar, live forever," came the obviously nervous reply at the other end of the connection.

"Cut the bull, man. What do you want?"

"Oh, sir, I'm sorry to interrupt you, but I was told to let you know that the Russian army has broken through our lines at the Lebanese border and is moving into Galilee."

Constantine swore, and kicked over a potted plant. He recovered somewhat and snapped, "Is that it, or do you have any more good news to share with us this morning?"

"Oh, forgive me, Great Caesar, but there is something else. The Euphrates River has completely dried up, and the Chinese army is moving across it along a wide front just north of Babylon."

Constantine swore again, more bitterly than before, and threw the intercom unit across the room and dashed it to pieces against the far wall. "Come on, Eli," he yelled, "let's get over to headquarters. We've got to stop those armies before they can reach Jerusalem!"[40]

[40] But news from the east and the north shall trouble him; therefore he shall go out with great fury to destroy and annihilate many (Daniel 11:44).

Chairman Chong was ecstatic. The Euphrates River had dried up entirely during the night, and before morning, he had ordered his armies to cross its sandy bed all along a fifty-mile front. Tanks, armored vehicles, and literally millions of men had stormed to the other side across the wet sand. They had encountered fierce resistance, but their sheer numerical superiority had eventually overpowered the enemy, driving them back from the river's edge.

Now, as his forces were pushing their way ever westward, many of the Federation defenders fled before them in panic; others retreated into the City of Babylon in an effort to hold off the invaders from behind its formidable walls. But their tactics were proving to be futile. Chong's generals had the rebuilt city surrounded, and were pummeling it with everything they had.

Chong stood on a low hill with his vassal kings and watched as his tanks and artillery pieces lobbed their destructive shells into the helpless city, blasting down its walls and pulverizing its structures within. He could have called for a ceasefire when the Federation defenders raised a white flag in surrender, but he was angry and frustrated with them for all the damage they had inflicted on his forces during the previous three days, so he ordered the shelling continued until the entire city was reduced to rubble, and its occupants buried beneath it. When the chairman was at last satisfied and ordered the shelling stopped, one could hardly recognize that a proud city had once stood where a huge mound of ruins now lay smoldering in the desert sun.[41]

At Chong's command, the Chinese forces turned westward to join their fellows in driving the remaining Federation defenders all the way back into Israel. They had brought thousands of armored personnel carriers with them, and they commandeered many more that had been left behind by the fleeing Federation troops. Therefore, the bulk of the Chinese army was able to move across the Iraqi and Jordanian deserts at a blistering pace. Barring significant armed resistance; they would be approaching the eastern borders of Israel by the next morning.

[41] Babylon has suddenly fallen and been destroyed (Jeremiah 51:8).
Babylon shall become a heap, a dwelling place for jackals, an astonishment and a hissing, without an inhabitant (Jeremiah 51:37).

CHAPTER FOURTEEN

The Battle

The fighting in Jerusalem was fierce. Federation forces struck, time and time again, at the 144,000 defending the Mount of Olives, only to be driven back each time. They had support from tank and mortar fire, but their bombardment did not inflict the kind of damage it should have. Few buildings collapsed, and few walls fell. Men were injured, and some were killed, but not in the numbers one would expect.

Although the 144,000 had no modern weapons, they more than held their ground. Aaron, and others who had rods and staves, stood on the tops of walls and buildings, and aimed their unlikely weapons at the attacking tanks and artillery pieces. Divine fire erupted from the ends of their wooden implements, and shot straight to the heart of their intended targets. After suffering heavy losses, the Federation commanders were forced to call back their tanks and heavy artillery lest they lose them all.

The scores of thousands of soldiers who swarmed up the slopes of the small mountain were driven back by a hail of sling stones, spears, and arrows. Their own bullets were unable to inflict the kind of punishment they should have. Although the air was literally filled with their fiery projectiles, few found their mark. Not nearly so many of the defenders were stricken as were those of the attacking hordes.

After the third wave of the attack had been successfully driven back, Aaron called for an offensive of his own. With the blasts from the rams' horns, and the shouts from the twelve commanders, the faithful charged down the slopes of the Mount of Olives and up into the heart of the City of Jerusalem. They drove back the Federation troops from the eastern wall of the city, and captured the temple mount. In the process, the temple was heavily damaged, and the Dome of the Rock was completely destroyed.

Aaron took special pleasure in leveling the golden-domed mosque himself with a blast of fire from the end of his rod. Constantine had converted the Muslim structure into a sacred shrine to glorify himself, housing every sort of picture imaginable of himself, documents he had signed, digital recordings of his public appearances, and even articles of clothing he had worn. Pilgrims, waiting for their turn to worship and pray to Caesar's image in the temple, had often spent hours in the Dome of the Rock, reveling in the plethora of information about their idol available to them there.

As he brought the abominable structure down on itself in a fiery implosion, Aaron thought back to four years before when he and Mark Robertson had damaged the same structure from across the Kidron Valley with a shoulder-fired missile. It seemed he had been a different person then, and living in another lifetime. Then, as a zealous Jew, he had fired the missile into a Muslim mosque in retaliation for the atrocities committed by Arab terrorists against the Jew's Great Synagogue. Now, as the leader of God's chosen 144,000, he delighted in obliterating the hellish shrine to the devil's own antichrist.

Yet, as gratifying as that was, it paled by comparison with the satisfaction he sensed when he pulverized, with his own rod, the demonic monstrosity in the Holy of Holies of the temple. Though heavily damaged, the temple building was still standing when Aaron cautiously approached it, and after dispatching the remaining soldiers inside, he approached the hideous idol itself.

It too, had been damaged in the firefight. Some of its circuits were blown, and it was malfunctioning. The life-sized image of Constantine Augustus was jerky in its movements, and its voice was comically distorted. "How fitting," Aaron thought to himself, "that the crowning achievement of the antichrist's genius should perform like a cheap carnival attraction."

He drew back his rod, and with fire in his eyes, he swung it with all his might, striking the mechanical monster squarely alongside its head, knocking it clean off. Sparks flew from the broken wires, and fluids spurted from the ends of the severed tubes, and the head shot across the room and smashed to pieces against the stone wall.

The headless monstrosity continued to jerk and twitch for several seconds while the remaining circuits shorted out, and then it slumped over and *died.* Aaron looked at the lifeless pile of junk and said, "If there's a hell for evil machines, may you burn in it forever!" And then remembering a line from an old science fiction movie he had seen as a boy, he added, "Hasta la vista, baby!" and he turned and walked out of the building.

When he had exited the temple, he stopped and looked at the magnificent structure, damaged, but still spectacular. Yet, he knew it was defiled by Satan's contamination, and it had to be destroyed. The Lord would build a much more holy and beautiful one in its place when He returned anyway. With a shrug, he drew back his rod one more time. He brought it forward with a powerful swing and smashed the end of it into the side of the massive building.

The huge wall instantly collapsed inwardly, bringing down the roof on top of it. Now unsupported, the other walls also collapsed, and in less than ten seconds, the once majestic temple was reduced to a pile of rubble.

Aaron jumped back as the stones came crashing down, and retreated toward the western wall. After the noise of the collapsing temple subsided, he became aware of someone calling his name. He looked and saw Mark Robertson at the wall, motioning for him to join him there. Aaron ran to his side, thinking his friend might be in need of immediate assistance.

When he arrived at Mark's side, his friend pointed over the low wall and said, "Look, Aaron. That's David and Joseph down there."

Aaron looked in the direction Mark was pointing, and saw the bodies of two men, lying in grotesque positions, about sixty-five yards west of the base of the wall, which was over fifty feet high at that point. The day was hot, and the bodies had already begun to swell, but he could clearly identify them as those of his two friends. His heart sunk as he saw them lying there, uncared for and unburied.

"We gotta go get them, Aaron," Mark urged. "We can't just leave them there to rot. God has protected us so far; surely He will be with us when we go after our own."

"No, I don't think so, Mark. The Bible says they have to lie in the streets of the city for three-and-a-half days for all the world to see; and God's Word is always true. Look at all the soldiers positioned around those bodies to keep anyone from tampering with them. If we sent our men out to get David's and Joseph's bodies, they would all be gunned down. As much as I hate it, we're going to have to leave them where they lie.

"Besides, look at all those TV cameras over there. It's just like the Bible says: the whole world will look at their dead bodies and rejoice in their deaths because they think they are the ones who brought all the plagues on them."[42]

"Yeah, I know all that stuff," Mark agreed, "but I still want to go get their bodies. I know it's only for a short time, but actually seeing them lying out there like that makes it so hard to accept. It just doesn't seem fair."

"It isn't fair," Aaron concurred, "but since when has anything been fair ever since this whole tribulation mess first began?"

"Yeah, you're right about that. The only thing that makes life bearable is knowing that God is still in control, and that He is going to work everything out for His own glory in the end. And I guess the fact that Joseph and David are going to be raised back to life should make it bearable knowing that their dead bodies are decomposing out there while the whole world is looking on and gloating. But it still isn't right."

"I agree. Now, come on, let's get back to the others and shore up our lines of defense and care for our dead and wounded. I've got a feeling the beast isn't going to be too happy when he finds out what we did to the shrines he dedicated to himself so his faithful followers would have places to come and worship and pay homage to him."

The beast was anything but happy. He ranted and raved and threatened to kill his own cousin.

"Eli, I'm going to execute you myself!" he bellowed, pulling his pistol from its holster. "You promised you would throw that bunch of Jewish rabble off the Mount of Olives by noon, but you fouled up again. Not only are they still in control of the mountain, but now they've taken the temple mount as well. In the process, they've blown up my sacred museum in the old mosque, and they've destroyed Caesar's image in the temple as well. What do you have to say for yourself now before I blow your brains out?"

[42] Then those from the peoples, tribes, tongues, and nations will see their dead bodies three-and-a-half days, and not allow their dead bodies to be put into graves. And those who dwell on the earth will rejoice over them, make merry, and send gifts to one another, because these two prophets tormented those who dwell on the earth (Revelation 11:9–10).

"Oh, Great One, have mercy," Eli pleaded. "Their apparent victory is but a temporary setback. I should have seen it before, but it appears we are to defeat all of our other enemies before we are to eliminate the Jewish rebels. I suggest we leave the Zionists where they are for now. The Russians are almost upon us, and the Americans will be here before dawn tomorrow. The Chinese have broken through our lines at the Euphrates, and they will arrive early tomorrow as well. As they come upon us, they will also have to encounter the Jews too. Let them destroy each other, and then we can eliminate whoever survives."

"You're right, Eli," Constantine conceded, lowering his pistol. "I was just thinking of something like that myself. We will keep our forces away from the Mount of Olives for the next couple of days, and we'll let the Russians and the Americans and the Chinese try to conquer it in order to get to us. With their combined strength, they should be able to eradicate those Jews in a matter of days, but not without suffering horrible losses themselves. I don't know where those rebels get their magic, but I must admit that they do have some. They will inflict terrible damage on our enemies, and then, when they have softened them up for us, we will swoop in and destroy them once and for all."

"A brilliant plan, your Majesty," Eli said enthusiastically. "It will work marvelously."

"It better. We're running out of time, my cousin. We must win this contest soon, while we still have the advantage. While the foolish Jews are unwittingly acting as our allies, and protecting our eastern flank, we will be able to concentrate on defeating our enemies to the north and south of us. Quick, inform our generals of the change in strategy!"

That night, the conflict began in earnest. Constantine's combined armies met the brunt of the Russian invasion in the Valley of Jezreel (also called Armageddon) and the battle raged throughout the night and into the next day, without letup. The casualties were enormous on both sides. Blood ran freely from a million wounds and formed crimson streams in the bottoms of the shallow ravines.

Before morning, the American armies battled their way up from the Negev and into the coastal plains of Israel. There, the Federation armies were waiting for them in full force, and a similar slaughter began, with both sides taking heavy casualties. Constantine's forces outmanned and outgunned the Americans, but the latter's superior strategy and maneuvering enabled them to hold their own. The carnage raged on, with neither side winning a decisive victory.

By noon the following day, more than three million corpses lay strewn across the soil of the western part of Israel, and the Chinese were adding to the total as they fought with Federation forces in the Jordan valley to the east. More men had already died than in any war in human history, and yet, everyone knew the battle had just begun.

The Russians and the Americans soon came to realize they would not be able to defeat the Federation forces by pushing straight ahead; the emperor simply had too many men and too many guns. They were killing more of the enemy than they were losing, but when their strategists made their calculations, they realized they would run out of resources before they could overrun the Federation positions. Therefore, they decided to send their armies around to the east, and join up with the Chinese forces to form one huge invasion force that would enable them to push the Great Caesar and his armies westward into the Mediterranean Sea.

President Lowell Renslow commanded his generals to push eastward into the mountains of Judea and to come at Jerusalem from the south, through Hebron and Bethlehem. At the same time General Borzov led his Russian forces eastward and into the mountains of Samaria. From there, he would push southward through Nablus and Ramalah, attacking Jerusalem from the north.

As the American and Russian armies fought their way ever closer to Jerusalem, the Chinese forces broke through the Federation lines at the Jordan River and took the fortified city of Jericho. From there, they began the torturous assent up the mountains that led to the Holy City. From an elevation of over 1000 feet below sea level, they had to climb to a height of nearly 3000 feet above sea level at Jerusalem. The Federation defenders hammered them relentlessly as they made their assent, and the casualties were enormous on both sides, but the sheer numbers of the Chinese attackers enabled them to gain slow and bloody progress up the twenty-mile incline.

By evening, all three armies were approaching the outskirts of Jerusalem. After heavy fighting, the Americans had taken Bethlehem, and were preparing for their assault on Mount Zion (the City of Jerusalem) and the Mount of Olives to the east of it. Meanwhile, the Russians had moved in from the north and had taken Mount Scopus, the site of the huge

Hebrew University complex. From there, they were ready to launch their own attack on the two mountains to the south.

By nightfall, the Chinese had battled their way to the eastern base of the Mount of Olives. The village of Bethany lay at the top of the mountain, and beyond it, Jerusalem spread out like a tempting vine, ready to be harvested.

To the west, from the temple mount in Jerusalem to the Mediterranean Sea, some fifty miles away, stretched the overwhelming Federation forces of Emperor Constantine Augustus. Although they had taken heavy losses, they still far outnumbered the combined strength of their enemies, both in numbers of troops, and in weaponry.

As the night deepened, the fighting tapered off, and then nearly ceased by midnight. Soldiers, on all sides, ate their meals, repaired and serviced their weapons, and got some much-needed sleep. They all sensed that with the rising of the sun, they would all be plunged into the worst battle the world had ever seen.

On the temple mount in eastern Jerusalem, and on the nearby Mount of Olives, what remained of the 144,000 worshipped God and prepared for the carnage that was to come. Over 10,000 of their numbers had already been either killed or seriously wounded, and they knew that the next day would be the worst by far.

Over two days had passed since Joseph and David had been killed, and their bloated bodies continued to decompose before the celebrating world, watching via television. Vile black liquid oozed from their multiple wounds, and thousands of eggs, laid by opportunistic flies, hatched, and their larvae feasted on the decaying flesh. The smell was overpoweringly nauseating, but the Federation soldiers continued to defend the site from anyone who might attempt to take the bodies. The news media representatives donned their gas masks and continued to maintain their vigil as well.

Aaron Muller grieved over the abomination created by Constantine Augustus, but he forced himself to concentrate on other matters, reminding himself that the end would soon come, and things would be drastically turned around. He met with the other eleven commanders well into the night in the lobby of the Inter-Continental Hotel, and planned their strategy.

It was decided that Aaron, Mark, Seth, and Ivan would lead their men in defending the temple mount and that section of eastern Jerusalem. Julio, Rico, Jabin, and their men would defend the Kidron Valley to the east; and the other five witnesses and the men of their tribes would defend the Mount of Olives and its surroundings. The combined forces of their enemies would outnumber them more than a hundred to one, but they were committed to hold their positions until the Lord came, or took them home; whichever came first.

The sun rose, blood red, over the distant Jordanian mountains to the east, and it was welcomed by the sounds of battle, already well underway. After giving their battle-weary troops some much needed rest at night, at first light, the Russians had attacked from the north, the Chinese from the east, and the Americans from the south. The combined Federation forces had counter-attacked from the west, and the battle had been joined. The fighting was unbelievably brutal, and the 144,000 were caught squarely in the middle.

The faithful had drunk little water from the Kidron Brook, they had eaten nothing, and had slept very little; yet the Lord renewed their strength. They stood their ground and fought like King David's mighty men of old, each killing his hundreds of God's enemies.[43]

They shot fire from the ends of their rods and staves, they launched their stones and spears and arrows at the attacking hordes, and they fought hand-to-hand with swords and clubs. They should have been overwhelmed in the first assault, but they were not. Time after time, the enemy attacked, and just as often, they were repelled. The 144,000 sustained their losses, but they slew their enemies by the thousands. Bodies of the fallen assailants began to stack up around the perimeters of their positions like a forest of dead trees toppled by hurricane-force winds.

While their enemies fought each other to the north and west and south of them, the 144,000 fought them all, on all four sides. Confusion reigned, and the carnage was unbelievable. Shells exploded, buildings were toppled, and soldiers died by the hundreds of thousands. Their

---

[43] 2 Samuel 23:8–39

[44] Then another angel came out of the temple which is in heaven, he also having a sharp sickle. And another angel came out from the altar, who had power over fire, and he cried with a loud voice to him who had the sharp sickle, saying, "Thrust in your sharp sickle and gather the clusters of the vine of the earth, for her grapes are fully ripe." So the angel thrust his sickle into the earth and gathered the vine of the earth, and threw it into the great winepress of the wrath of God. And the winepress was trampled outside the city, and the blood came out of the winepress, up to the horses' bridles, for one thousand six hundred furlongs (Revelation 14:17–20).

blood ran down the hills and into the valleys below. In some ravines, it flowed like rivers, several feet deep.[44]

It was not only the soldiers that died, however. Multitudes of hapless civilians suffered and perished in the onslaught. Those who were able to, sought shelter in the network of caves beneath the city, but others were not so fortunate. They were driven from their homes and into the streets, only to be mowed down or abused by the godless hordes that were destroying and looting the city.[45]

Those who were able to escape the city, sought to flee into the countryside, but there was really no place to hide. The mammoth battle raged virtually over the entire nation of Israel. The only place any refuge was found was in the territory controlled by the 144,000. Angels led the way and held back the throngs of evil men who sought to harm them while thousands poured into those areas. The battle continued to rage all around them, and many of them still fell victim to its carnage, but God's faithful welcomed them and gave them what protection they could. By the end of the day, some 20,000 civilians who had refused the mark of the beast now fled from his wrath and found refuge among God's 144,000. They huddled in whatever shelter they could find in Eastern Jerusalem, the Kidron Valley, and on top of the Mount of Olives.

The hostilities raged on throughout the day. By evening, millions more had died, but the lines remained virtually unchanged. Never in human history had there been such a day of suffering and death. Everything in and around the whole nation of Israel was engulfed in the holocaust. At last, it seemed the sun itself became exhausted with all the carnage, and sought refuge beneath the cooling waters of the Mediterranean Sea. Darkness fell, and only then did the combatants back off, and the devastation subside. But nothing had been decided. While the exhausted soldiers sought some desperately needed relief, their commanders met to plan their strategies for the coming day.

In the gymnasium of the Hebrew University on Mount Scopus, President Renslow, Chairman Chong, and General Borzov met in a heavily guarded meeting. The combined strength of their armies had been ravaged by the day's hostilities. They had lost nearly half of their men in the ravages of the excruciating battle. They could not afford to suffer similar losses the

[45] Behold, the day of the Lord is coming, and your spoil will be divided in your midst. For I will gather all the nations to battle against Jerusalem; the city shall be taken, the houses rifled, and the women ravished. Half the city shall go into captivity, but the remnant of the people shall not be cut off from the city (Zechariah 14:1–2).

following day or they would have no armies with which to pursue their objectives. They simply had to find some way to break through the Federation lines and strike a killing blow at the heart of the beast himself.

"But what about those barbarians in the eastern section of the city?" asked Chairman Chong. "My armies were powerless against them. For every one of them we were able to kill with our tanks and guns, they killed hundreds of us with sticks and stones. They must be some mercenary demons Augustus has hired to fight against us."

"No, Mr. Chairman, I think not," General Borzov responded. "From our position, we were able to observe the fighting between the barbarians on the temple site and the Federation troops to the west of them. It seems, whoever they are, they are fighting against both sides. And we too were unable to subdue them. We tried to drive down through the valley between them and to separate them from each other, but we were never able to do so. We finally gave up and directed our assault elsewhere."

"So did we," President Renslow interjected. "My men attacked them on all fronts, and were driven back every time. We suffered more casualties at their hands than we did from everything else the Federation threw at us. After getting our butts kicked by them all day, we gave up and went after the Federation troops. We found them much easier to kill."

"But who are they, and where did they come from, and what do they want?" Chong asked rhetorically. "It seems, at this time, they are more our enemy than is Constantine Augustus himself."

To his questions, the others had no answers; but with his evaluation, they both agreed.

Constantine Augustus and Eli Rothschild knelt in the middle of the floor in the subterranean conference room of the World Federation of Nations headquarters in the foothills west of Jerusalem. The Great Caesar had ordered all his military advisors out of the room, and had given strict orders that no one should disturb him and his prophet for any reason.

They had come to seek counsel from the great god Lucifer himself. The battle had not gone entirely as they had expected. It was true that the Jewish rebels had inflicted great losses upon the armies of the three invading nations, but perhaps they had been too effective. Towards the end of the day, all three armies had nearly ceased in their attempts to subdue the Jews, and had turned their guns almost exclusively upon the Federation positions. Even the Chinese had skirted the Mount of Olives, and had attacked Federation positions both to the north and the south of the temple mount.

The Federation had suffered heavy losses, and had failed to gain any ground. Constantine and Eli needed guidance to determine the direction in which they were to command their armies. The whole world was watching, and the two were convinced they needed to win great victories the next day in order to convince their subordinate countries that they were still in charge, and that total conquest would soon be obtained.

"Oh, great Light Bearer, Son of the Morning, hear my prayer, oh Lucifer," prayed Constantine, his head bowed, his eyes closed, and his arms outstretched. "We, your servants, wait upon you. Come, oh Great One, reveal yourself in all your glory!"

Just then, the room was filled with a dazzling light, and a presence descended upon the two kneeling men. It had the appearance of a man, and yet, it was not human. The creature's face would have been handsome, had it not been so dark and etched with evil. Robed in scarlet, the figure stood suspended above them, its arms extending down toward them.

"Arise, my son!" the creature commanded, looking into the eyes of the trembling Constantine. "Your prayers are heard, and I have come to strengthen you. Be of good cheer; the world lies at your feet. Come with me; there are those with whom we must speak."

Then turning his gaze upon the terrified Eli, he added, "Arise, oh prophet of god; come with us. We three shall turn the tide of human avarice and ambition. Your enemies will become your allies and, ultimately, your footstool. The hated Jews will be destroyed, and soon, you will reign supreme over all the earth."

Constantine rose to his feet, gaining confidence and strength. He reached down and assisted his cousin, who was struggling in weakness and fear. No sooner had the two of them stood erect, than they were caught up into the air; lifted up to join the creature in the center of the room, some fifteen feet above the floor.

Before they could realize what was taking place, the creature grasped their hands, and they felt themselves rising upward, through the steel-reinforced concrete floors above them, and out into the night air.

"Be strong, my sons," the creature said. "We travel to the camp of your enemies to turn their hearts and minds to you."

Unseen by the men who stood guard around the headquarters complex, the three empowered figures ascended into the air and sped off into the night. Straight to Mount Scopus they flew, and slowed to hover above the Hebrew University there. They made their descent through the roof of the gymnasium and came into the view of those assembled there.

Momentarily dazzled by the light, Lowell Renslow quickly recovered and realized that they had somehow been invaded. He didn't know how the three intruders had breached their perimeters and gained access to their command headquarters, but he was not about to wait around for them to launch an attack.

"Open fire!" he screamed, as he dove under the table at which he had been sitting, his fat buttocks and legs protruding out from beneath it. Chairman Chong joined him there in a flash, but General Borzov jumped to his feet and pulled his pistol from its holster. He aimed at the central figure, draped in red and staring at him through eyes that burned with fire. He pulled the trigger and fired, point-blank, into the body of the intruder.

At the same instant, dozens of guards, positioned around the perimeter of the table, opened fire with automatic weapons and sprayed the bodies of the three with hundreds of lethal bullets. But not one of them had any effect. The fiery projectiles, traveling at a speed of more than two thousand feet per second, simply passed unhindered through their bodies and smashed into the ceiling above them. It was as though the three were not there at all.

With a wave of his hand, the creature caused every weapon in the room to jam instantly. Then, at the nod of his head, each weapon turned fiery hot. Thirty-seven guns immediately clattered to the floor beneath them. Their owners stood, stunned and helpless, looking up at their uninvited and unwelcome guests.

"Fear not!" the creature spoke. "I am Lucifer, god of heaven and earth. We bear you no harm; we have come to bring you words of victory and peace. This is my beloved son, in whom I am well pleased. Hear him, for he speaks with my authority."

Coached by the creature on what to say during their brief flight over, Constantine opened his mouth and began to speak authoritatively.

"I am Constantine Augustus, son of the living god, and Emperor of the Revived Roman Empire. We have been enemies for three-and-a-half years, but tonight that must end. The real enemy of all of us is the lesser God Jehovah, and those are his people encamped on the two mountaintops in Jerusalem. I have already killed their two great leaders who brought all the recent plagues upon us and our people. On television screens, you have all seen their dead bodies lying in the streets of the city. Together, we can destroy the rest of them tomorrow."

"But how do we know we can trust you?"

It was the trembling voice of Lowell Renslow, who was backing out from beneath the table and lifting his portly frame to an unsteady standing position.

"Your appearance here has been mind-boggling, and it has scared the daylights out of me, but what assurance do we have that you will not turn on us after we've helped you get rid of those barbarians on top of those hills over there? You have been doing your best to destroy all of us for years"

"Yes, indeed," came the heavily accented voice of General Borzov, gaining confidence as he spoke. "Why do you wait to approach us now; now that we are threatening to overrun your positions? If you are so powerful, why do you not simply destroy them yourselves?"

"Silence, fools!" Constantine and Eli commanded simultaneously, waving their hands in a sweeping motion.

Instantly, every man in the room fell backwards and landed heavily on the hardwood floor. Unable to rise, they stared in fear at the three figures above them, not knowing what next to expect.

"If I wanted to destroy you, I could do it right now with a simple nod of my head," Constantine said, "but that is not how I choose to use my powers. Now, as before, my prophet and I have displayed our supernatural powers to confirm who we are and why we have come. But our conquest of the world must not be through the use of signs and wonders. All men must bow before us, but not because they have been convinced to do so through the use of our divine powers.

"And do not be so foolish as to think you have any sort of an advantage over me. You are powerless to defeat that Jewish rabble by yourselves, as you have already seen. Your numbers are being diminished drastically with every assault on their positions, and you have no reinforcements coming to replace your losses. My armies far outnumber yours even now, and they are increasing every hour as my ships arrive from the west and unload their cargos of men and machines. The end is inevitable. The Jews will wear you down, and then my forces will overwhelm you.

"I come to you, not because I need you, nor because I fear you, but because I have come to respect you as worthy adversaries, and I want to offer you one last opportunity to save your lives and those of your people. Submit to my leadership now, and I will spare you. Furthermore, I will bring your three nations into my inner circle and, together, we shall rule the world. But refuse my offer, and you shall surely die. After you and the Jews have further weakened each other, I will destroy both you and them, and then I will destroy the people of your nations back home."

"But, again," protested President Renslow, "what assurance do we have that you will not turn on us once we have helped you destroy the Jews?"

"Only this; that in the presence of the great god Lucifer, creator of heaven and earth, I swear. He who does all things well will hold me to my word. If I should betray your trust, he would consume me himself with fire from his mouth."

"So be it, my son!" boomed the voice of Lucifer. "I bear you all witness, and I shall hold you all accountable!"

Then, to punctuate his statement, he opened his mouth, and fire proceeded out of it and consumed the heavy table around which the three men had been sitting.

The three national leaders rolled to escape the flames, and shielded their faces from it with their arms. Trembling, they bowed before Lucifer and the two men suspended on either side of him.

It was Chairman Chong who first found his voice. "If you will swear to spare us and our people, and grant us a measure of autonomy under your government, I will agree to yield to your authority and serve you, oh Great Caesar."

"As will I," agreed President Renslow, too terrified to say otherwise.

"I do not have the personal authority to pledge all the resources of Russia," said General Borzov. "President Galinikov is gravely ill, but if he were here, I believe he would concur with the decision of my colleagues. Acting as his representative, I also accept your proposal, on the condition that you allow us to rule our own countries under your administration."

"I so swear!" Constantine affirmed. "And my prophet and my heavenly father are my witnesses. Tomorrow, we dispatch the Jews! And the day after that, we rule the world!"[46]

---

[46] And I saw three unclean spirits like frogs coming out of the mouth of the dragon, out of the mouth of the beast, and out of the mouth of the false prophet. For they are spirits of demons, performing signs, which go out to the kings of the earth and of the whole world, to gather them to the battle of the great day of God Almighty (Revelation 16:13–14).

CHAPTER FIFTEEN

The Discovery

Lucifer escorted Constantine and Eli back to the Federation Building in the same manner in which he had removed them. After reassuring them of their glorious destiny, his terrifying presence vanished as suddenly as it had appeared. Left alone, they continued to tremble at the thought of actually being in the presence of a god.

Had they actually risen bodily through the concrete barriers of the building, and had they, in fact, flown through the air? Such concepts were mind-boggling, but, then again, they could not deny their own experience. Or perhaps they had been taken out of their bodies altogether, and only their spirits had been transported by their master. That was more likely, they decided, but by whatever means, they had been with their god, and they had subdued their enemies.

They went to bed and slept soundly, assured that the morrow would bring them even greater success. Once the combined strength of all four powers had exterminated the Jewish vermin from the nearby mountaintops, they could celebrate the glorious victory with their new allies, and send them triumphantly home to their own people. It was certainly reasonable to allow their newly established friends that much freedom.

Yet, already, Constantine was plotting how he would beat them back into complete submission. The military prowess of the other three nations had been ravaged by the brief but devastating war, and the next day's hostilities would further weaken them. It would be an easy matter for him to crush them later one by one, and to punish them soundly for their rebellion, and for all the frustration they had caused him over the past three-and-a-half years.

So what if he had given them his word? Had they not also given him their word in this very room back at the beginning? Then they had all broken their word and caused him no end of embarrassment and delay. Soon, he would give them a taste of their own medicine. And he need not worry about Lucifer forcing him to honor his commitment. He was convinced his father would actually bless him for his shrewdness. After all, it had been his god who had taught him to use whatever means possible to accomplish his goals. Lying and cheating and stealing were only necessary steps toward achieving greater goals for the greater good.[47] No, he had no pangs of conscience or guilt. He drifted off into a pleasant sleep, his mind filled with dreams of total world domination at last.

There was little sleep to be had on the two small mountaintops in eastern Jerusalem. The 144,000 had been reduced to less than 100,000, and nearly all who remained alive were wounded. The trench Ivan had bulldozed out earlier had to be enlarged to contain all the bodies of their fallen comrades. The walking wounded gently laid the bodies of their friends in the common grave and left them uncovered. There were no more tarps available, and Aaron firmly believed the Lord's coming would be so soon that it would not pose a problem. If His return were to be delayed more than a day or two, then Aaron would have to order them covered over with dirt, but he didn't think that would be necessary.

It had been three days since Joseph and David had been killed, and the Bible clearly stated that they would be raised back to life after three-and-a-half days.[48] If their resurrection was to immediately precede the Lord's return, and Aaron thought that it would, then they could expect everything to come to a cataclysmic conclusion in the morning.

But just in case the faithful be disappointed in their hope, and the Lord tarry in His return, Aaron was forced to deal with the possibility of facing

[47] "You are of your father the devil, and the desires of your father you want to do. He was a murderer from the beginning, and does not stand in the truth, because there is no truth in him. When he speaks a lie, he speaks from his own resources, for he is a liar and the father of it." (John 8:44).
[48] Revelation 11:11

another day of brutal hostilities. He met with the other eleven commanders in what was left of the hotel lobby, and they assessed their situation.

Aaron himself had been struck by two bullets, one in the left leg and another in the right shoulder, and his head had been grazed by yet another. He had fought side-by-side with Ken Weinman until the same hail of bullets had struck his friend. Ken had actually stepped in front of Aaron to protect him, and had died giving his life for his friend. Aaron laid the big Scotsman's body in the grave and grieved over his death. Ken had been a good friend, and had saved his life another time on the same temple mount three-and-a-half years before. Perhaps in the morning, he would join him in death.

Aaron prayed with the other commanders and begged the Lord to come quickly, before too many more of their comrades were struck down. They also made plans to defend their positions until He came, or until they all died, whichever came first.

After their meeting, they went back to their positions to help care for the more severely wounded and to repair and replenish their weaponry. There were plenty of automatic rifles available to them, having been dropped by their slain adversaries, but they declined to use them. Their Lord had delivered them so far by means of their primitive arms, and they were determined to trust Him to continue to do so.

As Aaron dressed his wounds and prepared for the onslaught that would doubtlessly come at first light, his mind traveled around the world to another mountaintop. What had become of his loved ones there? Had they suffered? Had they survived? Oh, how he longed for the bloodbath to end that he might be reunited with them again. He prayed for their safety before exhaustion overcame him and he fell asleep sometime after midnight.

It was 4:15 in the afternoon in Los Angeles, and Colonel Tony D'Angelo was ecstatic. Finally, good news was coming in from every direction. He had just been promoted to his present rank by order of General Spangler from Israel, who had also informed him that the war there was progressing well, and the word was that total victory should be achieved the next day.

Tony had seen on television the dead bodies of the two terrorists in Jerusalem who had brought all the plagues on the world, and he had celebrated their deaths along with everyone else on his staff. What a relief it had been to know that his Caesar had killed them personally, and had put an end to all the suffering and death of innocent people.

But what had excited him most of all was the news he had received earlier that morning. He had agreed to take a phone call from a stranger calling from a pay phone at a ski resort up in the San Gabriel Mountains when his secretary told him that the caller had information regarding the family of Aaron Muller. He had refused to discuss the matter over the phone with the possible informant, but he had learned enough from him to be convinced that the man did indeed know something.

Now, Tony looked again at his watch and drummed his fingers on his desk. The man should have been here by this time. What was keeping him anyway? This could be the breakthrough he had been waiting for. If he could locate that bunch and apprehend them soon, he would be in a perfect position to receive special rewards and promotions from the conquering Caesar Augustus, who would surely be in a generous mood after his forces had vanquished all his enemies. Where was that guy anyway?

Just then, his secretary called and informed him that a man had just arrived who said he had an appointment with the colonel. Tony told her to send him right in.

"Come in; sit down," Tony said reassuringly to the timid fellow who opened the door tentatively and peeked inside. "Take a seat. Can I have my secretary get you anything?"

The young man appeared to be in his early thirties, but was probably in his mid-twenties (people had aged much more rapidly in the past several years). His sandy-colored hair was long and matted, and his scraggly beard had a reddish tint to it. He was dressed in shabby and dirty clothing, but it was obvious that he had made an attempt to wash his hands and face and smooth his unruly hair.

"Thank you, sir," he said hesitantly, taking a seat in the chair across the desk from the young colonel. "Yes, I could use a drink to calm my nerves. I haven't had one in a long time, and I sure am nervous."

"Relax, my friend," Tony said kindly as he went to his liquor cabinet and retrieved a bottle of scotch and a couple of glasses. "I'm Colonel D'Angelo, commander of the Federation forces here, and who might you be?"

"I'm George Wheeler," the young man answered, taking the drink from Tony and downing it in two quick gulps. "Thanks, I really needed that."

"You're welcome," Tony replied, taking a sip from his own drink. "Pour yourself another one whenever you're ready. Now, tell me again what it is that brings you in to see me today."

"Well, it's like I told you on the phone. Me and my friends are living up there in a burned out cabin in them mountains. You know, just tryin' to get by."

"Yes, I know. These are hard times; a man's gotta do what a man's gotta do to make it in this world. Now, what was it you saw last night?"

"Yeah, well like I tried to tell you," George replied, pouring himself another stiff drink, "I was out hunting for a deer or somethun last night, cause the moon was full and I could see pretty good, when I sees these two dudes slippin' along draggin' a deer between 'em. That wasn't too strange these days. Most folks up there in those mountains do their huntin' at night when the moon's full. But what really got me goin' was them night vision goggles they was wearin'. Those things are hard to come by. I don't know anybody who's got 'em."

"You're sure they were wearing night vision goggles?"

"Oh, yeah," George answered confidently, downing his second scotch. "I stayed low and followed 'em for a long ways. They was concentratin' on that deer and wasn't aware I was even around. I got a real good look at 'em."

"What did they look like?"

"They was big and strong and young lookin'. They had beards 'n' longer hair, but then again, everbody I know does too. Ain't that many barbershops open these days. And even if there were, who could afford 'em? Y'know what I mean?"

"Yes, I do," Tony lied, brushing back his own immaculately trimmed hair, and stroking his closely shaved chin. "Was there anything else about them that caught your attention?"

"Yeah, there was. I noticed they had bows and arrows slung across their backs. You sure don't see many of those up there in the woods. Everbody I know is packin' a rifle, or at least a shotgun."

"Are you sure about the bows and arrows?" Tony asked, trying not to let his excitement show in his voice. "It's very important that you were not mistaken."

"No way, man. I got a real good look at 'em, and they was packin' bows and arrows alright; no doubt about it."

"Did you see where they went?"

"Oh, yeah! I thought they might be the ones you guys're lookin' for, so I followed 'em to their hideout. When do I get my reward?"

"Not so fast, my young friend," Tony cautioned. "They might not be the fugitives we're looking for at all. And even if they are, we have to identify them and apprehend them before any reward can be given out.

But if you can lead us to them, and once they're in custody, you will become a very rich man."

George swore, clapped his hands, and jumped to his feet. "Well, what're we waitin' on, Captain?" he urged. "If we leave now, we can have 'em in the bag before dark. I followed 'em to a cave of some sort, and I know right where to find 'em."

"That's Colonel to you, George. And we will most certainly leave right away. You go ahead and pour yourself another drink, I'll make a couple of phone calls, and we'll be on our way."

Forty-five minutes later, a large convoy exited the Foothill Freeway and began its steady climb up the Angeles Crest Highway to the top of the San Gabriel Mountains. Colonel D'Angelo sat in the back seat of a luxury Humvee, driven by Manny Russo. Next to him sat George Wheeler, animated and urging Manny to drive faster. Next to the driver up front, sat Captain Gino Mantelli with an automatic rifle beside him. Behind their vehicle, followed three armored personnel carriers, in which more than sixty armed soldiers were jostled along. Tony was not going to take any chances this time.

As they wound their way up the steep slopes of the mountains, George chattered aimlessly, with no one paying him any attention. As they rode along, Tony was lost in his own thoughts. He remembered, three-and-a-half years before, when there had been a very similar situation. Manny was driving, Gino was riding shotgun, he was in the back seat with another man, and they were in hot pursuit of a group of fugitives. What had changed was that, now, he was the crime boss in charge of the expedition in place of the late Sal LaMata, and now, instead of himself, this weasel George Wheeler was playing the part of the sniveling informant.

Tony couldn't help but think about how much things had changed since back then, and yet, strangely, how much they had remained the same. Back then, things had not turned out at all as they had planned, and he could not shake the feeling that this present expedition was similarly jinxed, but he shook it off. This time, he was in charge, he had plenty of firepower, and he had the element of surprise. He kept telling himself that nothing could go wrong, but still, he could not quite convince the pessimistic voice that continued to talk inside his head.

In Jerusalem, it was just starting to get light, but already the battle had begun. After getting some necessary sleep during the brief hours of darkness, the enemy charged the two mountaintops at first light. What remained of the 144,000 fought bravely to protect those who had taken refuge with them. Virtually all of them were wounded and weakened, but their God gave them supernatural strength to engage in one last battle.

The Americans, the Russians, the Chinese, and the Federation soldiers all fought shoulder to shoulder. At last, they were united in their effort to rid, once and for all, the world of the filthy Jews. They would lose many men, but they were sworn to press forward until they had eliminated the enemy and had joined hands at the tops of the mountains.

Armed with powerful telescopic lenses, dozens of television cameras recorded every aspect of the battle from a safe distance. Then, via satellite, those images were beamed to millions of sets all around the world.

Soldiers climbed over the bodies of their unburied comrades in their frantic efforts to scale the heights of the mountains, but most of them fell back, mortally wounded, only to add their numbers to the already swollen ranks of the dead. Yet, still they came. The almost limitless numbers of their troops enabled them to slowly progress up the sides of those hills, made slick with the blood of the fallen.

Aaron and his men stood their ground for the first hour, pushing back the enemy every time they launched an attack. But soon it became apparent that they weren't going to be able to continue to resist their advances. It was a simple matter of mathematics. The attackers lost hundreds of men to every one of the defenders who fell, but their numbers were in the millions, and every time one of them fell, two more took his place.

Aaron's fighting men had been reduced by more than one-half, and it was apparent that in a short matter of time, they would be overrun. The Russians from the north, and the Americans from the south, were at the point of breaking through the Jewish lines in the bottom of the Kidron Valley and driving a wedge between the two mountaintops.

He couldn't let that happen, so Aaron ordered a retreat. Abandoning the temple mount, he led his men and the Jewish refugees down off the mountain and into the Kidron Valley. There, they helped their brothers push back the Gentile attackers long enough for the civilians to climb to the relative safety of the Mount of Olives. Then his soldiers themselves retreated up the slopes of the mountain to unite with what remained of the defenders there, and to help them hold the mountaintop for as long as they could.

Aaron ordered all the civilian refugees to be gathered in the center, on the very top of the mountain, and then he arranged his forces around the perimeter to defend them. There was no time to count heads, but it was apparent that less than 40,000 remained of the original 144,000, and they continued to lose more men with every enemy attack.

Having been shot twice more himself, Aaron feared that he would not be able to continue to lead his men. Already, he had learned that Julio, Rico, Seth, and three others of the twelve commanders had been killed, so he knew he could soon be joining them. But he refused to give up. With renewed strength, he held his ground, his fractured right arm hanging uselessly at his side. From the end of his trusted rod, divine flames continued to shoot out and consume his enemies.

As the battle raged on, he glanced towards the heavens to see if he could detect any sign of the coming of the Lord. He didn't want to be presumptuous, but he sensed that it had to be soon. If the Lord delayed His coming much longer, there would be none of His own alive to welcome Him. As he fought on, Aaron breathed a prayer, "Even so, come, Lord Jesus."[49]

Somewhat after seven o'clock, George identified the spot, and Tony ordered Manny to pull the Humvee over to the side of the road. The other vehicles followed, and soon the troops were offloading and assembling in the middle of the highway. At Tony's command, George started off through the woods, angling southeast toward Throop Peak. He assured his new boss that it was only a mile or two, and that they would be there in no time. He was pumped up on nervous excitement, and even Tony's seasoned troops had some difficulty in keeping up with him.

It was after eight when the company of soldiers came to a halt behind George as he stopped abruptly. He looked around carefully to make sure of his location, and then assured Tony that they had indeed arrived at their intended destination.

---

[49] He who testifies to these things says, "Surely I am coming quickly." Amen. Even so, come, Lord Jesus! (Revelation 22:20).

"Just behind them bushes up there, in front of that cliff, is a tunnel or somethun. I seen 'em go in there, and they never came out. I bet they're in there right now."

"For your sake, I hope you're right," Tony replied. "You're not going to enjoy at all what I have in store for you if you've led us up here on a wild goose chase."

"Oh, they're in there alright," George assured him nervously. "All you gotta do is go in there and round 'em up."

"Good. We'll do just that. But first, let's take a moment to check things out. We don't want to rush into this thing unprepared."

Tony allowed his men to sit down and rest a few minutes while he sent three scouts out to examine the area. He and Gino used that time to plan their attack.

It was nearly six-thirty in the morning in Jerusalem. The battle had been raging since before daylight, and the combined Federation forces had nearly reached the top of the Mount of Olives. Only a few thousand stubborn Jewish defenders continued to fight on to protect their mountain and the precious souls huddled around the top of it.

Most of the television cameras were focused on the hostilities taking place on that mountain, but two crews were still back in Jerusalem, monitoring the site where the bodies of the two hated witnesses continued to decompose. The fighting had ceased in that area, and all was quiet. If it were not for the awful smell of rotting flesh, it would have almost been described as peaceful.

Suddenly, without warning, the swollen, blackened bodies of David and Joseph were transformed. The swelling vanished, the stench disappeared, the color of their flesh returned to normal, and their chests heaved and drew in breaths of air. Glorious life filled their once bloated bodies. They stretched, rolled over, and rose to their feet.

The startled television crews riveted their cameras on them, and relayed every frame of this impossible phenomenon to the watching world. The rotting bodies of the world's worst enemies had just been transformed, and those two troublemakers were, once again, free to walk the streets of Jerusalem.

Constantine Augustus and Eli Rothschild shook with fear as they watched it all unfold on the screen of the monitor mounted in their luxury Humvee. The impossible had taken place. Their enemies were alive again. It could only mean that they would be coming after them. Now that they were so close to conquering the world, would they be gunned down by those two zombies, risen from the dead?

However, that was not to be. Joseph and David looked at each other and smiled; then they looked upward toward heaven and gave thanks to God. Suddenly, they heard a loud voice cry out from heaven, "Come up here!" In response, they began to rise slowly from the limestone pavement and to ascend into the heavens.

Constantine had been watching the progress of the battle on the Mount of Olives from the safety of his Humvee, parked on the deserted temple mount, when he saw the unbelievable take place on his screen. He opened his door and flew out of the vehicle and sprinted to the western wall, overlooking the site where the bodies of his enemies had lain.

"Shoot them!" he screamed. "Don't let them get away!"

The shocked soldiers, who had been transfixed before by the miraculous resurrections, were suddenly galvanized into action. They raised their rifles and emptied their magazines at the bodies of the two prophets who were rising slowly before them. Yet their bullets had no impact. They either missed, or went right through the transformed bodies of the two witnesses, having no effect at all.

In sheer panic, Constantine pulled his own pistol from his holster and fired it at their bodies as they passed by on their way to heaven. He fired, and fired again, and again, but to no avail. It had been so easy before. He had shot them, and they had died. Now, he shot them repeatedly, and he couldn't touch them. What had gone wrong?

David and Joseph passed above him, no farther than ten feet away, and still he couldn't hit them. He fired his last round, but he continued to pull the trigger, clicking on empty chambers, unaware that his weapon was even more useless than it had been before.

The two witnesses looked at him as they passed by. It was not a look of hatred or malice, but one of pity and sadness. Then they shifted their gaze, and looked upward. Their faces became transformed as they looked into heaven's glory, and expressions of joy and rapture flooded their countenances as they sped off to meet their Lord.

---

[50] Now after the three-and-a-half days the breath of life from God entered them, and they stood on their feet, and great fear fell on those who saw them. And they heard a loud voice from heaven saying to them, "Come up here." And they ascended to heaven in a cloud, and their enemies saw them (Revelation 11:11–12).

Constantine collapsed to the pavement as he looked up in horror. He watched until the bodies of his enemies disappeared into the clouds that canopied above him. He bent over and held his head in his hands and cried bitterly, "NO! NO! NO!"[50]

Tony D'Angelo was confident that he had done everything he needed to do. The scouts had reported that the freshest tracks around the cave were all heading toward it; there were none pointing away from it. All the members of the Muller family had to be in there somewhere. He had his men don their night vision goggles, and was about to send them stealthily into the cave so that they might overtake those inside by surprise.

Just then, they all heard a low growling sound coming forth from behind the brush. Then, the biggest, ugliest dog any of them had ever seen emerged into view and snarled at them, his white fangs gleaming behind his curled lips.

"Quick," Tony ordered a young man next to him, "take him out before he can alert the others inside!"

The young sergeant shouldered his sniper rifle and aimed though its telescopic sights. The silencer at the end of the barrel would reduce the sound of the shot so those inside would not be able to hear it. He aimed carefully, let out his breath, and gently squeezed the trigger.

At the instant the rifle fired, the big dog bolted to his left. Instead of striking him in the head, as the sniper had intended, the bullet tore into the dog's right hip. He let out a yelp and retreated, disappearing back into the brush.

Tony swore and struck the young shooter with his fist, knocking him to the ground. Now there was no time to lose; they had lost the element of surprise.

"Gino, take your men, and storm that cave!" he yelled. "We can't let them get away! Manny, you and George stay here with me and the rest of the men so we can cut them off in case any of them escape out the front."

The truth was that Tony wanted no part of going into that dark cave. He would stay outside where it was safe, with plenty of firepower to protect him. Besides, the fifty men that he had previously assigned to Gino would be more than enough to apprehend eight or nine people. Any more than that, and they would just be getting in each other's way.

Gino and his men put on their goggles, and hurried toward the entrance of the cave. As he watched his men follow their commander into the brush and through the cave entrance, Tony was already looking forward to having his way with pretty Miss Rachel later that night. Gone was any possibility of beguiling and seducing her, but he was determined to have her nonetheless. He had waited a long time for this, and he was going to enjoy every minute of it.

In spite of his pleasant thoughts of forceful conquest, he could not shake the ominous feeling of doom. But he refused to give into it. As far as he knew, there were only four women and four men in there, and they didn't have any modern weapons. What resistance could they possibly put up against his men? Besides, there was no way they could have known that they were going to be attacked. They couldn't have made an escape, or prepared a booby-trap as they had done before.

Furthermore, the thing that Tony took the most solace in was knowing that Aaron Muller was not about to show up and start killing his men and gunning for him. Tony had seen on television how all the Jewish rebels were defending a couple of mountaintops in Jerusalem. The commentator had identified them as the same group of troublemakers that had been causing so much havoc for the Federation all over the world.

Tony remembered how Aaron had vanished when he had shot him several days before. He didn't know how he had done it, but now he was convinced that he had somehow been transported over to Israel. He had to be one of those rebels fighting the Federation troops over there now; and if that were so, then he couldn't show up over here and cause any trouble. Tony kept telling himself that this time nothing could go wrong. Why then did he feel so uncertain about the outcome of this relatively simple endeavor?

CHAPTER SIXTEEN

The Appearing

The halls of heaven were filled with excitement. The time had come at last. The day of their Lord's return had finally arrived. Saints and angels were preparing to accompany their conquering King as He returned to reclaim the title deed to the universe.

The Lord Himself was riding upon what appeared to be a prancing white stallion, and He was surrounded by an innumerable host of angels, similarly mounted. Together, they formed a mighty army. Jesus was clothed in a dazzling white garment, but its skirts were dipped in blood. His normally loving countenance was replaced with a look of strong determination, and there was a glint of fire in His eyes.[51]

Behind the heavenly host was the army of the saints. They too were clothed in white and mounted on heavenly steeds. They would not lead into battle, but they would certainly accompany their Lord when He returned in triumph.[52]

Scott Graham and Candace Mercer rode side by side, thrilled to be about to participate in this great event, promised by Jesus Himself. The

---

[51] Now I saw heaven opened, and behold, a white horse. And He who sat on him was called Faithful and True, and in righteousness He judges and makes war. His eyes were like a flame of fire, and on His head were many crowns. He had a name written that no one knew except Himself. He was clothed with a robe dipped in blood, and His name is called The Word of God. And the armies in heaven, clothed in fine linen, white and clean, followed Him on white horses (Revelation 19:11–14).

[52] Thus the Lord my God will come, and all the saints with You (Zechariah 14:5).

blessed hope of believers down through the ages was about to be realized, and they were going to take part in it. In front of them rode Pastor Bobby Davis, with his sons Jamal and Marcus on either side. Before them, astride matching white stallions, rode Georgia Davis and Saul Frieberg, both young and strong, and their hearts ablaze with righteous anticipation.

Around them rode a vast host of believers from all over the world. The Singletons were there: Carl and Sarah, with their adult daughters, Tamika and Grace, riding between them. Bruce and Florence Graham joined the triumphant brigade, as did the saved members of the UCLA basketball team, and the saints from the Antioch Baptist Church in Compton. Of all the believers from all the ages, young and old, none was left behind; none, that is, with the exception of the members of God's 144,000 who had been killed. He had something special planned for them, and had sent them on ahead.

The heavenly army was assembled, and all were eager to get underway. As soon as the Angel Gabriel sounded his mighty trumpet, they would make their descent into the world of suffering mankind, a world devastated by wicked men and fallen angels. Judgment Day had come, and all were anxious to be present when their triumphant King brought down the devil's house.

Aaron Muller was weary, hardly able to stand. He had been struck by yet another bullet, this time in the chest. He didn't know how badly he was wounded, but feared the worst. His chest ached deep inside, he had difficulty breathing, and he was spitting up blood. Was this it? Was this the end?

He stumbled, his knees buckled, and he toppled over. On his back, he looked up into the heavens to commend his spirit to the Lord, but instead, his gaze was just in time to allow him to see Joseph and David ascend into the clouds.

"Amen!" he shouted, recovering some strength. "It can't be long now!"

He pulled himself back to his feet and shouted to his remaining men, most of whom were in as bad a shape as he was.

"Take heart, men! I just saw David and Joseph ascend into heaven in their glorified bodies. The Lord is coming soon. Fight on! Fight on till He Comes!"

From the mouths of the wounded and exhausted Jewish warriors came a shout so loud it actually stopped the hostilities for a moment. The enemy soldiers ceased their firing as they heard the massive battle cry echo across the Judean hills. Although they were gaining ground, and victory was within their grasp, they were overcome with a sudden sense of fear and doom.

Then a strange thing happened. Although it was early morning, it began to get dark. Inexplicably, the sun lost its brilliance, and the whole area became enshrouded in gloom. That was when the earthquake hit.[53]

The massive quake came without warning. It did not start with tremors and accelerate into heavy vibrations; it struck like a bolt of lightning. The earth heaved under its force and shook with such magnitude that things erect came crashing down: buildings, bridges, towers, and every soldier in and around Jerusalem.

The armies of the combined World Federation toppled headlong down the slopes of the Mount of Olives, all fight instantly knocked out of them. Thousands were buried under collapsing structures, and the cries of the injured echoed through the rubble.

The saints and refugees on top of the Mount of Olives were spared. They were badly shaken, but no one was crushed or stricken by falling debris. Their battle with ungodly men had finally come to an end. Their God had intervened and crushed their enemies and delivered His own. They looked up into the heavens and gave glory to God.[54]

The same earthquake was felt around the world; in some places it was more violent than in others, but no place escaped its wrath. As the earth convulsed below, the heavens erupted from above. The sky became as black as midnight, the heavens were filled with thunder and lightning, and devastating hail fell from the blackness above. In some places, the weight of individual hailstones approached one hundred pounds. They pulverized everything they struck, and ungodly men shook their fists toward the heavens because of the devastation. They cursed the Lord for the plague He had brought upon them.[55]

---

[53] I looked when He opened the sixth seal, and behold, there was a great earthquake. And the sun became black as sackcloth of hair, and the moon became like blood (Revelation 6:12).

[54] In the same hour there was a great earthquake, and a tenth of the city fell. In the earthquake seven thousand people were killed, and the rest were afraid and gave glory to the God of heaven (Revelation 11:13).

[55] Then the seventh angel poured out his bowl into the air, and a loud voice came out of the temple of heaven, from the throne, saying, "It is done!" And there were noises and thunderings and lightnings; and there was a great earthquake as has not occurred since men were on the earth. . . . And great hail from heaven fell upon men, each hailstone about the weight of a talent. Men blasphemed God because of the plague of the hail, since that plague was exceedingly great (Revelation 16:17–18, 21).

The numbers of unbelievers on the planet that had received the mark of the beast had been reduced drastically in the previous three-and-a-half years by constant warfare, famine, demon attacks, and the numerous plagues that had swept the earth. Those numbers were further depleted by this final outpouring of God's wrath. Between the earthquake, the lightning strikes, and the devouring hail, the once-burgeoning population of the ungodly outside Israel was finally reduced to few more than five hundred million hardened, twisted, demented souls. They hid in the rocks and caves of the earth and cursed God as the earth shook and crushed them from below and the sky rained down death from above. They cried out in their desperation that the earth might swallow them up and hide them from the wrath of the One they hated so much.[56]

Colonel Tony D'Angelo cowered beneath the big pine tree and hugged its sturdy trunk for support. The earth had finally quit shaking, but the thunder and lightning continued unabated, and the murderous hail continued to fall. He knew he wasn't supposed to stand under a tree during a thunderstorm, but he wasn't about to step out away from it. He would gladly take the remote chance of being struck by lightning by staying next to the tree over the almost absolute certainty of being nailed by a hailstone if he were to leave it.

The stones were falling everywhere, and they were enormous; they had already crushed several of Tony's men. The three soldiers that remained, plus George and Manny, were likewise clinging as closely as possible to their own trees to escape the white death raining down from the blackened sky.

Just then, a lone soldier stumbled out of the mouth of the cave and made his way through the brush that obscured it. Blood was flowing from an open wound in his head, and his left arm hung limply at his side. Tony recognized Gino Mantelli, and yelled to him to take cover, but the injured man was oblivious to the danger from above; he was too badly injured and too intent on escaping the danger from within.

"Cave in!" he yelled as he stumbled forward. "Everybody's dead! Everybody's gone!"

---

[56] And the kings of the earth, the great men, the rich men, the commanders, the mighty men, every slave and every free man, hid themselves in the caves and in the rocks of the mountains, and said to the mountains and rocks, "Fall on us and hide us from the face of Him who sits on the throne and from the wrath of the Lamb! For the great day of His wrath has come, and who is able to stand?" (Revelation 6:15–17).

He would have said more had not the huge hailstone struck him. As it was, the basketball-sized stone crushed his skull like a sledgehammer would smash a walnut. He never saw it coming, and he never felt it hit him. He died instantly and collapsed in a heap.

"Oh, no!" Tony cried as he curled up in a fetal position next to the trunk of the big pine tree. "Make it go away! Make it go away!"

But it didn't go away. It continued to unleash its fury for fifteen minutes longer. Manny Russo and another one of Tony's men were struck down in spite of the trees to which they clung. The hailstones picked them off by slicing in at an angle, and the trees they were hiding behind weren't big enough around to deflect the blows. Only after their deaths did the storm seem to be satisfied, and it began to abate. After a few more minutes, it finally ceased altogether.

Tony looked up carefully into the sky to make sure that there were no missiles lingering there, just waiting for a careless creature to venture out into the open. Convinced the sky was empty, he gingerly stepped away from his tree. The ground was covered with unevenly sized boulders of ice, already beginning to melt. They would have looked innocent and pure had not some of them been stained with the blood of their victims.

George Wheeler also crept out from beneath the tree he had been embracing so ardently, and looked around in disbelief. The violent storm had taken the lives of several men around him, and apparently, from what the one soldier had said, all those inside had also perished in the cave-in caused by the earthquake. That was bad news; he was sorry so many young soldiers had died, but what was even more disturbing to him was the fate of the fugitives they were looking for inside that cave.

"Excuse me, Captain," he said, "but do I get my reward now, or do I have to wait until they dig all them bodies out from underneath all them rocks inside that cave over there?'

"Reward?" fumed Tony incredulously. "You want your reward, do you? Well, there's no sense making you wait! You can have it right now if you like!"

He pulled his pistol out of its holster and shot the simple man dead before he had could open his mouth to protest.

"How's that for a reward?" he screamed. "Anybody else want a reward? Huh, how about you guys?" he yelled at his two remaining soldiers, pointing his pistol in their direction.

"No, sir!" they both assured him in unison. One of them added quickly, "We are here only to carry out your commands, sir," and that was probably what saved their lives, because it caused the crazed colonel to come to his senses. Without them, he realized, he would be all alone in these woods, and the full moon was already rising in the gathering darkness. No, they represented no threat to him, and he needed them and the guns they carried.

He grunted something in recognition of their promises and holstered his weapon. He ordered them to leave the bodies where they had fallen, and to assist him in getting back to the vehicles as soon as possible. There was nothing they could do for them now anyway.

He feared his Humvee had been taken out by the hailstorm, but was hopeful that at least one of the big armored personnel carriers was still in working condition. He could not bear to think of spending the night in these God-forsaken mountains. He was intent on getting back to civilization, or whatever might remain of it.

With the aid of their night vision goggles, they began to pick their way carefully through the maze of melting hailstones, broken tree branches, and up-heaved boulders. As they walked, Tony mourned his losses. He would not get Rachel and Anna after all, and neither would he be able to collect on any rich reward from Caesar Augustus. His military detachment had been obliterated, as probably had been everything else meaningful in his life; and yet, he did have several things to be thankful for.

For one thing, he was alive and uninjured. Somehow, he knew the violence he had just experienced had been poured out worldwide, and millions, perhaps billions, around the world had died in the past thirty minutes. Yet he had escaped unscathed; he was truly one of the lucky ones.

Besides that, among the dead, had to be Aaron Muller, his hated nemesis. Tony had been following the action on the Mount of Olives on the monitor in his Humvee on the ride up into the mountains, and he had seen how decimated the Jewish rebels had been on top of it. By the time Tony and his men left their vehicles, it appeared that the rabble-rousers were about to be overrun. If the Federation troops hadn't killed him, then the earthquake and the hail most surely would have.

Tony also took solace in knowing that all those close to Aaron were also dead. Gino had confirmed, before his own death, that everyone inside the cave had been killed. If Tony could not have the two young women, at least he was pleased in knowing that no one else would have them either. They and all their family now lay buried inside the heart of that mountain back there. There was a bitter sweetness in that knowledge.

He had emerged the victor. Somehow, he sensed that the last set of plagues had indeed been the final ones. His enemies had all perished and he had out-lived them all, and now he could look forward to the brave new world of peace and prosperity under the universal reign of Constantine Augustus. And he was bound to be promoted to a position of great importance, if for no other reason than due to the fact that there were so few good men left alive to choose from.

If that were all so, why then did he still have such a sinking sense of doom? And why was that demented hissing laughter still ringing in his ears?

Tim Frieberg led the way out of the narrow tunnel, carrying Millennium in his arms. The rest of the family followed him out into the evening air. They were badly shaken, but unhurt, having waited out the hailstorm just inside the exit of their escape tunnel. Although they had desperately wanted to get out of the convulsing mountain, they had not dared to venture out into the maelstrom of falling ice.

Thirty minutes earlier, they had all been gathered together around the dinner table in the central cave, when Millie started growling and headed off toward the main entrance. Tim and Steve excused themselves from the table and followed him out, having learned from experience to give careful heed to their dog's warning signals.

When they reached the entrance, Millie had already left the cave and was making his way through the brush that grew in front of it. They stopped momentarily to listen before following him. That was when they heard his growl turn into a vicious snarl. He had definitely spotted what he interpreted to be a threat to those he was committed to protect. Tim and Steve froze in their tracks, straining to either hear or see something that might reveal what it was that had agitated their friend so much.

Just then, they heard the muffled report of a rifle and, simultaneously, the yelp from Millie. In an instant, the big dog reappeared through the brush, limping badly in his right hindquarter. They saw the blood draining freely from the flesh wound. There was no sign of fear in the dog's eyes; instead there was a look of urgency. He was on his way back to warn his charges that they were about to come under imminent attack.

As Millie approached Tim, he knelt and gently picked the heavy animal up in his arms, and then the two young men raced back through the tunnel to warn the others in the cave.

They reached them in what had been their common home for the past seventeen months and ordered everyone to flee to the escape tunnel immediately. No one questioned them, or hesitated to comply. The looks on their faces, and the tone in their voices revealed the sincerity and the urgency of their commands.

Dropping everything, they all ran to the back of the cave, where they paused long enough for the men to put on the night vision goggles, and for Steve to grab both his and Tim's bows and arrows. Steve led the way, charting a course through the tunnel by the meager light given off by the cigarette lighter he held in his hand. He was followed by Tim, still carrying the wounded Millie in his strong arms. The others filed in behind him, each one holding on to the person in front of him so as not to lose contact with one another since the women were all quite blind in the near total darkness of the escape tunnel. Albert brought up the rear, keeping a sharp eye out behind him through his goggles for anyone who might be following them.

They had not gone far into the tunnel when they heard the sound of muffled voices back in the main cave. Their escape route would quickly be discovered, and their pursuers would soon be on their trail. They picked up their pace. They had to wind their way through the labyrinth of tunnels to the exit, some two hundred yards to the south, before those in pursuit of them were able to overtake them.

That was when the earthquake hit. It threw them all against the wall to their left, and then back to the wall on their right. They all fell to the floor of the tunnel, scraped and bruised, but basically unharmed. There, they waited for nearly ten minutes as the earth heaved and convulsed in the darkness. Small rocks were dislodged above them and fell on them, but they were not heavy enough to inflict any serious injury. They huddled together for comfort, and prayed for God's protection over them as they suffered through the most terrifying ordeal of their lives.

Those in the main cave were not so inclined to pray to the Lord; neither were they similarly protected by Him. The roof of the cave gave way under the relentless heaving of the earthquake, and tons of rock came crashing down on the hapless soldiers trapped inside. Some fifty men were crushed to death under the onslaught. Their cries were hideous, but brief. Gino Mantelli alone escaped their fate as he was bringing up the rear and was still in the access tunnel when the earthquake hit. Falling rocks hit and wounded him, but he was able to struggle back toward the entrance without being buried under the same avalanche that had entombed his men.

After the quake had run its course, the Frieberg family managed to get to their feet and made it the rest of the way to the emergency exit from the cave. They wanted desperately to get out of the tunnel before it too caved in, but they were forced to stay where they were until the icy death stopped falling from the sky.

Now, they stood outside in the gathering darkness, and realized that they had no place to go. The melting ice around them lowered the temperature to about forty degrees, and they began to shiver in their light clothing. As badly as they wanted to be away from the bowels of that murderous mountain, they realized they had best return to the escape tunnel. It was warmer there, and it provided the protection of walls around them and a roof over their heads, unstable though it may have been.

They had had the forethought to store some emergency provisions near the tunnel's exit in preparation for the possibility of just such a forced retreat. There, they found dried food, spare blankets, and a first aid kit. In the darkness, they bandaged their wounds, ate their food, and prepared to spend a long and troubled night. If God allowed them to see the morning light, they would then decide what they would do and where they would go.

Gabriel sounded a long blast on his trumpet (the blast long awaited by the saints down through the ages), and Michael shouted that the time had come. The armies of heaven fell in behind them and they began moving out from the portals of heaven, following their Savior. The Lord Himself led the way, followed by the two archangels, with the hosts of angels directly behind them. At the end of the procession rode the glorified saints, clothed in purest white and astride prancing white stallions. In their earthly lives, they could not have imagined such a thing; but here, it all seemed natural and fitting. They were thrilled to be included in the heavenly procession.

As the army of the Lord drew closer to the earth, the devil, filled with rage, summoned every demon under his command and ordered them to attack the oncoming invasion from outer space. Under no circumstances were they to be allowed to descend to the earth. Up, up, the innumerable masses of fallen angels rose with all the wrath of hell infuriating them. Satan himself took the form of a fiery dragon and led the charge, flames erupting from his hideous mouth.

Michael led the charge of God's angels and saints. He slowed not his assault when he saw the black hordes of hate rising up to meet them. Instead he produced a long chain and began swinging it around his head as he increased his speed and flew to meet his adversary. At the end of the chain were manacles that reflected the light from the sun as they spun around the head of the archangel.

The dragon snarled as it approached the angel and prepared to devour him with fire from its mouth, but it was not to happen. Michael threw the chain with all his might, and it wrapped around the head of the dragon, and its manacles snapped shut on its leathery wrists. The archangel took hold of the end of the chain and sped off, dragging the infuriated dragon behind him.

Before the dragon's leaderless army of fallen angels could disperse to seek places of refuge, Michael's heavenly host produced similar chains, and each one ensnared his own demonic prey. The heavenly cavalry then followed their leader to the very edge of the abyss, the gaping hole called the bottomless pit. It had long been the place of confinement of banished evil spirits, and the wails of those confined within drifted up from the lowest regions of its depths.[57]

The dragon roared and tried to break free, but Michael held fast to its chain. He produced a key from his dazzling white robe and unlocked the gate barring the way to the abyss. He flung it open and spurred his white charger out over the center of the pit, dragging the fuming, cursing creature behind him. Then he turned to look into the fiery eyes of the hideous creature he held captive.

"Be gone, Satan!" he shouted. "Be gone, oh evil one who troubles the nations, father of all iniquity, and master of the denizens of hell!"

Michael flung the chain with all his might, straight down into the gaping maw of the abyss, and it sank into its depths, carrying the screaming, writhing dragon with it.[58]

---

[57] For if God did not spare the angels who sinned, but cast them down to hell (the abyss) and delivered them into chains of darkness, to be reserved for judgment (2 Peter 2:4).

[58] Then I saw an angel coming down from heaven, having the key to the bottomless pit and a great chain in his hand. He laid hold of the dragon, that serpent of old, who is the Devil and Satan, and bound him for a thousand yours; and he cast him into the bottomless pit, and shut him up, and set a seal on him, so that he should deceive the nations no more till the thousand years were finished. But after these things he must be released for a little while (Revelation 20:1–3).

"I'll be back!" the monster screeched as it disappeared into the hungry blackness. "And when I'm free, I'll destroy you all!"

The legions of the damned began to beg and plead that they be spared the fate of their master, but it was to no avail. The holy angels followed their leader out over the center of the smoking pit and dropped their chains, sending their wailing captives plummeting into its depths. Their pitiful screams echoed out of the blackness below.

But just before the last of them were to be dispatched, strangely, Michael took a dozen of them aside and unclasped their manacles, setting them free.

"I banish you to the earth," he said. "My God will allow you to draw the nations to the final battle of Gog and Magog.[59] Be gone with you; seduce, beguile, and betray. Work your evil spells on the armies of the damned. Your time is short; be gone with you, now!"

The evil spirits did not hesitate. They screeched and laughed and flew like the wind, speeding off as fast as they could to escape the horrible fate that had befallen their master and their comrades. They were not really free; they could do only as Michael had commanded them. But at least they were not in the pit! They flew off to do what they did best: to deceive and defile the hapless wretches remaining who were ultimately condemned to hell.

Their tasks completed, Michael led his heavenly army away from the pit and closed and locked its massive gate. Then he led them back to rejoin his King and the army of his saints who were speeding their way to the waiting earth below.

Constantine Augustus and Eli Rothschild huddled together in the subterranean conference room of the Federation Building west of Jerusalem. They had fled Jerusalem the moment the earthquake hit. Their driver managed to somehow negotiate the arduous fifteen miles, avoiding the collapsing buildings and driving over piles of debris and bodies strewn in their way. The devouring hail pounded the reinforced roof of their Humvee, but did not cave it in completely.

---

[59] Thus says the Lord God: "Behold, I am against you, O Gog, the prince of Rosh, Meshech, and Tubal. I will turn you around, put hooks into your jaws, and lead you out, with all your army, horses, and horsemen, all splendidly clothed, a great company with bucklers and shields, all of them handling swords (Ezekiel 38:3–4).

On arriving, they found the Federation Building in ruins. The upper stories had collapsed in the quake and had destroyed everything and everyone below them, that is, everything except the conference room, four stories down. Constantine had designed it himself, and he had built it to withstand anything that could possibly be thrown at it. Yet there was no apparent way to access it. All elevators and stairways in the building had been destroyed when the building collapsed. But that did not deter Constantine. He knew of a hidden passageway.

During the construction of the building, he had secretly contracted the underground passageway to be built by an independent firm. Like the conference room itself, the tunnel was reinforced to withstand even the most severe earthquake or bomb blast. Its outside entrance was concealed inside a fake reinforced concrete tomb, and only he had keys to unlock its heavy steel gate.

The workmen who had built the passageway had been bribed and sworn to secrecy, and then, when they had finished their work, Constantine had them all executed on a phony charge of treason. No one knew of its existence except himself and his cousin Eli.

After arriving at the tomb entrance, Constantine summarily shot his driver and left him dying in a pool of his own blood. The Great Caesar could not afford to leave anyone alive who might later be able to lead others to their secret hideaway.

The conference room was self-contained, having its own air, water, and generated power supply. It had sleeping rooms and restrooms attached, and a well-supplied kitchen and food locker. Constantine was convinced that if he and Eli could reach this sanctuary, they would be able to hold out there indefinitely. They could monitor what was going on in Jerusalem by way of the huge television screen mounted into one of the walls, and they would emerge only when they knew it was safe to do so. And no one would think to look for them beneath the pile of steel and concrete remaining from the collapse of the Federation Building.

So here they sat, their eyes glued to the television set, praying to Lucifer that he would descend and rescue them and deposit the world at their feet as he had promised. But they heard nothing from him, and even Emperor Marcus Aurelius failed to come to their aid when they summoned him. Alone and terrified, the world's Great Caesar and his divine prophet shivered and held on to one another for support.[60]

[60] And he shall plant the tents of his palace between the seas and the glorious holy mountain; yet he shall come to his end, and no one will help him (Daniel 11:45).

On the Mount of Olives, Aaron Muller leaned on his rod. He could barely stand. The wound in his chest had collapsed one of his lungs and it was filling with blood. It was becoming increasingly difficult to breathe, but he refused to lie down and die. He remained propped up and vigilant.

Mark Robertson was by his side, he too bleeding from gunshot wounds. Vile fluid, mixed with blood, oozed from a bullet hole in his stomach, but he too stood his ground, leaning on his bow for support.

Along with their fellow witnesses, who were likewise wounded, they watched what remained of the united Federation armies dig out from under the rubble left from the earthquake and the hailstorm. They had hopes that the enemy had all been destroyed, but such was not the case. Indeed, multiplied thousands had perished in the onslaught, but even greater multitudes had not.

Much to the dismay of the faithful warriors on top of the mountain, they saw those surviving enemy troops assembling and preparing for yet another assault. As their numbers continued to grow, the outcome of the assault became more and more apparent. There was just no way the few wounded survivors would be able to hold off the crazed multitudes now preparing to charge up the hill at them.

Aaron reached out and took Mark's hand in his own. "It looks like this is it, my friend," he said softly. "We've fought a good fight, like the Good Book says, and we've kept the faith. If the Lord doesn't come beforehand, we'll go out in a blaze of glory and join Him in heaven.[61]

"Amen, brother!" Mark agreed, smiling through his pain. "Bring 'em on!"

President Renslow, General Borzov, and Chairman Chong gave the order to attack. They were filled with rage, and were mutually agreed that the filthy Jews on that hill, and all those they protected, had to be eliminated, regardless of the cost. Victory had been within their grasp when that freak earthquake and hailstorm had struck, and they were not about to give up just because of the damage that had been done.

---

[61] "I have fought the good fight, I have finished the race, I have kept the faith. Finally, there is laid up for me the crown of righteousness, which the Lord, the righteous Judge, will give to me on that Day, and not to me only but also to all who have loved His appearing (2 Timothy 4:7–8).

They had been watching the progress of the pre-dawn assault on the Jewish positions from the top of Mount Scopus to the north when the earthquake hit. They had run out into the open to avoid the collapsing buildings around them, and then the murderous hail had driven them back inside. From the safety of a bomb shelter at the Hebrew University, they waited out the storm together along with their aides, cursing their bad luck.

But now, the earth was still and the sky was vacant, with the exception of some scattered residual clouds, and apparently the majority of their troops had survived. Victory was still within their grasp. They had not come so far, nor paid such a heavy price, to turn back now.

After repeated attempts, they had still been unable to contact Augustus or Rothschild, and presumed them dead, crushed in the particularly massive destruction that had struck the temple mount where they had been. The thought of their deaths caused the three leaders no grief. With them gone, nothing could stand in their way. This morning, they would conquer the Jews; and tomorrow, they would conquer the world.

The signal was given, the guns started blazing yet again, and the enemy troops started their advance up the mountainside one last time. From all four directions the enraged hordes ascended the Mount of Olives. Nothing would turn them back this time.

Suddenly, a light shone from heaven and illumined the top of the mountain with a glorious brightness. The former darkness that had engulfed the area was dispelled in an instant. All hostilities stopped, and every eye was turned upward. The two television crews that had survived the divine judgments earlier had their cameras trained on the strange radiance above them.

A trumpet blast shook the earth, and the shouts of innumerable voices echoed throughout the Judean hills. The clouds parted, and, unbelievably, a single rider, clothed in a white robe and astride a white horse, appeared in the heavens. Rapidly, He made His descent until the hooves of His great steed pranced on the rocky soil on top of the mountain.

The television cameras followed His every move, and as the world watched, the rider dismounted. After nearly two thousand years of absence, the King of kings and Lord of lords stood with His feet firmly planted on top of the Mount of Olives.[62]

---

[62] Then the Lord will go forth and fight against those nations, as He fights in the day of battle. And in that day His feet will stand on the Mount of Olives, which faces Jerusalem on the east (Zechariah 14:3–4).

CHAPTER SEVENTEEN

The Judgment

The crushing earthquake and the pulverizing hail had destroyed power plants, substations, and power lines all over the world. The world was virtually without electrical power, and yet, the televisions worked. While the rest of their houses were shrouded in darkness, people on every continent huddled around TV sets, powered by divine energy, and gazed at the most astounding event in modern history. Many others who were not near a television were able to pick up the images on battery powered cell phones. Jesus Christ had returned to the Mount of Olives just as the angels had promised so many centuries before,[63] and it was witnessed by people all over the world.[64]

There was a great mourning because of the guilt experienced by those who dwelt on the earth, especially among the Jews. He had come before as their King, and yet they had rejected him. He had offered Himself to them, and they had crucified Him. Now, they saw Him in all His

---

[63] Now when He had spoken these things while they watched, He was taken up, and a cloud received Him out of their sight. And while they looked steadfastly toward heaven as He went up, behold, two men stood by them in white apparel, who said, "Men of Galilee, why do you stand gazing up into heaven? This same Jesus, who was taken up from you into heaven, will so come in like manner as you saw Him go into heaven." (Acts 1:9–12).

[64] Behold, He is coming with clouds, and every eye will see Him, even they who pierced Him. And all the tribes of the earth will mourn because of Him. Even so, Amen (Revelation 1:7).

splendor, the returning Sovereign of the world. Their hearts condemned them at first, but then they erupted in faith. God opened their eyes and their minds, and they believed with all their hearts. Their mourning was mixed with incredible joy.[65]

Shortly after the Lord set foot on the Mount of Olives, there was a corporate conversion of all the Jewish people who had sought refuge among the 144,000. They had refused the mark of the beast, but they had not previously accepted Jesus Christ as their own personal Messiah. Instantly, that all changed. En masse, they believed and were gloriously saved. And all over the world, watching on television, their brethren did the same thing. Salvation came to the house of Israel after centuries of spiritual darkness.[66] A wonderful combination of weeping and rejoicing took place among God's chosen people universally, but at no place was it more evident than on the top of the Mount of Olives. The newborn saints there gathered around their newly arrived Redeemer with heartfelt shame for their lifetimes of unbelief, coupled with unabashed joy over their salvation, newly found in Him.

The three ungodly rulers watched in disbelief on the television monitor in the bomb shelter to which they had returned when they saw the strange light starting to illuminate the mountaintop to the south of them. They had wanted no part of a revisitation of the earthquake and hailstorm, or even something worse. But no plague or catastrophe took place. All they could see was a solitary figure in the center of all those Jews over there.

"I don't know how that guy got over there, or who he thinks he is," huffed President Renslow, "but he's gotta go. While everybody over there has dropped their weapons to celebrate his arrival, we need to send our troops up there and wipe 'em all out."

"I agree, Mr. President," concurred General Borzov. "They appear to be completely unprepared to ward off an attack."

"Very well," agreed Chairman Chong, "but let us get on with it. We will not have the element of surprise for long."

---

[65] It shall be in that day that I will seek to destroy all the nations that come against Jerusalem. And I will pour on the house of David and on the inhabitants of Jerusalem the Spirit of grace and supplication; then they will look on Me whom they pierced. Yes, they will mourn for Him as one mourns for his only son, and grieve for Him as one grieves for a firstborn (Zechariah 12:9–10).

[66] And so all Israel will be saved, as it is written: "The Deliverer will come out of Zion. And He will turn away ungodliness from Jacob; for this is My covenant with them, when I take away their sins." (Romans 11:26–27).

So it was decided. The order went out, and the exhausted united Federation armies rose to their feet and prepared for the final assault on the mountain. But it never took place.

Before the first shot was fired, an unbelievable phenomenon was seen approaching from the west. The television crewmen turned their cameras in that direction, and their zoom lenses picked up what appeared to be four men flying unassisted more than a hundred feet above the surface of the ground.

It was David and Joseph, hurrying triumphantly to meet their Lord on the Mount of Olives, and in tow, they led none other than Constantine Augustus and Eli Rothschild. The latter two were screaming and protesting, but to no avail. Manacles were clamped around their wrists and strong chains were attached to them; the two witnesses had a firm grip on the other ends of the chains.

Constantine and Eli had been snatched bodily out of their luxury bunker beneath the collapsed Federation Building where they had been huddled in terror. They had been watching what was taking place on the Mount of Olives on the television screen when Joseph and David descended into the conference room through the solid reinforced concrete of its roof. They wailed in protest, Constantine shot at them with his pistol, but the witnesses approached them nonetheless, touched them, and transformed them. Their bodies instantly took on a spiritual and indestructible quality, the manacles were clamped tightly around their wrists, and they were lifted straight up, through the rubble of the building, and into the morning air.

Now, as they approached the true Christ of Israel, the antichrist and his false prophet shook with mortal terror. "Father Lucifer, help us!" sobbed Constantine as the two witnesses pulled their captives up short in front of the God of the entire universe, but the heavens were silent.

"It is too late, Oh wicked ones," spoke the Lord, His intense face ablaze with righteousness. "The god of this world has been judged and thrown into the abyss with his demonic hordes. Oh you who have deceived the nations and trafficked in the souls of men; it is time for you to share their fate. My two witnesses, whom you have hated and killed, will seal your doom. Depart from me, you who practice lawlessness, into everlasting fire, prepared for the devil and his angels!"[67]

[67] And the lawless one will be revealed, whom the Lord will consume with the breath of His mouth and destroy with the brightness of His coming (2 Thessalonians 2:8).

With that, the glorified witnesses departed from the Lord, dragging the pathetic beast and his prophet behind them. In what seemed to be a moment of time, they stopped over the surface of the boiling caldron called Gehenna, the lake of fire. The fire burned with infernal heat, but it put off no light at all; the lake was shrouded in absolute darkness. It belched out brimstone, and its acrid smoke reeked of sulfur.

The two condemned souls pleaded for mercy and wept tears of anguish and insincere repentance, but David and Joseph paid them no heed. They looked at their captives one last time with righteous contempt, and then dropped the ends of their chains. Like massive weights, the chains sank instantly into the boiling surface of the lake of fire, pulling their wailing captives in behind them.[68]

The screams of the beast and the false prophet were hideous as they echoed through the corridors of hell. Their suffering was unimaginable, but what was even worse, it did not consume them. In their indestructible bodies, they were destined to writhe in Gehenna's flames throughout the endless ages of eternity, with no hope of reprieve or release. The blackness was so intense they could not see each other in their torment. The other's screams alone reminded them that they were not absolutely isolated in the universe.[69]

Joseph and David sped back to rejoin their Savior on top of the Mount of Olives as He was about to execute judgment on the millions still remaining of the armies that had invaded the land. Hundreds of thousands were in and around Jerusalem, and the remainder of them swarmed over the land like locusts. Some were Chinese, some were Russians, others were Americans, and the remaining hosts were Federation troops from countries all over the world. But the one thing they all had in common was that they all hated God and His people Israel.

---

[68] And I saw the beast, the kings of the earth, and their armies, gathered together to make war against Him who sat on the horse and against His army. Then the beast was captured, and with him the false prophet who worked signs in his presence, by which he deceived those who received the mark of the beast and those who worshiped his image. These two were cast alive into the lake of fire burning with brimstone (Revelation 19:19–20).

[69] He himself shall also drink of the wine of the wrath of God, which is poured out full strength into the cup of His indignation. He shall be tormented with fire and brimstone in the presence of the holy angels and in the presence of the Lamb. And the smoke of their torment ascends forever and ever. And they have no rest day or night . . . (Revelation 14:10–11).

Their commanders were not sure just what to do. They stood outside their bunker and stared in disbelief toward the south. They had been adamant about swarming the Mount of Olives and destroying the Jews once and for all, but that had been before they had witnessed the unbelievable condemnation of Constantine Augustus and his stooge Rothschild. Now, the three of them stood on Mount Scopus arguing among themselves as to what they should do next. But the Lord made the decision for them.

The returned Messiah of Israel stretched forth his hands and cried out with a loud voice, "Let the wicked of this land perish before Your sight, Oh Father. Let their breath go forth from their mouths, and let their bodies become food for the beasts of the field and the birds of the air!"[70]

The attacking soldiers were not struck down by blows from unseen swords or spears. They simply began to decompose while they stood on their feet. The decomposition began at the point where they bore the mark of the beast, and it quickly spread. It struck their commanders first, and then manifested itself throughout the ranks of their armies.

President Lowell Renslow was the first to fall. The flesh on his pudgy right hand began to slough off and fall to the ground, followed quickly by the liquefying substance of the rest of his body. His evil eyes rolled out of their puffy sockets and dangled momentarily on his cheeks from their optic nerves before they liquefied and dropped in globs from his vanishing face. He did not—could not—speak. He groaned softly and pitched over backwards, landing in an oozing pile on his back. He was dead before his body struck the pavement.

General Borzov and Chairman Chong stared in horror, but before either could say or do anything, the same thing happened to them. Their decomposing bodies fell next to the mound that had been Renslow. Their dreams of world conquest melted away as did their vile bodies.[71]

The shadow of the angel of death passed over the armies of the damned, and the plague quickly spread throughout the entire ranks of

---

[70] And the rest were killed with the sword which proceeded from the mouth of Him who sat on the horse. And all the birds were filled with their flesh (Revelation 19:21).

[71] And this shall be the plague with which the Lord will strike all the people who fought against Jerusalem: their flesh shall dissolve while they stand on their feet, their eyes shall dissolve in their sockets, and their tongues shall dissolve in their mouths (Zechariah 14:12).

the enemy; no one escaped. From General Putnam, Admiral Hightower, Myron Spangler, and other ranking officers, to the lowliest buck privates and seamen, the death angel passed quickly, taking his grisly toll. In a matter of a few minutes, the millions of enemy troops were reduced to mounds of mushy flesh, literally covering the entire countryside. Even the bodies of those who had been killed days before began to slough away.

Great hordes of vultures, crows, magpies, and other scavenger birds swept across the land, gorging themselves on the rapidly decomposing flesh of the fallen. They ate their fill, but the decomposition devoured the bodies faster than the scavengers could. By evening there would be nothing left of the carcasses but the basic elements of which they were composed. Even the natural fibers of their clothing would disintegrate, leaving only bits of metal, plastic, and inert fibers where the bodies had been.

Aaron and Mark and their comrades gazed around them in amazement. So very much had taken place, it was impossible for them to take it all in. The Lord had returned, the Jewish people had been converted, and their enemies had all been destroyed. It seemed as though they had been witnessing those things for hours, but in reality, it had all happened in less than ten minutes. And it wasn't over yet.

Even as the death angel had wrought destruction among the hordes of the ungodly, the Holy Spirit gently swept across the ranks of His chosen ones, spreading healing. Instantly, Aaron and Mark and all the others who remained of the living 144,000 were made whole. Wounds healed, broken bones mended, and surging strength returned to their formerly exhausted bodies. They embraced their returned Lord in perfect health.

Their rejuvenation was spectacular, but what followed was even more mind-boggling. At the command of Christ, the same Spirit swept over the bodies of the remainder of the 144,000, those who had fought and died courageously for their Lord and His people. Instantly, the dead were raised to life again. The slain stood to their feet. Even those who had been dead for more than three days were made perfectly whole. From the huge trench Ivan had bulldozed, they clambered, rejoicing and praising God. From all over the top of the Mount of Olives, from the temple mount to the west, and from the depths of the Valley of Kidron, the dead stood to their feet.

They were not gloriously resurrected in their immortal bodies; rather, they were resuscitated to their former state of being, such as was Lazarus in the days of the New Testament. Although he had been dead for four days, he was raised to perfect health by the spoken word of the Lord.[72] So were the fallen of the 144,000 restored to life by the same power. They were mortal still, but they were made miraculously whole.

The 144,000 had a glorious reunion; laughing, hugging, and praising God. The Jewish believers who had newly been saved joined in the celebration. The Lord Jesus was the center of their attention, and He received all their adoration and praise. The great hosts of angels and glorified saints added their exaltations from their vantage point high above the Holy City. The spectacular celebration far exceeded even Christ's triumphant entry into the City of Jerusalem on Palm Sunday so many centuries before.[73]

The 144,000 gathered around Jesus, and He blessed them. The throngs of converted Jews joined them as the Lord walked with them and talked with them. The huge congregation made its way down through the Kidron Valley and up to the top of the temple mount. They spread out over the entire eastern portion of what was left of Jerusalem. Their Lord stood at the site of the demolished temple and spoke to His own of the glories of the new temple He would build, of the incredible fruitfulness the land of Israel would experience, and of the general greatness of His coming kingdom. His 144,000 worshipped Him there and sang of His glory and greatness.[74]

As they worshipped their Lord on Mount Zion, a rumbling sound could be heard to the east of them. At first it was barely audible, but it

---

[72] Now when He had said these things, He cried with a loud voice, "Lazarus, come forth!" And he who had died came out bound hand and foot with graveclothes, and his face was wrapped with a cloth. Jesus said to them, "Loose him, and let him go." (John 11:43–44).

[73] They brought the donkey and the colt, laid their clothes on them, and set Him on them. And a very great multitude spread their clothes on the road; others cut down branches from the trees and spread them on the road. Then the multitudes who went before and those who followed cried out, saying; "Hosanna to the Son of David! Blessed is He who comes in the name of the Lord! Hosanna in the highest!" (Matthew 21:7–9).

[74] Then I looked, and behold, a Lamb standing on Mount Zion, and with Him one hundred and forty-four thousand, having His Father's name written on their foreheads. And I heard a voice from heaven, like the voice of many waters, and like the voice of loud thunder. And I heard the sound of harpists playing their harps. They sang as it were a new song before the throne, before the four living creatures, and the elders; and no one could learn that song except the hundred and forty-four thousand who were redeemed from the earth (Revelation 14:1–3).

increased in volume until the noise of it drowned out the sound of their own celebration. Then it happened.

To the east, the Mount of Olives suddenly split in two, one half of the mountain moving to the south, and the other half moving to the north. A valley opened up between the two peaks and worked its way both to the east and the west. Then, as the mesmerized saints watched from the temple mount, streams of water, fed from underground springs, began to flow from the rupture in the Mount of Olives. The waters divided, and some of them flowed eastward and into the Dead Sea; others flowed westward, and eventually found their way to the Mediterranean.[75]

That day was like no other: the darkness, the earthquake, the hailstorm, the return of Christ, the destruction of the enemy, the resuscitation of the 144,000, and now, the cleaving of the Mount of Olives. And it was not over yet.

The Savior pointed toward the gurgling fountain that supplied the water for the two streams and said, "Just as those living waters flow to bring life back to this dry and dusty land, so does the Holy Spirit flow forth to bring life back to those who died during the great tribulation. Flow, Spirit, flow! And you, who were dead, arise! Arise from the dust of the earth! Arise, for your Lord has come!"

Suddenly, from around the world, the resurrected bodies of the multitudes who had been saved during the tribulation, and then martyred for the cause of Christ, appeared in the air above Jerusalem. The temporary bodies they had been given vanished, and the tribulation saints were reunited with their original, but now glorified, bodies.

Papa Saul Frieberg, President Dwight Honaker, and his friend Ben Hiestead reveled in their new bodies. Although the original ones of all three of them had been virtually annihilated by evil men during the

[75] And in that day His feet will stand on the Mount of Olives, which faces Jerusalem on the east. And the Mount of Olives shall be split in two, from east to west, making a very large valley; half of the mountain shall move toward the north and half of it toward the south. . . . And in that day it shall be that living waters shall flow from Jerusalem, half of them toward the eastern sea and half of them toward the western sea; in both summer and winter it shall occur (Zechariah 14:4, 8).

[76] And I saw thrones, and they sat on them, and judgment was committed to them. Then I saw the souls of those who had been beheaded for their witness to Jesus and for the word of God, who had not worshiped the beast or his image, and had not received his mark on their foreheads or on their hands. And they lived and reigned with Christ for a thousand years. But the rest of the dead did not live again until the thousand years were finished. Blessed and holy is he who has part in the first resurrection (Revelation 20:4–6).

tribulation, they were all now perfectly restored and glorified. The things they had suffered in the past seemed as nothing compared to the glory they were now experiencing.[76]

Such was also true for the millions of others who had also been martyred during those horrible three-and-a-half years. They had been taken immediately to heaven after their deaths, and had been given temporary bodies and comforted there, but they had still not been complete.[77] But now, clothed in their own resurrected and glorified bodies, they were totally and eternally whole.[78]

The angels and glorified saints filled the sky above the Holy City, the 144,000 surrounded their Lord on the temple mount, and the redeemed saints assembled as closely as they could around them. The rejoicing and celebration was unrestrained and glorious. The tribulation had just come to an end, and there was much to do to prepare for the coming of the Messiah's millennial kingdom, but those things could be postponed. The suffering of the saints had been great, and their wait had seemed interminable. Now was the time for them to celebrate their emancipation and triumph in their returned Lord.

Because they had not participated in the attack against God's people, the lives of the television crews had been spared. They scrambled to capture as many of the phenomenal scenes as they could. No one had ever seen anything like what they were filming with their cameras, and they didn't want to miss a single frame. Around the world, beleaguered saints watched on television sets and rejoiced in what they saw. Many of them failed to comprehend all that was happening, but they sensed that their time of hardship and suffering had finally come to an end.

Others were not so joyous. Millions of unbelievers survived the tribulation as well, and they were painfully disillusioned. They had placed their confidence in ungodly men, and they had waited anxiously in front of their TV sets to celebrate when those men led their armies to the

[77] These are the ones who came out of the great tribulation, and washed their robes and made them white in the blood of the Lamb. Therefore they are before the throne of God, and serve Him day and night in His temple. And He who sits on the throne will dwell among them. They shall neither hunger anymore nor thirst anymore; the sun shall not strike them, nor any heat; for the Lamb who is in the midst of the throne will shepherd them and lead them to living fountains of waters. And God will wipe away every tear from their eyes (Revelation 7:14–17).

[78] See Appendix Four for a more detailed study of the various resurrections mentioned in the Bible.

ultimate victory. But they had watched in horror as those ungodly men were destroyed one by one, and all hope of world conquest perished with them. Those people watched the unfolding events in Jerusalem with the combined emotions of disbelief, anger, and fear.

President Gregor Odin Galinikov sat up in his hospital bed in Ankara Turkey and stared in disbelief at the television set mounted on the wall of his room. The earthquake had badly shaken the building, but had not collapsed. The devastating hail had broken windows and severely damaged equipment on the roof, but the hospital remained essentially intact. Diesel generators supplied the electricity necessary to power the lights and medical equipment.

The sick man in the bed had not been aware of the devastation anyway. He had been deathly ill for nearly a week, and he had just awakened from a coma-like state into which he had lapsed three days before. The sweat dripped from his feverish brow, but he ignored it. It was not the ailment in his body that disturbed him; it was the images that were playing out before his bloodshot eyes.

Could it really be that his friend General Borzov had been killed, and that his entire army had perished with him? Had all the American and Chinese forces been destroyed as well? Was it also true that Augustine and all those he commanded had met the same fate? Was there no one left on the planet to take control besides that strange character in Jerusalem who had ridden in on that ridiculous white horse?

It appeared that this one called Jesus Christ and a small army of his Jewish rebels represented the only ruling class in the entire world. They were not many in number, but they possessed some powerful magic. They had apparently been able to defeat what remained of the combined military forces of all the countries of the world. That was powerful magic indeed.

Gog decided he would do nothing to anger this newly arrived king of the world. Rather, he would be quiet and submissive for the time being. The doctor had told him that he had turned the corner in his battle with his strange illness, and that he was going to survive, but he still had a long way to go before he was well and strong again. He would recover his strength, return to Moscow, rebuild his nation, and look for his opportunity to make his move.

If this new king turned out to be ruthless and invincible, he would have to learn to stay out of his way. But if he proved to be careless and vulnerable, then there would surely come a time for a patient and ambitious man to take advantage of a future opportunity to take over. Gog decided he would be that patient and ambitious man.

As he pushed the button on the remote and turned off the TV set, he lay back in bed exhausted and breathed a prayer to Odin. Surely the great Norse God of War would come to his aid and give him the ultimate victory he had promised him since he was a boy.

CHAPTER EIGHTEEN

The Reunion

The reigning Christ spent the day with His people in Jerusalem. They had waited so long for His return; He was not going to disappoint them by leaving again or by sending them away. There was much to be done, and He had already set things in motion, but He determined not to assign His weary saints any responsibilities right away. He allowed them the time to rest from their sorrows and labors, and to bask in the presence of their blessed Savior.

He sent his angels off to the far reaches of the universe to do His bidding, and He appointed His glorified saints to various responsibilities around the world. They were commissioned to defend the believers from any harm evil men might attempt to bring upon them. They were also appointed to destroy all weapons of war; to repair power plants, roads, and bridges; and to restore the infrastructure of society that the devastating tribulation had destroyed. They were not to work with bulldozers, jackhammers, and cement mixers; but rather with the spoken word, and the power of the Spirit of God.

But to the 144,000, and to the other mortal believers who had survived the tribulation, He gave no immediate assignments. Instead, He nurtured and comforted them. He produced bread, fish, and wine for them. He simply spoke the food into being and had members of the 144,000 distribute portions to everyone. More than 200,000 were fed that day as easily as the 5,000 were fed by the Sea of Galilee so many years before.[79]

It was a glorious day; the first day of peace and comfort any of them had known in a three-and-a-half full years, but toward evening, He called for their attention. He spoke in a normal voice from the top of the temple mount, but He was readily heard by all the people, some of them from as far as a mile away.

First, the Lord sent those who lived in the area back to their homes. They were to clean and repair them and spend the night there. In so doing, the saints were delighted to find that, amidst heaps and mounds of demolished buildings, they found their dwelling places intact. God's divine power had caused the homes of His elect to stand while stronger buildings collapsed all around them. The repair work was minimal, but the cleaning tasks were a bit more demanding. The happy people readily accepted their responsibilities, and soon they were settled into their tidy and secure dwellings for the first time in longer than most of them could remember. They would spend a restful night sleeping in their own beds.

Then, the Master spoke to His 144,000. He expressed His love and appreciation to them for their faithfulness to Him and His people throughout the tribulation. They had suffered more in His name, and had accomplished more for His kingdom, than any comparable group of people in the history of the world. They were assured of many crowns in glory.

Next, the Lord did an unexpected thing. He released them from their special commitments. Their work was done, and the 144,000 witnesses were no longer needed. They were restored to their former lives, and released to return to their families. No longer would they have supernatural powers, or enjoy supernatural protection; they would enter into the millennium as ordinary men. But He promised to provide them with one last special enablement. He would return them immediately and supernaturally to their families to prepare them for their return to the Promised Land.

Finally, since Mark Robertson and Rico Sandia had no earthly families to care for, the Lord assigned them the happy task of traveling to

[79] And Jesus took the loaves, and when He had given thanks He distributed them to the disciples, and the disciples to those sitting down; and likewise of the fish, as much as they wanted. So when they were filled, He said to His disciples, "Gather up the fragments that remain, so that nothing is lost." Therefore they gathered them up, and filled twelve baskets with the fragments of the five barley loaves which were left over by those who had eaten (John 6:11–13).

Masada and leading the residents there on their long, but triumphant, march back to Jerusalem. They readily accepted their assignment, looking forward to seeing those good people again and renewing friendships they had forged with them three-and-a-half years before. They set off immediately to find the Humvee David and Joseph had hidden away, determined to make it to the desert fortress before darkness fell.

It was seven o'clock in the morning when Aaron Muller found himself standing beside a tall fir tree in the San Gabriel Mountains above what remained of Los Angeles. A moment before, he had been praising his returned Messiah on the temple mount in Jerusalem in the late afternoon; and now here he was, squinting in the bright morning sunlight in a California forest, half way around the world. Such instantaneous travel was not a new phenomenon to him now, but he was still amazed when it took place.[80]

"I'm going to ask the Lord how He does that when I get the chance," he said out loud. "That has got to be the most amazing thing I've ever experienced. . . . No, maybe not," he corrected himself, "I've seen and done so many impossible things in the past few days, I would be hard pressed to single out which one of them was the most amazing. But it sure enough has to be one of them."

He looked around to see if he could recognize any familiar landmarks. He surmised that he was close to the cave where his family had been hiding. He reached that conclusion simply on the reasoning that the Lord would most likely deposit him close to his loved ones. Sure enough, he picked out Throop Peak through the trees. According to his hasty calculations, he was no more than 500 yards from the entrance of the cave. He set off quickly in that direction, making his way hastily through fallen trees, branches, and other debris. He realized that the earthquake had taken its toll in this part of the world as well.

That thought caused him to wonder what damage it might also have done to the cave where his family was taking refuge. He quickened his pace to keep up with the increased cadence in the beating of his heart.

When he approached the entrance of the cave, his heart sank. For strewn about the ground were mounds that surely must have been bodies the day before. Like what happened in Israel after the

[80] See Appendix Five for a more detailed discussion of instantaneous world travel.

judgment of the Lord, the bodies had decomposed quickly, and only bits of metal, plastic, and nylon remained in the piles of what resembled organic compost.

"Who were these people," he asked himself, "and what were they doing here? They had to be evil men. If they were Christians, their bodies would have been raised and they would be off serving the Lord somewhere right now. I wonder what they did to my family before the earthquake hit."

He made his way to the entrance of the cave, but it was pitch dark inside, and he discovered his night vision wasn't as acute as it had been a few days before. He called out, but his voice bounced right back at him. He fished the cigarette lighter out of his pocket he always carried and struck the flint to light its small butane flame. By its light, he slowly made his way down the narrow tunnel leading to the main cavern, but he never made it there. A solid wall of fallen rock stopped his progress about sixty feet into the tunnel.

"Oh, no!" he lamented. "Not this! Not now! Lord, You surely wouldn't keep them alive all these years, just to let them die in a cave in at the very end of the tribulation. Sure, if they did, they're already resurrected and with You now, but where does that leave me? I don't want to enter into the millennium all by myself. Please, tell me they're not all dead!"

Then, as though prompted by the Lord Himself, Aaron thought of the escape tunnel.

"Of course!" he exclaimed. "The escape tunnel! Thank you, Lord. Why didn't I think of that myself?"

Aaron retraced his steps out of the tunnel as quickly as he could, and raced the short distance around the base of the peak as fast as he could. Less than a minute later, and a little out of breath, he arrived at the place where he thought the escape tunnel made its exit. He couldn't identify its exact location, so he began to call out: "Mom! Dad! Anna! Anybody! Where are you guys?"

The Frieberg family, inside the narrow tunnel, had just finished eating some dried food for breakfast and were discussing what they should do and where they should go. Recognizing Aaron's voice, Anna Berger jumped to her feet and hurried to the tunnel's entrance.

"Aaron, is that you?" came a muffled reply from within the rocks of the mountainside somewhere. It was a female voice, and it sounded like Anna to Aaron.

"Yes! Yes, thank God, it's me. Come on out. It's safe. I'm alone."

From behind a rock outcropping, stepped the most beautiful young woman Aaron had ever seen. In truth, her clothes were worn and tattered, her hands and face could use a good washing, and her hair was tangled and uncombed. She even had several scrapes and bruises from the falling rock, but Aaron saw none of that. Instead, he saw the perfect teeth, set in a wide grin; and the bright hazel eyes, brimming with happy tears. He saw the woman he had loved with all his heart for the past three-and-a-half years, and to him, she looked drop-dead gorgeous.

They ran to meet each other and embraced with unrestrained exuberance. They hugged, they kissed, they laughed and wept. At last, they were together, and this time, they would not have to part. Aaron could not remember experiencing such overwhelming joy.

The rest of the family made their exit from the cave as well, yet they paused for a moment, giving Aaron and Anna some brief time together. But when Aaron looked up and saw them, they practically mobbed him.

His parents and his sister, his aunt and uncle and his cousins, and even limping Millennium, crowded around him to welcome him back and to express their love for him.

"What happened, Aaron?" his father asked. "There were soldiers. They shot Millie and were coming into the cave after us when we ran out the back. Then the earthquake hit . . . and then that awful hailstorm. Did you see any soldiers? Will they be coming back? How many more disasters are we going to have to live through?"

"Dad, it's over! It's all over!" Aaron gushed. "The Lord came back right after the earthquake and destroyed all His enemies. The dead have been raised, and the living Jews have all been saved. The tribulation is over, and the millennium is about to begin!"

"Are you sure, son?" his mother asked. "It has all been so terrible; are you really sure it's over?"

"Yes, I'm sure, Mom. I was over there and saw everything with my own eyes. The Lord just sent me back here to get all you guys. We're going home at last."

"You mean back to our homes in the city?" his uncle asked. "There couldn't be much left of them now."

"No, Albert. They were never really our homes anyway. We're going to our ancestral home. We're going home to Israel!"

Colonel Tony D'Angelo was at a loss. He had spent the night in the back seat of his luxury Humvee, which had amazingly survived the earthquake and the hailstorm after all, guarded by the two young soldiers that had survived the natural disasters with him. He didn't know where to go. The city of Los Angeles had basically been destroyed by the final display of God's wrath. Along with every other high-rise building in the city, the Federation headquarters building had collapsed in the earthquake, and its ruins were unrecognizable.

After retreating from the mountains the night before, Tony had ordered his driver to stop the Humvee at the bottom of the Angeles Crest Highway. In the dark, he didn't want to try to negotiate the nearly impassable streets of the city. Buildings had collapsed everywhere, street pavement had been broken and heaved up in mounds, and water and gas lines had been broken and were spilling their contents into the neighborhoods. Fires and flooding were commonplace, and the whole Southland was in a state of chaos.

Hundreds of thousands of people had been killed in the onslaught, but their bodies had mysteriously melted away. Seemingly, only a handful of people loyal to the Federation had survived. They were milling around in confusion, lost and terrified as a result of the things they had experienced.

Most of the people who survived seemed to be the poor and oppressed, those sought after and hounded by the Federation. From out of basements, safe houses, and storm drains they came; shaken up, but confident, and with an air of triumph. They joined together into ever-growing congregations, and moved toward Dodger Stadium, as though drawn by an inaudible voice. From all over the Los Angeles area, they came walking, singing, and praising God.

Tony had his young driver maneuver their vehicle slowly through the devastation left from the night before, intent on reaching the safety of the bomb shelter beneath the Federation Building in downtown Los Angeles. Once there, he would hopefully be able to meet with other officers and figure out what they were going to do.

He had followed the goings on in Jerusalem the night before on the television monitor in the back of his Humvee. As their vehicle lost altitude on its descent down the slopes of the mountain, his emotions sank to even lower depths. He watched in horror as the Great Caesar Augustus and his prophet Eli Rothschild were hauled bodily away and presumably destroyed. Then he lost all hope when he saw the vast armies of the nations of the world destroyed by the spoken word of the central figure who had arrived on a white horse.

He had also seen his hated enemy Aaron Muller. He and others like him were with the one on the horse, and they appeared to be badly wounded. He felt some little consolation, seeing Aaron staggering and bleeding like that. When that dirty Jew finally toppled and died, Tony anticipated the satisfaction he would experience, but even that was not to be. At the last moment, the strange figure in the white robe spoke again, and the wounded were instantly healed and all the dead Jews were raised back to life. Tony saw Aaron restored to health and strength right before his eyes. Oh, how he hated that man, and how he now despaired for his own life.

Tony abandoned any hope of victory. It was apparent that the Federation was now out of business, and for that matter, so were all the other national governments around the world. No, he was not going to win, but he was determined not to lose either. Survival had now become his top priority.

As they picked their way painstakingly through the torn streets of the city, they encountered several groups of happy pilgrims, making their way to the west. These freaks had been Tony's enemies, and he had put thousands of their ranks to death in the past. Now, those who had survived greatly outnumbered him, and they had every reason to turn on him and take vengeance for all the suffering they had endured at his hands.

When they came upon the first large group, Tony instinctively reached for his pistol, but he found the holster inexplicably empty. He ordered the two soldiers to shoulder their weapons and disperse the crowd, but they too were unable to locate their automatic assault rifles. The weapons had been in the vehicle the night before, but now they were nowhere to be found. Defenseless, the three terrified Federation soldiers locked their doors and hoped that the rabble would not be able to break through and get at them.

What Tony had no way of knowing was that the glorified saints of God had gone about unseen in the night collecting all guns and instruments of war. They had transported them to steel mills all over the world to be melted down and converted into farm machinery and household tools. By order of the King of kings, there were no weapons of warfare on the planet left available to the hands of ungodly men.[81]

---

[81] For out of Zion shall go forth the law, and the word of the Lord from Jerusalem. He shall judge between the nations, and rebuke many people; they shall beat their swords into plowshares, and their spears into pruning hooks; nation shall not lift up sword against nation, neither shall they learn war anymore (Isaiah 2:3–4).

Without a means to defend themselves, Tony and his men braced for the attack, but they needn't have bothered. The jubilant throng passed them by without paying them any serious attention. Some of them actually smiled at them, and a few of the children waved. These people obviously had more pressing things on their minds than exacting vengeance on their former enemies.

The young man who was their apparent leader was unknown to Tony. Derek Uptain looked at the troubled young Federation officer, and instructed his people to ignore him and his men. He understood that the tribulation was over and everything had changed. They were under divine protection now, and they had nothing to fear from those who had terrorized them in the past. Instead of hatred, he felt pity toward the confused followers of a defeated foe. He was content to let the Lord take care of the people of the beast; he was intent on getting his own flock to the rallying point at Dodger Stadium.

More confused and deflated than ever, Tony ordered his driver to continue on his course to the bomb shelter downtown. He no longer feared for his immediate safety, but his hopes for the future were clouded in mystery and confusion. And try as he would, he could not shake the sound of that demonic laughter that continued to echo in his mind.

Aaron and his family enjoyed a brief time of reunion and fellowship in the open air outside the exit of the escape tunnel. They had only the clothes on their backs, a few blankets, and some dried food, but they acted as though they were the wealthiest people on the planet. And in a way, they were. They were alive, well, and together, after three-and-a-half years of hell on earth. Papa Saul's presence was sorely missed, but they all knew he was now in his glorified body, and they all took comfort in knowing that he was young and strong and busy serving his Lord somewhere.

Aaron explained that he had been told to transport his family to Dodger Stadium where instructions would be given to the surviving saints who would be assembled there. They needed to leave right away if they were going to get there in time to greet the others who would soon be arriving.

He bent and picked Millie up in his strong arms and began carrying him in the direction of the highway off to the north. The rest of the family joined in behind him, and the surviving members of the Frieberg family took their first steps in their long journey home.

On reaching the pavement, Aaron spotted the three armored personnel carriers, parked beside the road about a hundred yards away.

"Those must be the vehicles the soldiers came in who attacked you last night," he said, "and unless I miss my guess, Tony D'Angelo was behind it. But I doubt if he got caught in the cave in. He's much too big a coward to have risked going in there. He's probably still out there somewhere, but he's been defeated, and he'll be too busy trying to cover his own backside to pose any danger for us. Let's see if we can get one of these babies started."

The first vehicle had taken a direct hit in the engine from a giant hailstone and was rendered inoperable, but the second one fired right up after Aaron hotwired it. He asked Anna to ride up front with him and he carefully put Millie in between them. The big dog was improving rapidly. The bullet had gone clean through without hitting a bone or a major blood vessel, and the wound had already closed and was healing nicely. In a few days he should be almost as good as new.

The remainder of the family took their places in the back, and Aaron drove the heavy vehicle carefully down the steep mountain grade. Their progress was slow because of all the devastation caused by the events of the previous night, but the truck had plenty of power and four-wheel-drive, so they eventually reached what remained of civilization.

There, their progress slowed even more noticeably because of all the disabled vehicles and debris in the roads, but they continued on their course. By two in the afternoon, they climbed the hill above Interstate Five, just north of downtown Los Angeles, and into Chavez Ravine, the location of the famed Dodger Stadium, which had been divinely protected from any earthquake or hail damage.

Others had arrived before them and the stadium had already begun to fill. Aaron parked their vehicle next to the ticket booths on the east side of the stadium, and he and his passengers got out and made their way through the gates, leaving Millie to rest inside and to discourage anyone who might want to borrow their means of transportation.

Once inside the stadium, Aaron led his family to the infield, near the pitcher's mound. There, they sat down and watched and waited. By four o'clock the place was packed. More than 100,000 people were jammed into the stadium that was designed to seat about half that many. Every seat was taken, and people spilled over into all the aisles and flooded the entire playing field. The only spot left unoccupied was the pitcher's mound, and that wasn't vacant for long.

Suddenly, a hush fell over the massive, happy crowd, and two figures appeared, apparently out of nowhere, at the rubber on the pitcher's mound. Instantly Aaron recognized them as Scott Graham and Candace Mercer. They were wearing white robes and had glorified bodies, but they were unmistakable. Scott spotted Aaron, who was standing right in front of him, and they smiled at each other in mutual recognition and appreciation, but there was no time for a reunion. The Master's business had to be attended to.

Scott opened his mouth and spoke distinctly, but he did not shout. Amazingly, his voice carried throughout the stadium, and he was heard clearly by every person there.

"Beloved of the King," he proclaimed, "I bring you greetings from the Lord Jesus Christ and all the glorified saints of God. Our Savior has returned, the enemy has been vanquished, and the saints have been raised. The horrible tribulation is over, and the glorious millennium is about to begin."

On hearing that, the entire stadium erupted into a celebration so enthusiastic and loud that it could be heard miles away. It would have gone on indefinitely, had not Scott raised his hand after about thirty seconds and called for silence. Abruptly the shouting and clapping ceased and quiet was restored.

Candi spoke and said, "Dear ones, we have instructions from our Lord in Jerusalem. You who are sons and daughters of Jacob are called home to Israel. You are to make your way to the Los Angeles Harbor at San Pedro and board ships waiting to take you to the Holy Land. Take whatever clothing, supplies, and treasures you may desire from the vacant stores you will pass on your journey to the docks. Our Lord has willed it that you should spoil the heathen even as they have spoiled you. You shall enter into your Promised Land with great abundance.[82] But make no provision for what you shall eat, for the Lord will supply all the food you will need on your voyage."

Scott continued, "You, our Gentile brothers and sisters, are instructed to leave this cursed city and make your way northeast to the Antelope Valley and northwest to the San Joaquin Valley. There you will till the land and operate small businesses in the towns and small cities there.

---

[82] Now the children of Israel had done according to the word of Moses, and they had asked from the Egyptians articles of silver, articles of gold, and clothing. And the Lord had given the people favor in the sight of the Egyptians, so that they granted them what they requested. Thus they plundered the Egyptians (Exodus 12:35–36).

The Lord will bring abundant rain and the land will bring forth plentifully. You will live in peace and harmony, and you will enjoy the bounty of our Lord.

"To demonstrate our Lord's power and love, He has prepared a feast for you even now. At all the concession stands, and at all the exits, meals are waiting for you, my friends. As you leave, take as much as you can eat, and as much as you can carry with you."

"And do not be afraid as you leave," Candi concluded. "Even in the dark, the saints and angels will watch over you, and no ill will befall you. Go in peace, and God bless you, my brothers and sisters in Christ."

Then, just as abruptly as they had appeared, Scott and Candi vanished from their sight. The huge congregation was spellbound for a moment, and then erupted in a thunderous roar of approval. The saints rose to their feet and stomped and cheered for several minutes. It had been a long time since they had experienced much to cheer about, and they were determined to enjoy every second of it.

Finally, they began to find their way to the exits. They were hungry and thirsty, but there was no pushing or shoving. It took over two hours for everyone to be fed and supplied, but the task was accomplished without incident. Glorified saints served up hundreds of thousands of meat-filled rolls and plastic bottles of purified water. Where it all came from was a mystery, but no one was incredulous. They considered it a small feat for the One who changed the water to wine, and fed the multitude with a few loaves and fishes. They consumed all they desired, and filled their backpacks with as much as they could conveniently carry. Then they set out for their destinations: the Jewish believers toward the harbor to the south, and the Gentile saints toward the rich farmlands to the north.

On their way to the parking lot, Aaron and his family met up with Derek Uptain and those he was leading, and the two of them had an emotional reunion and farewell. Derek was amazed and delighted to see his mentor and friend alive and well, and was pleased to finally meet the members of the family about whom he had spoken so often. Aaron was also thankful that his young friend and assistant had indeed survived the tribulation, along with nearly all the members of his own *family* of misfits and fugitives.

Derek told Aaron he and his people were headed to the Bakersfield area, about a hundred miles to the north, on the other side of a mountainous region called the Grapevine. He had lived in Bakersfield for a few years while he was growing up, and he was looking forward to a more simple life there, away from the painful memories of life in the slums of Los Angeles.

Aaron led their combined group in prayer, thanking God for delivering all of them through the horrors of the tribulation, and asking for His blessing and direction in their lives in the future years of the coming kingdom. Before parting, he hugged Derek to his chest in a strong embrace, and then held him at arms length and said goodbye.

"So long, my ragged friend. We've been through a lot together these last several years, you and I. God bless you and your people, Derek, as you grow carrots and potatoes in Bakersfield. Find yourself a good wife and raise a big family, and be happy and prosper. And I'm sure, sometime in the next thousand years or so, we will meet again."

"You can count on it, Aaron. Even if I ain't Jewish, I'm plannin' on making a pilgrimage to Israel just as soon as I can. And I'll be sure to look you and your family up in your own little kibbutz there."

"Good, I'll be looking forward to it," Aaron said, releasing his friend and sending him and his people on their way. "May God bless and keep you until we meet again," he added, before he turned and led his family toward their waiting vehicle.

Upon arriving, Aaron loaded his family into the personnel carrier, and then filled the room that remained with as many of his countrymen as he could comfortably fit inside. With their vehicle thus fully loaded, they set out for the harbor. They would arrive long before the others, most of whom would be making the journey on foot, and Aaron was determined to use the time wisely. They would assist whoever was at the docks in making preparations for the others when they did arrive.

What happened in Los Angeles was repeated in similar fashion in major cities over the entire world. Believers who had survived the tribulation were assisted by God's glorified saints and His 144,000 to assemble in public places. There, they were encouraged, fed, and sent away to begin their lives in the Lord's coming millennium. The Gentiles were sent to the surrounding countryside, primarily to farm the soil, but also to perform various other necessary tasks. But no one was commissioned to run major corporations or huge conglomerates. Life in the kingdom was destined to be much simpler.

And in every city, the Jewish believers were called to return to Israel. Most of them had never been to their ancestral land, but their Lord called them home nonetheless. Those closest to Israel were instructed to make the journey overland, but most of them were sent to the nearest harbor to complete their journey by ship. They also were instructed to confiscate and take with them whatever items they might desire from the vacant stores they encountered along their way.

Within two weeks, every Jewish believer in the world was destined to take his spoil with him and establish his residence in the expanded land of Israel. Even so, their numbers were not staggering. No more than five million pilgrims would make the journey.

The Jewish population had been ravaged by the tribulation. Multitudes had been deceived by the antichrist and had taken his mark. They were lost forever. Multitudes more had rejected the mark, but they had perished in the devastations of that horrible three-and-a-half-year period. Those who were saved among them were now raised and glorified, but they would not be joining the ranks of the mortals who were privileged to return to their Promised Land. Only those who had lived through the entire tribulation, and were saved either before, or at the time of the Lord's return, would be returning home.

Coupled with the approximately one million Jewish saints who had survived the tribulation in Israel itself, there would be about six million Jews in Israel to begin the millennium. That was, more or less, the population of the nation prior to the rapture. However, that number now would represent the entire population of Jewish people living on planet earth. It wasn't many, but it was a start. They were destined to prosper and multiply during the fruitful thousand years that lay before them.

CHAPTER NINETEEN

The Home Coming

When Aaron Muller and his small congregation arrived at the docks in San Pedro, they discovered things were buzzing with activity. It was late in the day, but there was no sign of things beginning to slow down. Trucks were arriving continuously, and were being unloaded by what appeared to be thousands of happy laborers. The pallets, piled high with food and equipment, were offloaded from the trucks and then moved by forklifts to the staging areas where large cranes hoisted them onto the decks of the waiting ships.

Upon investigation, Aaron discovered the workers were none other than a large detachment of the glorified saints, assigned by the Lord to assist His people in their homeward journey. They were busy helping themselves to whatever treasures the Federation forces had left behind, and seeing to it that those things were transported to Israel to assist the Jewish emigrants in getting established there.

Along with vast amounts of food and other expected materials, Aaron saw other things being loaded onto the ships that amazed him. A large assortment of plants and trees that the Lord had protected from the devastation of the tribulation were being carefully taken aboard, as well as herds of various types of livestock. Cars and trucks and farm machinery were also being hoisted aboard. Aaron was nearly overwhelmed to see so much activity going on, and so much *stuff* being loaded onto the dozens of waiting ships.

He approached a nearby worker who was in the process of leading a Holstein milk cow toward a corral that had been constructed on the docks to see if there was anything he and his companions could do to help. When the man turned around and looked at him, Aaron was shocked to see that it was Carl Singleton. He just stood there for a moment, dumbfounded and unable to speak.

He had been in a Bible study with Carl and his wife Sarah back before the rapture, but all the believers had been transformed and taken to heaven, and he hadn't seen him in years. And so very much had happened since those days back in the conference room in the Antioch Baptist Church in Compton.

"Hi, Aaron," the big African-American saint called out happily, a broad smile creasing his handsome face, "we've been expecting you." He left the cow to fend for herself and hurried over and gave his bewildered friend a big hug. "And welcome, all of you," he said to those with Aaron, who were standing back and looking on quizzically.

"The Lord has called upon us super saints to sorta watch out for you mere mortals while you make your voyage back to your homeland. We got assigned to our old stompin' grounds; so here we are, longshoremen for the Lord, loadin' ships for the chosen people of Israel."

Then Carl turned and called to others who were working nearby, "Hey, you guys, Aaron and his family are here. Come, and say hello."

From the immediate area, Aaron gasped as he saw the familiar faces of friends he had not seen for three-and-a-half years. They stopped what they were doing and made their way to greet their newly arrived brother. First to approach was a big black man who stopped the forklift he was driving and hopped down and opened his arms wide.

"See, I told you so, Aaron," chirped Marcus Davis, giving his friend a big hug. "I knew you was gonna be one of those 144,000 dudes, even if you didn't believe me back then. Now, look at you, all bearded up and battle scarred. You're a real hero, man. Everybody's been talkin' about all the cool things you've done."

"I'll say," agreed Jamal, Marcus' younger brother, who gave Aaron a hug of his own. "That night we got raptured, I could see you in the back seat of Dad's old car, signing up for duty. You've done well, my friend. We're all proud that a member of our old Bible study turned out to be the one who duked it out with the devil himself and lived to tell the tale."

"Well, well, well, just look at you," came the unmistakable voice of Georgia Davis. Aaron turned and embraced the beautiful black woman who had come up behind him; she appeared to be in her mid-thirties. "I knew taking that bullet for you back in The Corner Store was the right thing to do, but I had no idea who you was, and who you was gonna become. My lands, boy, you've not only become a hero, you've done made one outta me too." Then she laughed that wonderful laugh of hers that filled all those gathered around with pure delight.

Suddenly, Aaron and his family were surrounded by all the believers he had known and studied with before the rapture. Pastor Bobby Davis was there, hugging and congratulating his former student; Scott Graham and Candi Mercer enthusiastically welcomed their friend with open arms, and Sarah Singleton joined Carl and introduced their two grown daughters to him.

"Wow!" gasped Aaron. "I remember Tamika, but she was just a little girl. And I don't even remember you having another child."

"Silly, of course you do!" laughed Sarah. "I was so big and pregnant I could hardly sit at that table in Pastor Bobby's conference room. Well, Grace joined us at the rapture, all grown up and beautiful, as you can plainly see."

"I remember how awkward you were back then, young lady," said Saul Frieberg, who had quietly joined the group. "I think it was one of your pregnant cravings that sent Carl out to my store that rainy night so long ago."

"Papa Saul!" shouted Aaron as he threw his arms around the handsome man who had been his elderly grandfather before the rapture. "I can't believe it's you. You look so young and strong and handsome. Getting yourself killed and resurrected is the best thing you ever did."

"Watch yourself, young man," Saul teased. "You may be one of the famed 144,000 and all, but in this supercharged body I've got now, I could turn you over my knee and give you a good whipping if I had a mind to."

Aaron laughed and hugged him again. He was nearly overcome with wonder and joy, but he did recover enough to think to introduce his family to all the glorified saints he had known before the rapture, and who had helped mold and prepare him for what then lay ahead for him. There was an enthusiastic and joyful celebration that attracted the pleased attention of other glorified saints who were passing by.

"What are you all doing here," Aaron asked Pastor Bobby, still naturally looking to him for answers to his questions, "and why are all these other people loading all that stuff onto those ships?"

"Well, son, as you already know, the Lord is calling all the Jewish people back to the Holy Land, and He doesn't want you going home empty handed. That place has really been torn up over the past several years, but He has plans to turn it into a paradise. And He's sending you home with everything you'll need to turn it into one."

"Yeah, that makes sense," Aaron agreed. "And I imagine the same thing is happening in other cities all over the world, right?"

"You got it, my young friend. The world hasn't seen anything like this since Moses led the children of Israel into Canaan Land, loaded down with the treasures they took out of Egypt."

"But it must take millions of you glorified saints to get all this work done all over the world."

"Sure it does, but with a few billion of us, we've got millions to spare. Actually, only about a third of us are gathering supplies and helping the surviving saints like we're doing. Another third are busy rebuilding and repairing stuff that got destroyed in the tribulation. You know, things like roads, bridges, power plants, and such. They should have the Panama Canal up and running by the time your ship gets there in a few days. Then, the other third is busy confiscating all the guns, tanks, bombs, and stuff in the world, and either destroying them or melting them down to be made into useful vehicles and machinery. So you can see, we're all gonna be real busy for awhile."

"What about all the Gentile believers?" Aaron asked. "A bunch of them left on foot on a long walk to farm land to the north. They could get real tired and hungry and thirsty before they get there."

"Don't you worry your pretty little head about a thing, Aaron," Georgia said. "There's more of us helping them right now. They'll have plenty of food and water and blankets for their journey, and when they get there, they'll find everything they'll need to set up house and start farmin' the land. My Father takes care of all His children."

"Wow!" Aaron breathed. "And to think, we hurried down here to help get things loaded onto the ships. I don't think there's really much for any of us to do."

"You got that right," Marcus chirped. "Just you stand back and let the professionals do their jobs. We never get tired, hungry, or thirsty; and we never have to take a restroom break. Aaron, you just gotta try one of these glorified bodies. Personally, I wouldn't leave home without one."

That brought a laugh from everyone, and Bobby made an excuse for his son, explaining that he wasn't sure he had been completely glorified yet. That brought a playful scowl from Marcus and another laugh from everyone else.

"Seriously, Aaron" the preacher said, "there's nothing you need to do here. Why don't you take your people on a shopping spree so they can pick up some clothing, personal items, and maybe even some nice jewelry for the ladies? It's been a long time since any of you had anything new. I'll personally take that dog of yours and get him settled into one of your rooms. Go ahead, have a good time."

That suggestion met with universal approval. So Pastor Bobby took Millie aboard the ship, the rest of the glorified saints went back to their work, and the mortal saints got back in their big vehicle and drove into what was left of Long Beach. There, they took whatever they needed from the demolished and deserted stores that lined the congested streets, strewn with battered and abandoned vehicles.

The city was abandoned. The believers who had survived the tribulation had all either migrated north, or were on their way to the ships in the harbor. The unbelievers who survived had gathered together in little huddles and were in the process of making their way to the downtown area of Los Angeles. The news had spread that there was food and protection there.

Later that evening, Aaron and those with him were all comfortably aboard the *Coral Queen*, a former cruise ship that, before the tribulation, had escorted vacationers in luxury from the Los Angeles area to and from the resorts along the western coastline of Mexico. They had been shown to their staterooms, where they were able to take showers and change into the first new clothes they had worn in over three-and-a-half years.

Joseph and Miriam Muller had their own room, as did Albert and Nora Frieberg. Anna Berger shared a room with Rachel Muller, and Aaron bunked in with Tim and Steve. After their showers, the three young men took turns cutting each other's hair and trimming one another's beards. It wasn't perfect, but their appearance was light years ahead of what it had been just a few hours earlier.

That night, their dinner was prepared and served by some of the glorified saints. This would be their last contribution in Los Angeles to the Jewish pilgrims before they began their long journey home. After the rest of their people arrived from Dodger Stadium, and they got under way in the morning, they would be on their own. Various members of their own numbers would be assigned the necessary tasks to facilitate a pleasant voyage to Israel.

But that night was special . . . unbelievably special. Formerly beleaguered saints were scrubbed and groomed and clothed in fine apparel. They sat around tables bedecked with linen, china, silver, and crystal; they were served by glorified saints in shimmering white robes; and the food . . . the food was fabulous. After most of them had eaten little else besides bits and scraps of scavenged food for years, they could scarcely believe their eyes . . . or their taste buds.

They ate steak and broiled salmon, steamed vegetables, mashed potatoes and gravy, and freshly baked rolls. And for dessert, they indulged themselves in rich chocolate and delicacies they had long since forgotten existed on the planet. It was like a dream come true. No one was in a hurry to finish. Each person wanted to savor every sight and sound, and every aroma, texture, and taste. They lingered for a long time around the tables, talking, laughing, reminiscing; but most of all, praising God for His wonderful protection and provision.

After others had finally retired for the night, Aaron and Anna continued to sit at their table. Aaron looked especially handsome, neatly trimmed and groomed and in his new clothes. And Anna was simply ravishing in every way. They talked of many things, but most especially, they talked of marriage. They had been in love for years, but they had not heretofore been able to pursue it, or even to really consider it. Aaron had been a member of God's chosen 144,000, and he had been afforded precious little time or energy to pursue anything other than the Lord's immediate directives. But he had now fulfilled his high and holy calling, and had been released. He was finally free to follow his dreams.

They held hands and spoke of marriage plans in Israel after the transition period was over and the millennium had fully begun. It would be a matter of a few months at most, but it seemed like forever to them. They had waited for so long already, they were not excited about waiting any longer.

As they lingered, Scott Graham and Candace Mercer approached their table and asked if they might join them.

"Absolutely!" Aaron exclaimed, standing to his feet and pushing back the chair next to him. "I was hoping we would have a chance to talk with you two before we got underway in the morning."

Scott didn't bother assisting Candi as they took their seats. In their glorified state, there was no difference between the status of male and female, and acts of chivalry were neither expected nor performed. In their identical white robes, there was not that great a difference between them, even in appearance.

Aaron introduced them to Anna, and they all exchanged a few pleasantries before Scott came to his point.

"Candi and I want to express our appreciation and admiration to you, Aaron, for all you did for our Lord and His people during the tribulation period."

"Thank you," Aaron replied, "but it is I who should be thanking you. If it hadn't been for your encouragement and support during that Bible study back in Pastor Bobby's church, I probably never would have stuck it out. And, Scott, I'm sure witnessing your conversion just before the rapture helped prepare me for my own decision when it did take place a couple of days later."

"You don't need to be thanking us," Scott said. "It was the Lord who was at work in all our hearts to bring us to Himself at His own appointed time. Now that we have been with Him personally for a time, we have come to realize even more how He is in control of absolutely everything that takes place. He had us all chosen from the beginning of the world, and He simply called us to Himself at different times, through different means."[83]

"Yes, I'm sure that's true, but it's a little harder for us to see it because we haven't been glorified yet and our minds haven't been totally enlightened like yours have."

"That reminds me of something I've been wondering about," interjected Anna. "Aaron has told me how much in love you two were before the rapture took place, and how you were looking forward to getting married and raising a family together. I know how you must have felt because Aaron and I are feeling that same way right now. But all your dreams were canceled at the rapture, and now you'll never be together as husband and wife. Don't you feel cheated somehow, or at least disappointed?"

Candi laughed and said, "That's exactly how we would have felt had God not changed us so radically at the time of the rapture. But the things that were so important to us before suddenly lost interest for us after the rapture, and the things we couldn't even imagine back then have be-

---

[83] Just as He chose us in Him before the foundation of the world, that we should be holy and without blame before Him in love, having predestined us to adoption as sons by Jesus Christ to Himself, according to the good pleasure of His will (Ephesians 1:4–5).

But when it pleased God, who separated me from my mother's womb and called me through His grace, to reveal His Son in me, that I might preach Him among the Gentiles . . . (Galatians 1:15–16).

come our whole lives. Now I have much better things to do than wonder what people might think of my married name: 'Mrs. Candygram'."

That brought a laugh from everyone, and any discomfort Aaron and Anna may have felt at being in an intimate conversation with glorified saints melted away.

"But, seriously," she continued, "it's impossible for us to try to explain it to you; you'll just have to experience it for yourselves. So enjoy your present lives together to the fullest. Drink deeply from the streams of love and romance, marry and raise a large family, but remember one thing: the best is yet to come!"[84]

"Amen!" Scott agreed. "Candi and I are even more in love with each other now than we were back then, but not in the same way. Our love is deeper, fuller, and richer now than ever before. God is so good! He never takes anything away from you that He doesn't replace with something even better. So don't feel sorry for us. We did get to get married after all . . . we're married to Christ, and we're still on our honeymoon. And it's been great!

"Which reminds me," he continued, changing the subject, "we need to be getting back to our Bridegroom right now. He has much for us to do to get ready for the glorious kingdom He has planned for all of us. We just stopped to say goodbye for now. But I'm sure we'll be seeing each other a lot in the future in the Holy Land."

Then suddenly, without warning, Scott and Candi simply vanished. One instant, they were sitting at the table with Aaron and Anna; and the next, they were gone.[85]

Anna gasped in disbelief, but Aaron, having become somewhat accustomed to the Lord's unconventional means of transportation, assured her that everything was okay, and that it was just God's special way of moving Himself and His people from place to place whenever there was an immediate need to do so.

"Well, why doesn't He just zap us all over to Israel like them?" she wanted to know. "It would be a whole lot faster and easier than having us sail all the way over there on this ship."

---

[84] When I was a child, I spoke as a child, I understood as a child, I thought as a child; but when I became a man I put away childish things. For now we see in a mirror, dimly, but then face to face. Now I know in part, but then I shall know just as I also am known (1 Corinthians 13:11–12).

[85] Now it came to pass, as He sat at the table with them, that He took bread, blessed and broke it, and gave it to them. Then their eyes were opened and they knew Him; and He vanished from their sight (Luke 24:30–31).

"I learned a long time ago," Aaron replied, "that God expects us to do for ourselves whatever we are capable of doing; He only steps in and does for us the things that we cannot do, or that which He wants done immediately. We don't have the antichrist and his crowd after us anymore, and we are perfectly capable of getting to Israel on this ship without any divine assistance, so He isn't going to transport us over there supernaturally just because it would be more convenient and efficient.

"Besides," he continued, taking her hand in his, "I'm looking forward to spending the next week or so courting you on the *Love Boat*, with no emergencies to meet, and no bad guys to fight."

"Yes," she agreed, snuggling up to him, "that will be rather nice, after all."

By the next day, all the returning Jews had arrived at the docks, and the four ships were able to get underway. Those with nautical experience manned the control towers and the engine rooms, and the other responsibilities were delegated out to the remainder of those on board. Again, Aaron was selected by his shipmates to lead and direct in those matters. So, with the help of his family, he assigned everyone a responsibility, and established the schedule so each person had a four-hour shift each day. Everyone was given a job to do, but no one was overworked, and each happy saint could look forward to plenty of free time to enjoy the pleasant journey home.

What took place at the Los Angeles Harbor was duplicated at similar facilities all over the world. Thousands of ships of various descriptions were loaded with emancipated Jews, anxious to return to their ancestral homeland, a place most of them had never visited before.

Some of the vessels had to wait a longer period of time for all their passengers to arrive, but within a few days, all the ships were steaming their way toward the tiny nation of Israel.

The Lord could certainly have arranged for many of them to fly directly to Israel on commercial airplanes, but He was in no hurry to get them there. His people needed time to rest and recover on their ocean voyages, and He needed time for His saints and angels to prepare for their arrival.

Nearer the Holy Land itself, returning Jews were making their exodus overland. They boarded trains, busses, trucks, automobiles, and even horse-drawn wagons. By whatever means available, scores of thousands of delivered Jews began making their way from Southeastern Europe, Northeastern Africa, and Western Asia. God's glorified saints assisted them on their journey as they wound their way over mountains, across rivers, and through valleys and deserts. They would all arrive within the two-week timeframe their returned Lord had established.

Furthermore, the returning Jews were not coming home empty-handed. Along with their families and personal possessions, they brought with them vast resources of all sorts. Ships and trains were loaded with livestock, potted plants, and bags of seed grain. Building supplies and industrial equipment were also loaded on in abundance. Vehicles, furniture, household items, clothing, office equipment, and countless other commodities also found their way into the bellies of the massive armada steaming its way to Israel from all over the world. In addition to that, incredible treasures of gold, silver, and precious stones were carefully loaded onboard. The greater part of the remaining wealth of the world was being systematically transferred to the ravaged land of Israel on the eastern shores of the Mediterranean Sea.

By the third day, the first ships started arriving, and from then on, the ports at Haifa, Tel Aviv, and Elat were bustling with activity around the clock. Millions of people, and even greater numbers of plants and animals, were being offloaded, not to mention the other vast resources stowed in the cargo areas. Cranes and forklifts were operated non-stop as crews took turns at the controls. Much work was being done, but no one complained. Those good people, along with their homeland itself, had gone through three-and-a-half years of hell on earth, and they were overjoyed to be allowed to participate in the arduous efforts necessary to bring about the rebirth of their nation.

Thankfully, they did not have to labor unassisted. God's glorified saints went before them, destroying weapons of war; restoring devastated roads, bridges, and buildings throughout the land; and revitalizing the pulverized temple mount. The temple area was first cleared of all rubble and debris; and then the courtyard, walls, and eastern gate were rebuilt in splendid fashion. Finally, the largest and most glorious temple ever constructed was being erected at the exact site where the three previous temples had stood.[86] The returning saints would not see a war torn land, emaciated by the tribulation. Rather, they would enter an emerging paradise, prepared for their families and their farms, their machinery and their merchandise, and for their edification and enjoyment. Indeed, the Lord's kingdom could not be far away.

---

[86] Ezekiel, chapters 40–42

Mark Robertson and Rico Sandia had found the Humvee right where David Rosen and Joseph Roth had said it would be. They had loaded two heavy coils of rope into its back seat, and had driven it down good roads, already restored by the Lord's glorified saints, and made their way to the desert fortress of Masada, towering above the western shore of the Dead Sea.

It was the second day after the Lord's return, and the day was breathtaking. The sun had risen through dissipating clouds that had watered the land with a soothing rain during the night; the air was pristine, no longer choked with acrid smoke and the stench of decaying flesh. There was a wonderful quietness that lay across the Judean hills, uninterrupted by the sounds of rattling tanks and exploding bombs. The songs of birds and the buzzing of insects were the only things the two young men heard when they turned off the engine and stepped out of the Humvee at Masada's parking area.

The glorified saints had not yet done any rebuilding in the area, and the signs of devastation were everywhere. The remains of the tourist center, the cable car system, and the tour bus lay strewn about the desert floor. In addition, there appeared to be hundreds of huge craters where artillery shells and aircraft missiles had impacted around the perimeter of the mountain itself. But the flat-topped mesa itself appeared to be intact. Perhaps it had indeed escaped the ravages of the past three-and-a-half years of warfare.

Rico shouted with all the volume he could muster, and his voice echoed back from the sheer walls of the bluffs before him. But before the sound of his own voice had completely dissipated, a similar greeting echoed back from the top of the mountain.

They glanced upward and saw several figures looking down at them from the top of the bluffs, and their numbers were increasing with every passing second. Soon the whole rim was bedecked with happy people, shouting greetings down and waving enthusiastically from their lofty perch.

Thus encouraged, Mark and Rico began their brief, but challenging, climb up the side of the mesa. Carrying their ropes with them, they picked their way carefully up the old snake path and over the rim of the bluff. After forty minutes of arduous climbing, they arrived, sweaty and winded, but filled with excitement and anticipation.

They were practically mobbed by the enthusiastic residents of the mountain hideaway. They were the first to visit the remote desert sanctuary in three-and-a-half years, and the people were eager to extend a hearty welcome. They were hugged, kissed, and pounded on the back by young and old alike; and then they were escorted to the main assembly area on the north side of the mountaintop.

There, ancient Zecharias, the high priest, threw his arms around them and wept for joy. The long ordeal of his people had at last come to an end. He pumped his two young guests with dozens of questions as hundreds of his expectant congregation crowded around them to hear the answers.

Mark and Rico answered as many as they could. The most important of them were: yes, the tribulation was finally over; yes, the Lord Jesus had indeed returned; and yes, they had been sent to lead the Masada saints back to their homes. Their answers were greeted with exuberant cheers and praises to the Lord.

The two informed David's family that Constantine Augustus had killed both David and Joseph, but that the Lord had gloriously raised them back to life. They had actually been the ones to take the defeated beast and his false prophet and cast them into hell. Mark assured them that they would be waiting to greet them when they got to Jerusalem.

That answer seemed to raise a question shared among all the mountaintop dwellers: "What are we doing, standing around on top of this mesa in the wilderness when we could be going home?"

At Zecharias' instruction, over twelve hundred people scurried excitedly back to their respective dwelling places to gather together what meager possessions they intended to take with them. As they did, Rico and Mark looked around in amazement at how good everything appeared.

The fields atop the mesa were green and teeming with a wide variety of vegetables, the structures appeared sturdy and the tarps were still intact, the people were healthy and robust, and even their clothing and shoes showed little sign of wear.[87] God had indeed preserved and protected His people during those long years of war and devastation.

Thirty minutes later, Mark and Rico were assisting the eager pilgrims as they made their slow descent off Masada's steep bluffs. The two long ropes made it possible for them to help the people down the abrupt drop-off at the rim, and then they were able to carefully descend the winding snake path unassisted.

---

[87] "And I have led you forty years in the wilderness. Your clothes have not worn out on you, and your sandals have not worn out on your feet." (Deuteronomy 29:5).

It took them several hours, but by mid-afternoon, the entire congregation was assembled in the parking area, southeast of the towering plateau that had been their home for the past several years. As they turned to follow their two young guides on their long walk home, none looked back longingly. They were indeed grateful that their God had provided a sanctuary for them at Masada while the rest of the world was being devastated by the wars and plagues of the tribulation, but now they were anxious to leave its narrow confines and finally return to their real homes.

It would take them nearly three days to make the journey, but no one complained. They carried plenty of food with them, abundant water could be found in pools along their way, the full moon would give them light at night, and they were all strong and healthy. And most importantly, they had plenty of time, and no evil men were pursuing to do them harm. Their Messiah had returned, His kingdom was about to begin, and they were anxious to get home and dwell under His glorious administration.

Not all of the earth dwellers were as ecstatic about the coming of the Lord and his rapidly approaching kingdom as were the Jewish saints who were returning to their ancestral homeland. Unsaved survivors of the tribulation crawled out from their hiding places with no place to go and nothing meaningful to do. Their lives had been spared, but the world, as they had known it, had disappeared. Jesus Christ had destroyed Constantine Augustus and his World Federation of Nations, and indeed, the newly arrived Prince of Israel had dissolved all other national governments as well.

Tony D'Angelo huddled with a growing congregation of dissidents in the devastated downtown area of Los Angeles. He still wore the dirty uniform of a Federation colonel, but he had no army to command. Instead, he found himself in charge of a defenseless rabble that had been drifting in over the past two days. They would all be sitting ducks if the followers of the Lord sought to retaliate against them; they had no weapons, or any other way of defending themselves. However, their enemies seemed to be busy with other things, and were content to ignore them for the present time.

They had food reserves, and were in no immediate danger, so they were content, for the time being, to simply wait and watch to see what was going to happen. Tony was a survivor. He tried to convince himself that he would somehow find a way to weather this present storm, and emerge on top of things once again. But, at the moment, he did not have a clue what that way might be.

CHAPTER TWENTY

The Jericho Road

The Lord's return took place during the third week in August, in the middle of the Jewish month of Av. Fifteen days later would mark the beginning of the month of Tishri, the first month in the traditional Jewish year. The reigning Christ set aside Rosh Hashanah, the Jewish New Year's Day, as a national day of celebration for all His regathered people. By that time all of them would have arrived from other parts of the world, and would be busy setting up their homes, farms, and businesses.

Those fifteen days were passing quickly. Ships, trains, and trucks continued to arrive daily, and were relieved of their precious cargos of returning Jews and their spoils of war. Glorified saints met all the new arrivals at the docks and informed them of the Jewish tribe to which they belonged, and which geographical section of the land was available to them. For just as the land had been divided among the twelve tribes of Israel after Joshua had led them to conquer it following their exodus from Egypt,[88] so the Lord chose to divide the land among His people returning home after the tribulation.

After a wonderful ten-day voyage from the west coast of America, Aaron Muller and his family arrived in Tel Aviv a few days before the big celebration scheduled for Rosh Hashanah. They were greeted by Papa Saul Frieberg, who was delighted to see them. He confirmed what Aaron

[88] Joshua, chapters 14–20

had already told his family: they were of the tribe of Benjamin, and that the historical territory occupied by their tribe was located to the east and north of Jerusalem.

After conferring among themselves for a few minutes, they agreed with Aaron's suggestion that they make their home in the area of Jericho. It was located at the southern end of the Jordan Valley, not far from the north end of the Dead Sea. It had rich soil and plenty of water and a long growing season, and it was only a little more than twenty miles east of Jerusalem. It seemed like an ideal location for their new farming operation.

They had spent the past three-and-a-half years hunting and farming and living off the land, and they had grown fond of its simple challenges and pleasures. They were given the use of two trucks to transport what they would need to set started.

Into the first one, a large moving van, they loaded the things they had chosen from huge supplies stored in warehouses: furniture, food, household items, clothing, and a wide assortment of potted plants and seedling trees. Into the other one, a flatbed with stock racks, they loaded the livestock they had selected from large corrals and holding pens: horses, cattle, sheep, goats, and crates of chickens. They weren't at all sure where they would put everything when they got to Jericho, but they were confident that the Lord would provide quite nicely for them.

What really amazed them was that Millie, now fully recovered from his gunshot wound, showed no hostility toward any of the other animals. He had been trained to stalk and kill such creatures, and he had done so with deadly precision. But now he simply sat passively on his haunches and watched the animals being loaded onto the truck. The coming of the Lord had definitely changed his behavior toward what had formerly been his prey.[89]

Papa Saul assisted them until they had everything loaded, and then gave them all a hug and returned to greet the next family assigned to him, which had just walked down the gangplank of a newly arrived ship.

---

[89] "The wolf also shall dwell with the lamb, the leopard shall lie down with the young goat, the calf and the young lion and the fatling together; and a little child shall lead them. The cow and the bear shall graze; their young ones shall lie down together; and the lion shall eat straw like the ox. . . . They shall not hurt nor destroy in all My holy mountain." (Isaiah 11:6–9).

Aaron informed his family that he would be driving the livestock truck, and he asked Anna to join him and his parents in the cab. It would make for a tight fit, but they could manage. In fact, he rather looked forward to having her sitting that close to him for the fifty-plus miles of their journey.

He asked his uncle Albert to drive the other truck, to be accompanied in the cab by his wife Nora and Aaron's sister Rachel. Tim and Steve volunteered to ride in the back with Millie to help keep things from falling over and breaking. Soon, they were all loaded up, and the little caravan began its journey eastward and upward.

As they wound their way up the slopes leading from the coastal plains to the mountaintops around Jerusalem, Aaron couldn't help but remember a similar trip they had taken some three-and-a-half years before. At the very beginning of the tribulation, he had led a similar caravan up the Angeles Crest Highway, into the San Gabriel Mountains, overlooking the Los Angeles Basin below. Then, they had been fleeing for their lives, trying to escape the wrath of the devil's antichrist, which was soon to be unleashed upon the world. But that was then, and this was now.

Now, they were delivered from any threat from the deposed and destroyed antichrist, they were at home in their ancestral land, and they were on their way to the inheritance God had prepared for them. Instead of being filled with thoughts of uncertainty and apprehension, they were rejoicing with hearts full of gratitude and keen anticipation.

Aaron drove into the northern outskirts of Jerusalem, approaching the walled Old City. Before he turned left and connected to the rebuilt road that would take them down the mountain eastward to Jericho in the Jordan Valley below, he pulled over to the side of the road and stopped his truck. Albert pulled his vehicle in behind him.

Aaron jumped out and called for the rest of his family to follow. They readily complied, and soon Aaron was leading them on a short walk up to the top of the hill overlooking the bustling city behind it. None of them had been to Jerusalem before, and they were awestruck by its size and present condition.

The effects of the devastating battles that had taken place there during the recent tribulation had virtually disappeared. The multitudes of glorified saints, who never grew tired or hungry, had worked feverishly to remove the debris left behind by enemy attacks from without, and from divinely administered plagues from above. At the same time, other saints were busy rebuilding and restoring the city to a state that far exceeded any glory it had ever known in its long and troubled history.

The newly arrived pilgrims stood in awe, overlooking the city that might have been called Phoenix had it been in need of a new name. For indeed, it was rising from its own ashes like the legendary Phoenix Bird, and was in the process of emerging into the glorious thing God had long promised it to be. Its streets and buildings were being restored to a condition far superior to their former state, and parks and promenades were being added that had never existed before. A huge stadium was being built in the valley north of Jerusalem, and the once-demolished temple mount was nearing complete restoration. Its walls were already rebuilt and its eastern gate was restored and open for the first time in a thousand years. But the thing that really fascinated the onlookers was the emerging temple itself.

In the center of the mount, stood the most magnificent building any of them had ever seen. Though not yet fully completed, the millennial temple dominated the entire eastern sector of the city. It was far bigger and far more glorious than any of the other three temples that had occupied that holy ground before it. The hated Dome of the Rock was gone and the new temple shared the top of the mountain with no other structure. Soon it would be completed and dedicated, and the living Messiah would rule and reign from its throne for the next thousand years.

Aaron's family was fascinated and could have stayed there for hours, watching the emerging city taking form before their very eyes, but Aaron knew they would have plenty of opportunities to observe and explore the Holy City in the future. Right then, they needed to locate their new homes and get somewhat settled in before darkness fell. He escorted his reluctant charges back down the hill and into their respective vehicles to resume their eastern trek.

Forty minutes later, they were at the outskirts of the city of Jericho, which itself had been nearly completely restored from the devastation it too had suffered during the past tribulation period. Aaron pulled his truck to a stop in front of a checkpoint and was greeted by a smiling attendant who looked vaguely familiar.

"Greetings, friends, welcome to New Jericho," he said warmly. "How may I assist you?"

Aaron replied, "We're the Frieberg and Muller families from the Los Angeles area. We're from the tribe of Benjamin, and we would like to settle in Jericho, if that's okay with you."

"Absolutely! We've been expecting you. Here, let me check my list. Yes, indeed, here you are right at the top. Let's see . . . nine people . . . three homes required, right?"

"Yes, there are nine of us," Aaron replied, "but we really only need two houses at the present time."

"But won't you be needing another one to fix up for when you and Miss Anna get married?"

"How did you know about that?" Aaron asked incredulously. "We haven't even formally announced it to anyone!"

"Oh, you would be surprised how much we know about you. As the leader of the 144,000, you're a national hero. We've been looking forward to your arrival ever since the reconstruction began. You probably don't remember me, but I sure remember you."

"You do look familiar, but I've been struggling with trying to remember where we met before."

"I'm Doran Stuben. I was one of the soldiers who joined with the refugees you helped lead up to the top of Masada back at the beginning of the tribulation. I'll never forget watching you standing on that wall, shooting lightning bolts out of the end of that rod of yours and knocking down the enemy's planes and guns."

"Of course! Now I remember. You and Levi were of great help to us in getting all those people settled on top of that mountain."

"Do you still have that rod?" Doran wanted to know.

"Sure do; it's in the back of the truck right now. It don't think it has any lightning bolts left in it anymore, but it's like an old friend; I'll hang on to it forever. But what have you been doing, and what brings you here?"

"I stayed at Masada throughout the tribulation, and God blessed me so much. I met one of David Rosen's sisters, and we got married nearly two years ago. We have a one-year-old baby now, and we're expecting another one early next spring.

"After the Lord finally came back and destroyed all our enemies, Mark and Rico came to Masada and led us all back to Jerusalem. There, I found out that I was from the tribe of Benjamin, so Elizabeth and I decided to make our home here in Jericho. We moved in last week, and since then, I've been helping new arrivals like you get settled."

"Praise the Lord! That is so cool!" Aaron practically shouted, giving Doran a big hug "Come here, I want you to meet my family."

Aaron had those with him get out of the trucks and he proudly introduced them all to Doran. There was an enthusiastic display of immediate love and acceptance all around. The young Jewish soldier and his family were destined to become some of their dearest friends.

"I was told a lot about you and that you would be coming soon, so I took the liberty of picking out some places for you to look at near where we live," Doran said as he noticed some more vehicles coming down the road toward them. "I have to get back to work here, but you can go on down and check them out. Stay on this road, past the city, take the third road to the left, and follow it to the end. You can't miss it. I'm confident you will like the houses and farmland. The only drawback is you may have some trouble with your other neighbors."

"What do you mean?" Aaron asked as he and his family began returning to their vehicles.

"Oh, you'll see," Doran said with a wave and a smile as he turned to greet those in the vehicles who were braking to a stop behind him.

A bit puzzled, but filled with eager excitement, Aaron got everyone back in the trucks and drove off, following the directions Doran had given him. Albert was right behind him as he turned at the designated intersection, and both vehicles headed north on a graveled road toward the properties his new friend had told him about.

It was the last day of August, and it should have been hot and dry in the Jordan Valley, nearly a thousand feet below sea level, but Aaron noticed that the air was only pleasantly warm, and the ground was moist from a recent rain. Many of the fields they passed on their way had been recently planted, and were already bursting forth with shoots of new grain. Things had certainly changed since the Lord had returned, and Aaron was eager to take full advantage of the wonderful opportunities that lay ahead for him and his loved ones. His hands trembled a little with anticipation as they steered the truck down the road toward a group of buildings he could see in the distance.

He had driven past Jericho on his left, and was well north of the city when he slowed his vehicle. They were approaching the end of the road, and what appeared to be a large estate spread out before them. Aaron identified three separate houses, along with several barns and other outbuildings. He drove beneath a beautiful arched gate and around a large circular driveway, pulling to a stop in front of the second of the three houses. It was the largest of the three structures, and it appeared to contain well over three thousand square feet of living space. It was at the top of the circle drive to the north, with another house on either side, one on the east, and the other on the west.

The entire property had been restored and prepared for its new occupants. The flat-roofed houses were sturdy, and showed no signs of having been through three-and-a-half years of violent warfare and devastating plagues. The team of glorified saints that had restored the estate had not only repaired the buildings; they had also planted grass and flowers to add a special atmosphere of beauty and hospitality.

The occupants of the two trucks got out eagerly and gazed in wonder at their new surroundings. It was hard for them to imagine that they were looking at their new homes. They had lived in similar houses before the tribulation, but that seemed like it was in an entirely different lifetime. Ever since the rapture had taken place, they had been homeless, existing wherever they could find a measure of comfort and security. For the past year-and-a-half, the rest of them had lived in a cave, and Aaron had possessed no place at all to call his home. Now, they were looking at large and beautiful houses that were groomed and vacant, just waiting for their arrival.

The family members walked around slowly and marveled at their new surroundings, but Millennium was not so restrained. The big dog was happy to be freed from the cramped confines of the back of the truck, and he expressed it by romping around, barking, and marking his territory on nearly every shrub on the estate.

Choosing to ignore Millie's antics, Aaron gathered his family around him, and they held hands in a circle as he led them in a prayer of heartfelt love and gratitude for everything their Lord had done for them in the past, and for all He had now provided for their glorious future. When Aaron said his amen, they all echoed his sentiments, and hugged one another for sheer joy.

There was simply no question as to who was in charge, and Aaron continued his leadership role by deciding which family would occupy each of the three houses. He directed Albert and Nora to take the house in front of them, since it was the largest. They would need room for the four in their family, and for Anna as their temporary guest. He directed his parents to the large home to the west of them. It was a little smaller, but it would do nicely for the four in the Muller family. Besides, he didn't plan to be living there for very long anyway. The smallest of the three homes, the one on the east side of the circle drive, was reserved for himself and his bride after they were married.

With that readily agreed upon, the families divided to inspect their new places of residence. They were overjoyed to discover that they were already partly furnished. The furniture and household utensils were not new or extravagant, but they proved to be exactly what was needed. What the family had been able to load into the van would not have begun to furnish three large houses such as these, but added to what was already there, they would apparently lack for nothing. They were all delighted with everything that had been provided for their use.

Aaron and Anna walked hand in hand through their new home. It was quite modern by Palestinian standards; the previous owners had doubtlessly been very wealthy. The house had three large bedrooms and an office. There were two full bathrooms, a large kitchen, a dining room, and a huge living room. Anna playfully said it would do for a start, but Aaron would need to start adding on a bedroom wing to accommodate the many children she planned to bear him.

Aaron hugged her tightly and kissed her. He had rarely dared to dream of a moment like this. The tribulation had been so horrible, and their very existence had been so precarious, the possibility of them sharing this kind of life together had seemed like a fairytale. Yet here they were at last. They lingered in their embrace, savoring every moment of it.

However, they knew there was much to be done. The men needed to unload the trucks, and the women needed to put things away and prepare their evening meal. So they went outside and called everyone over and Aaron gave out the appropriate assignments.

Aaron helped Joseph and Albert put the livestock in their proper corrals and pens. Millie assisted them in their efforts by keeping the animals in line, still showing no sign of aggressiveness toward any of them. When they were finished, Aaron assisted Tim and Steve who were offloading the other truck, and made sure that everything had been deposited correctly in the respective buildings. Joseph and Albert pitched in and helped their wives get things unpacked and properly put away.

Aaron was pleased to discover that a large outbuilding was filled with farming machinery. There were three tractors, two combines, two wagons, and a wide assortment of other necessary implements. In an adjoining building, he discovered pallets stacked high with sacks of seed grain. It appeared they had already been provided with everything they would need to begin their farming operation.

The three young men walked out to the east and looked over the flat fields that stretched before them, extending all the way to the Jordan River. They were barren at the moment, but the future farmers could envision them soon teeming with vibrant new growth.

After a wonderful meal was shared at Albert and Nora's home, and after the dishes were done, the entire family sat around their vast living room and talked about their past experiences, but mostly about their dreams for the future. The men were anxious to start working the ground and tending their livestock. The women were anxious to decorate their homes and plant their trees and shrubs. Aaron and Anna announced their plans to be married just as soon as the transition period was over and the millennium had officially begun.

Their announcement came as a surprise to no one. The only question anyone had was why they were going to wait so long. Aaron just laughed and told them there were still a lot of things that needed to be done before he and Anna would have time to get married and settle down. He didn't tell them the real reason. He didn't want to spoil what had been an absolutely fantastic day by telling them that there were still some dark and uncertain days that lay ahead before any of them could expect to enter into the uninterrupted blessedness of their Messiah's kingdom. Until that time arrived, he would not be free to invest his time and energy into his pursuit of marital bliss.

It was not late, but everyone was tired, and they knew they had a full day ahead of them that would start early in the morning. So they were about to retire to their respective rooms and get some much-needed sleep, when they heard a loud knock at the front door.

Aaron rose, a bit surprised, and went to the door. Out of habit, he picked up his rod and carried it along with him. He opened the door, and before he knew it, he was picked up in two strong arms, hugged to a broad chest, and turned around and around.

"Tharr ya arre, laddie. I've been waitin' farrr ya to get herre. Ya cun put duwn yerr rod if ya like. I'm na gunna do ya no harrm."

It was Ken Weinman, the big Scotsman who had been Aaron's good friend and fellow member of God's chosen 144,000. Aaron laughed and playfully punched him in the stomach as Ken set him back down on the front porch.

"Ken, it's great to see you too!" he exclaimed, leaning his rod against the side of the house. "But what are you doing here?"

"Ah, mon, do ya na remember? I'm of the tribe of Benjamin too. Me farrm is just duwn the rroad. We're gunna be neighbors, you und I."

"Of course I remember. And you're left-handed too. You're the one who taught me how to use the sling. Come on in and meet my family."

"Naa, it's late, und I best be gettin' on home. I'll be meetin' alla yer kin in the marnin'."

But Aaron would hear none of it. He practically dragged his big friend into the house, and there he introduced him to each one of his family members. Ken was polite and charming, and he delighted everyone with his rough highland brogue. He was friendly to everyone, but he was awkward around the young women. When he was introduced to Anna and Rachel, he became embarrassed and blushed; his cheeks momentarily matched the red of his hair and the plaid tartan sash he had draped across his right shoulder.

The family took to him right away. He was handsome and charming, and most importantly, he was a trusted friend of their Aaron. They were especially enamored with him when Aaron told them all how Ken had stepped in front of him in the final battle on the Mount of Olives and had taken the bullets that had been intended for him. Ken had sacrificed his own life to save that of his friend.

"But it was na a big deal," Ken protested. "I wus only dead farr a lit'le while. The Lard soon came, und rraised me back oop. Und now I'm as good as new. It wus just like I took a wee nap in the midst of the bat'le."

Everyone had a good laugh, and it was apparent to all that Kenneth Weinman was destined to become their dear friend and neighbor. They all expressed a desire to meet the rest of his family, and it was arranged that he would bring them all over in the morning. He insisted that they bring breakfast with them as a "welcome to the neighborhood" gift.

Ken was eager to express his hospitality toward Aaron's family, partly because it was in his basic nature to do so, but especially because it would give him an opportunity to introduce them to his own fiancée, the lovely Mary Turner, whom he had loved since was a teenager. He promised to see them all early in the morning and bade them all a good night.

The next day fairly flew by. Ken and his family arrived early, bringing a delicious breakfast with them. Ken introduced everyone to Mary, his cute and lively young fiancée with dark hair and eyes. She was as dark as he was fair, and as short as he was tall, but in spite of their differences, they made a perfect couple. Ken also introduced everyone to his parents, Robert and Hanna, and to his younger sister Betty and his little brother Hamish. Betty was twenty-one, a pretty girl, pleasantly plump, and with red hair and freckles like the rest of her family. Hamish was nineteen and a bit smaller than Ken, but in nearly every other way, he was a carbon copy of his older brother.

After breakfast, while the older adults did the dishes and got better acquainted, the younger ones paired up and went their separate ways. Ken and Mary went for a walk back to the Weinman home so Ken could retrieve some preserves his mother had intended to give to Aaron's family, but had neglected to bring along. Ken volunteered eagerly to retrieve the two jars, as it would give him a rare chance to be alone with the woman he loved.

Tim and Betty sat awkwardly on the front porch and made polite conversation. They were mildly attracted to each other, but neither one of them was interested in rushing into any kind of a relationship. So they sat and talked, and thoroughly enjoyed getting to know each other.

Steve and Hamish took off with Millie on a long hike to the Jordan River. They took along their swimsuits and a sack lunch. They planned to do some swimming and exploring, and they didn't expect to return until well after noon.

Aaron invited Anna to accompany him back to Tel Aviv. He had decided that they would keep the truck with the stock rack. It would prove useful in the future in hauling livestock and crops to market and in transporting various pieces of farm equipment, furniture, and what have you. But he was going to return the larger moving van to the docks so it could be used by other new arrivals. He planned to exchange it for a smaller vehicle that their whole family could ride in.

They informed everyone that they planned to do some shopping before they returned, and they made a long list of things various family members requested they pick up for them. They took some gold jewelry they had picked up in Los Angeles to pay for their purchases, and they left together at about ten o'clock.

Their drive to the coast was pleasant, but uneventful. They enjoyed just being alone together. They spoke of the future and made some tentative plans for their wedding, but Aaron informed her that his study of the Bible indicated that there would be a major conflict soon, and that they could not plan anything until all of that had been resolved.

In Tel Aviv, they again met up with Papa Saul, who promptly called over most of the other glorified saints they knew. Aaron and Anna enthusiastically greeted Scott and Candi and the others. Saul explained that after the glorified saints had assisted the Jewish pilgrims in getting onto the ships and leaving for the Holy Land, they were transported here to Israel to help the same people get settled once they arrived.

Aaron thanked them for their help, and began to tell them about all they had done since they had arrived the day before, and how the

Lord had provided so wonderfully for their family. However, in their glorified state, the others already knew about all those things. They expressed their love and approval, but they were clearly focused on other things: spiritual and invisible things that Aaron and Anna could not comprehend.

Aaron turned the large moving van back over to Saul and received permission to select something else from the vast assortment of vehicles that had been imported from all over the world. They chose a large white fifteen-passenger Ford van that would easily transport their entire family in comfort. They hugged Papa Saul and the others and invited them to come and visit them when they were able to get away. After being assured that they would be seeing them soon, they took their leave and drove into the city to do their shopping.

They exchanged some of the jewelry for freshly minted currency that bore the image of the newly constructed temple. That currency was replacing all others in the world, and would be used as the sole medium of exchange in the coming kingdom. With it, they were able to purchase everything they needed. The shops in Tel Aviv were fairly bursting with merchandise of every sort imaginable. Factories were already up and operational all over the world, and much of what they produced was destined for the bustling market places in Israel.

With the back of their van nearly filled with food, clothing, household items, and sundries, they started back home. Home . . . how wonderful that word sounded. Home had been an idea they had talked about, dreamed about, but had doubted whether or not would ever materialize. Now they already had beautiful homes for their families awaiting them at Jericho, and another one that, one day, would be their very own to share. They were eager to go home!

They stopped in Jerusalem and toured the Old City. Aaron told Anna briefly what had taken place there only two weeks before, but she could not grasp the devastation he described. The city had experienced a new birth, and it showed it everywhere they looked.

They were not allowed to enter the temple area. It was still under construction, and for their own safety, all but the heavenly workers were kept outside the chain link perimeter fence. After it was dedicated, they would all be welcome to tour the courtyards and to worship in the glorious temple itself. And judging by the way the work was progressing, that day would not be too far away.

It was late afternoon when Aaron and Anna arrived back at their estate. Joseph and Albert and Tim were still out on the tractors, working the ground in preparation for planting, but the rest of the family happily jumped in and helped unload the van. They all approved of the selection of the vehicle, and Steve insisted on taking it for a spin so he could go show it to his new friend Hamish.

Before he left, Steve told Aaron that he and Hamish had met someone at the Jordan River who was his cousin's old friend. His name was Mark Robertson, and he had established his home on the other side of the river in the ancient land of the tribe of Gad. Aaron was delighted to hear that his friend would be living so close, and made plans to visit him personally as soon as he was able.

Later that evening, after the supper things were done, Aaron and Anna sat on the front porch of the house that would be theirs and watched the sun settle gracefully behind the mountains of Samaria, rising to the west of them. They held hands and talked of things that had been, of things that now were, and of things as they anticipated them to be.

It was a glorious evening, with the setting sun painting crimson the clouds gathering in the western horizon. Those clouds would further congregate to bring a refreshing rain and water the earth later during the night, but for the moment, they seemed to be content to bask lazily in the glow of the setting sun.

The two young lovers lingered until the clouds' last dusky hew of color gave way to the gathering folds of darkness. Then they kissed goodnight and returned to their respective homes, quietly longing for the time when they would simply be able to retire to their own bedroom together.

CHAPTER TWENTY-ONE

The Festivals

Rosh Hashanah occurred early that fall. At the end of the first week in September, representatives from all the Jewish settlements in Israel were called to assemble in a nearly completed stadium in Northeastern Jerusalem. It was constructed after the return of the Lord for the purpose of accommodating the assembling of large groups of people. It was located just north of the temple mount where two valleys joined together. The natural contours of the merging valleys, along with their steeply sloping walls, were modified to accommodate the largest arena in the world.

Thousands of glorified saints had constructed the Great Hall in less than two weeks. It was not yet finished, nor was it elaborate. It had no grass yet in the infield, the comfortable seats had not yet been affixed to the concrete risers, and the concession stands and restroom facilities had not yet been completed. In the days that followed, all those things would be completed, and the Great Hall would become great indeed. During the approaching kingdom reign of Christ, it would serve as the favorite place for citizens and pilgrims to enjoy sporting events, concerts, and worship services, but at the present, it was simply a place where more than 500,000 people could assemble at the same time.

The evening before, the tiniest sliver of a new moon had been seen in the western sky, and ram horns had been sounded throughout the land, signaling the beginning of the month of Tishri. The next morning, tens of thousands of Jews traveled to the capital city and began filing into the Great Hall. By noon, there were in excess of 600,000 people sitting on the concrete risers and standing in the infield.

There was a platform constructed at the west end of the hall, but only a small orchestra was seated there, playing spirited Jewish folk music. The area around the podium was curiously vacant. The happy congregants visited with one another as they waited for their Lord to arrive. Millions more watched from their homes as the proceedings were being broadcast on local television stations.

All of the 144,000 were in attendance, and the assembly afforded them the opportunity to see one another again. Aaron and Ken had gone across the Jordan to visit Mark Robertson the day before and had invited him to accompany them to Jerusalem. He had readily agreed, and had returned with them and spent the night at Ken's place. The three of them had driven up in Aaron's van, along with several men from the tribe of Benjamin, and the three were able to make contact with many of the witnesses from the other tribes. Out front, they met Rico Sandia, Ivan Feldsin, and Julio Otero, and on the way in, they bumped into Jabin Weisler and Seth Goodman. It was great to learn that each of their friends was experiencing the same measure of success and happiness in getting settled into their new homes and occupations as were Aaron and Ken and Mark.

As they were talking with one another, suddenly, the Lord appeared behind the podium. He did not descend out of the heavens, He did not emerge from an underground passageway, He was just simply *there.*[90] He was not particularly tall or handsome, but rather ordinary in appearance. He was dressed in a white robe, but it was not dazzling in its whiteness, neither did His face shine with any sort of radiance. Yet there was a divine presence about Him that drew everyone's attention to Him.

An immediate hush fell over the vast assembly, and for a full minute, not a sound could be heard. Then, simultaneously, the entire congregation broke forth into thunderous sounds of praise and adoration. The 144,000, and a few of the others present, had already embraced their returned Messiah, but for the large majority of those assembled, this was the first time they had seen the Lord with their own eyes. Words could not express the unmeasured joy they experienced in their hearts.

The entire congregation was on its feet, cheering and clapping, and the celebration could have easily gone on all afternoon, had not the

[90] After eight days His disciples were again inside, and Thomas with them. Jesus came, the doors being shut, and stood in their midst, and said, "Peace to you!" (John 20:26).

Lord raised His hand and asked for their quiet attention. Again, the noise ceased instantly, and a hush fell over the stadium as before.

"Greetings, My beloved!" He began, His unamplified voice being clearly heard by everyone in attendance. "Welcome to the land I promised to Abraham, Isaac, and Jacob. Today marks the beginning of a new year, but not just any year. This is the year that will usher in My kingdom, in which we will live and prosper together for a thousand years in the land of your forefathers. I will pour out on you all the blessings I promised to them so many centuries ago.

"My kingdom is fast approaching, and you will soon enter into it with Me, but it is not yet here. What you have experienced thus far is merely the period of transition and preparation. Have you found it to your satisfaction?"

Again, the Great Hall erupted into roars of praise and thanksgiving. It was not entirely reverent. Sounds of cheering, clapping, stomping, and whistling could be heard throughout the stadium. Those gathered there were at a loss as how to express their feelings in an appropriate manner, but as before, a word from the Master silenced them before they could get out of hand.

"For the next two months," He continued, "we will continue to remove all vestiges of war and death, and we will continue to prepare the land for the glory that awaits it during My coming kingdom. Three sacred days are set aside for you to observe.

"The first of those will be ten days from now. Yom Kippur, the Day of Atonement, will be the day we will dedicate the new Millennial Temple. It will not be a day of repentance and fasting as it has been in the past. There will be no need to make sacrifices for the atonement of sin, since I made atonement for all sin, for all time, when I bore it in My own body on the cross. Instead, sacrifices will be made as thank offerings and praise offerings to your Father in heaven for that atonement I made for you once and for all.

"Then, five days later, on the fifteenth of Tishri, we will celebrate the Feast of Tabernacles together. Representatives from peoples all over the world will join us we commemorate together how your forefathers dwelled in tents for forty years in the wilderness. In recent years, you too have dwelled in the wilderness in tents and in caves, in the tops of trees, and beneath great rocks. In the midst of your plenty, we will remember the hardships through which you have come.

"Finally, at the end of the second month, we will celebrate the great harvest, and the beginning of My thousand-year reign here on this earth.

Already, you have planted your crops, and they have begun to grow. At that time you will reap a harvest of such abundance there will be no place for you to store your increase. You will be able to send a portion to your Gentile brethren over the entire world.

"The great tribulation was on the earth for 1260 days, just as it was promised by My servant John.[91] Most wicked men were destroyed at My coming, but there are yet many on this earth who cannot understand My words, nor are they destined to enter into My kingdom. They will yet rise against you, but do not fear them. Just as My prophet Daniel predicted so long ago, there shall be a purification and refinement for you righteous ones who live to celebrate the Feast of Tabernacles at the end of the 1290 days. Then there is a special blessedness reserved for you when you reap the great harvest and enter into My kingdom at the end of the 1335 days.[92]

"Do not be afraid when you yet hear of rumors of war. These things must come to pass that all righteousness be fulfilled. Be fruitful, My beloved, and prosper. Sow your seed and reap your harvest. Make no provision to defend yourselves, nor give any thought to your safety. At the end of the 1335 days, your enemies will be destroyed, and you will enter into My rest.[93]

"Return to your homes, My children. Celebrate with your families. A new month and a new year have begun, and soon a new millennium will follow. I will see you again on Yom Kippur, the Day of Atonement."

And then, just as suddenly as He had appeared, the Messiah of Israel vanished from their sight. The huge congregation sat spellbound for a short time, and then the orchestra began to play again, and the people began to make their orderly exits from the complex, talking quietly about the things they had just heard. Some were expressing concern over the Lord's words about a coming conflict, but the 144,000 encouraged them to be of good cheer. They had served Him for the past three-and-a-half years, and had never known Him to fail them. If He had said there was

---

[91] Then the woman fled into the wilderness, where she has a place prepared by God, that they should feed her there one thousand two hundred and sixty days (Revelation 12:6).

[92] "Many shall be purified, made white, and refined, but the wicked shall do wickedly; and none of the wicked shall understand, but the wise shall understand. And from the time that the daily sacrifice is taken away, and the abomination of desolation is set up, there shall be one thousand two hundred and ninety days. Blessed is he who waits, and comes to the one thousand three hundred and thirty-five days." (Daniel 12:10–12).

[93] See Appendix Six for a more detailed discussion of the mysterious numbers at the end of Daniel, chapter twelve.

nothing to fear, and that no harm would come to them, then that is exactly how it would be. They had nothing to fear, and no harm *could* come to them.

Aaron and Ken and Mark were engaged in an animated discussion during their drive home. Things had changed so very much since they had been in Jerusalem together before. Scarcely more than two weeks earlier, they had stood, shoulder to shoulder, bruised and bloodied, fighting for their survival in the midst of unspeakable devastation. But their Savior had appeared and turned certain defeat into glorious victory. Now His saints and angels were transforming the city into a paradise. Their Lord's presence had made all the difference in the world. They decided they would encourage their families to trust Him, and Him alone, for their safety and protection during the uncertain days ahead.

When they arrived home, after dropping off their other passengers, they were plied with questions from various family members, wanting to know more about the conflict the Lord had mentioned in His brief address. They told them not to concern themselves with any of those things. That was an area the Messiah had assumed complete responsibility over, and they could rest assured that He would be able to handle it quite nicely without any help from them.

That seemed to satisfy them, and the subject was dropped. The remainder of the day was spent in celebration. Aaron invited Ken and Doran and the others who lived in their proximity to bring their families and come over to Glory Land Estates, as Tim and Steve had decided to name their property. He also insisted Mark spend the rest of the day with them since he had no immediate family with him at his own home. Eventually, nearly fifty people had come together in the circle separating the houses, and everyone stayed well into the night, thoroughly immersed in feasting, singing, and folk dancing. None of them could remember a time when they had experienced so much unadulterated joy.

During the evening, Mark and Rachel slipped away and sat on the front porch of Aaron and Anna's soon-to-be home. They had been attracted to each other as soon as they had been introduced. They each had a deep love for Aaron, which gave them common ground to begin with, and he was tall and handsome and she was strikingly beautiful, but there was something more that drew them together. Perhaps the Lord had simply intended them for each other because the bond between them was formed immediately, and it would quickly grow into a deep love in the weeks ahead. Mark promised to visit her as often as he could.

The two joined the others in the circle, but stayed close to each other the rest of the fun-filled evening. Mary Turner turned out to be as exuberant and uninhibited as was her fiancé, and the highlight of the evening was when she and Ken performed a duet on their bagpipes, and tried to teach the others how to dance the highland fling.

The next ten days saw the entire land of Israel come alive. The divinely orchestrated demolition and construction projects were completed, and no evidence of the previous three-and-a-half years of warfare and suffering could be seen anywhere. All buildings, machinery, and weapons of war had been either destroyed or converted into things peaceful and productive. All damaged buildings, roads, bridges, and other structures had been restored to a condition far better than they had been in before the rapture had taken place. The Great Hall was completed, and it was magnificent, but it was dwarfed in glory by the Millennial Temple that dominated the hilltop above it. The temple was the last building completed, and it was splendid beyond anyone's imagination. It made the previous structure that the antichrist had dominated seem like a woeful warehouse by comparison.

The Land of Israel itself had blossomed into an exquisite dreamland. Every available plot of ground had been planted, and crops were growing at an amazing rate. Within a few weeks, the fields of grain and produce would be harvested in such abundance that there would be no storage facilities large enough to contain it all. The hillsides, watered by the frequent rains, were lush with grass, and fat livestock grazed lazily on their slopes. Orchards and vineyards were revitalized, and their branches drooped heavily, laden down with ripening fruit.

Even the Dead Sea was coming to life. The waters that had started flowing forth from the temple area when the Lord returned, continued their flow. Fed by underground springs, a veritable river flowed forth from beneath the temple mount, down the Kidron Valley, and eventually into the Dead Sea to the east. Where the river emptied into the sea, it was having a cleansing effect on the stagnant and polluted waters, pushing most of the suspended salts to the southern end where they settled to the bottom, leaving the waters at the northern end no saltier than those of the Mediterranean Sea.

Like everything else that had perished in Israel, the Dead Sea was being brought back to life, and in a short time, the entire body of water would be reclaimed. Already, ocean fish had been planted at the river's mouth, and they were beginning to multiply. During the coming kingdom, a huge fishing industry would flourish in the once-poisoned waters of the Eastern Sea.[94]

Industry was booming in the Holy Land as well. Bombed out factories were rebuilt, and others were newly constructed. Together, they were already pumping out useful products at an amazing rate. Shops were filled with newly produced clothing, appliances, household items, luggage, and dozens of other types of needful things. Soon the large industrial plants would be up and running as well, producing trucks and automobiles, farm equipment, heavy machinery, and even airplanes. The little nation of Israel was already the world's leading industrial power, and it would soon become even more productive.

The returning Jews had brought with them treasures from all over the world. Israel's national vaults contained most of the world's gold reserves, and its national museums displayed vast numbers of rare art treasures, precious gems, and fine jewelry. In addition, the majority of the working trucks and automobiles had been transported to Israel. The world's remaining ships sailed under the Israeli flag, and most of the limited airplanes that had survived the tribulation were sitting on airfields or in hangers in the Holy Land.

Yom Kippur, the Jewish Day of Atonement, was not a day of fasting and self-affliction, with offerings for the atonement of the sin of the people. Instead, it was a day of unparalleled celebration. People from all over the land assembled in Jerusalem. The Great Hall, the temple square, and the streets and parks of the city were all filled to capacity.

The Lord Himself appeared on the porch of the newly completed temple. Those of the tribe of Levi, who lived in the area surrounding the holy sanctuary, and were destined to serve as priests and attendants, were privileged to fill the temple courtyards and see their Messiah face

[94] Then He said to me: "This flows toward the eastern region, goes down into the valley, and enters the sea. When it reaches the sea, the waters are healed. And it shall be that every living thing that moves, wherever the rivers go, will live. There will be a very great multitude of fish, because these waters go there; for they will be healed, and everything will live wherever the river goes. It shall be that fishermen will stand by it from En Gedi to En Eglaim; they will be places for spreading their nets. Their fish will be of the same kinds as the fish of the Great Sea, exceedingly many." (Ezekiel 47:8–10).

to face.[95] Others watched on large screens that were set up all over the city. Virtually the entire population of Israel was in and around the capital city on that historic day. They stood spellbound as their King addressed them.

"Greetings, My children. Welcome to My city and to My house. I am the Greater David, promised to you by the prophet Ezekiel. I have come to reign over you and to bless you forever.[96] On this day, we will dedicate My house, and it will be a place of worship for you and for your children in the age to come. We will sacrifice animals on this altar, but it will not be for the remission of sin. It will be as a memorial for the sacrifice I made for the sin of the world. And in the future, as often as you offer sacrifices in My name, you will show forth My death, by which you were healed."[97]

Then the Lord Jesus had old Zecharias, the high priest, to come forward and perform the necessary sacrifice. A young bull was led forth to the altar where the priest killed it by slitting its throat. Its blood was caught in a basin, and he used it to sanctify the temple and its altar.[98] The animal was then dressed out, skinned, and dismembered; and its body was burned on the altar of sacrifice.

It was the first time an acceptable animal sacrifice had been offered since before the Lord had died on the cross. But neither at that time in

---

[95] "So this is the district you shall measure: twenty-five thousand cubits long and ten thousand wide; in it shall be the sanctuary, the Most Holy Place. It shall be a holy section of the land, belonging to the priests, the ministers of the sanctuary, who come near to minister to the Lord; it shall be a place for their houses and a place for the sanctuary." (Ezekiel 45:3–4).

[96] "David My servant shall be king over them, and they shall all have one shepherd; they shall also walk in My judgments and observe My statutes, and do them. Then they shall dwell in the land that I have given to Jacob My servant, where your fathers dwelt; and they shall dwell there, they, their children, and their children's children, forever; and My servant David shall be their prince forever." (Ezekiel 37:24–25).

[97] "You shall daily make a burnt offering to the Lord of a lamb of the first year without blemish; you shall prepare it every morning. And you shall prepare a grain offering with it every morning, a sixth of an ephah, and a third of a hin of oil to moisten the fine flour. This grain offering is a perpetual ordinance, to be made regularly to the Lord. Thus they shall prepare the lamb, the grain offering, and the oil, as a regular burnt offering every morning." (Ezekiel 46:14–15).

[98] Thus says the Lord GOD: "In the first month, on the first day of the month, you shall take a young bull without blemish and cleanse the sanctuary. The priest shall take some of the blood of the sin offering and put it on the doorposts of the temple, and the four corners of the ledge of the altar, and on the gateposts of the gate of the inner court." (Ezekiel 45:18–19).

history, nor at this time in the present did the sacrifice itself have any atoning value. In the past, the offering was made in anticipation of the ultimate sacrifice to be made by their Messiah; and this offering was made in grateful commemoration of that sacrifice. The knowing participants on both occasions knew full well that the blood of the animal sacrificed was only symbolic of the blood of a much greater sacrifice made for them.[99]

Once the fire had consumed the body of the bull, the priest Zecharias returned to the podium and led the people in adoration and praise to their exalted Lord and Savior. Jesus welcomed their worship and blessed them all. Before He dismissed them to return to their homes, He looked into the cameras and blessed the remainder of His people throughout the world. He assured them of His love, and that He would be with them as they pursued their new lives in His emerging kingdom. He promised to visit them in their cities soon, and He invited them to come to Israel when they were able.

He addressed the unredeemed as well. Scattered throughout the large cities of the world, unsaved survivors of the tribulation huddled together for mutual support and protection. They had not been executed, nor had they been punished in any way. The Lord's glorified saints had prevented them from committing any outward acts of aggression or rebellion against His people, but they had otherwise been left alone.

"You were deceived by the god of this world," He told them, "and to further your own lives, most of you received the mark of his beast. Your eternal destiny is sealed, but I will not destroy you at this time. If you abide by my statutes, you will be allowed to live in peace during My kingdom. You will be allowed to live in your own communities, and to govern yourselves, but you will not be allowed to follow the dictates of your sinful hearts.

"My commandments will be strictly enforced, and any breach of them will be quickly and severely punished.[100] My saints have prevented

---

[99] And every priest stands ministering daily and offering repeatedly the same sacrifices, which can never take away sins. But this Man, after He had offered one sacrifice for sins forever, sat down at the right hand of God, from that time waiting till His enemies are made His footstool. For by one offering He has perfected forever those who are being sanctified (Hebrews 10:11–14).

[100] "Ask of Me, and I will give You the nations for Your inheritance, and the ends of the earth for Your possession. You shall rule them with a rod of iron; You shall dash them to pieces like a potter's vessel." (Psalm 2:8–9).

you from sinning against My people, but they have not punished you for the vile acts you have committed among yourselves. However, after the great harvest is over, and My kingdom officially begins, any overt transgression of My law, in any form, will not be tolerated.

"You are hereby commanded to send representatives from each of your communities to meet with Me in Jerusalem at the Feast of Tabernacles, beginning five days from now. I want you to see the beauty and abundance in the Land of Israel. I want you to see the fruit of righteousness and peace. Select a representative from each of your cities, and they will all be flown here to see the glories of My emerging kingdom.

"At that time, I will give them my promise to share in the great harvest soon to be reaped in Israel. Arrangements will be made to send portions of the abundance to you at the beginning of My kingdom. Furthermore, I will give to you My promise of fair weather and rain on your own crops. But if you fail to send your representatives to worship Me during the Feast of Tabernacles, you will not share in My harvest, neither will I send rain from heaven. The skies will become as brass, and your crops will wither before your eyes."[101]

The citizens of the world sat spellbound before their television sets. The Lord's address had been promised for two weeks, and few indeed were those who missed it. People everywhere heard the same message, but their response to it was divided into two distinct categories.

The redeemed rejoiced and gave thanks to God for every word. They rejoiced in the Lord's triumph over the forces of evil, over His emerging kingdom wherein righteousness would reign, and in the promise of peace and abundance in the future.

In the scattered camps of the ungodly, such was not the case. They sat in shocked silence, with mixed emotions running through their minds. They were relieved beyond measure to learn that they were not to be targeted for attack and annihilation because of their former opposition against the Lord and His people. They were pleased as well with the prospects of actually prospering in the years to come, but they were dumbfounded and infuriated with His demands that they worship this self-appointed King of the world, and keep His stifling

---

[101] And it shall come to pass that everyone who is left of all the nations which came against Jerusalem shall go up from year to year to worship the King, the Lord of hosts, and to keep the Feast of Tabernacles. And it shall be that whichever of the families of the earth do not come up to Jerusalem to worship the King, the Lord of hosts, on them there will be no rain (Zechariah 14:16–17).

commandments. How could they possibly bring themselves to live under such impossible conditions?

CHAPTER TWENTY-TWO

The Feast

Gregor Galinikov stared at his television set in stunned disbelief. He had recovered completely from his recent near-fatal illness, but he was far from well in his heart and mind. He, who had been on the very threshold of ruling the world, was now reduced to the rank of a mere second-class citizen. He sat in his soiled and torn tee shirt, a three-day growth of beard on his face, and with an open bottle of vodka in his grimy hands.

Indeed, those who were prospering and being promoted to positions of prominence in Russia were those wretched followers of that Nazarene in Jerusalem. Their health was robust and strong, their fields were green and growing, and their shops were fairly bursting with both goods and customers. They went about constantly praising God and talking of His glorious kingdom to come. The whole thing sickened him.

But he, the great Gog, the one-time Crown Prince of the Kremlin, was now nothing more than one among millions of other dissidents, who were outwardly tolerated and inwardly taunted by the stupid Christians who surrounded them. The former rulers were now ruled, and the former victors were now vanquished.

Gog sat in his one-room flat in what was left of the once-great city of Moscow. He and others like him had gravitated into the hearts of the inner cities for mutual protection, and to get away from the sickening syrupy sweetness of the do-gooders who farmed the countryside and ran their shops in the suburbs. The farther they could get away from them, the better they liked it.

Whoever was rebuilding the nation's infrastructure had neglected the inner cities, and they lay in ruins. Yet Gog and his companions didn't mind that so much. There, at least, they were pretty much left alone. They found work only as menial laborers in the steel mills and factories, but at least, it was a living. And as long as they didn't try to venture out and cause trouble in the forbidden territory of the pious, they could drink, do drugs, and party as much as they pleased. But that was all about to come to an end.

If he had understood that Jesus character correctly, his partying days were soon to be over. He and his people would be forced to worship the Man in Jerusalem every year or they would be punished, and they would be forced to keep all of His stupid commandments under penalty of death. Gog had become the man that he was through lies, deceit, and brutality. There was no way he would, or could, become a man of righteousness and purity. Something simply had to be done.

Just then, as he sat mumbling to himself on his dirty hide-a-bed, his thoughts were interrupted by a once-familiar guest.

"Greetings, my son," said Odin, the Norse God of War. "Why is your countenance fallen?" He stood tall and straight, dressed in full battle garb, his long hair and beard flowing beneath his horn-studded helmet.

"Oh there you are! Where have you been?" Gog demanded. "I've been rotting in this cesspool for weeks, and you have abandoned me."

"No, my son, I have not abandoned you. I have been preparing the way for your rise to power at last. Everything is falling into place quite nicely, and soon you will receive everything that I have always promised you."

"Why should I believe you now? You made me promises before, and what did it get me? I nearly died in that filthy hospital in Turkey, my armies were annihilated, and that Man in Jerusalem now rules the world. Did I miss something, or have things turned out a bit differently than what you promised?"

"No, I promised you that you would rise to power," Odin said reassuringly, "and rise you shall. What happened before was only to get Augustus and the others out of your way. I have already set things in motion for you to turn the tables on that imposter in Jerusalem. It was I who caused your illness. I was forced to set you aside so you would not be destroyed in the overthrow in Israel. Yes, your losses were great, but greater still will be your final triumph."

"Triumph! Excuse me, but does this look like triumph to you?" Gog countered. "I have no army any more. I have no resources. I have only a few underlings in this rat hole that I have been able to bully into submission. What kind of triumph is that?"

"Silence! You forget yourself. I am the god here; you are but a man. Still, I am prepared to make you the greatest and most powerful man in all the world, but you must trust and obey."

"Forgive me, Odin, but you must understand my frustration. You promised me the world, and this is what I have become: a steel worker by day, and a drunkard and whoremonger by night. The world I rule over is much smaller than I had imagined. What would you have me do . . . charge the world with my gang of forty thieves?"

"No, my son, nothing so foolhardy as that. No, I want you to sober up, shower and shave, and dress yourself properly. I want you to journey to Jerusalem to celebrate the Feast of Passover with the rest of the faithful. I want you to bow in humility and allegiance to the Son of David that sits on the throne there. I want you to receive His pardon and blessing."

"What! You must be joking! I could never do that! And even if I could, what good would that do?"

"You can . . . and you will!" You will give every appearance of submission and respect. You will win the confidence of those who rule there, and while you are there, I want you to observe two things."

"And what might those things be?" Gog wanted to know, suddenly interested in what his god had to say.

"I want you to see the incredible wealth available in that small part of the world, and I want you to assess the military strength that is amassed to defend it. Do you think you can manage that?"

"Yes, of course, but what is the purpose of these things?"

"That, you will discover when the time is right, my son. But this, I can tell you now. While you are in Jerusalem, you will meet with like-minded people from all over the world. You will form alliances that will soon lead you to conquer the world."

In other cities, in other parts of the world, other infidels were visited by other demons; disguising themselves as gods and heroes, prophets and popes, and ascended masters and ancestors. They lured their subjects with the same tantalizing message of world conquest.

In Los Angeles, Tony D'Angelo, broken and bewildered, and working in the same rendering plant where he had disposed of Saul Frieberg's body, was visited by the spirit of Alexander the Great. The intimidating specter convinced the cowering, foul-smelling laborer that he too must journey to Israel to celebrate the Feast of Tabernacles. There, he would make the necessary connections that would eventually propel him to the elusive greatness he had always sought.

In the Muslim world, Mohamed won the hearts and minds of the dissidents there and propelled them on a holy pilgrimage to Jerusalem. In Southeast Asia, Buddha and Krishna urged their followers to make the journey as well. Confucius and Genghis Khan did the same thing in the northern Asian latitudes. Napoleon and Hitler and others motivated the Europeans to turn their thoughts toward Israel, and still others brought languishing infidels out of their doldrums all over the world and set their feet on the paths leading to Jerusalem.

When the Feast of Tabernacles arrived, the Jewish citizens in Israel celebrated with immense enthusiasm. They harvested some of their earliest crops, and rejoiced in their abundance. They erected tents and lean-tos in their yards and on their rooftops, and dwelt in them for seven days as Moses had commanded them.[102] They rejoiced and feasted and made merry as never before in their lives. They were so happy; they found it hard to believe that the millennium had not yet officially started. How could things possibly get any better?

Aaron and Tim and Steve cut willows from the banks of the Jordan and constructed huts on the tops of the three homes on their estate. Their parents stayed in the huts above their respective houses, and Anna and Rachel shared the one on top of the third one. The young men built themselves a lean-to against the main barn and slept in it. The weather was mild, and the light from the brilliant stars and the full moon gave them plenty of light.

The lone disruption in their otherwise idyllic experience came the one night when it rained. At about three in the morning of the third day of the feast, the clouds opened up and began to drop a steady blanket of

[102] "Also on the fifteenth day of the seventh month [first month of the civil year], when you have gathered in the fruit of the land, you shall keep the feast of the Lord for seven days. . . . You shall dwell in booths for seven days. All who are native Israelites shall dwell in booths, that your generations may know that I made the children of Israel dwell in booths when I brought them out of the land of Egypt: I am the Lord your God." (Leviticus 23:39, 42–43).

rain. The huts were anything but waterproof, and their occupants were immediately awakened by the cool water in their faces.

Laughing at their predicament, Aaron and the Frieberg brothers scampered out of their lean-to and assisted their families as they fled the nearby rooftops. Carrying their blankets with them, they climbed down the ladders in the rain and made their retreat into the barn. Aaron didn't feel it would be proper to seek the warmth and comfort of their homes in the midst of a week when they were supposed to be roughing it, but they couldn't very well stay out in the rain, so he suggested the barn as an appropriate compromise.

He built a fire in the middle of the floor, and they all stood around it until they dried out. They used the time to pray and sing and give praises to their Lord for His love and grace, and for His sense of humor. An hour later, they spread their blankets on the soft hay in the loft, and were lulled to sleep by the sounds of the gentle rain on the roof overhead and the lowing of the cattle in their stalls beneath them.

Aaron and Anna slept side by side for the first time then, surrounded by seven other family members, and separated by an affectionate Millie who had curled up and lain down between them. It was hardly a romantic setting, but they were pleased nonetheless. They drifted off to sleep with their hands touching and their hearts joined in their maturing love for each other.

The entire land of Israel was filled with people living out of doors. The residents were observing the Feast of Tabernacles, and the visitors were simply camping out because there was no room for them anywhere else. Millions had journeyed to the Holy Land from all over the world to celebrate the feast. Most of them were believers who had come with hearts of genuine gratitude and reverence, but a few of them were obstinate infidels who were there out of obligation and curiosity, one representative from each of the three hundred pagan cities. Members of the latter group made their way to the Negev region in the south and camped apart from the rest of the people.

They made their appearances in Jerusalem at the required times, and they bowed humbly before the King of kings. They said their prayers, pledged their allegiance, and paid their respects, but their hearts were in none of it. They were especially incensed by what the King told the crowds about the lifestyles He was dictating for everyone during the coming kingdom.

The thousand-year reign of Christ was scheduled to begin at the new moon, less than a month-and-a-half away. By then, all repair and reconstruction would be completed, and the greatest harvest in the history of the world would be gathered in. The kingdom would begin in a beautiful world, filled with order and abundance. Most of the overflow would come from Israel initially, and the delegates were encouraged to return at the time of the harvest to fill their ships with food to take home to their people.

The infidels detested the idea that they would be dependent upon the charity of the Jews, and that they would have to return to Israel regularly in the future to worship and pay tribute in order to avoid disciplinary action; but what they really hated was the long list of rules they were going to be expected to obey.

During the millennium, no acts of violence or aggression in any form would be tolerated; neither would be allowed any abuse of alcohol nor the use of tobacco or drugs. But worst of all, no sexual immorality of any sort was to be permitted. To the ungodly delegates, who were used to every sort of abuse and vice imaginable, the coming kingdom was going to be a thousand-year-long Sunday school picnic.[103] To them, such a life would be unthinkable.

On the other hand, what they were really impressed with was the incredible wealth they saw everywhere they looked. The countryside looked more like Ireland than Israel, covered with lush crops, green and growing in the warm sun. Fat livestock by the millions grazed the verdant slopes even in the formerly barren regions of the Negev. The factories in Israel were turning out vehicles, machines, and consumer goods at a pace unmatched anywhere in the world. And what tantalized them most were the reports of the vast amounts of gold and riches stored in the national vaults. Israel was a fat plumb indeed, just waiting to be plucked.[104]

---

[103] They shall not hurt nor destroy in all My holy mountain, for the earth shall be full of the knowledge of the Lord as the waters cover the sea (Isaiah 11:9).

[104] "*You have come* to take plunder and to take booty, to stretch out your hand against the waste places that are again inhabited, and against a people gathered from the nations, who have acquired livestock and goods, who dwell in the midst of the land. Sheba, Dedan. The merchants of Tarshish, and all their young lions will say to you, 'Have you come to take plunder? Have you gathered your army to take booty, to carry away silver and gold, to take away livestock and goods, to take great plunder?'" (Ezekiel 38:12–13).

What was even more intriguing was the total absence of any evidence of national security. There were no military personnel; no military ships, aircraft, or land vehicles; and no weapons of any sort to be seen anywhere. The land was simply left with no means whatsoever of defending itself. The visiting infidels found that fact most interesting.[105]

One night toward the end of the week, a council of the appointed representatives met under a big tent provided for them courtesy of the nation of Israel. They resented the nation and all it represented, but they appreciated the tent. Under lights powered by a nearby generator, the council met to decide what they were going to do. Demonic sentries guarded the perimeter to make sure there were no uninvited guests present. The conversation among the three hundred men went well into the night, with no apparent agreement reached. Then Gregor Galinikov stood to speak.

"My friends," he said in heavily accented English (they had chosen to use that language since it was the only one known to all of them), "we have come to an impasse. We all agree that we detest the terms dictated to us by that tyrant who sits enthroned in Jerusalem. We will not be allowed to succeed in business unless we pay homage to Him. We will not escape punishment unless we abide by His strict moral code. I fear we will not be able to breathe unless He grants us permission."

That last comment brought laughter and words of agreement from the others. He went on to say, "But who does He think He is? He has no warships with which to assault our shores, no warplanes with which to bomb our cities, and no armies with which to invade our lands. How can He expect to enforce His demands upon us? I believe He has left us with no choice. We must not agree to live under His rules; we could not, even if we attempted to do so. We must rise up and throw off His yoke of bondage and assert ourselves as men."

"But how can we do that?" Mustafa Karemi wanted to know. He was a tall, swarthy man who had once been a prominent military leader in Lybia. "We all know what happened to those that opposed Him last month. Without any military weapons, He destroyed them down to the

---

[105] "After many days you will be visited. In the latter years you will come into the land of those brought back from the sword and gathered from many people on the mountains of Israel, which had long been desolate; they were brought out of the nations, and now all of them dwell safely. . . . You will say, 'I will go up against a land of unwalled villages; I will go to a peaceful people, who dwell safely, all of them dwelling without walls, and having neither bars nor gates.'" (Ezekiel 38:8,11).

last man. What would prevent Him from doing the very same thing to us if we dared to oppose Him now?"

"Yeah," agreed Tony D'Angelo, rising to his feet. "We all watched on TV when He dissolved all those soldiers into mush with just the words spoken from His mouth. No way do I want that happenin' to me. I refuse to live in that puritanical pressure cooker He has designed for us, but I'm not ready to sign my own death warrant either. What makes you think we can throw off His hand of oppression without being crushed under His foot of retaliation?"

"I am not sure, my young friend," replied Gog, "but I believe it can be done. And what do we have to lose? We are as good as dead men already. I would rather die as a soldier in battle than to wither away in some oppressive religious concentration camp. Besides, look at what we have to gain if we should be successful. I have never seen such wealth as I see in this land. My Russia is a wasteland compared to this place. I am prepared to fight to take this home with me. I was once the president of my country, and with the spoil I take from Israel, I will be its new czar."

"That all sounds very tempting," said Hatif Ajar, a hatchet-faced Iranian. "I too would like to return to my former status in my country, and I must admit that there is a great desire within me to plunder this overripe piece of fruit called Israel, but what of the risks? That tyrant who sits enthroned here has some powerful magic. I fear we would meet the same destiny as those who invaded this land before. They came with millions of men and the most powerful military weapons in the world, and still they were defeated. We have no weapons at all. How could we ever hope to be successful?"

For a moment, Gog was frustrated in his attempt to reply convincingly; then an idea flashed into his mind. He said, "I have been visited by a spiritual messenger who has instructed me to come here, and has promised me ultimate success. How many of you have entertained a similar guest from the spirit realm?"

No one moved initially, each one being reluctant to be singled out for ridicule; but after about five seconds, a hand was raised in the back, then another on the right side, and then another near the front. Soon, hands were being raised all over. After thirty seconds, Gog looked over the group and could not see a person who did not have a hand in the air.

"It is just as I thought," he said with growing confidence. "Something supernatural is at work among us. There are powerful spiritual forces that have appeared to each one of us, and they have brought us together here tonight. They have survived the wrath of this new King in

Israel; therefore, they must be more powerful than He is. If He could have defeated them, He would have done so by now. That leads me to believe that they have the power to give us the victory over this usurper."

Murmurings swept throughout the gathering, and voices started being raised, some in agreement, and some in opposition. Before the confrontation could become heated, Gog called for everyone's attention. It was given to him immediately. Although no nomination had been made, and no vote had been taken, the powerful man from Russia had clearly emerged as their leader.

"It is late, my comrades," he said. "Let us not debate this matter further tonight. Let us return to our tents and get some rest, and we will speak more on this matter tomorrow. But before you go to sleep, invite your spirit guide to speak to you. Ask him what our course of action should be. If we all receive the same response, then we will know for sure what we must do."

That suggestion met with everyone's immediate approval. They adjourned their meeting without further discussion, and all of the representatives were anxious to get alone and confer with the mysterious messengers who had already captivated them by their apparent knowledge and power. There was a new air of optimism and anticipation in the camp of the damned that night.

The next morning, they met again. Each man was excited and anxious to share his experience with his new companions. The tent was buzzing with animated conversation when Gog walked to the front of the gathering. He called for, and received, their attention, and asked each of them to take his seat. They did so in unison, anxious to hear what their leader had to say.

"Good morning, comrades," he said warmly. "I trust you all slept well. As for me, I was up most of the night with Odin, the Viking God of War. How many of you entertained a similar guest?"

Every hand under the tent immediately shot into the air, accompanied by enthusiastic affirmations, and even shouts and whistles. In actuality, the twelve demons had been at work through the night, impersonating about thirty different ascended masters each, thoroughly convincing their subjects that Gog's plan was divinely ordained and worthy of their full support.

"My god assured me that this Jesus has no lasting power," the bold Russian continued. "He is over-confident now because of His past successes, and has been divested of any powers He once had. He and His people are vulnerable and can easily be defeated. How many of you were pleased with the results of your own consultations with your mentors? How many of your spirit guides agreed with mine?" he demanded in a booming voice.

This time, his congregation leapt to its feet and cheered wildly, giving him a rousing standing ovation. He welcomed their applause, and reveled in it for a few moments before raising his hands and calming them down. He thanked them and asked them to again take their seats.

"Excellent! Now then, let us get down to the business of formulating our strategy."

And that is exactly what they did. For the remainder of the day, Gog led his new allies in a spirited mapping out of their plans for world conquest. They decided that they would do nothing at the present time. They would pay their respects to the King of Israel, and make any promises He demanded of them. They would return peacefully to their respective cities and show no outward signs of rebellion. No one observing them would be able to tell that they were quietly preparing for a massive invasion.

Outwardly, they would be preparing to return to Israel just as the King had invited them. They would obtain whatever vehicles they could find from the scarce supply, but mostly, they would prepare wagons and secure horses to pull them. They would transport them to Israel by ships, or trains, or by whatever means available. They would come under the pretense of filling their vehicles and wagons with grain and produce from the great harvest that would be ready within a month's time, and they would promise to return to their cities peacefully with their vehicles filled with their charitable donations.

In truth, they would be filling hidden compartments in the wagons with weapons of all sorts. Since all modern weaponry had been destroyed and none was available anywhere in the world, they would fashion their own primitive ones: swords, spears, clubs, and bows and arrows. In light of the fact that there were no weapons of any kind and no defenses whatsoever in the entire land of Israel, such homemade weapons would be more than adequate to destroy their enemies. There were no more than six million Jews in the land, and the dissidents were confident that they would be able to assemble at least five times that many men to come up against them. By the time the meeting was over, all the representatives were confident that they would indeed be able to orchestrate a massive coup against the Jewish King on the very eve of the beginning of His proposed kingdom.

Before they adjourned, there was one more question they needed to address. How were they going to communicate with one another after they returned to their respective nations? They would need to share a great deal of information in order to coordinate their attack, but all conventional modes of communication were controlled by those loyal to the Jewish King. Any contact made by way of telephone, telegraph, or over the Internet would be subject to monitoring. Absolute secrecy had to be maintained, so, what were they going to do?

"Don't worry, my comrades," Gog assured his new friends, "We already have an absolutely secure means of communication at our disposal."

"And what might that be?" asked Tony. "Did I miss something here, or do you have a carrier pigeon in your pocket?"

The other men laughed at Tony's ridiculous inquiry, but they agreed with his apprehension, and they voiced their own misgivings about the existence of any such means of communication.

"It is all so simple," Gog laughed, obviously pleased with his grasp of the apparent facts that eluded the others. "We all have access to a spirit guide of some sort; that fact was proven last night when we all spoke with them. They inhabit the same spiritual realm, and they most certainly have contact with one another. Each one of us can simply talk to his spirit guide, and then he can pass the information on to the others, who in turn, can communicate it to the rest of us. We can have almost instant access to one another, and no one will be able to intercept our messages."

"What if the other side has spiritual agents of some sort?" Tony wanted to know. "Couldn't they interfere somehow with our communications?"

"Yes, they certainly do," Gog replied. "Odin has told me of their existence, but they are weak and disorganized. They are busy trying to prepare things for their Champion's kingdom, and they are totally unaware of the activities of our ascended masters who are allied against them. They think their side has won the final battle, and they do not think it is even possible for any rebellion to be mounted against them. They pay no attention to the activities of our spirit guides, and are ignorant of our present activities as well."

His response satisfied Tony's misgivings, as it did for the others gathered under the tent that morning. They unanimously appointed Gog as their captain and appointed him to coordinate their activities over the coming month to prepare for their worldwide rebellion. They adjourned their meeting and started making preparations to return to the temple for the closing ceremonies of the Feast of Tabernacles, and then to return to their respective cities. They all agreed to behave as inconspicuously as possible so as not to attract any undue attention to themselves.

They would pay proper respect to the Jewish King, and they would inform Him that they planned to return the next month to take advantage of His generous offer for them to share in the bounty anticipated from the enormous crop already ripening in the fields and orchards of Israel.

As he packed his bags, Tony could not help but think about how much more he planned to take back from Israel besides a wagonload of grain. There was so much more available here, and it would all be ripe for the picking.

CHAPTER TWENTY-THREE

The Spiritual Realm

The millions of glorified saints who had returned to the earth with their Lord had experienced an eventful month. They had been privileged to make their entrance riding on majestic white horses,[106] but that is where the fun had ended and the work had begun. In heaven, they had been comforted and blessed, and had no real tasks to perform, not even providing care for the horses. The gallant steeds had not been stabled in heaven throughout eternity; they had not even been there until the Lord spoke them into existence when it was time to leave. Neither were they necessary to provide them with a means of transportation; the Messiah and His armies were perfectly capable of making the transition from the heavenly realm to the earthly one unassisted.

The Father simply provided them with the horses to enhance the majesty of the event, and to give pleasure and satisfaction to those who rode upon them. After the heavenly cavalry had all assembled in the skies above Israel on that fateful day and watched their Savior dispatch His enemies with nothing more than the spoken words from His mouth, the horses disappeared, both His and theirs.[107]

---

[106] Now I saw heaven opened, and behold a white horse. And He who sat on him was called Faithful and True, and in righteousness He judges and makes war. . . . And the armies in heaven, clothed in fine linen, white and clean, followed him on white horses (Revelation 19:11, 14).

[107] See Appendix Two for a more detailed discussion of the place of animals in heaven.

Not only had the presence of the horses not been necessary to provide transportation, neither was the presence of the heavenly armies of saints and angels necessary to assist the Lamb of God in subduing His enemies. They had been allowed to accompany Him simply so they might witness His glorious return and His victory over the hosts of darkness. They comprised an unseen gallery of unsurpassed numbers, assembled in the skies above the war-torn land of Israel to witness the triumph of righteousness over evil on the earth. It was a majestic experience indeed to watch the forces of evil destroyed in a moment's time after they had dominated the earth for so many centuries, and had inflicted such pain and suffering in the lives of the saints of God.

The glorified saints witnessed it all. Their hearts thrilled as they watched their Savior dispatch His enemies. Their voices were unheard on earth, but the heavens were filled with their shouts of triumph. The saints who had been tortured and put to death for the cause of Christ experienced an overwhelming sense of vindication as they saw the wicked wither and die under the sword of the Spirit, the invincible Word of God!

After celebrating the triumphant return of Jesus Christ, most of the heavenly angels departed to resume their responsibilities elsewhere in the universe, and the saints who had accompanied them to earth were assigned to various posts throughout the world. They were destined to rule and reign with their Lord during the millennium, but first, there was a lot of clean up work that had to be done.

The saints were assigned responsibilities in areas near where they had lived their mortal lives. Then, with the speed of divine thought, they were instantly separated and relocated to strategic places all over the world. The first task for many of them was to confiscate all weapons of war, and they went about their duties with amazing efficiency.

In their glorified bodies, they found they possessed incredible abilities: abilities such as they could not have imagined in their former lives. They could move about in the air effortlessly. They had no wings, and couldn't actually fly; but they navigated flawlessly by the mere power of thought. And they didn't have to actually lift anything either. By simply willing an object to move, and by believing it would happen, they were able to lift and move virtually anything they wanted to.[108]

[108] "Assuredly, I say to you, if you have faith as a mustard seed, you will say to this mountain, 'Move from here to there,' and it will move; and nothing will be impossible for you.'" (Matthew 17:20).

In addition, they could conceal their presence from mortals by simply willing themselves to be undetected by them. They could clearly see one another and communicate openly, but mortals were oblivious to their presence, being able neither to see nor hear them.

Thus equipped, they easily went about confiscating weapons of all sorts. By night, they slipped guns from the hands and holsters of sleeping pagans, and just as effortlessly, they lifted huge tanks and artillery pieces and hauled them away to steel mills where they would be melted down and transformed into useful vehicles and pieces of machinery. In the same manner, they took over warships and military planes, and after the terrified occupants had fled their crafts, they gutted them of any weapons onboard, and converted them into vessels capable of carrying only passengers and cargo.

While the weapons were being destroyed or neutralized by some of the glorified saints, the remainder of their numbers were given other assignments. Some were given the responsibility of repairing roads, bridges, buildings, and other structures that had been destroyed during the horrors of the tribulation. All over the world, repairs were made with amazing speed since the saints didn't actually have to do the work by hand. They simply willed the actions to take place and coordinated the progress by the power of their minds. Interestingly, they were told not to make any repairs in the hearts of the three hundred largest cities in the world. They left them, and the unsaved masses that were migrating to them, in their miserable state in which the devastation of the tribulation had left them.

Others of the glorified saints were charged with the necessary task of monitoring the activities of the unbelieving hordes streaming into those huge cities. For the time being, they were not instructed to compel them to obey the Lord's mandates for godly living, which commands were already in force elsewhere in the world, and which would become mandatory universally just as soon as the millennium officially began. Temporarily, they were to allow the heathen to continue in their wicked ways within the confines of the large metropolitan areas. They could harm and abuse one another so long as they stayed within those areas, but they could commit no crimes or transgressions outside the city limits, and certainly not against any believer.

For that reason, few of the unsaved ventured out. They left the urban centers only if their menial jobs required them to, or to purchase food and other necessities. They hurried back to the *safety* of their inner city ghettos just as quickly as they could. The heavenly saints were there to make sure that they did just that.

Other groups of the glorified saints were given the responsibility of assisting the surviving Gentile believers as they relocated to rural areas and small urban centers away from the large cities. Some of the people were to be assisted in setting up farming operations. Others needed help in getting started in small businesses and in opening up retail shops. Still others were destined to operate larger industrial plants, and the saints assisted them in getting them up and running. It was pleasant work for all as glorified and mortal saints worked side by side to accomplish the monumental tasks.

The remaining numbers of saints who had returned with Christ were privileged to assist the surviving Jews in their return to the Holy Land. The first ones selected were obviously the Jewish saints who had already gone on to be with the Lord and had returned with Him. But along with them were many Gentile believers who had established special relationships with Jewish people before they had been taken to heaven by either their deaths or the rapture. Among these were Scott Graham and Candace Mercer and all the members of the Davis family.

Their first assignment was to assist the Muller and Frieberg families in their journey from the San Gabriel Mountains and over to Dodger Stadium. They kept any bands of heathen marauders away and cleared a path for them through the wreckage and debris that congested the streets. At the stadium, Scott and Candi appeared to the saints who had survived the tribulation and gave them encouragement and instructions. Then they retreated to the docks in San Pedro to begin loading the ships there with whatever their friends would need to establish their new homes in Israel.

At the docks and on one of the ships, they were able to talk personally with their friends and assure them that they would continue to assist them on their journey and help them get established once they arrived in the Holy Land, which they did. During the sea voyage and at the docks in Israel, they protected them and assisted them in procuring what they needed to get established in their new lives.

It had all been pleasant work, and they had thoroughly enjoyed it. Their hearts thrilled to see the land of Israel transformed before their very eyes. The remains of years of war and devastation were removed, and in its place, new signs of life, growth, and progress were springing up everywhere. All had been wonderful, that is, until the heathen hordes had arrived during the Feast of Tabernacles.

Now, the glorified saints were troubled. They sensed that something was wrong. The visiting representatives from the three hundred pagan cities all acted as though they were submissive and responsive to the Lord, and to the requirements He had placed upon them, but there was something about them that troubled the saints who observed them. God's glorified children remained undetected and were able to listen in on the conversations of the visitors, and they detected all was not as it appeared to be.

Scott asked Candi to accompany him, and the two of them approached the camp of the heathen in the Negev to learn what they could of the evil plans they were sure were being formulated there. They were invisible to the human eye, but they were still not able to gain entrance to the large tent in the center of the compound. The entire site was surrounded by a number of ferocious demons who had stationed themselves there for the specific purpose of keeping out any unwelcome guests. It appeared to Scott that every evil spirit the Lord had spared from the abyss was assembled there. Their presence confirmed his suspicion that foul play was indeed afoot.

The two saints sped back to their friends and informed them of the ominous goings on in the Negev. They all agreed that something was amiss, and that they needed to look more closely into it. They decided that they would observe closely the activities of those nefarious delegates from the dark side that afternoon at the closing ceremonies at the temple.

As the Feast of Tabernacles came to a close in Jerusalem, the city was packed with joyous worshippers. The greatest of the Old and New Testament saints were seated on either side of the King who sat on a majestic throne situated in the middle of the temple courtyard. Abraham, Moses, David, Paul, Timothy, and several others were so honored. Seated in front of Him, on identical chairs, were His twelve disciples. Hosts of other glorified saints were also in attendance. Scott and Candi, the Davis', and Singletons spent many happy hours worshipping and celebrating with the Mullers and the Friebergs near the Messiah's throne.

Scott and Candi called Aaron aside and spoke with him privately. They told him of their suspicions about the intentions of the three hundred delegates from the heathen cities of the world. They also told him what they had witnessed at their campsite in the Negev and warned him not to be fooled by their display of piety. They were up to something rotten, and they were not to be trusted.

Toward the close of the festivities, the representatives from the heathen cities of the world made their entrance. They worked their way to the center of the temple courtyard and bowed before the presence of the Jewish King. They gave every appearance of being His humble and obedient followers. They deposited their offerings in the temple treasury and pledged their allegiance to the King of kings and Lord of lords. Before they left, their spokesman, a man they called Gog, stepped forward, kneeled, and spoke to the King.

"My Lord, we are Your humble servants. We thank You for sparing our lives and allowing us to live in our own cities. We regret that we opposed You and Your people in the past, but we were deceived and misled by the devil and his angels. We now know the truth, and the truth has made us free.[109] We promise to obey Your rules and keep Your peace during Your coming kingdom. We will return each year at this time to bring our offerings and worship You. And if it pleases You, my Lord, we will return next month with many of our people to fill our vehicles with grain and produce as You have invited us to do. We are making progress in our cities, but we are not yet self-sufficient. Your generosity will help sustain us until such a time as we become so."

The vile words nearly stuck in his throat, but he managed to get them out in an Oscar-winning performance. He sounded so humble and so sincere; his rehearsed speech impressed nearly all who heard it. All, that is, with the exception of Scott and Candi, and especially Him who sat on the throne.

"Be it as you have said," the Master replied. "Go in peace; live in peace, and you shall be spared. Return with your people and share in the bounty of our harvest, and your little ones will be fed. We are at last a world at peace after so many ages of war. Whoever honors that peace shall live; whoever breaks that peace shall surely die. Do I make Myself understood?"

"Yes, my Lord," Gog replied weakly. His voice broke and his body visibly trembled. It had not been planned; he was simply not able to control himself in the presence of that strange being on the throne. He was frustrated with himself for his lack of self-control, but on second thought, he decided his actions added to the humble and broken image he was trying to portray. Pleased with his performance, he rose to his

---

[109] Then Jesus said to those Jews who believed Him, "If you abide in My word, you are My disciples indeed. And you shall know the truth, and the truth shall make you free." (John 8:31–32).

feet, bowed, and retreated from the courtyard. His men followed behind him, each of them doing his best to appear both meek and pious.

Tony D'Angelo was pleased with Gog's performance. He himself would have been swayed by it had he not known better. He was confident the King and all his followers had bought it all. They were leaving with His blessing, and they would be welcomed when they returned with their trucks and wagons the following month. The King and His people would be totally caught by surprise, and they wouldn't know what hit them. A feeling of confidence flooded his being, and he was having difficulty maintaining his humble posture. He wanted to strut and swagger.

Just then, someone stepped in front of him and forced him to stop. He had been looking down in an attempt to appear meek and harmless, and had not seen the man before he almost bumped into him. He wanted to push him out of his way, but he decided that would not be a fitting response for the pious person he was attempting to portray, so he looked up to ask the intruder to please excuse him and let him pass. As he did so, he gazed squarely into the eyes of Aaron Muller.

"Hello, Tony," Aaron said coldly, forcing himself to remain calm. "How've you been?" He had purposefully worked his way through the throngs of people and positioned himself at the gateway so he could intercept his former friend, whom he had spotted in the crowd earlier. Now he was looking into the eyes of the man who had killed his grandfather and his aunt and uncle, and had attempted to kill both him and all of his loved ones. It was all he could do to keep from strangling his adversary with his bare hands.

"Uh . . . hi, Aaron . . . uh . . . it's good to see you," Tony managed to get out. Gone were his former feelings of confidence and bravado. Suddenly, he found himself trembling with fright. He was afraid he was going to wet his pants as he shook uncontrollably in the presence of his hated nemesis. He could not look him in the eyes; he lowered his gaze and braced himself for the attack he was sure to come. He cowered and flinched, but the blows never came.

Aaron was experiencing a measure of self-control he never dreamed possible. He had grown to despise Tony with an intense hatred, and had longed for the day when he could get his hands on him. In his dreams, he had literally torn him limb from limb, and now, he had him cowering right in front of him. He would have felt justified in dispatching his enemy right then and there, but he restrained himself. If his Lord and Master had been willing to let these evil men walk away, then who was he to take vengeance into his own hands? Instead of grabbing Tony by the throat, he extended his open hand in a gesture of friendship. "It's been a long time," he said in measured tones.

Tony was flabbergasted as he reached out and shook Aaron's hand weakly. "Are you living here now?" he asked, not knowing what else to do or say.

"Yes," Aaron replied. "My family and I have made our home in some farmland northeast of Jericho. You'll have to come visit us the next time you're in Israel."

"I'd like that," Tony lied. "Maybe we can plan on it."

"Yes, let's do that. In fact, next month when you come back with some of your people, bring them down to our farm. Our barns aren't big enough to hold everything we're going to be harvesting. You're welcome to take as much as you want."

"Thanks, I think I'll take you up on your offer," Tony responded weakly. Then overcome with emotion, he began to break down and weep. "Aaron, why are you doing this after all I've done to you and your family? I don't understand."

"I don't know, really. I hated you for what you did, and I wanted to kill you, and I would have if I could have got my hands on you, but that was in a different age. You were deceived and misled and not totally responsible for what you were doing. If my Savior is willing to let all the evil done to Him and His people go unpunished, then I feel compelled to follow His example. As long as you come in peace, you will be welcome to visit our home and to share in our harvest."

"I can't believe this, Aaron. You really are a Boy Scout. I'm sorry for all the rotten things I did back then. You're right, I was deceived and misguided; I didn't really know what I was doing. But I'm much better now; I've seen the light, as you say. If you're willing to forget about the past, then so am I. You don't have to worry about any threats or attacks from me anymore. I'm a changed man. I am; you'll see."

"I hope so, Tony. For your sake, I sincerely hope so."

With that, the two former friends shook hands once again and parted. Tony had a puzzled look on his face and his thoughts deeply troubled him as he hurried to rejoin his comrades. Aaron turned and walked back to his friends and family again. Many thoughts raced through his mind as he made his way through the crowd, wondering just how that brief conversation would play into what happened in the future.

Later that afternoon as Gog boarded his plane for Moscow, he was alive with excitement. All that Odin had promised him had come to pass. He was convinced that his god was drawing him to return to this land and subdue it. He had made many new allies from various areas of the world who would assist him in his conquest. Most of them would come from Eastern Europe, the Middle East, and Northern Africa;[110] but some from Western Europe, Asia, Australia; and even others from North and South America would join them. He was particularly impressed with that young man D'Angelo from Los Angeles. He was sure he would find him useful in coordinating his coming assault on Israel.

He was confident he had convinced the new King of Israel that he and his people were defeated foes, and that they would be submissive and obedient in the future. When they returned with their soldiers and weapons the following month, he was sure that they would find the people of Israel totally caught off guard and unprepared to defend themselves.

He would not be able to sleep on the flight to Moscow. His mind was racing with plans already fomenting in preparation for the campaign that lay ahead. He retrieved a pad from his carry on bag and began to jot down his thoughts so none of them would be lost.

At the same time, Tony D'Angelo was on a similar flight destined for New York City. He would change planes there, and sometime in the middle of the night, he would touch down at LAX. He too was filled with anticipation. He had recovered from the shock he had experienced when Aaron Muller had surprised him, and he was even more confident than before.

He concluded that their King Jesus really was a good person, and that Aaron was too. He was amazed that they had been so willing to forgive those who had lashed out against them and sought to destroy them. But he also concluded that their love and forgiveness were their greatest weaknesses. Their naïve and trusting goodness would leave them completely vulnerable when the armies of Gog and his allies came upon them.

Aaron may have been willing to forgive him for what he had done to him and his relatives, but he was not about to forgive that dirty Jew for all the suffering he had caused him. He rubbed the scar on his cheek and thought about how he would take vengeance on him and his unsuspecting family the following month when he looted their barns and burned their homes.

---

[110] "I will turn you around, put hooks into your jaws, and lead you out, with all your army, horses, and horsemen, all splendidly clothed, a great company with bucklers and shields, all of them handling swords. Persia, Ethiopia, and Libya are with them, all of them with shield and helmet; Gomer and all its troops, the house of Togarmah from the far north and all its troops—many people are with you." (Ezekiel 38:4–6).

For the first time in weeks, he felt that he was once again on the winning side. Instead of facing a future of bondage and deprivation, he was excited about destroying his enemies and rising to great power. He leaned back in his seat and drifted off to sleep, thinking about the possibility of ruling over the entire Western United States (maybe over the whole country) and enjoying a life of incredible wealth and decadent indulgence.

The assembly of the demons from hell was a ghastly one. The dozen hideous creatures gathered in a circle in the most remote region of Antarctica. It was absolutely dark in the sun-deserted continent at the bottom of the world. And it was cold: so cold no mortal creature could survive for more than a few minutes in its wind-swept, icy clutches. But the fallen angels felt no discomfort. As creatures of the night, they loved the darkness, and even the bitter cold posed no danger to them. It was the threat of the fires of hell that sent chills down their twisted spines.

The demons had gathered there to escape any possible detection by the nosey spies sent out by the other side. They were not overly concerned; it appeared that the King in Jerusalem had sent His angels off to other realms in the universe, and few of them were even in this part of the solar system. And His so-called glorified saints were all too busy cleaning things up and preparing for His coming kingdom to be snooping around in this God-forsaken part of the world. The fallen ones were confident that they were entirely alone.

Their leader, the one they called Apollyon,[111] the one who impersonated Odin, Marcus Aurelius, Alexander the Great, and a dozen others, cackled and gloated, "There are few of us left, but we shall overcome. Lucifer and our comrades may be in chains, but we shall bring about the final victory on their behalf. We have escaped the Nazarene's snare and we are now free to work our will in the world of mankind. We shall yet lead the followers of our god to defeat those fools who believe in Jehovah. We shall overcome Him who sits enthroned in Jerusalem. We shall steal His keys and unlock the gates to the abyss and let our god and our brothers go free. Then we shall destroy Jehovah and His minions once and for all."

---

[111] And they had a king over them the angel of the bottomless pit, whose name in Hebrew is Abaddon, but in Greek he has the name Apollyon (Revelation 9:11).

"So it seems, oh Great One," snarled the drooling creature to his left. "They seem so foolish, and they are so unprepared; it should be an easy victory. But what if it is a trap? What if they have anticipated our actions and are somehow prepared against us and our human shields? Their Book says they will destroy us and banish us in the end."

"I know all that!" Apollyon groaned, his grotesque features twisted up in a frown, his sunken eyes burning as lamps of fire. "But their Book was written by mere men—their men. Of course they are going to insist that their side wins. Our books read differently. We must trust in them and draw on all the powers of hell to rise up this last time and win the final victory."

"But what if we fail?" demanded his reptilian-looking antagonist.

Apollyon snarled and cursed and spat and bellowed, "Then we all go to hell and burn forever! But at least we get to take multiplied millions of souls with us, and that's not a bad consolation prize. However, I'm not willing to settle for that. We will win this war! We must win this war! You shut up and join in with us right now, or so help me; I will tear you to pieces where you stand! I will tolerate no dissention! Do you hear me?"

The other demons roared and screeched their approval, and the lizard-looking one abandoned his protest and joined in with them in their demonic revelry. They were committed to each other and to their fallen comrades in the abyss. They would carry out this final coup, or they would die eternal deaths trying.

After a brief time of consultation and planning, they flew off to their appointed groups of cities to continue to beguile and seduce their human stooges. Time was drawing short and their god Lucifer was counting on them to pull this off. The destinies of all of them depended on their success, and they were determined not to fail.

The feast was over and all the celebrants had returned to their homes. Night had fallen and the waning moon had not yet risen. Clouds were gathering as they often did at night to refresh the earth with gentle rain, and they blocked what little light the stars afforded, so the temple courtyard was shrouded in almost complete darkness. No mortal, had one been in the area, could have detected the presence of the three individuals gathered at the throne in the center of the square.

"My Lord," said the tall handsome figure who was standing before the throne. "Thank You for agreeing to meet with us here. I don't want to be disrespectful, but I must inform you of what I believe to be a plot being orchestrated against You and Your people even as we speak."

"My son," replied the One seated on the throne, "I have been such a long time with you, and still you do not know Me? I am well aware of the intentions of those who walk the darkness. Their demonic aspirations are not hidden from Me."

"Forgive me, Master," said Scott Graham, "but I assumed You had divested Yourself of Your omniscience in Your new role as King of Israel during Your reign here on earth. Why else would You tolerate the insurrection that is being formed against You even before Your kingdom begins?"

The glorified Christ smiled knowingly, his facial features lit up by the light that seemed to emanate from within Him. He replied lovingly, "I thank you for your concern, Scott, but nothing is being planned beyond My perception, and nothing is taking place beyond My control."

"Why then haven't You intervened, my Lord?" asked the other saint, standing to Scott's left. She was tall and beautiful and clothed in purest white.

"Candace, I am pleased with the concern that both of you have demonstrated for Me, but I assure you, everything is going as I have expected."

"Forgive me, Master, but I don't understand," Candi replied. "Why is it then that You have done nothing to prevent it from taking place. We feel sure there are wicked demons right now seducing the unbelievers living in large cities all over the world. If nothing is done, they could send millions to attack Israel in the near future."

"Yes," added Scott, "and Your people here have no way of defending themselves. They have no weapons of any sort. Since You have known all about the things we've just discovered, why have You allowed it to continue to go on? I never understood why You allowed those demons to escape when Michael and his angels threw the rest of them in the bottomless pit in the first place. You surely could have prevented that from happening, right?"

"Of course, My child. Their escape was not due to any oversight on the part of my heavenly host. They went free only because I willed it so, and they will remain free only as long as I will it so."

"I'm sorry, Master, but I really don't understand," Candi interjected. "If You're planning to imprison those demons too, why did You let them go free in the first place? And if You're planning to destroy the unbelievers in those cities in the future, why didn't You just destroy them along with the others when You came back to the earth last month?"

"I know this must be difficult for you, My friends, but I assure you there is, as you say, a method behind My apparent madness. At My coming, I destroyed only those who were actually warring against My people in Israel. I spared the lives of the rest of the ungodly around the world so they might understand full well what they are doing before they make their final choices. They will hear the voices of the fallen angels persuading them to rebel, and they will have their own carnal natures encouraging them to do so as well, but they will also hear from Me.

"After the next forty days have passed, they will have heard and observed, for a full seventy-five days since My return, the extent of My power, the depth of My love, and the glory of My approaching kingdom. They will have been completely informed from both sides before they decide whom they will follow."

"Begging your pardon, my King," Scott said, "but are we just going to sit and wait to see what happens? In forty more days they could launch a massive invasion against Your defenseless people here in Israel. If it was up to me, I would put a stop to this right now before things get out of hand."

"But it is not up to you, My son, and My ways are not your ways.[112] Do you believe that I am who I say I am, and that I can do what I claim I can do?"

"Yes, of course," Scott readily agreed.

"Then I am simply asking you to trust Me to handle things when they materialize. I must allow those fallen mortals every opportunity to repent, even if it might put those I love in jeopardy. I thank you for your concern, but I must fulfill all righteousness according to My Father's will. You must believe in My ability to complete His will even when my actions, or lack thereof, make no sense to you.[113] Can you do that?"

"Yes, my Lord," replied Scott and Candi in unison as they bowed before Him in submission and reverence. Before they left Him, Scott

---

[112] "For My thoughts are not your thoughts, nor are your ways My ways," says the Lord. "For as the heavens are higher than the earth, so are My ways higher than your ways, and My thoughts than your thoughts." (Isaiah 55:8–9).

[113] Oh, the depth of the riches both of the wisdom and knowledge of God! How unsearchable are His judgments and His ways past finding out! For who has known the mind of the Lord? Or who has become His counselor? Or who has first given to Him and it shall be repaid to him? For of Him and through Him and to Him are all things, to whom be glory forever. Amen (Romans 11:33–36).

assured his Savior and King that they would simply trust and obey, and that they would encourage their mortal friends to do so as well.

Their Lord embraced them both before they departed, and they left with a sense of complete confidence in His knowledge of the situation, and of His absolute ability to handle it without any further input or assistance from them. Later, they discussed the conversation they had just had with their Lord, and they agreed that Pastor Bobby had been correct when had he taught them about a Russian-led rebellion taking place between the end of the tribulation and the beginning of the millennium.[114] At the time, they had not been convinced; but now, they agreed that they could see the stage being set for just such a massive confrontation.

[114] Ezekiel 38–39

CHAPTER TWENTY-FOUR

The Harvest

The next thirty days passed quickly. Gregor Galinikov wasted no time in carrying out his plans. He was in constant communication with the other representatives of the pagan cities of the world, and they, in turn, were giving directions to the millions who were under their control. No official census was taken, but there were between one and two million people in each of the large pagan cities, bringing the total population of infidels in the world to more than five hundred million. Those numbers were nearly equal to the total number of believers who were living on farms and in small cities around the world. Gog was confident he would be able to lead his forces to victory over those of Him who sat on the throne in Jerusalem.

The first thing he did was to orchestrate a propaganda war. He instructed his subordinates secretly to print up millions of flyers to be distributed throughout their cities, being careful not to let any of them fall into enemy hands. The flyers were to decry the horrible conditions under which they would be forced to live if they accepted the demands of the despot in Israel. They would be robbed of their freedom of speech and conduct, and forced to live by an impossible moral code, which none of them could tolerate. They would be expected to swear allegiance to a foreign king who had done nothing for them in the past, and who would do little for them in the future. They would have to worship Him and pay tithes to Him, and in return, they would receive a few scraps that fell from the tables of the fat Jews He pampered.

The flyers reminded the residents of the inner city ghettos to compare their living conditions with those of the Jews in Israel, whose opulent lifestyles were regularly depicted on their television sets. The dissidents languished in poverty within the demolished ruins of what had once been great cities while the Jews wallowed in ease and luxury. The drastic contrast had its desired effect, bringing the ire of the infidels against the Jews and their Messiah to a boiling point.

Also described in the flyers was the incredible wealth now stored in the Holy Land. The great treasures of the world had been looted from the nations by the wicked Jews, who had then smuggled them into Israel where they were being kept illegally. The citizens of the world had every right to go and take back what was rightfully theirs. They were encouraged to begin equipping an army to do just that.

The flyers also assured the infidels that they would encounter little resistance when they invaded the homeland of the Jews. There were simply no weapons or defenses there of any kind. The fat and lazy Jews would be sitting ducks, armed only with pitchforks and hammers when the attack began. And their so-called Messiah had divested Himself of any powers He might have had. He was no longer a returning warrior; instead, He sat enthroned as a fat cat, ruling over a kingdom of docile mice. They would all be caught totally off guard, and by the time they knew what had happened, it would all be over. The usurper King would be dethroned, and His deceitful followers would be finally eliminated, which is what should have happened to them centuries before.

Within a short time, virtually the entire population of all three hundred cities had been won over. The people were clamoring for war against Israel, and there were more men volunteering to fight than could possibly make the journey. Gog determined that he would not need as many soldiers as he had first thought. Five million men would be more than enough to conquer the unsuspecting and unprepared Jewish gaggle in the Holy Land. Besides, if he sent more than that, it would certainly arouse suspicions. After all, it would take only a limited number of pilgrims to go to Israel and bring back food for the hungry inhabitants of their cities; if many more than that went, it would generate unwanted inquiries and investigations.

Gog sent the word out that certain cities should send more soldiers than others. The ones in proximity to the Middle East should send as many as a hundred thousand troops overland to Israel, while those that would require ship transportation were limited to no more than ten thousand from each city. However, the entire population of all the cities was to prepare for war, because just as soon as the dirty Jews in Israel were eliminated, the Gentile Christians in the rest of the world would be targeted. Therefore, everyone with a desire to kill believers would have his chance.

The first two weeks were spent in manufacturing weapons and securing the necessary number of carts and wagons to bring home the spoils of war. The weapons were crude and homemade, consisting of swords, spears, axes, clubs, shields, and bows and arrows. Such primitive weapons would normally be considered woefully inadequate, but since the Jews would have none whatsoever, they would do quite nicely.

Tony D'Angelo suggested to Gog that they not attempt to take motorized vehicles to Israel. In the first place, they were in extremely short supply and notoriously undependable. Secondly, they would require an enormous amount of gasoline, which was not readily available to them. Finally, millions of men driving large trucks into Israel would arouse too much suspicion. He suggested they secure crude carts and wagons that would be drawn by horses or oxen. They would get the job done, and no one would be the wiser. Besides, weapons could easily be hidden away in the bottoms of them and no one would be likely to look for them there.

Gog saw the wisdom in Tony's words and immediately agreed. He sent the word out for his people to go out among the Gentile Christians in their vicinity and borrow or purchase from them the necessary vehicles, and the animals to pull them. This they did, and they discovered that the foolish believers were all too willing to assist them. Most of the wagons and livestock were freely loaned to them by the gullible dupes whom they would soon destroy.

Within two weeks, everything was in readiness. From distant lands, men and animals and crude, weapon-laden vehicles were being transported to seaports and loaded onto more than a thousand ships to begin their voyages to the shores of the Middle East. Closer to Israel, even greater numbers of would-be pilgrims loaded what they had onto trains and trucks to transport it close enough to the Holy Land so they could complete their journeys overland to the land flowing with milk and honey. Within another three weeks, they would all converge in the heart of Israel, ready to partake of a rich harvest: a harvest of foodstuffs and livestock, of gold and treasures, and especially, a harvest of the lives of their unsuspecting enemies.

Gog and Tony stayed in close communication with each other, coordinating their movements and planning their future attack. They needed no electronic equipment whatsoever, and there was no way for their messages to be intercepted. Gog simply talked to Odin on a daily basis, and Tony communicated with Alexander the Great just as often. And since Apollyon impersonated both spirit guides, he was able to inform and influence both men with devilish efficiency. Everything was falling into place exactly as the wicked demon had planned, and better than either man had dared to hope.

In the rest of the Gentile world, the Christian population thrived under the leadership and protection of God's glorified saints. Their crops were growing in the fields, and some of the early produce was already being sold in the marketplaces. Manufacturers were producing goods at a rapid pace, and happy consumers were buying their wares in busy shops everywhere. There was no such thing as poverty and unemployment. All able-bodied people were working and providing for their households, and no one lacked for any good thing.

Also, everyone appeared to be healthy and strong. Illness seemed to be a thing of the past; the plagues and diseases that had destroyed so many during the tribulation were strangely absent. Medical clinics were maintained only for the purpose of treating those injured in accidents, and for assisting women in childbirth. And there were simply no undertakers or funeral homes. Deaths occurred so seldom, family members cared for their own during those rare occasions.[115]

Small fire departments were maintained to put out the accidental fires that occurred on occasion, but arson and acts of terrorism were simply unheard of. There were no police forces, National Guard units, or military detachments of any kind. They simply were not needed; the Lord provided His own police force. All the people were truly born again, and they strove to live together in love and harmony, however, they were not yet perfected or glorified. They were still human and still possessed carnal natures, and they were perfectly capable of sinning against one another. Therefore, in those isolated cases when one person attempted to harm or cheat another, the otherwise unseen glorified saints administered swift and severe punishment. The mortal saints soon

[115] No more shall an infant from there live but a few days, nor an old man who has not fulfilled his days; for the child shall die one hundred years old, but the sinner being one hundred years old shall be accursed (Isaiah 65:20).

learned what the Lord meant when He said He would rule the nations with a rod of iron.[116]

It was true; the Lord ruled the world of the redeemed as their benevolent dictator. There were no houses of parliament or other legislative bodies anywhere. There were no elections or courts of appeal. The rules were simply distributed from the King's throne in Jerusalem, and His people everywhere were expected to obey them. It took a little getting used to, but soon the believers thrived under the new regime. In their hearts, they really wanted to do what was right anyway; now, they received strong reinforcement from the Lord and His saints to yield to the desires of their new natures and to resist the carnal urges of their old ones. Overt acts of sin were quickly becoming rare occurrences indeed.

The Lord's thousand-year kingdom had not officially begun yet, but His subjects were already becoming well adjusted to how things would be when it did commence. They lived in peace and harmony in their own communities, and they stayed completely away from the vile inner cities where the heathen continued to dwell. They didn't discuss it much, but they wondered how the Lord was going to deal with the unbelief and lawlessness that continued to fester there. Ultimately, they concluded He would handle it all according to His own will, and in His own time. They decided not to concern themselves further with the matter, and they went on living their happy lives, praising their Redeemer and serving one another.

In Israel, the land was indeed flowing with milk and honey . . . and with about every other good thing imaginable. The limbs of the trees and vines bent low, weighed down by the heavy load of fruit tugging at them. Fields were choked with massive crops of grain, alfalfa, and cotton; produce of every sort literally covered the ground.

The harvest started early in October, and continued through to the end of the month. Joyous citizens worked long hours during those weeks, bringing in the largest harvest ever gathered in the history of civilization. By the time it was completed, every warehouse, barn, and storage shed in the nation was filled to the brim.

---

[116] "Ask of Me, and I will give You the nations for Your inheritance, and the ends of the earth for Your possession. You shall rule them with a rod of iron; You shall dash them to pieces like a potter's vessel." (Psalm 2:8–9).

At no place in the entire nation did the land bring forth more plentifully than at Glory Land Estates. The rich soil, abundant rainfall, and nurturing sunshine all combined to produce an unbelievable amount of vegetation. In many fields, the crops stood well above the heads of those who set out to harvest them.

Aaron Muller and the other men worked fourteen-hour days, getting into the fields before sunup and not calling it a day until well after dark. They hired six young teenagers who were not otherwise employed and let them bunk out in the vacant house. With the eleven-man crew, working extra long hours, they were still able to barely keep up with the staggering demands placed upon them. They stopped for breakfast at about eight in the morning and again for lunch at one in the afternoon, but it was well after nine at night before they were able to sit down to a sumptuous dinner before retiring to bed to recover their strength in order to face the challenges of the following day.

The four women were kept busy all day preparing meals, cleaning up afterwards, and keeping up with the laundry. There was no time for leisure pursuits and precious little time even for conversation. Breakfast and lunch were consumed with haste in order for the men to get back into the fields as quickly as possible; dinnertime was the only exception. During the meal, the tables were alive with conversation about the work of the day, the weather, and what was going on elsewhere in the nation and the world. Afterwards, the hired help, exhausted from the long day's work, usually made their way directly to bed and immediately to sleep. But the family lingered for an hour or more, the men helping the women with the dishes and the cleanup, and then sitting in the large living room of the Frieberg home and sharing from their hearts the joy they were all experiencing.

The one day that was different from the rest was the Sabbath. No matter how much remained to be done in the fields, no work was done on the seventh day of each week.[117] Those days were set aside for rest and worship and fellowship. The Glory Land Estates seemed to be the natural gathering place for the people of that area, and long hours of pleasant relaxation were spent there by scores of people.

[117] Thus says the Lord; "Keep justice and do righteousness, for My salvation is about to be revealed. Blessed is the man who does this, and the son of man who lays hold on it; who keeps from defiling the Sabbath, and keeps his hand form doing any evil." (Isaiah 56:1–2).

Ken and Doran and their families were always there, and since he had no immediate family of his own, Mark Robertson chose to make his way across the river and join them every week as well. He was completely stricken with Rachel Muller, and he took advantage of every opportunity he could to see her. Rachel had likewise fallen for him, and welcomed his advances. They too were talking of getting married as soon as the harvest was over and the millennium had officially begun. But for the present, there was simply too much work to be done for anyone to be doing much of anything else.

The work was hard, but not exceptionally so, and the rewards from their labor more than made up for the effort required to gain them. By the third week, the barns and sheds were completely filled, and Aaron had Steve use the truck to haul their excess grain and produce to large community barns and granaries in Jericho. Requests were coming in from all over the world for the excess food produced in Israel, and as it was sold, they received a good portion of the price credited directly to their accounts in the National Bank of Israel. By the time the harvest was coming to an end, they already had more money in the bank than they would need for the coming year, and their barns were still filled to the brim.

The financial gains were amazing, but they were not the greatest benefit from those weeks spent in harvest. The work agreed with them, and they all gained in strength, stamina, and in general health and wellbeing. They all ate well, slept well, and felt well; it was such a contrast to the way they had lived over the previous three-and-a-half years. However, the physical gains weren't the most significant benefits either.

What amazed and blessed them most was the freedom and security they experienced. Instead of running and hiding and fighting to stay alive, they worked openly under the warm sun without fear of being discovered and attacked by some fearful enemy or opportunistic bounty hunter. That incredible sense of wellbeing was a common topic of conversation between Aaron and Anna late in the evenings as they sat on the front porch of the Frieberg home: that and the plans for their upcoming wedding. They rejoiced over all God had done for them in the past, how truly blessed they were at the present time, and how much they were looking forward to the future because of His grace.

But on one particular night, the conversation took on a more somber and ominous tone. Something was beginning to take place over the entire State of Israel that was causing Anna to feel strangely uncomfortable, and maybe even a little fearful.

It was now November and the harvest would soon be over. Already, foreigners were beginning to arrive in Israel. They were coming in carts and wagons drawn by horses and oxen, accompanied by others riding on horses. They were coming to fill their wheeled vessels with some of the overwhelming abundance produced in Israel. They were arriving in great numbers, some from ships anchored in the Mediterranean Sea and the Gulf of Aqaba, but most of them coming overland from all directions. They were beginning to fill the land; some of them were already camped on the estate property next to the Jordan River.

"Aaron, all these people coming here are making me really nervous," Anna confessed. "I know the Messiah invited them to come, and they really need the food, and we have more than we can ever use, but still, it makes me nervous. I guess it's because they were the ones who tried to destroy us believers during the tribulation, and I don't know whether they've really had a change of heart or not. Please tell me that everything's going to be all right."

"Yes, I can do that, Anna," Aaron assured her. "Everything will be perfectly all right . . . but I'm afraid it might take awhile."

"What do you mean by that?"

"Well, there are hundreds of millions of people out there living in those cities all over the world that were the sworn enemies of our Lord and His people. Most of them received the mark of the beast. From what I understand from the Scriptures, those people can never be saved. I don't see them living in peace and harmony with God's people for the next thousand years."

"What are you saying, Aaron? Are they here to attack us? Why would God allow them to do that after everything we've already been through?"

"You know how gracious our Lord is. He wants to give everybody every chance to get saved. He could have wiped all those people out when He came back at the end of the tribulation, but His great heart of compassion wanted to give them a chance to see how wonderful the millennium will be, and give them the chance to repent and be converted. He just couldn't destroy them all without giving them one more chance to believe."[118]

"That's good for them, but it might not be so good for us. What if they decide not to believe, and they refuse to live under the Lord's strict

[118] The Lord is not slack concerning His promise, as some count slackness, but is longsuffering toward us, not willing that any should perish but that all should come to repentance (2 Peter 3:9).

moral laws? What if they're here to start a rebellion? We have no weapons or fortifications of any sort in the whole nation. How would we be able to defend ourselves against them?"

"We couldn't. If we were on our own, we'd be overrun in no time, but we're not on our own, and we never will be. The Lord knows what He's doing, and if it comes down to a fight, He's more than able to take care of Himself, and us too. Here, let me read you the second psalm; it's one of my favorite, and I was just reading it this morning before we went into the fields."

Aaron picked up his Bible, which he had left early that morning on a small table next to the porch swing where they were sitting. He found his place and began to read:

> *Why do the nations rage, and the people plot a vain thing? The kings of the earth set themselves, and the rulers take counsel together, against the Lord and against His Anointed, saying, "Let us break Their bonds in pieces and cast away Their cords from us."*
>
> *He who sits in the heavens shall laugh; the Lord shall hold them in derision. Then He shall speak to them in His wrath, and distress them in His deep displeasure; "Yet I have set My King on My holy hill of Zion."*
>
> *"I will declare the decree; the Lord has said to Me. 'You are My Son, today I have begotten You. Ask of Me, and I will give You the nations for Your inheritance, and the ends of the earth for Your possession. You shall break them with a rod of iron; You shall dash them to pieces like a potter's vessel.'"*
>
> *Now therefore, be wise, O kings; be instructed, you judges of the earth. Serve the Lord with fear, and rejoice with trembling. Kiss the Son, lest He be angry, and you perish in the way, when His wrath is kindled but a little. Blessed are all those who put their trust in Him.*

"This tells me that if any of those infidels out there are planning to attempt to overthrow the Messiah's rule in the world, they will be in for a big disappointment," Aaron concluded as he closed the Bible and took Anna's hand in his. "Pastor Bobby Davis taught me in that Bible study of his that there will be a final rebellion staged by a leader from Russia; it will occur after the tribulation ends and before the millennium officially begins. I think all the pagans who're coming into Israel right now might well be planning on taking more home with them than a few wagonloads of grain and vegetables. Unless I miss my guess, they want to destroy us all and steal everything we have. But God only laughs at their rebellious plans, and He will destroy them instead. I like that last verse that says the Son's enemies will perish, and *"Blessed are all those who put their trust in Him."* We have put our trust in Him, and I'm confident we can depend on Him to bless us and keep us from all harm."

"Yes, you're right," Anna agreed. "Even though it scares me to see so many men with wagons and horses flooding into our land, I will trust the Lord with all my heart. He has brought us this far; He won't abandon us to our enemies now. But I'm still going to pray that those people have truly had a change of heart, and that all they want is to take home to their families some of the good things God has blessed us with. That is possible, isn't it?"

"Of course, my love," Aaron said, trying to sound optimistic. "With God, all things are possible." But in his heart, he feared the sound of war cries would soon begin to be heard throughout the land.

Gregor Galinikov stepped down from the wagon in which he had been riding. He stretched and walked around to work the kinks out of his joints and muscles. He had been riding in that wagon every day for the past two weeks, and he was relieved to be at the end of his journey. Since they had offloaded their wagons and horses from the train in Turkey, it had seemed as though his slow-moving caravan would never arrive in Israel, but here they were, finally at a campsite in the Valley of Jezreel. It was late Wednesday afternoon, so he ordered his men to set up camp and prepare the evening meal. He would rest the remainder of the day, and in the morning, he would survey the surrounding area.

They were at the northern edge of the famous valley called Armageddon where such intense fighting had taken place at the end of the tribulation, but it looked nothing like a battlefield at the present time. From east to west, as far as the eye could see, nothing but rich farmland stretched before him. Most of it had already been harvested, but there remained a few fields where the laborers were still at work. Gog decided he would stay right where he was, and would coordinate the attack from that strategic location.

His initial decision was confirmed the next morning as he rode one of the horses to the top of the hill behind their camp and surveyed the area. Others of his people were moving into the valley and setting up camps as well, and their numbers would continue to increase. By Saturday, the day he and Tony D'Angelo had chosen to launch their nation-wide attack, they would have sufficient numbers to easily subdue the local residents. He could see several farmhouses from his vantage point, but there were no walls or fortifications around them. They would be easy to invade and overrun.

East and south of the valley of Armageddon, Tony was looking for a campsite of his own. He had remembered the words of Aaron Muller, and decided to take his former friend up on his invitation. He had led his group of carts and wagons up a dirt road that paralleled the west side of the Jordan River until he reached a point directly east of a group of farmhouses that looked to be exactly where Aaron had said his estate was located.

Tony decided to set up camp in a large grove of cottonwood trees that grew beside the river. It would provide them with shade and plenty of firewood, and they could draw all the water they would need from the nearby Jordan. He decided it was a perfect spot. What made it so perfect was not the shade and the firewood and the water the location provided, but it was its proximity to his hated nemesis. All the way over on the long boat ride, he had thought of little else besides how sweet would be his revenge at long last.

As others were setting up the camp, he walked out into the harvested field to the west and looked into the distance at the group of buildings at the end of a road more than a mile away. That had to be the place where he would find Aaron and all those close to him. On Saturday morning, when the dirty Jews were enjoying their day of rest, and with the rising sun at his back, he would lead his small army of men across those empty fields and into the rats' nest over there.

He imagined how gratifying it would be to attack those unarmed people who had given him so much grief over the past several years. Divested of his special wartime powers, Aaron should be easy to overcome, and the rest of the gaggle should put up very little resistance, if any at all. He could almost sense the taste of victory in his mouth, and he could hardly wait to have his way at last with that lovely thing Rachel. And he reminded himself, while he was at it, he would also take Aaron's fiancé, or wife, or whatever she was. That would add even further insult to injury to Aaron before he killed him. He had waited a long time, and he had suffered greatly, but he would have his revenge and gratification at last.

CHAPTER TWENTY-FIVE

The Staging

Over the next two days, the harvest was completed throughout the land of Israel. By noon on Friday, every field was bare, and every barn and storage facility in the land was filled to the brim. Great feasting and celebration was taking place around banquet tables in every farmhouse and in every home in the cities and villages. The harvest was in; the Lord's glorious kingdom could not be far off.

Landholders reached out to those camped on their property and shared their bounty with them. The foreign visitors accepted their food and gifts gratefully, but declined to visit any of the Jewish homes or join in on any of their celebrations. They told them they would remain in their camps and respect the Jewish Sabbath the next day, and then on the first day of the week, they would drive their wagons and carts over and begin filling them from the excess contained in their overflowing facilities. They all expressed their seemingly sincere gratitude and appreciation to the residents of the land for their generosity and hospitality, but that did not express the true sentiments of their hearts.

The invaders actually loathed the wealthy Jews in whose land they now camped. As always before, the Jews had taken advantage of innocent people and had profited from the sufferings of others. They had grown fat while the rest of the world suffered and did without. The foreigners were anxious to finally finish what Hitler and Stalin had failed to accomplish: the total and complete annihilation of every Jew on the planet.

Their plan was to eradicate all the people throughout the rest of the land of Israel first, and then march en masse on Jerusalem and destroy the King and His followers there. The plan was a simple one, and it should work perfectly. The stupid Jews were rolling out the red carpet for them: carpet that would soon be stained with the redness of their own blood.

Ivan Feldsin rode one of his horses out to meet those who were camped on his property. He had established his farm in the middle of the Valley of Jezreel (also called Armageddon), and was more than willing to share its incredible abundance with those visiting him. He had known of the presence of his visitors, but before, he had been too busy with his harvest to take time out for a social visit. Now, as he drew near their camp on Friday afternoon, he saw a man riding out to meet him on a horse of his own. As the two approached each other, the hair on the back of Ivan's neck began to stand up. He recognized the visitor as none other than Gregor Galinikov, the wicked ruler of Russia who had personally tried to kill him only a few months before.

Ivan was momentarily speechless, unable to decide what to say or do. He had seen and heard this man in Jerusalem at the Feast of Tabernacles, but prior to that, he had experienced personally his incredible wickedness and cruelty in Russia; he knew of multitudes of his fellow believers who had been killed by him. He would not have hesitated to destroy him a few months before if he had been given the chance, but things were different now; the Lord had come, and He had offered clemency to His former enemies. How could Ivan lash out against this evil man now? He did not look aggressive, and was apparently unarmed; perhaps he had experienced a change of heart. Ivan seriously doubted it, but he decided he would be willing to give him the benefit of the doubt.

"So, Gog, we meet again," he said warily. "As long as you come in peace, you are welcome on my land." He did not, however, extend his hand in a gesture of friendship.

Gog was relieved that he was not assaulted. He recognized the young man immediately as one of those troublesome Jewish rebels who had given him so much resistance during those years leading up to the campaign against Constantine Augustus. He knew him to have had special powers, and would never forget seeing him disappear before his very eyes just as his firing squad had shot their rifles at him. Even though he was a hardened soldier himself, he feared he would be no match for the younger man if he decided to attack him.

"Thank you, my young friend," he said as humbly as he could. "We were enemies before, and you were a worthy opponent, but that was a long time ago. Much has happened since we last saw each other, and believe me, I am a changed man now. I have come to know the error of my ways, and I bear you no harm. Forgive me for the evil I brought upon you and your people in Russia; I was deceived and did not know what I was doing."

"Personally, I am not so sure I believe you, comrade," Ivan replied, "but I am willing to follow the instructions of my King and extend to you the welcome He requires of me. You are free to stay on my land as long as you like, and to fill your wagons with as much as you need. The Lord has blessed me beyond measure and I have much more than I will be able to use. I would invite you and your men to join us for dinner tonight, but we are even now preparing for our Sabbath celebration. However, I would be happy to send some food out to you."

"Thank you; you are very kind, but that will not be necessary. We have plenty, and my cook is preparing our own meal as we speak. We will remain in our camp tomorrow as you observe your holy day, and then, with your permission, we will drive our wagons over to your barns on Sunday and fill them as you have said."

"Of course. Our people will assist you with whatever you may require. But I must warn you; if you have plans to attack and destroy us, you will be destroyed instead. Do I make myself clear?"

"Perfectly. But you do not need to worry. We would not be so foolish as to attempt such a thing; not after your King has been so gracious and generous with us. We are His loyal subjects, just as you are—you will see. Now, if you will excuse me, I must be getting back to my camp."

"Yes, of course. Shalom. I will see you Sunday morning."

With that, the two men turned their horses around and returned in the direction from which they had come. When he was far enough away from the arrogant young Jew so as not to be heard, Gog spat on the ground and cursed him out loud.

"Who do you think you are? How dare you, a filthy peasant, speak down to the Czar of Russia and, soon to be, the ruler of the world. You have no weapons, and you have no army. When I have destroyed everyone in your miserable family, and I have you beaten down to the ground, I will take great pleasure in killing you personally with my own hands."

Later that afternoon, Mark Robertson arrived at the Glory Land Estates east of Jericho. He had made a habit of spending the Sabbaths there because of his friendship with Aaron Muller, and especially because of his love for Aaron's sister Rachel. He had personally strung a cable across the Jordan with a chair suspended from it on a pulley so he could cross the river easily, and the path across the fields between their farms was well trodden by this time.

On this occasion, he was especially anxious to arrive at the Muller home. He had met some visitors on Aaron's side of the river of whose presence he wanted to make sure Aaron was aware. He sought out Rachel and embraced her warmly, but he quickly took Aaron aside and talked with him privately.

"Did you know you had some foreigners camped in the big cottonwood grove next to the river over there?" he asked, pointing to the east.

"Yes, but I haven't gone out there yet. We just finished bringing in the last of the hay this afternoon. I was planning on driving out there when you showed up. Why? Did you meet them?"

"Only one of them, but he seemed to be their leader. He saw me crossing the river and came over to check me out. He's about our age, I'd say; and quite a looker too, I might add. He would be about perfect if it weren't for a big scar on his nose and cheek."

"So he accepted my invitation after all," Aaron said, more to himself than to Mark.

"Do you know the guy?"

"Yeah, we go way back. We swam on the same team in college and were in a Bible study together before the rapture."

"He's not the same dude who was trying to kill you and your family during the tribulation is he?"

"Oh yeah, I forgot I'd told you about him. Yeah, that's Tony D'Angelo. I talked to him briefly the last day of the Feast of Tabernacles in Jerusalem and invited him to visit us here, but I didn't think he would actually take me up on it."

"You think he's gotten saved, Aaron?"

"No way! He was as hardened as anyone I've ever known. He took the mark of the beast immediately, and has been serving the devil ever since."

"Why did you invite him here then?"

"I'm not sure. I guess it was partly because our Lord invited him, and all the people like him, to come, and He expects us to welcome them and share our harvest with them."

"Yeah, I know," Mark agreed. "I remember He told us that these invaders would be coming, but their presence here still makes me uneasy. These pagans have flooded our nation. There're more of them than there are of us, and have you seen them up close and personal like? They look more like an invading army than they do a bunch of hungry pilgrims, and we don't have any way of protecting ourselves. Remember, we can't dodge bullets anymore, and you can't still shoot fire out the end of that rod of yours. If they should attack us, they could easily mow us down, and then there would be nothing standing between them and our loved ones. I shudder to think what they could do to them."

"Yeah, I've thought about that too," Aaron admitted, "but that's the other reason I invited Tony and his bunch to come to our farm. I would actually be surprised if they don't attack us. It's scary, but it's also exciting; I guess that's what faith is all about. I have complete confidence in the Lord Jesus Christ. He knows what He's doing, and He invited them here. If they turn on Him, and us, then I believe He will be perfectly capable of taking care of the situation. All we have to do is hide and watch; and personally, I guess I wanted Tony here so I could see for myself what God's gonna do to him."

"You're actually excited about taking that kind of chance? Remember, we're not just talking about our own skins here. There's all your family here too. Are you willing to risk the lives of your parents and relatives, and that of Anna and Rachel too?"

"Yeah, I guess I am. After all the Lord has seen us through already, I'm convinced we can trust Him to deliver us from whatever evil these foreigners might have in mind for us."

"So, you really want them to attack us so you can see the Lord destroy them, is that it?"

"No, I've got mixed feelings about all this, if you know what I mean. The new man in me wants to see Tony and those like him actually have a change of heart and come to Christ. Even after all he's done, I would be willing to forgive him if he really got saved, and I'd help him load his wagon with our food and send him home with my blessing. I don't even want to think about the eternal torment he'd go through if God were to pour out His divine wrath on him. But the natural man in me wants to see him burn for all the misery he's caused me and my family.

"I'm glad it's not my call, Mark. It's up to Tony and all those who came with him. . . . No, I guess it's really up to the Lord. He can either soften their wicked hearts and bring them to repentance, or He can confirm them in their hardness and destroy them. Personally, I'm betting on the latter. At any rate, I want to be there when it happens, and I'm convinced the Lord is able to protect His own. We're kinda like Moses and the children of Israel during the Exodus. God would never deliver them out of Egypt and across the Red Sea only to destroy them with hunger and thirst in the wilderness. Neither will He deliver us out of the horrors of the tribulation only to waste us in His Holy Land on the eve of His millennial kingdom."

"Yeah, I see what you mean," Mark agreed. "We've trusted the Lord and obeyed His instructions; we can certainly depend on Him to keep His word and see us through this ordeal, no matter how it turns out. But you really think they're planning to attack us, don't you?"

"Yeah, I do. In fact, I think God is actually bringing them here to allow them to follow the dictates of their depraved minds. He gave them an extra forty days to repent, but since they had all taken the mark of the beast, their wicked hearts would not allow their minds to believe. They're confirmed in their infidelity, so the Lord is bringing them here to stage their final rebellion so He can rid the planet of them before He begins His glorious kingdom."

"I think I remember studying about that in a prophecy class I attended back in that Bible college in Philadelphia," Mark said.

"Yeah, Pastor Bobby mentioned it as well," Aaron added. "I just read in Ezekiel again last night where God puts hooks in their jaws and draws them here to Israel to let them stage their assault on His people before He pours out His wrath on them.[119] If this is what that passage is talking about, and I think it is, then it explains why the Lord has allowed so many of His enemies to come into this peaceful land and surround His defenseless people. They hate Him anyway, and they would never consent to live under His strict rules during the kingdom, so He's just drawing them here, using our prosperity as bait, and soon He'll spring the trap."

"I think you're right, Aaron, and if you are, those heathens will probably attack us tomorrow on the Sabbath when they know we will be most vulnerable. I better get back across the river and encourage our people over there. You oughta see the motley crew who've moved in around us on the other side."

---

[119] Thus says the Lord God: "Behold, I am against you, O Gog, the prince of Rosh, Meshech, and Tubal. I will turn you around, put hooks into your jaws, and lead you out, with all your army, horses, and horsemen, all splendidly clothed, a great company with bucklers and shields, all of them handling swords." (Ezekiel 38:3–4).

"Yeah, I think that's a good idea. I'll give you a ride over to the river. I want to see Tony anyway before tomorrow. Maybe I can get a better idea of what to expect after I actually talk to him again.

Aaron went to a shed and started up the ATV he had recently purchased to provide quick transportation to remote sectors of their farm, and he pulled up on it in front of the Frieberg's home. Mark had gone in to say goodbye to Rachel and to pray with her before he left. He came out, looking confident and determined, and climbed on the ATV behind Aaron, and the two of them headed out toward the river. As they rode eastward together, Aaron thanked God for Mark. He had been a faithful friend to him through the horrors of the tribulation, and he couldn't think of anyone he would rather have as a brother-in-law to care for his sister.

When they arrived at the Jordan, they dismounted and knelt beside the ATV and asked the Lord to work His perfect will in their lives, to protect their loved ones, and to defeat their enemies if it came to that. They rose and hugged, and Mark set out for his cable crossing while Aaron walked toward the grove of trees to his right. As he approached the grove, a familiar figure walked out to meet him.

"Hello, Aaron. I thought you might be dropping over," Tony D'Angelo said in a friendly voice.

"Hi, Tony. I see you decided to take me up on my invitation," Aaron replied. "I would have been over sooner, but we really had to hustle to get the last of the hay in before the Sabbath tomorrow. Do you need anything out here? I can bring you about anything you might want."

"No thanks, we're fine. We brought a lot of food with us, and the river is supplying us with all the water we need. We've even been able to rig up some fishing poles and catch some nice fish; tilapia, I think. I hope that's okay."

"Sure, help yourself. The river's full of them. We've been enjoying them ourselves whenever we've had a chance to get away and do some fishing. So, what are your plans, Tony? When do you want to come over and fill your wagons? We have more than we will ever be able to use."

"Tomorrow's your Sabbath, right?"

"Yes, in fact, it'll start in about an hour, just as soon as the sun goes down. I'd invite you and your men to join us for supper, but it will include a lot of praise and worship, and your people would probably be pretty uncomfortable."

"No thanks, you guys go right ahead. Like I said, we're fine right here. You do your Sabbath thing tonight and tomorrow, and we'll stay here and finish making the repairs and modifications we'll need on our wagons. Then, if it's okay with you, we'll drive 'em over Sunday morning and start filling 'em up."

"That'll be fine; we'll be there to help you get loaded up. But before I go, Tony, there's one more thing."

"Yeah, what's that?"

"Just a word of caution. Over a year ago, you tried to deceive my family in order to capture and destroy them in an effort to get at me, but it all blew up in your face. Unless I'm mistaken, that's how you got that scar on your face, right?"

"Yeah, that's right," Tony answered coldly, fingering the scar as he tried to hide the hatred he felt in his heart for the man standing before him who was responsible for it being there. "That's a night I would like to forget, let me tell you."

"No, I don't want you to forget it," Aaron said flatly. "I want you to think about it tonight. In case you and your people plan to take more than some of our food, I want you to think about it real good."

"What are you talking about, Aaron?" Tony demanded.

"You know very well what I'm talking about. We've got a lot more here in Israel than just food. All this abundance must look real good to you guys who've been doing without. We have no army and no weapons to defend ourselves with, and it must be real tempting to just move in and take whatever you want and do whatever you want."

"No way, man!" Tony blurted out, trying to sound convincing. "We all learned our lesson back during the tribulation, or whatever it was. Your side won and our side lost; it's as simple as that. Like Galinikov said back during your feast: we've surrendered, and we've accepted the terms your King set forth. We're just happy to be alive and to be allowed to share in your harvest. We've brought no weapons, and we mean you no harm, believe me."

"I'm not sure I believe you, Tony," Aaron said, looking his former friend squarely in the eyes, "but I'm willing to accept your answer for now. However, I should warn you; for your own good, don't try any funny stuff. We may not have any way of defending ourselves, but we are by no means defenseless. Our Messiah sits enthroned in Jerusalem, and He will not allow anything to happen to His people. Do you understand what I'm saying here?"

"Yes, perfectly; but like I said, you don't have anything to worry about. We're here to get some food, and that's all. We'll be gone by Monday, and you can get back to building your kingdom, or whatever it is you're doing here."

"Very well," Aaron said, extending his hand. "We'll see you on Sunday morning then."

Tony agreed and shook Aaron's hand, hoping his own hand didn't feel as weak and trembling to the other man as it felt to him. The two parted; Aaron got back on his ATV and returned to his loved ones for his Sabbath meal, and Tony returned to his comrades-in-arms to finalize their plans for the next day. He would need a long session with Alexander the Great later that night to bolster his courage and renew his resolve.

His spirit guide assured him that Aaron was pleading in desperation to save his own skin and that of his family. The new King of Israel had lost all of His divine powers, as had Aaron and all those other Jew boys who had served the weak Jehovah back during the former conflict. They were totally defenseless now, and Aaron knew it. He was just bluffing in an attempt to persuade Tony not to take the vengeance on him that he so well deserved, and which was so long overdue.

Finally convinced that everything was as it should be, Tony retired for the night. But, lying on his back, gazing up into the vastness of the starlit heavens, sleep eluded him. He could not shake the sense of impending doom from the corners of his mind, and he was sure he could hear faint echoes of that sinister hissing laughter that had haunted him for so very long.

CHAPTER TWENTY-SIX

The Overthrow

During the hours of that long night in Israel, people started leaving the large cities of the world. Relatively few slipped away, and most of them were women and children, but the exodus was undeniable. Within a twelve-hour period, nearly half a million people worldwide left those wretched places. No formal decision was announced, and few even talked with others about their intentions, but a strange sense of peril drove them from the relative security of their ghettos out into the deserted areas surrounding the cities.

They took with them only what they could carry. They would journey to the Christian settlements in the countryside and ask for asylum, not knowing what would befall them there. Those were the ones who had not formerly received the mark of the beast, and whose hearts had not been permanently hardened. The Spirit of God drove them out of those cities; the same Spirit who would later open their hearts to the gospel and grant them the precious faith to receive its saving message.

As the sun slowly inched its way above the eastern hills, the citizens of Israel were up and alert. Although it was their Sabbath, they somehow sensed it would not be a day of leisure and fellowship like the ones they had enjoyed in the past. Something was about to happen, and they could all sense it. The men in the families walked out of their houses and stood looking toward the encampments of the foreigners who had descended upon their land. They had no weapons in their hands, but there was a look of steely resolve in their faces.

Aaron Muller stood at the back of the house that would be his and Anna's, and looked eastward toward the river. His father and uncle joined him there, as did his younger cousins, Tim and Steve. Millennium paced back and forth in front of them, his eyes always looking in the direction the river, his lips peeled back, exposing his teeth, and a rumbling growl resonating from deep within his massive chest.

"You sense it too, don't you, boy?" Aaron said, kneeling down and putting his arm around the big dog's powerful neck. "They're out there somewhere, aren't they? We can't see 'em, but you've gotten wind of 'em, haven't you, big fella?

Millie whined nervously, and pulled away from Aaron's embrace, which he normally would have welcomed eagerly. He sensed something was definitely about to happen, and he wanted to be ready to respond to it when it did. He walked out to the back gate and stood looking off to the east, his hind quarters quivering with nervous energy, and the hair on the back of his neck standing straight up.

Aaron held his rod in his left hand, not so much as a weapon, but more as a trusted friend. Tim and Steve had picked up pitchforks from the barn, and Joseph and Albert both had shovels in their hands. The five of them were not really armed, but they felt they should not be standing out there empty-handed. They did not speak as they stood gazing across the barren fields; the early morning silence was broken only by the occasional chirping of birds and Millie's steady growl.

Gregor Galinikov sat astraddle his big black horse and checked his watch again. He had sent the word through Odin to the other encampments that they would all launch a coordinated attack on the Jewish settlements at exactly seven in the morning. It was less than two minutes before that hour, and the would-be Russian czar was alive with excitement and anticipation. He held a heavy sword in his right hand, and a wooden shield hung across his saddle horn.

He was surrounded by his best men, similarly armed and mounted on horses of their own. They comprised a cavalry of nearly a hundred horsemen, and they would lead the charge. They would be followed by another hundred foot soldiers, armed with spears, clubs, and bows and arrows. As he looked across the empty fields at the settlement to the south of them, he concluded that there could not be a total of more than a hundred able-bodied men and boys living there. Many of them would still be in bed, and those who were up, would be unarmed and totally unprepared. This was going to be easier than he had hoped.

He checked his watch again and mentally assisted the sluggish second hand in its climb to the top of the dial. When it finally reached the twelve, he raised his sword over his head, dug his heels into the flanks of his mount, and shouted at the top of his voice. His men joined in the battle cry immediately, and they spurred their horses as well. The dust rose in the field as the big steeds churned up the ground. Their riders were careful not to let them break into a gallop, as they did not want to outrun their infantry and divide their forces. Together, more than two hundred warriors closed in on the sleepy little settlement in the middle of the Valley of Jezreel.

All over the land of Israel, similar bands of marauders descended upon similar Jewish settlements. Their hands were filled with crude weapons, and their hearts were filled with cruel hatred. They would kill, rape, pillage, and destroy; and there was no one to stop them. The taste of Gog's revenge would be a sweet one indeed.

On the western bank of the Jordan River, Tony D'Angelo also ordered his men to attack. He insisted he was not accustomed to riding horses, so he let others lead the cavalry charge. He would follow with the other foot soldiers. The truth was he wanted no part of the initial attack. He had more than a hundred soldiers, and he estimated no more than forty men were in the cluster of farmhouses strung out along the road to the west of him, but he didn't want to take any chances.

Although the Jews didn't have any weapons, they were still likely to put up a fight, and he didn't want to run the risk of getting a pitch fork run through his belly or a shovel handle broken across his skull. He would let the more adventurous ones up front break down the Jews' resistance, and then he would be right there to assist in the mop up.

As he jogged across the soft field, following those on horseback, he stayed near the front—but not too near. He wanted to be there to finish off Aaron Muller personally, and he carried a spear in his hand that would run him through quite nicely. After he had dispatched his hated foe, and any of his male relatives who were still alive, he would find a secluded place and have his way with the two young women at last. He had given strict orders for no one else to touch them.

Through the dust raised by the horses in front of him, he could see a gaggle of pathetic Jews beginning to form somewhat of a skirmish line on the east side of the road. There were even fewer of them than he had estimated. This was going to be a piece of cake.

As they drew within bowshot, he ordered his men to halt and his archers to ready their bows. They would probably be able to take out half of the enemy's numbers with their arrows before they even had to enter into hand-to-hand combat. Tony ordered them to draw their bows, which they did in unison, but not a shot was fired.

Suddenly, a mighty voice was heard throughout the entire land of Israel. It appeared to emanate from the heavens themselves. Every soldier froze where he was, and every person in the land heard these words as they boomed forth from the sky above:

> *Behold, I am against you, O Gog, the prince of Rosh, Meshech, and Tubal; and I will turn you around and lead you on, bringing you up from the far north, and bring you against the mountains of Israel. Then I will knock the bow out of your left hand, and cause the arrows to fall out of your right hand. You shall fall upon the mountains of Israel, you and all your troops and the peoples who are with you; I will give you to birds of prey of every sort and to the beasts of the field to be devoured. You shall fall on the open field; for I have spoken.*[120]

Appolyon and his cohorts were frozen in place. They had been busy manipulating their human stooges in their attack against the hated people of Israel, and had been confident of an overwhelming victory, but those words struck horror into their hardened hearts. This was not supposed to happen; Jehovah and his angels were supposed to be preoccupied with other things. They had not been bothered by any of them for weeks, and they had been confident that they would not show up now. The wicked demons looked warily toward the heavens, fearful of what they might contain.

The sound of a mighty blast from a trumpet filled the air, and Michael led his angels in an assault against Appolyon and his scattered comrades. The demons screeched in terror and tried to flee, but chains were thrown about their leathery necks, and they were pulled up short. Michael himself tightened his grip on the chain about Apollyon's neck and started pulling him, writhing and cursing, upward in the air.

[120] Ezekiel 39:1–5

The fallen angel fought to free himself, but he was held fast. He sought to lash out against his captor, but he was powerless against him. Finally, his depraved mind snapped as he gave into the inevitable. He and those like him were being led off to be cast into the blackened abyss, and they were destined to burn in hell forever; but, at least, they had succeeded in seducing Gog and his millions. That was half a billion more souls they had been able to snatch away from the hated Jehovah, and that fact gave him a sick sense of consolation and gratification. As he ceased pulling against his chain and surrendered to the inevitable, he laughed out loud at the thought of all those tortured souls he had been able to beguile into damnation.

Tony D'Angelo was horrified. He too had heard the disembodied voice thundering from the heavens, announcing the impending destruction of Gog and all those who rode with him. Suddenly, all the Scriptures that Pastor Bobby Davis had shared with him flooded his mind, and he remembered clearly all the efforts that black preacher and Scott Graham had made to get him to accept Jesus Christ as his own Savior. But he had rejected Him back then, and he still rejected Him now; and now, he was forced to come to grips with what he had refused to consider before: that he was eternally doomed, and that judgment day had come. But what terrified him most was the sound of Appolyon's maniacal hissing laughter. The sound that had haunted him for years in the back of his mind was now ringing loudly in his ears, confirming his doom and paralyzing him with fear. Then the earthquake hit.

It did not begin slowly and then escalate in magnitude; it struck like a bolt of lightning. The earth heaved in a powerful convulsion that sent seismographic needles off the charts, and sent every standing creature reeling to the earth. Horses and their riders, foot soldiers, and spectators alike, were catapulted to the ground as their legs were knocked out from under them. Weapons were dropped as terrified invaders reached out to break their fall.

Mountains were shaken to their foundations and massive boulders cascaded down their throbbing slopes, the waters of the lakes and rivers were thrown over their banks, and walls everywhere collapsed into piles of rubble. Thousands of Gog's men were either crushed by falling objects, drowned by engulfing water, or swallowed up by huge fissures that the quake opened in the surface of the earth.

Had it not been for God's divine protection, many of His own people would have perished too, and every building in Israel would have collapsed in a matter of a few cataclysmic seconds.[121] As it was, they shook violently, but the Lord's glorified saints and angels banded together to keep them from tumbling to the ground, and the people inside were protected from harm.

The earthquake that ripped through Israel was felt throughout the rest of the world as well. The three hundred cities from which the marauders had come simply disappeared. Those on the seacoasts sank instantly below the ocean waves as the foundations beneath them were destroyed by the massive tremors. The great inland cities, even those in the mountains, did not escape. Great chasms opened in the ground beneath those cities, and the entire metropolitan areas tumbled into the fiery depths in the heart of the earth, dragging their horrified inhabitants with them. In a matter of a few minutes, nearly five hundred million people were swallowed into oblivion. Their last thoughts were of the awesome power of God's wrath, and of their own eternal damnation.[122]

Back in Israel, the destruction of the wicked was not so instantaneous, but it was no less thorough. The power of the mighty earthquake heaved tons of dirt into the air, reducing visibility to near zero. The believers who were outside hurried indoors to the protection of their houses, but the infidels were left out in the open.

They picked up their scattered weapons and struggled to their feet. They groped around in the semi-darkness, trying to regain their bearing. Terror and confusion from the Lord had gripped their hearts, and they had lost all sense of control. In the dim light, they mistook one another as enemy assailants, and they lashed out to defend themselves. For the next several minutes, invaders hacked and stabbed and pum-

---

[121] "And it will come to pass at the same time, when Gog comes against the land of Israel," says the Lord God, "that My fury will show in My face. For in My jealousy and in the fire of My wrath I have spoken: 'Surely in that day there shall be a great earthquake in the land of Israel, so that the fish of the sea, the birds of the heavens, the beasts of the field, all creeping things that creep on the earth, and all men who are on the face of the earth shall shake at My presence. The mountains shall be thrown down, the steep places shall fall, and every wall shall fall to the ground.'" (Ezekiel 38:18–20).

[122] "And I will send fire on Magog and on those who live in security in the coastlands. Then they shall know that I am the Lord. So I will make My holy name known in the midst of My people Israel, and I will not let them profane My holy name anymore. Then the nations shall know that I am the Lord, the Holy One of Israel." (Ezekiel 39:6–7).

meled one another until less than half of them remained standing.[123] But even they did not escape the wrath of God.

The dust had hardly settled, and the godless hordes had barely realized that they had been slaughtering one another, when the darkened skies opened up and poured destruction on the miserable heathen who remained. Overwhelming rain devoured many of them, bowling them over and drowning them in depressions in the earth. Others were crushed to death by mammoth hailstones that fell to the earth like boulders launched from mighty catapults. Still others were consumed by fiery balls of burning sulfur that fell to the earth, strangely mingled with the driving rain and relentless hailstones.[124]

In less than one hour, the mighty invading forces of Gog and his followers were devastated. Well over five million men lay dead or dying across the length and breadth of the land. Gog himself lay mortally wounded, having been pierced by a spear and struck by a hailstone. Blood was running from his wounds, and life was draining from his body when Ivan Feldsin found him lying beside his dead horse in the open field.

"You win!" he groaned. "I could not kill you before, and I could not kill you today. Your God is greater than mine. I have been deceived, and now, I have been destroyed. My dreams die with me, and together, my dreams and I must burn in hell forever."[125] He cursed bitterly, coughed up blood, and died, staring blankly into the blackened heavens above him.

Back at Glory Land Estates, Aaron Muller told his family to stay inside the house and to keep Millie with them as he grabbed his rod and bolted for the door. The onslaught from heaven had not yet completely ended; the rain had nearly stopped, but scattered hailstones and balls of burning brimstone were still falling from the sky, yet he felt compelled to locate his hated nemesis and dispatch him with his own hands. He had seen Tony D'Angelo, back in the pack giving orders to the archers, just before the Lord had spoken from heaven, and he was pretty sure where he would be able to find him. He sprinted out the door and made his way out into the field, his progress hampered by the muddy ground and the mass of bodies strewn across it.

---

[123] "I will call for a sword against Gog throughout all My mountains," says the Lord God. "Every man's sword will be against his brother." (Ezekiel 38:21).

[124] "And I will bring him to judgment with pestilence and bloodshed; I will rain down on him, on his troops, and on the many peoples who are with him, flooding rain, great hailstones, fire, and brimstone." (Ezekiel 38:22).

[125] "Thus I will magnify Myself and sanctify Myself, and I will be known in the eyes of many nations. Then they shall know that I am the Lord." (Ezekiel 38:23).

He paid no attention to the hailstones and burning brimstone that continued to fall to the earth around him. They were decreasing in frequency and magnitude, and he sensed that they were not intended for him anyway. Surely his God could protect him from danger as he sought out the enemy He had finally delivered into his hand. As David of old had been unconcerned with any threat from the Philistine army as he approached the fallen giant Goliath to cut off his head with his own sword, so Aaron was oblivious to the falling objects about him as he approached his stricken enemy.[126]

He spotted Tony, writhing in the mud up ahead of him, and he quickened his pace so he could get there and dispatch him before his enemy died of his own wounds first. He tightened his grip on his rod and mentally prepared himself for the task that was long overdue. He had not lashed out against Tony when he had met him before because his King had granted amnesty to the infidels who had come to Israel in peace. But those evil men had now displayed their intentions to kill and plunder, and the Lord Himself had destroyed them. Surely, he had the green light now to finish the job, and he was looking forward to it. But that was before he saw him up close.

When Aaron reached Tony's side and looked down at the miserable creature before him, his desire to destroy him drained from his heart, and it was replaced by an overwhelming sorrow and pity. For, before him lay the once healthy and handsome young man now reduced to a quivering mass of dying flesh. His body had been hacked and pierced by weapons wielded by his own men, and a falling hailstone had apparently crushed his left shoulder. But worst of all was the damage done by the burning brimstone that had scorched the right side of his head. The hair and most of the flesh had been burned away, exposing the raw bones of his skull and jaw jutting through the charred remains of tissue.

Tony looked up at Aaron with his remaining left eye, and it was an image the latter would never forget. Gone was the look of cockiness and pride Aaron had seen so often in their college days. Gone too was the

[126] Then David put his hand in his bag and took out a stone; and he slung it and struck the Philistine in his forehead, so that the stone sank into his forehead, and he fell on his face to the earth. So David prevailed over the Philistine with a sling and a stone, and struck the Philistine and killed him. But there was no sword in the hand of David. Therefore David ran and stood over the Philistine, took his sword and drew it out of its sheath and killed him, and cut off his head with it. And when the Philistines saw that their champion was dead, they fled (1 Samuel 17:49–51).

look of hatred and malice he had seen there when Tony had tried to shoot him to death a few months before. Now there was only the appearance of agony and terror.

"Aaron, is that you?" Tony gasped, reaching out toward the man now kneeling at his side.

"Yes, Tony, it's me," Aaron answered, taking the fallen man's bloody hand in his own.

"Oh, Aaron, help me! For God's sake, help me!

"Tony, I'm so sorry, so very sorry," Aaron said, tears now filling his eyes and spilling down his cheeks, "but I'm afraid there's nothing I can do for you now."

"You can help me to believe," Tony replied through a gurgling sound deep in his chest. Pastor Bobby said that's all I had to do, Aaron. . . . I'm ready to do that now. . . . Can you help me . . .? I can't seem to do it by myself."

"Oh, I wish I could, Tony!" Aaron choked out, now weeping openly. "I really wish I could! But you made your choice long ago, and you reconfirmed it time and time again. I fear you must now accept the consequences of that choice. I'm so sorry!"[127]

"Oh, no . . . it's too late for me, isn't it . . .? Too late," Tony whispered weakly as the life drained from his stricken body. The ever-resourceful, self-confident man had finally come to the end of himself, and there was none to help him. His back arched, his breath stuck in his throat, his eye rolled back in his head . . . and he died.

Aaron looked down through his tears at the pitiful mass of scorched flesh before him, and his heart broke. He picked up Tony's head and shoulders in his strong arms and held them to his chest. He sat there in the mud and the blood, rocking back and forth, his body racked with sobs. As he mourned the loss of the man who had once been his friend, all animosity toward him was gone. His emotional pain was compounded by the fact that Tony represented multiplied millions just like him who now lay dead across the face of the land. He felt pity and sorrow for

---

[127] "Because you disdained all my counsel, and would have none of my rebuke, I also will laugh at your calamity; I will mock when your terror comes, when your terror comes like a storm, and your destruction comes like a whirlwind, when distress and anguish come upon you. Then they will call on me, but I will not answer; they will seek me diligently, but they will not find me. Because they hated knowledge and did not choose the fear of the Lord, they would have none of my counsel and despised my every rebuke." (Proverbs 1:25–30).

them, but he was overwhelmed with a consuming hatred toward the devil and his angels. They had seduced and deceived so many billions of people, and now they had not only destroyed their lives, but they had also managed to doom their souls to an eternity in hell. The anger, frustration, and sense of helplessness were almost more than he could bear.

After some time, Aaron was shaken from his anger and grief when he heard his name being called. He looked up and saw that the wrath from heaven had completely ended and people were emerging from the buildings. Tim and Steve were making their way out to him to see if he was okay.

He released Tony's body and stood to his feet. He waved to his cousins and called to them that he was fine; he would be coming in shortly. That satisfied them and they turned around and returned to the rest of the family standing next to the house. There was nothing pleasant to see out in the field, and they had no desire to stay out there among so much death if they didn't have to.

Aaron looked around him. The darkness of God's wrath was dissipating from the skies and the sun was beginning to shine through again. The air was filled with a wonderful stillness, so reassuring after it had been choked with the awful sounds of chaos only a short time before. The wicked had been destroyed, and God's people had been spared. The time of threats and danger was over, and the reign of peace and prosperity was about to begin.

He turned away from Tony's body and started walking back to his loved ones. Already, his mood was changing. Being yet in his mortal state and not having the mind of Christ, accepting God's divine wrath against His enemies was not automatic for him, but he was beginning to accept things as they really were. Tony had made his decision long ago, as had all those slain across the mountains and valleys of Israel, and they had come into this land only to kill, plunder, and destroy. They had received from God only that which they sought to inflict upon others.

Aaron wiped his eyes with his sleeve and quickened his pace. He would leave the wicked where they had fallen and grieve for them no more. As he walked through their bodies strewn about him, he praised God for His righteous indignation poured out upon His enemies, but he praised Him even more for the marvelous grace He had continually demonstrated toward those unworthy sinners who had placed their confidence in Him—among whom he considered himself chief.

He broke into a run, wanting to distance himself as soon as possible from the death in the field, and to embrace the life waiting for him at the edge of it. In the arms of his family and the woman he loved, he would erase the last vestiges of the grief he had experienced over the death and damnation poured out on the enemies of his God.

CHAPTER TWENTY-SEVEN

The Kingdom

The reigning Christ sent word through His glorified saints for His people to remain in their homes for the remainder of the Sabbath day. They were to ignore the bodies of the men and beasts that surrounded them on that fateful day, and they were to spend the time in rest, praise, and thanksgiving. This they did, although it was difficult to ignore that which was so painfully obvious. They drew their shades to blot out the sight of the carnage outside, and they worshipped their Redeemer with a sincerity and fervor they had not known before.

On Sunday, it was a different story entirely. The Lord instructed his people to attend to that which surrounded them. They were to bury the bodies of the men and beasts that lay scattered throughout their land, and they were to collect and destroy all their weapons of war. It was a monumental job, and it would not be accomplished quickly.

With bulldozers and earthmovers, huge mass graves were dredged in a deserted valley east of the Dead Sea, and every truck in Israel was employed in hauling the bodies to that remote site. With virtually every able-bodied citizen involved in the corporate task, most of the bodies were buried within three days, but the burial process would go on for months. Gog's forces had literally covered the land, and many of them had fallen on the tops of mountains, down in gorges, and in other hard-to-access places.

Detachments of searchers were organized to canvass the entire nation to discover every dead body—even small portions thereof—and to set up markers at the site of every discovery to be seen by burial crews who followed behind them. They would collect the bones and transport them to the burial site. It would be a full seven months before every bone, of every body, of every invader, was securely buried in the valley that came to be known as Hamon Gog (literally *the multitude of Gog*).[128]

To get rid of the weapons of war that Gog and his hordes had brought into the land took even longer. The Lord instructed His people to melt down the swords and spearheads and other metal objects to make farming implements,[129] but He told them to burn the wood in their stoves and fireplaces. The amount of wood in all the shields, spears, clubs, and bows and arrows—not to mention that in the carts and wagons—came to an enormous amount. It would take a full seven years for all of it to be used up.[130]

But the kingdom of God was not postponed until all that was done. Indeed, the Sabbath following Gog's attack and subsequent destruction, the Lord declared the official beginning of His glorious thousand-year reign on the earth. It was in early November, a full 1335 days since that Friday when Constantine Augustus had defiled the temple in Jerusalem and the tribulation had begun.[131]

During those few horrible years, there had been more suffering and death than in all the wars of the world since the beginning of civiliza-

---

[128] "It will come to pass in that day that I will give Gog a burial place there in Israel, the valley of those who pass by east of the sea. . . . They will set apart men regularly employed, with the help of a search party, to pass through the land and bury those bodies remaining on the ground, in order to cleanse it. At the end of seven months they will make a search. The party will pass through the land; and when anyone sees a man's bone, he shall set up a marker by it, till the buriers have buried it in the Valley of Hamon Gog." (Ezekiel 39:11, 14–15).

[129] They shall beat their swords into plowshares, and their spears into pruning hooks; nation shall not lift up sword against nation, neither shall they learn war anymore (Isaiah 2:4).

[130] "Then those who dwell in the cities of Israel will go out and set on fire and burn the weapons, both the shields and bucklers, the bows and arrows, the javelins and spears; and they will make fires with them for seven years. They will not take wood from the field nor cut down any from the forests, because they will make fires with the weapons; and they will plunder those who plundered them, and pillage those who pillaged them," says the Lord God (Ezekiel 39:9–10).

[131] "And from the time that the daily sacrifice is taken away, and the abomination of desolation is set up, there shall be one thousand two hundred and ninety days. Blessed is he who waits, and comes to the one thousand three hundred and thirty-five days." (Daniel 12:11–12).

tion. A few more than half a billion mortals continued to live on the earth out of more than six billion who had inhabited it prior to the rapture. Yet it had not all been bad, not by any means.

About a third of those who had perished had come to know Jesus Christ as their own Savior and Lord before their deaths, and they were now glorified and reigning with their King. The others who had perished—the wicked ones who had been beguiled by the devil and his angels—had been permanently removed, along with the foul spirits whom they served, and there was no threat of evil anywhere on the planet. The time of pain and misery had finally come to an end, and the long-promised era of peace and prosperity had arrived at last.

Even as the bodies of the wicked were still being located and buried, and their weapons were being broken down and burned, the permanent order of the kingdom was being put in place. The first thing the Lord did was to appoint His original eleven disciples (plus Matthias who had later been chosen to replace the fallen Judas[132]) to rule over the twelve tribes of Israel. Each of those glorified saints would assist their sovereign Lord in governing the nation, sitting on large thrones in the temple courtyard, from which they would handle matters brought to them from members of their respective tribes.[133]

Aaron and his family were thrilled to learn that the apostle Paul was also being promoted to one of the highest positions in the kingdom. On official occasions, he and King David were to sit at the places of honor on either side of their Lord. But when not needed in Jerusalem, he was free to dwell among his people, and being from the tribe of Benjamin,[134] he had chosen to care for his kinsmen in Jericho. The people in and around that city who had come to know and love him rejoiced to see their friend and benefactor so honored.

---

[132] And they prayed and said, "You, O Lord, who know the hearts of all, show which of these two You have chosen to take part in this ministry and apostleship from which Judas by transgression fell, that he might go to his own place." And they cast their lots, and the lot fell on Matthias. And he was numbered with the eleven apostles (Acts 1:24–26).

[133] "But you are those who have continued with Me in My trials. And I bestow upon you a kingdom, just as My Father bestowed one upon Me, that you may eat and drink at My table in My kingdom, and sit on thrones judging the twelve tribes of Israel." (Luke 22:30).

[134] If anyone else thinks he may have confidence in the flesh, I more so: circumcised the eighth day, of the stock of Israel, of the tribe of Benjamin, a Hebrew of the Hebrews; concerning the law, a Pharisee (Philippians 3:4–5).

The other glorified Jewish saints were assigned other responsibilities throughout the land of Israel. They were busy repairing the damage the earthquake and the onslaught from heaven had done on earth, and were available to serve their Lord and assist their mortal brethren in whatever way they could. They were not to interfere with the daily lives of the people, but whenever special assistance might be required, they would lend immediate assistance. The kingdom would truly be a time when no one lacked for any good thing.

The first official act of business of the new government in Israel was to distribute the excess food still stored in the barns and warehouses across the land. Happy laborers loaded truckload after truckload onto the waiting ships that Gog's minions had left at anchor in Israel's harbors. They, in turn, would transport the precious cargos to Christian communities all over the world. The needs of believers who had survived the tribulation would be more than supplied until they reaped more of their own harvests.

The glorified Gentile saints were assigned responsibilities in those communities of the faithful all around the world. Scott Graham and Candace Mercer, the Singletons, and the entire Davis family were given assignments in the area where Los Angeles had once stood. The former wicked inhabitants had been swept away when the western part of the city had sunk beneath the waves of the Pacific Ocean, but much of the uninhabited outlying areas remained. Those areas were already being restored, and soon families would be moving back into them. A thriving metropolis would soon flourish where only evil had dwelt for the previous several years.

All over the world, the same thing was taking place. The scars where the evil cities had once stood would soon be erased, and their existence would be nothing more than a distant memory in the minds of those dwelling in the cities of righteousness being built in their place. Men and beasts would live together in perfect harmony, and there would never be any cause for fear or dread. All people would know the Lord, and that knowledge would set them free from the painful consequences of ignorance and sin.[135]

[135] The nursing child shall play by the cobra's hole, and the weaned child shall put his hand in the viper's den. They shall not hurt nor destroy in all My holy mountain, for the earth shall be full of the knowledge of the Lord as the waters cover the sea (Isaiah 11:8–9).

Christ's kingdom was to be highly organized and extremely efficient. Everything would flow from His throne in Jerusalem and then be communicated universally through a sophisticated network of glorified saints. Righteousness and justice would flow like refreshing streams throughout the world.[136]

Since the time of the Lord's return, the earth had begun to produce bountifully in Israel, but with the official onset of the kingdom, nearly that same degree of fruitfulness was to be evidenced throughout the rest of the world as well. Gentle rains would water the fertile soil, and farmers would reap bumper crops in record time. There would never be a shortage of food for the world's population, which would soon begin to grow at an exponential rate.[137]

Israel and its people were destined to be at the very center of all that was good. For an untold number of centuries, they had been hated and persecuted and driven from their land, but that was a thing of the past. They had all returned to their ancestral home, and they would prosper there, and they would never be uprooted from it again.[138] In fact, the Jews were to be honored and welcomed by all wherever they traveled. People everywhere would seek them out and show kindness to them because they would know that God's special favor rested on them, and they wanted perhaps some of it to rub off on them.[139]

The people of the kingdom were still human, and as such, were still capable of sinning, but evil deeds would be a rarity, and sin would be dealt with quickly and severely. People were destined to live extremely

---

[136] Of the increase of His government and peace there will be no end, upon the throne of David and over His kingdom, to order it and establish it with judgment and justice from that time forward, ever forever. The zeal of the Lord of hosts will perform this (Isaiah 9:7).

[137] "Behold, the days are coming," says the Lord, "when the plowman shall overtake the reaper, and the treader of grapes him who sows seed; the mountains shall drip with sweet wine, and all the hills shall flow with it." (Amos 9:13).

[138] "I will bring back the captives of My people Israel; they shall build the waste cities and inhabit them; they shall plant vineyards and drink wine from them; they shall also make gardens and eat fruit from them. I will plant them in their land, and no longer shall they be pulled up from the land I have given them," says the Lord your God (Amos 9:14–15).

[139] Thus says the Lord of hosts, "In those days ten men from every language of the nations shall grasp the sleeve of a Jewish man, saying, 'Let us go with you, for we have heard that God is with you.'" (Zechariah 8:23).

long and incredibly healthy lives. Some of the young perhaps would live throughout the entire thousand-year period.[140]

But even under such ideal conditions, the curse of sin was not completely removed. The babies born to the citizens of the kingdom would still have a sin nature, and they would need to be saved as they grew older and became aware of their need. Initially, almost all of them would, but as the centuries passed, more and more of them would become hardened in their unbelief. They would conform outwardly—there would be nothing else they could do—but inwardly, they would long to fulfill the lust and greed that raged in their unregenerate hearts.

At the end of the thousand-year kingdom, the devil would be loosed for a short time, and he would lead a huge rebellion against the Lord and His people similar to the one that had just been put down (so similar, it would be called by the same name). And similarly, the final rebellion would end with the ultimate destruction of the wicked.[141]

However, such an event was so far in the future, no one at the beginning of the millennium gave it so much as a second thought. They were completely absorbed with the amazing spiritual and tangible abundance surrounding them; they could not be troubled with what could happen a thousand years in the future.

No place on earth was happier or more prosperous at the beginning of the millennium than was Glory Land Estates, the thriving little community northeast of the ancient city of Jericho. As soon as the dead bodies had been removed from the fields and the soil had dried sufficiently, the men were on their tractors working the ground and planting their winter crops. The women were busy preparing for the upcoming weddings.

---

[140] "No more shall an infant from there live but a few days, nor an old man who has not fulfilled his days; for the child shall die one hundred years old, but the sinner being one hundred years old shall be accursed. . . . For as the days of a tree, so shall be the days of My people, and My elect shall long enjoy the work of their hands." (Isaiah 65:20, 22).

[141] Now when the thousand years have expired, Satan will be released from his prison and will go out to deceive the nations which are in the four corners of the earth, Gog and Magog, to gather them together to battle, whose numbers is as the sand of the sea. They went up on the breadth of the earth and surrounded the camp of the saints and the beloved city. And fire came down from God and out of heaven and devoured them (Revelation 20:7–9).

They completed furnishing and decorating the houses that would be the newlyweds' homes, they sewed festive attire for all those who would be participating in the wedding, and they cooked and baked like women obsessed. After all, not one, but two couples, were being married (at one time, the number had been three). Of course, Aaron and Anna were to be wed; their marriage had been planned since shortly after the rapture, but Mark and Rachel had consented to join them in the ceremony. At first, they had planned to postpone their own wedding until afterward so as not to take anything away from the other couple's celebration, but Aaron and Anna had insisted they join them in a double wedding. Ken Friedman and his fiancée Mary had been invited to join them to make it a threesome; and they had originally agreed, but they later decided they didn't want to wait that long. They had been married earlier in a simple backyard ceremony, and they were away on their honeymoon as the preparations were ongoing for the lavish affair that Miriam Muller and Nora Frieberg had planned.

Mark spent as much time as he could with Rachel's family at Glory Land, but he was so busy planting his own crops and making his own home comfortable for his bride-to-be, that he wasn't able to visit very often. But he still saw Rachel nearly every day, as she and her mother came over often to help prepare the future bride's new home. He even recruited some help and constructed a footbridge over the Jordan River to replace the awkward cable chair contraption that the women had so much difficulty operating. It was a wise decision, for in the years to come; many adults and happy children would use the bridge and beat down the path between the two farms.

Those were good days indeed. The pleasant autumn sun warmed their bodies, and the joys of the millennial kingdom warmed their souls. Tim had grown quite fond of Ken's sister Betty, and they were beginning to talk of wedding plans in the future. Even Steve, at nineteen, had begun dating Doran's cousin Emma. It would not be long before every able-bodied adult in Israel was married and the land would be awash with the sounds of little children playing in the orchards and fields, and in the streets of the cities.

Even the dog Millennium was not to be left out. He had encountered a big female mastiff-cross down the road and they had become inseparable. His mate's name was Molly, which the family found greatly amusing. It was clear from the swelling around the female's midsection that Millie and Molly would be welcoming young ones of their own into the kingdom, come next spring.

Gentle rains watered the fields regularly, and the crops thrived in them; strangely, weeds did not grow at all. Work was not arduous, and it was soon done for the day, leaving much time for leisure. Long walks were taken by young lovers in the fields and along the riverbanks, and long talks were enjoyed by the older adults in porch swings in the afternoon shade.

There was much to be done for pure fun and entertainment. Aaron and his family enjoyed riding the horses and the ATVs and swimming in a deep hole in the Jordan River. Tim and Steve rigged a huge swing in a cottonwood tree that could launch the more adventurous users two-thirds of the way across the river. But the family's favorite recreation spot was the Dead Sea (now called the Eastern Sea, since it was certainly no longer dead).

Cleansed by the healing waters that continued to flow from the temple mount in Jerusalem, the sea was now awash with life and teeming with ocean fish. The family purchased a ski boat and kept it docked permanently at the water's edge. They were not concerned about it being stolen, never even bothering to take the key out of the ignition. During this kingdom age, theft—along with other overt crimes—was simply unheard of. Whenever they got the chance, the family headed for the sea to enjoy their boat.

The young adults soon became accomplished water-skiers, and everyone enjoyed the fishing. The catch of the day was often served up on the dinner table that evening. They had to be careful not to catch more fish than they could use or give away. There was no legal limit to the number of fish they could catch, and there was certainly no limit to the number of fish available in the sea.

In the days before their wedding, after supper, Aaron and Anna often drove down to the sea and went out on the boat. They watched the sun set beyond the mountain of Masada and listened to the gentle plops of the fish jumping in the water around their boat. As darkness settled in on the peaceful scene, they enjoyed drifting on the smooth surface of the Eastern Sea under the light of the waxing moon. They spoke of many things during those evenings they spent together.

"Aaron," Anna said softly as she snuggled up to him at the back of the boat one such evening, "We're going to be married two days from now. I can hardly believe it's really going to happen. There were times when I was sure I would never see you again."

"I know what you mean," Aaron agreed. "The tribulation was truly hell on earth, and there were plenty of times when I thought I was a goner . . . and you too. I'll never forget how awful I felt when I thought you and my family had been blown up in that cabin back in those mountains. But that's all behind us now. The tribulation is over, the devil and his angels are in the bottomless pit, the beast and the false prophet are in the lake of fire, and the wicked men of this world have been swept away into Hades. Christ has returned and is reigning in Jerusalem, His saints and angels are assisting Him in maintaining absolute justice and harmony, and we're enjoying perfect peace and prosperity. I guess it just couldn't get any better than this."

"Oh, yes it could!"

"How do you mean?"

"Well, smarty pants, I don't know about you, but as far as I'm concerned, it won't be complete until we're married and live together in our own home and start raising our own family."

Aaron laughed. "Of course, my dear," he said playfully. "I was assuming those things when I said things were about as good as they could get. My life wouldn't be complete if I couldn't be with you. There would be no millennium at all for me if I couldn't spend it as your husband, and as the father of our children.

"But this spot is way too secluded, and this atmosphere is way too romantic," he quickly added. "And unless we want to get an early start on raising our children, I suggest we head for the docks."

Now it was Anna's turn to laugh. "You're absolutely right, my love. Our relationship has been wonderful up to this point, and I want our wedding night to be that way too. There's no sense messing things up now by getting carried away in the back seat of the car."

"It's a boat, my dear," Aaron laughed as he got up and went to the driver's seat and started the big inboard engine. It responded eagerly as Anna settled into the seat opposite him and took his hand in hers.

"I love you, big guy," she said as the boat did a u-turn and headed back toward the distant docks.

"I love you too!" Aaron responded as he smiled in the darkness and squeezed her hand. He felt his heart beating in his chest with absolute joy as they skimmed across the surface of the water in silence under the silvery glow of the harvest moon.

CHAPTER TWENTY-EIGHT

The Wedding

The day of the wedding was simply splendid, from the eager rising of the sun to the reluctant going down of the same. Only a few scattered fluffy clouds interrupted the continual flow of the warm autumn sunshine, and singing birds added their melodies to the already festive mood of the day.

Glory Land Estates was indeed glorious on that eventful day. Flowers and balloons and streamers were everywhere. Next to a platform erected in front of Aaron and Anna's home, a small orchestra was playing, and children were dancing and singing along with the familiar Jewish folksongs. Guests had started arriving shortly after eight o'clock, and by ten, there was hardly a place to sit or stand in the large circle between the three houses. The smell of a whole beef and two lambs being barbequed was tantalizing the taste buds of the well-wishers, and the array of food being placed on the serving tables was a sight to behold.

Most of the guests were from the immediate area, but many had come from some distance. Along with Ken, who had returned early from his honeymoon to serve as Mark's best man, Joseph Roth and David Cohen were in attendance, as were the grooms' closest friends among God's 144,000 witnesses: Ivan, Rico, Julio, Seth, and Jabin. Many of their family members were there as well to add to the numbers of local guests. Papa Saul Frieberg, who would serve as Aaron's best man, was also there, and from as far away as the United States, several other glorified saints had arrived for the occasion.

Along with his mother and sister who had been saved prior to the rapture, Mark had requested the presence of Dwight Honaker and Ben Hiestead, and they had been happy to oblige. The two men were seated near the front in a section reserved for family and honored guests. Next to them was Keith Thompson, the young helicopter pilot, who had flown in from his home in Denver at Mark's request.

Aaron also had guests there from the States. Derek Uptain had flown in from Bakersfield with several members of his *family* to honor his friend. Scott Graham and Candace Mercer were there to offer their congratulations, as were the Singleton and Davis families. Actually, Pastor Bobby Davis was a special honored guest, as he was the minister chosen to perform the double ceremony. Since nearly all of the participants in the ceremony, as well a great number of the guests in attendance, had lived in the U.S. prior to the rapture, those to be married had decided on an American-style wedding rather than a typically Jewish one.

The weather was perfect, the setting was ideal, and the guests were beaming with love and support. But what made the event absolutely perfect was the arrival of the two guests who appeared just before the wedding began.

Saul of Tarsus, better known as the apostle Paul, arrived with several others of the glorified saints. Although he was a highly esteemed member of the Lord's millennial administration, he considered it an honor to attend the wedding of two of the most outstanding of the 144,000 who had stood for the Lord and His people during the horrific years of the tribulation. He was in his glorified body, and no longer suffered from the physical limitations that had plagued him during his earthly ministry. He was young, handsome, and full of righteous exuberance. His presence created quite a stir, but it was soon eclipsed by the fervor created by the last guest to arrive.

The Lord Jesus Christ, the reigning Messiah of Israel, appeared at the rear of the large congregation. He did not drive up in a chauffeured limousine, neither did He ride in on a donkey, nor did He walk humbly into their midst. He was simply *there*. He was dressed in a simple white robe and had sandals on his feet. His dark hair and beard were neatly trimmed, but they did not shine in the morning sun. His features, though pleasant enough, were not remarkable. At first glance, one might mistake Him for just another one of the celebrants, but there was something special about Him—something regal—something divine.

Perhaps it was His countenance that revealed His true identity, for there was a deep radiance emanating from within His brown eyes that spoke volumes about His person. One could not look into them without realizing he was in the presence of God. Also, the way He carried Himself revealed the divine essence that moved within His human frame.

The word quickly spread throughout the crowd, and people began to leave their places and gather around the Lord. He raised His hand and called for them to return to their places. He was there, not to draw attention to Himself, but to honor two of His choicest servants on the day of their weddings. He declined a seat offered to Him in the front row, insisting rather on standing at the rear of the congregation. He even drew a laugh from the crowd when He observed that His services were not really needed anyway, as the hosts had provided plenty of wine for everyone.

At precisely 10:30, the orchestra stopped performing, and the lady at the harp began to play beautiful strains from the classic song *Exodus.* Then Zelma Parsons, by special request from Aaron Muller, stepped to the platform and started to sing, "This land is mine, God gave this land to me." Although a microphone was there, she did not use it. Her powerful voice carried the moving message of the song throughout the entire congregation. Having heard her sing at Gloria Davis' funeral, Aaron had decided that, if at all possible, she would be there to sing at his wedding, and here she was—her glorified voice even more enthralling than it had been before. She was not Jewish, but she was an anointed child of God, and everyone thrilled at her presentation.

As she continued her song, Tim and Steve ushered in Miriam Muller and Mark Robertson's glorified mother and sister. After seating them all in the front row, they went over and took their places in the second row beside their mother Nora Frieberg. After they were seated, Reverend Robert Davis led Aaron and Mark, accompanied by Papa Saul and Ken Weinman, as they walked over from the Frieberg home. Pastor Bobby was dressed in a stunning navy blue suit with a carnation in the lapel. Although the others normally wore western attire as well, on this special occasion, they were all dressed in festive traditional Jewish robes.

As soon as they had taken their places on the platform—with the pastor in the middle, and Aaron and Mark and their best men positioned to his right and his left respectively—two ladies emerged from the house behind the platform. Ken's wife Mary led the way and came and stood opposite her husband on Mark's right. She was followed closely by Ken's sister Betty, who took her position across from Papa Saul, who was standing next to Aaron.

As Zelma began the last verse of the song, Joseph Muller stepped from the house and led his daughter Rachel on his arm to join Mark on the platform. They were followed by Albert Frieberg and Anna Berger. Since Anna's parents were not among the redeemed, she had asked Albert, who had become like a father to her over the past several years, to give her away. He was delighted with the honor, and couldn't have been more proud had she actually been the daughter he had always wanted. He had tears of joy in his eyes when he placed her hand in that of his beloved nephew Aaron Muller.

The two maids-of-honor were dressed in soft yellow dresses, and the brides were stunning in their long white wedding gowns. Rachel was a little taller, and her features were a little darker than Anna's, but they were equally radiant, and equally beautiful.

After the two fathers-of-the-brides had taken their seats beside their wives, Zelma finished her song and stepped down to take her seat next to Georgia Davis. Bobby Davis approached the microphone and thanked her for her contribution. He said it brought back fond memories of the ministry they had shared together at the Antioch Baptist Church back in Compton, California. Bobby welcomed all the guests and led them in a prayer of praise and thanksgiving for the lives and testimonies of the two couples now standing before him.

He went through the preliminaries of having the fathers give the brides away, and asking if anyone had any reason that should prevent either marriage from taking place. Then he talked about marriage in general, giving biblical references for the principles of undying love, self-sacrifice, and fidelity. Those who had heard him preach before agreed he had never before come across with so much spiritual sincerity, insight, and power. There was something about being in a glorified state that perfected every aspect of one's person, including a preacher's ability to communicate the Word of God.

Then, turning to Aaron, he said, "Son, I knew there was something very special about you the moment I got to know you. You had a hunger for spiritual knowledge and zeal for God I had never seen before. I count it a great privilege to have been allowed to lend some small assistance along your spiritual journey. Your exploits have become legendary; there's not a person in heaven or earth who does not know of Aaron Muller, the leader of God's chosen 144,000 witnesses. And now, you have again honored me by asking me to help launch you into your next great adventure. And, though it may have its challenges, believe me, it's going to be much more pleasant than your previous one."

That last comment brought laughter and shouts of affirmation from the large congregation. Bobby continued, turning to Mark Robertson, "And Mark, we have not met before today, but I have known you through Aaron, and I have prayed for you for years. You too have distinguished yourself as a chosen vessel of the Lord. Years ago, the two of you stood side-by-side as you brought down that hated Dome of the Rock, you fought side-by-side on the Mount of Olives before our Lord returned, and now, on the day of your wedding, you stand side-by-side again. And with your farms adjoining each other, you're destined to raise your families side-by-side throughout this glorious kingdom age.

"And ladies," he said, turning his attention to Anna and Rachel, "it was a great honor to meet you after the Lord's return, and to assist you and your family in your journey to your new homes here in the Holy Land, but I have never seen you looking so lovely. Thank you for allowing me to have a part in this great event in your lives."

Then the preacher had the couples face each other and join their hands together. They looked lovingly into each other's eyes as they repeated their wedding vows. Bobby had performed many weddings before, and he had always had some apprehension when he administered phrases like, "for better or worse," "for richer or poorer," and, "in sickness and in health," not knowing what those couples might face in the future, but not so today. During God's perfect millennial kingdom, there would be no calamity, neither poverty, nor infirmity. In fact, he didn't even include those phrases in their vows, knowing that only goodness and mercy would follow them all the days of their lives.

First Mark and Rachel, and then Aaron and Anna, repeated their vows and pledged to each other their undying love and devotion. They exchanged simple gold bands, and again, sealed their unions with solemn and heartfelt promises. With tears of joy in his eyes, Pastor Bobby pronounced them man and wife, and gave the new husbands the customary permission to kiss their new brides.

Amid thunderous applause and shouts of approval, the two happy couples embraced and initiated their long and blessed marriages with an enthusiastic kiss. But before he presented them to the congregation eager to congratulate them, Bobby did something that hadn't been done in nearly two thousand years. He asked the Lord Jesus to bless a marriage.[142]

---

[142] On the third day there was a wedding in Cana of Galilee, and the mother of Jesus was there. Now both Jesus and His disciples were invited to the wedding. . . . This beginning of signs Jesus did in Cana of Galilee, and manifested His glory; and His disciples believed in Him (John 2:1–2, 11).

Although it had not been previously arranged, the Lord was willing to oblige. He made His way through the crowd as they parted and bowed before Him. As He walked onto the platform, everyone on it knelt before Him. Jesus insisted they stand, which they did, but they remained with their heads bowed before His majesty. Even though they were now in the Lord's millennial kingdom, and He had been living among them for nearly three months, none of them felt worthy of being in His presence.

Jesus embraced all of those on the platform, and then He stepped between Aaron and Mark and laid His arms across their broad shoulders and rested His nail-scarred hands on the heads of their brides. They, in turn, reached out and drew the rest of the wedding party in around them.

Thus arranged, the Lord began by quoting Himself from Matthew 25:21, *"Well done, good and faithful servants; you were faithful over a few things, I will make you ruler over many things. Enter into the joy of your Lord."* He continued by individually thanking them for their faithfulness during the tribulation period, and for their continued obedience and loyalty during the months of transition.

Then he smiled and looked at the two beaming young couples and blessed them. He then brought Ken and Mary into the circle and lovingly said to them all, "Aaron and Anna, Mark and Rachel, Kenneth and Mary, you are not only My faithful servants, you are My intimate friends. Be blessed, be fruitful, multiply, and replenish the earth. The grace of your Lord Jesus Christ, the love of God your Father, and the communion of the Holy Spirit be with you always. Amen."[143]

With that, He embraced and kissed all six of them. Then he turned and blessed the entire congregation and presented the newlyweds to them. There was even a greater celebration than before, and it went on for several minutes. The Lord had to raise His hands and call for order before they finally settled down. While they were all still in their places, He called the apostle Paul to come to the platform to close in prayer.

The apostle was eager to respond, and he bounded to the platform. He hugged Pastor Bobby and embraced the three couples as well, and then asked everyone to bow in prayer. He prayed a simple prayer of thanksgiving to God the Father, and again asked His divine blessing on the lives and families of the three special couples before him. He

[143] 2 Corinthians 13:14

blessed the food and the time of celebration that would follow, and then said amen.

When the people echoed the amen and raised their eyes, they were surprised to see that both the Lord Jesus and the apostle Paul had vanished. They had not wanted their presence to distract in any way from those who had just been married, so they simply willed themselves back to the temple in Jerusalem.

Pastor Bobby Davis shouted a hearty, "Hallelujah! Praise the Lord!" Then he said, "It gives me great pleasure to present to you three wonderful couples: just married today are Aaron and Anna Muller and Mark and Rachel Robertson; and married just a week ago, Kenneth and Mary Weinman. Whom God has joined together, let no man put asunder!"

With that, the orchestra began playing a lively number and Aaron and Anna walked briskly off the platform to join the congregation in front of it, followed closely by Mark and Rachel and Ken and Mary. They were then followed by Saul and Betty, with Bobby descending the steps behind them. They did not actually form a receiving line in front of the platform; their family and friends simply surrounded them and spent the next thirty minutes hugging and kissing and congratulating all those who had participated in that unusual, but magnificent, wedding.

Papa Saul hugged Aaron for the longest time. Finally, he released him and said, "Son, I'm so proud of you, and so thankful for you. God used you to deliver me and my family from the hell of the tribulation, but more importantly, He used you to bring us to faith and salvation. I can never thank Him and you enough. You deserve every blessing He will bestow upon you in the years to come."

Georgia Davis grabbed him from Saul, saying, "Don't you be keepin' him all to yourself, you old goat. You gotta' be sharin' him with the rest of us." Then she gave Aaron a big kiss and laughed that wonderful laugh that was uniquely hers.

"Aaron," she said, "you're about the best thing that ever happened to me. Don't get me wrong; I thank God for my son and grandsons, and I did a few things right by them, but steppin' in front of that bullet for you is the best thing I ever did. My dyin' allowed you to live and do all those amazing things you did for all those people in the world. Now you and your sweet wife be happy, enjoy life to the fullest, and fill this valley with your children." She laughed again, hugged him tightly, and released him to other well-wishers as she embraced and congratulated Anna.

Normally, the glorified saints and the mortal believers did not socialize a great deal with one another during the millennium (their interests being so vastly different), but this was an exception. The large congregation was about equally divided among them, and one would be hard pressed to distinguish one from the other. They ate and drank and danced and celebrated together for the rest of the day with not so much as a thought as to who had been glorified and who had not. The food was delicious, the music superb, the dancing enthusiastic, and the celebrating was totally unabashed. Such pure joy and merry making had not taken place in Israel since the events surrounding the return of the Lord Himself.

Toward evening, the two newly wed couples excused themselves, changed their clothes, and loaded their van in preparation for their drive to Tel Aviv. One more time, they hugged their parents, family members, and dear friends. Then they boarded the van, and Tim and Steve drove them to the coastal city where they would be staying in separate hotels. Mark and Rachel were staying near the airport so they could catch their plane in the morning for their flight to South Africa where they would be spending their honeymoon surrounded by the country's breathtaking beauty and abundance of exotic wildlife.

Tim would then drive Aaron and Anna to their hotel on the beach, which would put them close to the docks where they would board their cruise ship in the morning. They had decided to sail the Mediterranean Sea for their two-week honeymoon, stopping at all the famous ports-of-call.

They hugged all around one last time and wished each other well. They would be apart for a short time, and each couple was looking forward to spending that special time completely alone and away from family and friends. But they would be back together again in two weeks, and would be neighbors for perhaps hundreds of years to come. They all welcomed that happy thought.

As Aaron waved goodbye to them and got back into the van with Anna for the short trip to their hotel, he was filled with joy and approval concerning the other couple. His little sister, in whom he thoroughly delighted, was now married to his best friend, to whom he had trusted his life on several occasions. He could not have been more pleased with the match. He looked forward to raising their families together on adjacent farms, separated only by the faithful flow of the scenic Jordan River.

That night, after a light supper, Aaron and Anna sat together, hand-in-hand, in lounge chairs on the balcony outside their hotel room. They looked out at the vast Mediterranean Sea, watching the last faint glow of light fade from the western sky. They sat there for a long time, enjoying the soft warm breeze from the sea as it caressed their faces, sharing their love, and recounting the many miraculous things God had done in their lives over the past four years. They had gone from the breaking off their relationship because of his crazy religious fanaticism, on to the horrors of the tribulation and the blossoming of their love for each other, then to the coming of the Lord and the beginning of His glorious millennium, and now, to the joining of their lives together in marriage, blessed personally by the apostle Paul and the Lord Himself.

Aaron looked over at his bride and smiled. He told her softly, "Now I really don't see any way it could possibly get any better than this. At the risk of sounding corny, this is where someone needs to say, 'And they all lived happily ever after.'"

"And I suppose, after that, someone else ought to say, 'The End,'" Anna added laughing. "But we can't have that, my love; not in light of the fact that this is only the beginning."

She rose from her chair and gently took the hand of her husband and drew him to her side. She kissed him softly on the lips and then led him back into their hotel room and closed the sliding glass door and drew the heavy drapes.

Appendices

APPENDIX ONE

Life in the Millennial Kingdom

Few subjects are as controversial among evangelical Christians as is the matter of the kingdom of God. The reason for the controversy is that although the word "kingdom" occurs hundreds of times in the Bible, it doesn't always carry the same connotation. Usually, in the Old Testament, the word was used to depict the realm of a particular nation, most often that of Israel, either as it existed in the days of the prophets, or as they saw it materializing in the future. But in some of the Psalms and in other poetic passages, the kingdom takes on a more spiritual or heavenly dimension. David said in Psalm 103:19, *"The Lord has established His throne in heaven, and His kingdom rules over all."*

In the New Testament, the spiritual aspect of the kingdom is emphasized even more. In many passages, "the kingdom of God" is a phrase used to express the way God relates to His people at any time, and they to Him. In Romans 14:17–18, Paul tells us, *"For the kingdom of God is not eating and drinking, but righteousness and peace and joy in the Holy Spirit. For he who serves Christ in these things is acceptable to God and approved by men."* And in some places, "the kingdom of God" is used almost interchangeably with the concept of heaven itself. In John 3:5, Jesus told Nicodemus, *"Unless one is born again, he cannot see the kingdom of God."*

In light of the fact that the Bible, especially in the New Testament, uses the term "kingdom" so often to convey spiritual truths, many scholars have come to the conclusion that we are to understand the kingdom of God as being entirely spiritual in nature. They would have us to believe that there will be no tangible kingdom of God on the earth in the future: that the kingdom is purely spiritual, and that we are in the kingdom of God right now. Such scholars are called amillennialists (meaning *no* millennium).

Other scholars disagree. They concur that the word "kingdom" is often used to convey spiritual and heavenly truths, but they insist the concept of a future, physical kingdom is so overwhelmingly taught in Scripture that it must be understood as tangible. It will be manifested on earth after the Lord returns at the end of the tribulation period. Such scholars are called premillennialists (meaning the Lord will return *before* the millennium).

If you have read *Gog's Revenge*, you know that I agree with the premillennial scholars. I believe the Bible clearly confirms what the Jewish scholars have always taught: that we are in a present evil age of sin and suffering, which will be followed by an intense time of judgment and tribulation, which will, in turn, be followed by a wonderful age of peace and prosperity. We have names for these three periods: the present church age, the coming great tribulation, and the following millennial kingdom of Jesus Christ.

In this short appendix, we will not have space to examine this question thoroughly, but we will take a look at two specific aspects of it. First, we will summarize the extensive biblical teaching concerning the coming of a literal, thousand-year kingdom on earth. Then, we will consider some of the objections to such a kingdom posed by the amillennial scholars, and we will offer some answers to those objections.

Support for a Literal Kingdom

The Permanent Return of the Scattered Nation of Israel

There are literally dozens of Old Testament passages that prophesy concerning Israel's destiny. For the sake of brevity, we will look at only one of them. In the ninth chapter of the book that bears his name, the prophet Amos, writing in the ninth century B.C., reveals the nation's future in three distinct phases.

First, he predicts that because of Israel's continual rebellion against her God, He will uproot her from her land and scatter her among all the nations of the world. Yet in all of her dispersion, she will not be destroyed; her integrity as a people will be preserved:

> *"Behold, the eyes of the Lord God are on the sinful kingdom, and I will destroy it from the face of the earth; yet I will not utterly destroy the house of Jacob," says the Lord. "For surely I will sift the house of Israel among all nations, as grain is sifted in a sieve; yet not the smallest grain shall fall to the ground. All the sinners of My people shall die by the sword, who say, 'The calamity shall not overtake nor confront us.'"* (Amos 9:8–10)

History reveals that is exactly what happened. Israel suffered captivity in the Old Testament days at the hands of the Assyrians and the Babylonians because of their sinfulness, but it was the Romans, in the New Testament, who finished the job. After the Jews rejected and crucified their Messiah, the Lord allowed the Romans to destroy Jerusalem, raze the temple, and disperse the people throughout the world. After the final dispersion in A.D. 135, for over 1800 years, the people of Israel wandered the earth without a homeland. But as the prophet predicted, they did not perish; they maintained their culture, their language, and their religion.

Secondly, the prophet predicted that the Lord would bring His people back and establish them in their ancestral homeland once again. He would bless them with incredible fruitfulness and power over the other nations:

> *On that day I will raise up the tabernacle of David, which has fallen down, and repair its damages; I will raise up its ruins, and rebuild it as in the days of old; that they may possess the remnant of Edom, and all the Gentiles who are called by My name," says the Lord who does this thing. "Behold, the days are coming," says the Lord, "when the plowman shall overtake the reaper, and the treader of grapes him who sows seed; the mountains shall drip with sweet wine, and all the hills shall flow with it. I will bring back the captives of My people Israel; they shall build the waste cities and inhabit them; they shall plant vineyards and drink wine from them; they shall also make gardens and eat fruit from them.* (Amos 9:11–14)

That too has taken place, at least in part. At the end of the nineteenth century, the Zionist movement began, and Jews by the thousands began to return to Palestine. After World War II, the United Nations established the Nation of Israel in a portion of the land that had been theirs two thousand years before. Over fifty years later, in spite of the concerted efforts of their hostile Muslim neighbors to drive them out, they are still there. And they are prospering. For its size, Israel has the strongest military and the most productive economy in the world.

Finally, the prophet Amos predicts that the people of Israel will possess their land permanently, and that nothing, and no one, will be able to uproot them again: "*'I will plant them in their land, and no longer shall they be pulled up from the land I have given them,' says the Lord your God.*" (Amos 9:15).

Amos' prophecy is in the process of being fulfilled before our very eyes. It has all come true literally and historically up to this point; why would we not expect the full realization of their promised kingdom to be realized in any other way?

The Unique Details of the Promised Kingdom

Another reason we believe the kingdom will be literal and tangible is because the Bible describes in detail a period of time that has definitely not existed in the past, and can only be realized in the future. Again, for the sake of brevity, we will look at only two Old Testament passages and one in the New Testament.

In the book of Zechariah, the prophet describes what can only be the final battle at the end of the tribulation, and the literal return of Christ to the Mount of Olives:

> *Behold, the day of the Lord is coming, and your spoil will be divided in your midst. For I will gather all the nations to battle against Jerusalem; the city shall be taken, the houses rifled, and the women ravished. Half of the city shall go into captivity, but the remnant of the people shall not be cut off from the city. Then the Lord will go forth and fight against those nations as He fights in the day of battle. And in that day His feet will stand on the Mount of Olives, which faces Jerusalem on the east.* (Zechariah 14:1–4a)

Then the prophet goes on to describe a natural phenomenon that has never occurred in the past and can only find its fulfillment in the future kingdom:

> *And the Mount of Olives shall be split in two, from east to west, making a very large valley; half of the mountain shall move toward the north and half of it toward the south. . . . And in that day it shall be that living waters shall flow from Jerusalem, half of them toward the eastern sea; and half of them toward the western sea; in both summer and winter it shall occur.* (Zechariah 14:4b, 8)

Zechariah continues by telling us that the Jewish King will reign in Jerusalem, and all nations will be required to go there periodically to worship Him, and they will be punished if they refuse to do so:

> *And it shall come to pass that everyone who is left of all the nations which came against Jerusalem shall go up from year to year to worship the King, the Lord of hosts, and to keep the Feast of Tabernacles. And it shall be that whichever of the families of the earth do not come up to Jerusalem to worship the King, the Lord of hosts, on them there will be no rain.* (Zechariah 14:16–17)

Zechariah gives many other descriptions of this kingdom, and sadly, we don't have space to pursue them all, but from what we've already considered, he can only be describing a time in the future since nothing he reveals has ever taken place in the past. So many of the other prophets do the same thing. Ezekiel devotes the last twelve chapters of his prophecy to describing a kingdom that has never existed anywhere in the history of the world.

In Chapter 37, Ezekiel describes the Spirit of God descending upon a lifeless valley and miraculously producing a vast army of vibrant soldiers from the heaps of dry bones scattered about in the dust. The prophet can only be prophesying concerning the phenomenal rebirth of Israel and its return to its homeland.

Then in chapters 38–39, he describes the invasion of the peaceful and prospering Israel by an overwhelming force led by a dark prince out of the far north. As Ezekiel describes it, this Battle of Gog and Magog has never taken place in history, but it fits perfectly into the transition period immediately after the Lord returns at the end of the tribulation, and before He actually sets up His kingdom on earth.

After that, in chapters 40–48, the prophet launches into a very detailed description of the kingdom age that follows the battle. He first gives graphic descriptions of the massive and elaborate temple that will be built in Jerusalem (chapters 40–42). Then he describes in detail the order of worship conducted at the temple site, complete with its elaborate dedication, regulations for the worshipers and priests, and the many sacrifices they will offer (chapters 43–46). Finally, he concludes by describing how the river from the temple mount will flow into the Dead Sea and will heal its poisoned waters, and how the expanded dimensions of the land will be divided among the twelve tribes of Israel (chapters 47–48).

Ezekiel's descriptions of Israel's future kingdom are both detailed and extensive, and they are also completely meaningless unless they are describing actual places and events. So are all of the other Old Testament passages that describe the kingdom in detail. The New Testament confirms, rather than explains away, the kingdom prophecies initiated in the Old Testament; we will look at just one of its passages.

In the book of Revelation, John devotes most of his attention to describing the details of the great tribulation that will engulf the earth in the near future (chapters 6–19), but in chapter 20, he tells of the Lord's kingdom that will follow His return to earth and His defeat of all His enemies. He does not give a great deal of detail about the kingdom, but one thing he says is of great importance. Five times, he states that the duration of that period will be specifically one thousand years:

> *He laid hold of the dragon, that serpent of old, who is the Devil and Satan, and bound him for a thousand years; and cast him into the bottomless pit, and shut him up, and set a seal on him, so that he should deceive the nations no more till the thousand years were finished. . . . And I saw thrones, and they sat on them, and judgment was committed to them. . . . And they lived and reigned with Christ for a thousand years. But the rest of the dead did not live again until the thousand years were finished. . . . Now when the thousand years have expired, Satan will be released from his prison.* (Revelation 20:2–7)

There is a generally accepted rule of biblical interpretation that deals with numbers. It states that if a numerical coefficient is used with a word, that word is to be understood in a literal sense, and is not to be taken spiritually or symbolically. Such terms as "the day of the Lord," or "the day of vengeance of our God," can be understood as long periods of time, and not as literal twenty-four hour days; but when numbers are used, that is not the case.

God created the heavens and the earth in six literal days. It rained literally for forty days and forty nights in the days of Noah. Methuselah lived precisely nine hundred and sixty-nine years. And the coming kingdom of Jesus Christ will last for a full one thousand years. To consider Christ's kingdom in any other light is to destroy any significance that numbers have when used in biblical revelation.

The Living Conditions During the Kingdom

The prophets of the Bible describe a future time when life on earth will be like no other time since Adam and Eve lived in the Garden of Eden. Their explanations are not set in figurative terms, but are penned in clear, descriptive language. Isaiah records how the Lord will destroy His enemies through the words of His mouth and He will rule his kingdom in righteousness and equity. Then the prophet describes living conditions under His reign:

> *The wolf also shall dwell with the lamb, the leopard shall lie down with the young goat, the calf and the young lion and the fatling together; and a little child shall lead them. The cow and the bear shall graze; their young ones shall lie down together; and the lion shall eat straw like the ox. The nursing child shall play by the cobra's hole, and the weaned child shall put his hand in the viper's den. They shall not hurt nor destroy in all My holy mountain, for the earth shall be full of the knowledge of the Lord as the waters cover the sea.* (Isaiah 11:6–9)

> *He shall judge between the nations, and rebuke many people; they shall beat their swords into plowshares, and their spears into pruning hooks; nation shall not lift up sword against nation, neither shall they learn war anymore.* (Isaiah 2:4)

Besides describing a time of incredible peace and harmony among men, and even in the animal world, another thing the prophet reveals is that people will live for an incredibly long time in the coming kingdom:

> *No more shall an infant from there live but a few days, nor an old man who has not fulfilled his days; for the child shall die one hundred years old, but the sinner being one hundred years old shall be accursed. . . . For as the days of a tree, so shall be the days of My people, and My elect shall long enjoy the work of their hands.* (Isaiah 65:20,22)

The question we must ask is this: If the Lord did not want us to understand the coming kingdom as being a literal one, complete with all the astounding characteristics Isaiah has just depicted for us, then why did He direct him and the other prophets to describe it so explicitly? God is certainly not the author of confusion, which is exactly what we would get if we tried to explain that God didn't really mean what He said, even though He said it clearly over and over again.

Objections to the Literal View

Those amillennialists who choose to spiritualize all of the passages we have examined thus far (and a host of other ones as well) insist that the kingdom of God is not to be understood as a real period of time in the future in which Christ will actually rule the world from Jerusalem. They understand it rather as a spiritual state of mind. To them, Christ has already come in a spiritual sense, and we are already in the spiritual realm of His kingdom. All the benefits of the kingdom are not to be realized in a tangible way, but are to be experienced spiritually in the inner man. They point to three main arguments for support. We will examine them briefly and give answers to them.

The Kingdom Is Not an Earthly One

They insist that Christ never taught that His kingdom was going to be a tangible, earthly one. Supposedly, He taught his disciples that the kingdom was spiritual in nature, and that it was to be experienced immediately, not at some time in the distant future. They point to such Scriptures as Luke 17:20–21, where we read:

> *Now when He was asked by the Pharisees when the kingdom of God would come, He answered them and said, "The kingdom of God does not come with observation; nor will they say, 'See here!' or 'See there!' for indeed the kingdom of God is within you."*

The statement about the kingdom being within you seems convincing at first, but a closer look at the passage and its context will reveal that the Scriptures do not support their conclusion at all.

The Greek phrase, translated *within you* in Luke 17:21, is more accurately translated *in the midst of you.*[144] Jesus was not saying the kingdom was a spiritual thing, only to be realized in their hearts. What He was saying is that they should not be overly concerned with when the kingdom might someday come, especially in light of the fact that the King was already in their midst. The King, without whom there would be no kingdom, was standing right before them.

Luke then removes all doubt concerning what Christ meant in the sixteen verses that follow. Through the end of the chapter, Jesus explains how the actual coming of His kingdom will be sudden and without warning just as in the days of Noah's flood and the overthrow of Sodom and Gomorrah. The Savior assured them that He would be coming in judgment to set up His kingdom; they would just not know when to expect it.

Another passage they point out is found in John, chapter eighteen, where Jesus was examined by Pontius Pilate. The Roman governor asked Him if He was the King of the Jews and if He was guilty of the insurrection of which the Jewish leaders had accused Him. In verse thirty-six, Jesus answered, "*My kingdom is not of this world. If My kingdom were of this world, My servants would fight, so that I should not be delivered to the Jews; but now My kingdom is not from here.*"

They insist Jesus taught that His kingdom was merely a spiritual one, and they find it sad that both the people of His day, and most evangelical scholars since their time, have failed to grasp His meaning. They feel we are misguided and without true biblical support when we insist on looking forward to an earthly kingdom.

However, on closer inspection, we discover that when Jesus said, "*My kingdom is not of this world,*" He was not saying that His kingdom would never be realized in tangible form; He was simply saying it was not scheduled to be manifested in that particular setting, and that He would do nothing to establish it at that time. He was on trial for His life before the governor Pontius Pilate, and He offered no resistance or defense. That was because He had repeatedly stated that His mission at that time was to suffer and die and to be raised back to life,[145] not to set up His kingdom. But only hours earlier, He had clearly confirmed that in a future time He would most certainly come and set up His kingdom.

When He was arrested and brought before the high priest, Caiaphas asked Him if He were the Christ, the Son of God, and He answered, "*It*

[144] George Ricker Berry, *Interlinear Greek-English New Testament*, (Grand Rapids, Michigan: Baker Book House, 1981), 286.
[145] Matthew 16:21, 17:22–23, and 20:18–19.

is as you said. Nevertheless, I say to you, hereafter you will see the Son of Man sitting at the right hand of the Power and coming on the clouds of heaven," (Matthew 26:64). Christ's kingdom was indeed coming, but He would do nothing to establish it at the time of His arrest and trial because it was not the proper time, neither were those the proper circumstances. Therefore, he told Pilate, *"It is not of this world."*

If Jesus had never intended to set up His kingdom on earth, He had plenty of opportunities to clarify the matter. In Matthew 20:21, the mother of James and John asked Jesus if her sons might be granted to sit on His right and left hand when He established His kingdom. If there were to be no literal kingdom, the Lord would surely have told her so; instead, He said, *"To sit on My right hand and on My left is not Mine to give, but it is for those for whom it is prepared by My Father,"* (Matthew 20:23).

On the day of Christ's ascension, His disciples asked Him, *"Lord, will You at this time restore the kingdom to Israel?"* (Acts 1:6). If there were to be no such kingdom, He would plainly have told them so. Instead, He told them, *"It is not for you to know times or seasons which the Father has put in His own authority,"* (Acts 1:7). Instead of saying there would be no kingdom, He confirmed there would be one, only they would not be allowed to know when it was coming.

Rather than denying the coming of a literal kingdom, our Lord gave specific instructions and details concerning it. At the night of the Last Supper, He told His disciples, *"And I bestow upon you a kingdom, just as My Father bestowed one upon Me, that you may eat and drink at My table in My kingdom, and sit on thrones judging the twelve tribes of Israel,"* (Luke 22:29–30). If there was to be no kingdom, His words were absolutely meaningless and confusing.

Hence, in spite of a few passages that have been taken out of context and given meanings that are without justification, Jesus clearly taught of a coming kingdom, which will be literal, tangible, and earthly.

The Kingdom Worship System

Amillennial scholars take great exception to the descriptions of how worship will be conducted in the promised kingdom of God. As we pointed out above, Ezekiel goes to great lengths in chapters 40–46 of his prophecy to describe the millennial temple and all of its articles of furniture. He pays particular attention to describing the responsibilities of the priests and the nature of the various sacrifices they will offer. What disturbs the scholars most is that animals will be sacrificed in great numbers for the sins of the leaders and the people:

> *And on that day the prince shall prepare for himself and for all the people of the land a bull for a sin offering. On the seven days of the feast he shall prepare a burnt offering to the Lord, seven bulls and seven rams without blemish, daily for seven days, and a kid of the goats daily for a sin offering.* (Ezekiel 45:22–23)

They rightly point out that, "*It is not possible that the blood of bulls and goats could take away sins,*" (Hebrews 10:4). They also remind us that "*This Man, after He had offered one sacrifice for sins forever, sat down at the right hand of God. . . . For by one offering He has perfected forever those who are being sanctified,*" (Hebrews 10:12,14). And they claim that any additional offering for sin beyond what Christ supplied once and for all is not only unnecessary, it is totally unacceptable. They insist, "*Now where there is remission of sin, there is no longer an offering for sin,*" (Hebrews 10:18).

To those scholars, the idea of a millennial kingdom where animal sacrifices would be a daily experience is unthinkable. They rightly insist Christ's supreme sacrifice put a permanent end to all other sacrifices, and they maintain that any description of animal sacrifices in a future kingdom must be understood in a spiritual sense, not a literal one.

These critics make a valid point, and a strong argument. It really doesn't seem reasonable that God would reinstitute animal sacrifices so long after Jesus made a final offering for sin. Yet their argument is not ironclad, and there is a plausible explanation.

The only answer that makes any sense is that those sacrifices will be offered as a memorial, commemorating the one great sacrifice of the unique Lamb of God. Animal sacrifices are completely out of the question in our present church age, but they may not be in the coming kingdom of the Jewish Messiah. A close examination of Old Testament kingdom passages reveals just how very Jewish that age will be. There will be an enforced observance of the Sabbath and all the annual Jewish feasts and holy days. There will be a fully furnished temple, complete with an altar of sacrifice, with a multitude of attending priests. Animal sacrifices would seem much more natural in such a setting.

We Christians observe communion as a memorial to Christ's death. We partake of the bread and the cup in remembrance of His sacrificed body and His shed blood. The apostle Paul put it this way:

> *For I received from the Lord that which I also delivered to you: that the Lord Jesus in the same night in which He was betrayed took bread; and when He had given thanks, He broke it and said, "Take, eat; this is My body which is broken for you; do this in remembrance of Me." In the same manner He also took the cup after supper, saying, "This is the new covenant in My blood. This do, as often as you drink it, in remembrance of Me." For as often as you eat this bread and drink this cup, you proclaim the Lord's death till He comes.* (1 Corinthians 11:23–26)

Just as partaking of communion on a regular basis is the Christian way of commemorating Christ's death, so may the animal sacrifices of the kingdom be the Jewish way of doing the same thing. Such sacrifices could never be offered to actually atone for sin, but they could certainly be offered symbolically, to remind the Lord's covenant people of His supreme sacrifice on their behalf.

Unrealistic Descriptions of Life in the Kingdom

Some of the amillennial scholars use our own arguments against us. They insist that the descriptions of life in the kingdom are so idyllic and supernatural that they actually do more harm than good to our position. Above, I described some of those supernatural characteristics as evidences that the kingdom must be future because nothing like that has existed on earth since the days when the prophets revealed them. But instead of being convinced, or even impressed by such descriptions, those scholars contend that they are so unrealistic they cannot be describing actual conditions, and they must be understood only in a spiritual or allegorical way. We will consider two examples of the types of things that disturb them most.

They maintain that it is not reasonable to believe that the basic nature of animals will be changed throughout the world. They find unbelievable the idea that carnivorous animals that attack and kill other animals for food could be changed into herbivorous ones. Lions and leopards are simply designed to be meat-eaters. There is no plausible way they could survive on a diet of plants. The scholars insist we must look at such passages as spiritual allegories depicting how children of God's spiritual kingdom lose the desire to bite and devour one another, and former enemies are able to dwell together in harmony and love.

Answering that argument is not difficult to do. God created all animals to be herbivorous in the beginning. There wasn't a meat-eater in the bunch. We read in Genesis 1:29–30:

> *And God said, "See, I have given you every herb that yields seed which is on the face of all the earth, and every tree whose fruit yields seed; to you it shall be for food. Also, to every beast of the earth, to every bird of the air, and to everything that creeps on the earth, in which there is life, I have given every green herb for food;" and it was so.*

After the Fall, God cursed man and the natural world in which he lived. He obviously changed the nature of some of the animals, and carnivorous beasts began to roam the earth. When He blesses the world during the coming kingdom, it will be an easy thing for an infinite God simply to change the beasts back to the way He had created them in the first place.

Another teaching about living conditions in the kingdom sticks in the craw of the amillennial scholars. As we saw above, Isaiah depicts life as being drastically extended during the reign of the Messiah. One who dies at one hundred years of age will be considered a child, and a person's lifespan will be comparable to that of a tree. Many trees live hundreds of years, some well over a thousand years, but the average human lifespan has been well under a hundred years for millennia. They maintain that ever since the Flood changed the atmospheric conditions on our planet, it has been scientifically impossible for humans to live as long as Isaiah claims they will.

The scholars' explanation again is that such language must be understood symbolically. The extended life, of which Isaiah speaks, must be referring to the spiritual vitality experienced by the believer in this life, and of the endless nature of the one to come in heaven.

Such a spiritualized interpretation of man's long life during the kingdom is not logical, and neither is it necessary. The thought that mortal men will be able to live hundreds and hundreds of years should not come as any great shock. A look at Genesis, chapter five, will reveal that men lived an average of about nine hundred years before the time of Noah's flood.

However, critics are quick to point out that before the Flood, a vapor canopy covered the earth (the waters that were above the atmosphere, in Genesis 1:7), and they filtered out all the harmful rays from the sun that cause aging. They say that after the Flood, when that canopy collapsed and fell to the earth in the form of torrential rain, it would have been physiologically impossible for mortal humans to live so long without its filtering effect. But that is simply not so.

That vapor canopy had little or nothing to do with how long people lived on the earth. After the flood occurred, and the canopy was gone, Noah lived an additional three hundred and fifty years (Genesis 9:28). And his son Shem lived an incredible five hundred years after the flood occurred (Genesis 11:11). Ten generations later, men were still living twice as long as they do today; Abraham died at the age of one hundred seventy-five (Genesis 25:7), and his son Isaac at one hundred eighty (Genesis 35:27). People lived as long as God intended them to live, not just as long as their environment would allow them.

The Lord gradually decreased the length of men's lives down to the time of Israel's exodus from Egypt. Moses wrote Psalm 90:10, in which he reveals, "*The days of our lives are seventy years; and if by reason of strength they are eighty years, yet their boast is only labor and sorrow; for it is soon cut off, and we fly away.*" For the past thirty-five hundred years, man's natural life expectancy has remained virtually unchanged, but that is not to say it will always be so.

The same Lord who originally allowed men to live for many hundreds of years, and then shortened their years to less than a hundred, could just as easily lengthen them again in the days of His coming kingdom. What is impossible under our present living conditions becomes entirely feasible when we factor in God's good will toward His people during the coming kingdom and His infinite power to accomplish that will.

Conclusion

The Bible gives long and detailed descriptions, both in the Old and New Testaments, of a coming glorious kingdom: a kingdom of universal peace, abundance, and incredible blessedness. It describes that kingdom in simple prose, not using allegories and symbolic language, which would suggest something other than a literal interpretation. It appears indeed that the Holy Spirit intended us to understand it just as it was written.

However, there are those who insist otherwise. In spite of the vast amount of biblical information concerning the coming kingdom, they would have us to believe that it will never actually come about; that it is to be experienced only in the hearts of believers in a spiritual sense. But as they do that, they impugn the accuracy of everything else written in the Book. For if there will be no future kingdom on earth for Israel, if Christ will not actually reign from His throne in Jerusalem, and if the world will not experience a thousand years of peace and prosperity; then how can we be sure that Jesus really died for our sins, that He rose from the dead, that He ascended into heaven, and that He will return to earth again? Who's to say? Perhaps those things are to be understood only in a spiritual sense as well.

No, God does not toy with His people. If He wants us to understand a passage in a spiritual or allegorical sense, He makes it clear by the language used and the context in which it occurs. When He reveals something in plain language, clear and straightforward, that is exactly how He expects us to interpret it. The Scriptures teach about a real kingdom. Arguments against it are weak and unconvincing. There will be a kingdom, literal and earthly, just as the Bible describes it. To believe otherwise is to cast a huge shadow of doubt over everything else we read in the Good Book.

APPENDIX TWO

Will There Be Animals in Heaven?

Do animals go to heaven? Is there some provision for our faithful pets and companions to enjoy the blessings of the after life? These are not questions of great importance, and we will not spend a great deal of time answering them. But they do deserve some consideration, if only because of the fact that so many Bible-believing Christians feel in their hearts that their animal friends will indeed join them in glory.

Many Christians fuss over their pets, in life and in death. They give them funerals of sorts, bury them in pet cemeteries, and they fully expect to see them in heaven. We will examine their reasoning for believing as they do, and then we will see what the Bible really has to say on the subject.

Reasons for Believing They Will

Those who believe animals go to heaven rarely point to any Scripture references for support. To them, it is not a matter of doctrine; it is a matter of logic and common sense. Their reasoning usually goes something like this:

1. My dog was a good friend to me, faithful and true.
2. He never did anything really wrong; he never actually sinned.
3. God is a loving Father, giving His children what they want.

4. Heaven would not be perfect if my dog were not there.
5. God is able to raise my dog and give him eternal life.
6. Therefore, it stands to reason that He will do so.

If animals are not capable of committing willful acts of sin, then they cannot be found guilty or condemned. They surely don't deserve judgment or punishment, so why would they not go to heaven? They have personalities and souls; if they don't go to heaven, what then will happen to them? Heaven is a big place, and God is a big God; He is certainly able to provide the means whereby man's faithful companions will be able to enjoy the glories of the afterlife with him. Heaven would be a dull place indeed if happy animals were not bounding about its vast expanses. How could heaven be perfect if it lacked the warmth and companionship that faithful pets have always supplied their masters?

Although their arguments mostly come from their emotions and human reasoning, advocates of animals in heaven are not totally without biblical support. They are quick to point out that we know for sure there are horses in heaven, and if they are there, then there must be other animals also.

When Elijah was translated and taken into heaven, a horse-drawn chariot accompanied him. In 2 Kings 2:11, we read, "*Then it happened, as they continued on and talked, that suddenly a chariot of fire appeared with horses of fire, and separated the two of them; and Elijah went up by a whirlwind into heaven.*" If those glorified horses were in heaven, then it stands to reason that there must be other such animals up there too.

Furthermore, when Jesus comes again, He will be riding on a white horse, and a great heavenly army will accompany him on white horses as well. We read in Revelation 19:11, 14:

> *Now I saw heaven opened, and behold, a white horse. And He who sat on him was called Faithful and True, and in righteousness He judges and makes war. . . . And the armies in heaven, clothed in fine linen, white and clean followed Him on white horses.*

If that army includes all of the Lord's holy angels and/or all of His glorified saints, then the number of horses required to transport them is mind-boggling. If there are billions of horses in heaven, there simply must be room for all sorts of other animals as well.

Reasons for Doubting They Will

The primary reason for doubting that animals will be in heaven is that the Scriptures are absolutely silent about any provision made for them to be there. Christ became a man, to die for man's sin, to grant man salvation, that man might go to heaven. He made provisions for no one else. We read in Hebrews 2:14–16:

> *Inasmuch that as the children have partaken of flesh and blood, He Himself likewise shared in the same, that through death He might destroy him who had the power of death, that is, the devil, and release those who through fear of death were all their lifetime subject to bondage. For indeed He does not give aid to angels, but does give aid to the seed of Abraham.*

God made provision for the seed of Abraham (mankind), but He did not provide aid for the fallen angels. If He did not make it possible for the once-glorious angels to go to heaven, then on what authority can we assume He made provision for beasts?

Furthermore, there is a clear distinction between the three types of life on this earth. Plants have only a physical dimension, a body, through which they can relate only to the earth. In addition to bodies, animals have souls (the seat of intellect, emotions, and will), through which they can relate to others around them. But only mankind has the additional attribute called a spirit, through which he can relate to God and spiritual things. Only man can think in the abstract. Only he can contemplate such things as righteousness and sin, salvation and condemnation, and heaven and hell. If animals have no capacity to comprehend spiritual things, then on what basis can we assume they will be incorporated into God's spiritual heaven?

The Scripture makes a clear distinction between men and animals when they die. Although they are both destined to perish, and their bodies to decay, there is a definite difference in the destiny of their immaterial essence. In Ecclesiastes 3:19–21, we read:

> *For what happens to the sons of men also happens to animals; one thing befalls them: as one dies, so dies the other. Surely, they all have one breath; man has no advantage over animals, for all is vanity. All go to one place; all are from the dust, and all return to dust. Who knows the spirit of the sons of men, which goes upward, and the spirit of the animal, which goes down to the earth?*

If the spirit, or soul (often the words are used interchangeably in Scripture) of men go upward to heaven, and that of the animals goes downward to the earth, then we are hard pressed to assign them the same station in the afterlife. It is my impression that animals will simply die, and there will be no conscious existence for them beyond their earthly lives.

As for the horses that are seen in heaven, there is nothing to indicate that they are permanent residents there. They may very well be nothing more than temporary instruments used by God to accomplish a specific task. They may well be like the physical bodies God used from time to time in the Old Testament as He sought to communicate on a tangible level with His people.

Now we know that God is spirit (John 4:24) and that He has no physical body; but He took on Himself a physical form when He ate with Abraham in Genesis 18:1–8, when He wrestled with Jacob in Genesis 32:24–32, and when He walked with Shadrach, Meshach, and Abed-Nego in the fiery furnace in Daniel 3:19–25, just to name a few.

The bodies that God used were not those of human beings who had been born as babies and had grown up to adulthood. Neither is it likely that they existed as permanent human bodies, hanging around in heaven someplace, like clothes in a closet, just waiting for the Master to have need of them. It is evident that God simply willed those bodies into being in each case to accomplish His particular objective, and then they simply ceased to exist when He no longer had need of them.

I believe God used, and will use, horses in a similar way. There is no need for us to imagine billions of horses, stabled and pastured in heaven throughout eternity. God simply wills them into existence when He has need of them, and then He wills them into oblivion when He has no further need of them.

Conclusion

As we have seen, there is no clear evidence that animals exist on a permanent basis in heaven. And there is absolutely no indication that animals that lived and died on earth will somehow be transported or resurrected into heaven to provide pleasure and companionship for their former masters. To believe such a thing may appeal to our emotions and give us a sense of warmth and satisfaction, but it is totally lacking in biblical support. I'm afraid it is but another one of the heartwarming heresies that we believe simply because we want to, and because they make us feel good.

Yet, could there be animals in heaven? Yes, it is certainly possible. Heaven will be a wonderful place, filled with all sorts of things to enhance the pleasure and enjoyment of those who dwell there. In Revelation, chapters 21–22, John gives us a glimpse into its wonders, but he includes no reference to animal life. He speaks of a glorious city with gates of pearl and streets of gold (but no mention of dogs or cats dwelling there). He speaks of a river of life (but no reference to it being filled with fish). He speaks of trees that line the river, teeming with all manner of fruit (but no description of birds or squirrels perched in their branches).

If there are animals in heaven—and there may well be—it will come as a pleasant surprise to serious students of the Word. God makes no statement as to them dwelling there, and we must not insist on their presence without biblical support. But He is sovereign, and He is free to include them for our enjoyment if He so chooses. Wouldn't that be nice?

APPENDIX THREE

The Supernatural Conception of the Antichrist

In *Aaron's Rod,* the second book of my end times trilogy, I introduced the idea that the antichrist will be supernaturally conceived, that he will be born of the physical union between a young woman and the devil himself in bodily form. I did not examine that concept further in the appendices in that book, so I will attempt to do so here. I have been challenged as to whether such a thing could be true, and if the Bible could support such a bizarre occurrence. I admit it sounds more like the plot of a horror movie than it does a revelation from God's Word, but I believe we can demonstrate that there is indeed biblical justification for holding such a position.

We will first look at the evidence that supports my position, and then we will answer some of the arguments put forth by those who would disagree.

Supporting Evidence

Arguments from Reason

Admittedly, I was attracted to the idea of the antichrist being the literal offspring of the devil because it would add intrigue and suspense to the development of my novel, but that is not the reason I decided to actually pursue it. When one understands what the Bible teaches about the person and work of the devil, it makes perfect sense for him to bring forth his own son into the world if he were allowed to do so.

Satan has been an impostor and counterfeiter from the time of his fall. He has always wanted to be like God. In Isaiah 14:12–14, we read what ambitions caused him to rebel against his creator:

> *How you are fallen from heaven, O Lucifer, son of the morning! How you are cut down to the ground, you who weakened the nations! For you have said in your heart: "I will ascend into heaven, I will exalt my throne above the stars of God; I will also sit on the mount of the congregation of the farthest sides of the north; I will ascend above the heights of the clouds, I will be like the Most High."*

From the beginning, he has tried to be like God and to rise above Him. He is a counterfeit god, with a counterfeit gospel, offering a counterfeit heaven. It only stands to reason that he would want to create his own counterfeit trinity and bring into the world a counterfeit Christ.

The Bible presents the one true God as manifesting Himself in the three persons of the Father, Son, and Holy Spirit. It makes sense that the devil would try to produce his own unholy trinity, and he will do just that. In Revelation 16:13, we read, *"And I saw three unclean spirits like frogs coming out of the mouth of the dragon, out of mouth of the beast, and out of the mouth of the false prophet."* The devil, described as the dragon, will present himself, his antichrist, and his false prophet as the threefold god of the tribulation period.

When God sent forth His Son into the world, He sent Him by way of Mary's conception by the Holy Spirit, and the resulting virgin birth. God truly became a man. The beloved apostle puts it this way in John 1:14: *"And the Word became flesh and dwelt among us, and we beheld His glory, the glory as of the only begotten of the Father, full of grace and truth."*

If the devil were able to pull it off, it is reasonable to expect that he would try to counterfeit the virgin birth as well. What better way to seduce men into accepting his lies than to become flesh and dwell among them? With a man directly sired by the devil himself, complete with supernatural strength and cunning, sitting enthroned in the temple in Jerusalem, Satan would be in an excellent position to conquer the world. In 2 Thessalonians 2:3–4, Paul describes just such a man as one who definitely sees himself as divine, and one who demands that others honor his divinity as well:

Let no one deceive you by any means; for that Day will not come unless the falling away comes first, and the man of sin is revealed, the son of perdition. Who opposes and exalts himself above all that is called God or that is worshiped, so that he sits as God in the temple of God, showing himself that he is God.

The question then arises: "Is it possible for the devil or another fallen angel to impregnate a mortal woman and bring forth a viable offspring?" We will examine that question next.

Arguments from Scripture

It is my contention that in the sixth chapter of Genesis, we see an incidence of fallen angels cohabiting with mortal women. Their unholy union and the grotesque offspring produced thereby directly contributed to the complete moral collapse in those days, prompting God to decide to destroy the entire human race through the universal flood. We read in Genesis 6:1–7:

Now it came to pass, when men began to multiply on the face of the earth, and daughters were born to them, that the sons of God saw the daughters of men, that they were beautiful; and they took wives for themselves of all whom they chose. . . . There were giants on the earth in those days, and also afterward, when the sons of God came in to the daughters of men and they bore children to them. Those were the mighty men who were of old, men of renown. Then the Lord saw that the wickedness of man was great in the earth, and that every intent of the thoughts of his heart was only evil continually. And the Lord was sorry that He had made man on the earth, and He was grieved in His heart. So the Lord said, "I will destroy man whom I have created from the face of the earth, both man and beast, creeping thing and birds of the air, for I am sorry I have made them."

The union of the demonic and human races, and the powerful and incredibly wicked offspring they produced, brought about the total corruption of the human race (with the exception of Noah and his family), and the consequential destruction thereof. But was such a union really possible?

The objective reading of the passage in Genesis certainly seems to convey such a conclusion, and other passages in Scripture help to confirm it. In the Old Testament, the phrase "sons of God" refers to angels, not to men. Let us look at a couple of the clearest examples.

Job 1:6 reads, "*Now there was a day when the sons of God came to present themselves before the Lord, and Satan also came among them.*" This is a heavenly scene, and the sons of God could be none other than angels. An even more convincing passage is found in Job 38:4–7. There we read:

> *Where were you when I laid the foundations of the earth? Tell Me, if you have understanding. Who determined its measurements? Surely you know! Or who stretched the line upon it? To what were its foundations fastened? Or who laid its cornerstone, when the morning stars sang together, and all the sons of God shouted for joy?*

These verses tell us that the sons of God were present when the foundation of the earth was laid. Obviously, this was before any human being was created, so the sons of God here had to be angels who rejoiced at the work of God's creation.

Furthermore, the concept that fallen angels could cohabit with women is supported by a couple of passages in the New Testament. The first one is found in 2 Peter 2:4–6, where we read:

> *For if God did not spare the angels who sinned, but cast them down to hell and delivered them into chains of darkness, to be reserved for judgment; and did not spare the ancient world, but saved Noah, one of eight people, a preacher of righteousness, bringing in the flood on the world of the ungodly; and turning the cities of Sodom and Gomorrah into ashes, condemned them to destruction, making them an example to those who afterward would live ungodly.*

Here, in these verses, we see three separate incidents closely linked together. The sin of the angels not only brought great condemnation upon themselves, it also seems to be closely associated with the destruction of the world through Noah's flood, and with the overthrow of Sodom and Gomorrah because of their ungodliness. Sexual perversion seems to be the common denominator that brought on all three instances of judgment.

The next passage, Jude 6–7, makes that association even more evident:

> *And the angels who did not keep their proper domain, but left their own abode, He has reserved in everlasting chains under darkness for the judgment of the great day; as Sodom and Gomorrah, and the cities around them in a similar manner to these, having given themselves over to sexual*

immorality and gone after strange flesh, are set forth as an example, suffering the vengeance of eternal fire.

Here, the association is unmistakable. The sin of the fallen angels is directly compared to the sin of the people of Sodom and Gomorrah. In both cases, the perpetrators were guilty of *going after strange flesh.* In the case of the former, it was a matter of sexual perversion: fallen angels cohabiting with mortal women. In the case of latter, it was a similar moral transgression: the sin of homosexuality, men cohabiting with men.

For a serious student of the Bible who reads the Word objectively, the point is firmly established. Somehow, fallen angels of old cohabited with women, and brought forth powerful and wicked offspring. And since it was possible at that time, then there is a strong possibility that it could be done again. Satan could indeed bring forth his own son through an ungodly union with a mortal woman.

But there are some who insist that such a thing is not possible, and that there is a better interpretation to that passage in the sixth chapter of Genesis. We will consider their arguments at this time.

Answering Objections

Angels Cannot Procreate

Many scholars reject the idea that angels could have cohabited with women in the days of Noah, and they most certainly object to the notion that Satan would be able to directly sire his own supernatural son to rule the world as the antichrist during the tribulation. They direct us to a passage in the gospel of Matthew to prove their point.

In Matthew 22:23–28, certain Sadducees, a sect which denied the resurrection, tried to trap Jesus by telling Him of the hypothetical case where seven brothers, one after the death of another, had all married the same woman. After all the brothers and the woman had died, the Sadducees wanted to know whose wife she would be in the resurrection.

Jesus responded to their question in the next two verses by telling them, "*You are mistaken, not knowing the Scriptures or the power of God. For in the resurrection they neither marry nor are given in marriage, but are like angels of God in heaven.*" Obviously, she would be a wife to none of them since people in heaven would be like the angels who have no marital relationships.

The scholars insist that this passage proves that angels are sexless, and thus, incapable of procreation. The fallen angels could not have cohabited with women in Noah's day, neither could the devil sire his own evil offspring.

They make a valid point, but there is one detail they fail to consider. The Lord is careful to specify that they are *the angels in heaven* who have no experience in marital relationships. It is true, there are no holy male and female angels; and they do not have chubby little cherub offspring that fly around and shoot people in the heart on Valentine's Day to make them fall in love. Godly angels are always depicted as male, and they are apparently totally celibate. But that tells us nothing about wicked and perverted fallen angels.

It is entirely possible that the demonic beings in Noah's day were able to somehow manifest themselves in human form and cohabit with women.

Pagan myths are almost always the distorted perversions of ancient biblical truths passed down from generation to generation. Virtually every culture in the world has a tradition of a massive flood that destroyed the world of men. Those often-bizarre traditions had their roots in the true biblical account of Noah's flood. In like manner, the vast number of pagan legends of powerful demigods (half god and half man) almost surely had their origin in the biblical account of the supernatural offspring of fallen angels and mortal women in the sixth chapter of Genesis.

The Sons of God Were Men

Those who reject the conclusion that the sons of God were fallen angels are quick to point out that there is another interpretation for the Genesis account, which they feel is much more reliable. They contend that the *sons of God* in Genesis 6:2 were the offspring of the godly descendents of Seth who lived in the area of the Garden of Eden in the Middle East, while the *daughters of men* were descendents of the evil Cain who established his civilization to the east in the distant land of Nod (Genesis 4:16).

Those scholars maintain that the two civilizations remained separate for about two thousand years, but eventually, they discovered each other, and the intermarrying between them corrupted Seth's godly line and brought about God's judgment on the entire human race.

That is an interesting theory, and I admit it is a much more palatable explanation than that of demons cohabiting with women, but does it really square with Scripture? Does the objective reading of the passage naturally lead us to that conclusion? The answer is no; it does not. Let us look at Genesis 6:1–2 again:

> *Now it came to pass, when men began to multiply on the face of the earth, and daughters were born to them, that the sons of God saw the daughters of men, that they were beautiful; and they took wives for themselves of all whom they chose.*

There is nothing in the context that suggests that the two groups represented two different human civilizations, and it is a great stretch of the imagination to believe that they could have remained isolated from each other for so many hundreds of years, especially since Nod was located nearby *on the east of Eden* (Genesis 4:16). To maintain such a thing is nothing more than a dodge to escape the almost unthinkable conclusion, which is actually demanded by the plain reading of the text.

An objective reading of the passage would never lead one to believe that the godly male descendents of Seth went out on a scouting expedition one day, and discovered the heretofore-unknown beautiful and wicked female descendents of Cain, and that they each took one of them to be his wife.

The obvious interpretation is that mankind in general began to multiply on the earth, and that multitudes of female offspring were born to them. The fallen angels, in their perverted state, lusted after the women and were somehow able to cohabit with them. The hypothetical civilizations of Seth and Cain never enter the picture.

Besides that, the offspring produced from the unholy union cannot be explained by the simple intermarrying of two human civilizations. The children born were not only called giants because of their physical stature, they were also called mighty men, men of renown, because of their superior intellects and leadership abilities. And perhaps most convincing of all is their incredible wickedness. The very thoughts and intents of their hearts were only evil continually. That is perfectly understandable if they were the offspring of wicked demons, but it doesn't make any sense if their fathers were merely the descendents of the godly line of Seth.

The Antichrist Cannot be Jewish

I have maintained that the antichrist will not only be the spawn of the devil himself, but that he will also be the son of a Jewish mother. I have been challenged on that point, and since the two questions are related, I will attempt to answer it here.

Those who challenge my assumption, point out that there is no place in the Bible which indicates that the antichrist will be Jewish. In fact, they say the Scripture suggests just the opposite. In Revelation 13:1, the first beast seen by the apostle John is rising out of the sea, which could refer to the sea of the Gentiles. That interpretation becomes even more intriguing in light of the fact that in verse eleven, a second beast is seen coming out of the earth, which could very well refer to the land of Israel. A careful reading of the context makes it clear that the first beast is the antichrist, and that the second one is his false prophet. Therefore, the common assumption is that the antichrist will be a Gentile, rising out of the pagan world, and that he will be allied with the Jewish false prophet.

That interpretation is certainly possible, but it is by no means proven. The antichrist will most surely arise out of the Gentile nations, but that doesn't necessitate that he himself be of Gentile extraction. My reasons for believing otherwise are logical, rather than biblical, but I believe they are worthy of consideration.

In the first place, as I mentioned above, the devil is a counterfeiter. He always tries to produce that which is as close to the original as possible, only bearing his mark rather than God's. For that reason, it is perfectly logical to expect that his antichrist will not only be supernaturally conceived, as was Christ; but that he will also be born of a Jewish woman, as was our Savior.

The other reason I believe the antichrist will be Jewish is due to the very fact that he will be a counterfeit of the true Jewish Messiah. If the devil expects his antichrist to deceive the Jewish people, *"So that he sits as God in the temple of God, showing himself that he is God"* (2 Thessalonians 2:4), then his imitation messiah must be Jewish as well. There is no conceivable way the Jewish people would accept a Christian or pagan Gentile as their Messiah, much less an Arab dictator from the hated Muslim world, as some scholars have suggested.

Conclusion

The Scripture does not conclusively prove either that the antichrist will be the supernaturally conceived child of the devil or that he will be born of a Jewish mother. Other scholars strongly reject both concepts, especially the notion that Satan could take human form and cohabit with a mortal woman to produce such a child. Admittedly, even I find such a concept absurd, and would certainly reject it if there were a strong biblical reason to do so. But there is not. On the contrary, the Scripture strongly suggests that the man of sin will indeed be the spawn of the devil himself.

The Bible reveals that there were many occasions where spiritual beings took upon themselves fleshly bodies. Holy angels did it, and even God Himself walked, talked, ate, and wrestled with men in human form. Why then must we insist that it be impossible for evil spirits to do the same thing? The plain reading of the text in Genesis, chapter six, indicates that is exactly what happened with fallen angels back in Noah's day when they took human women to themselves. Besides that, two New Testament passages seem to confirm it as well. Although God has not allowed demons to duplicate those perverted acts since that time, it seems clear that He did back then.

Besides that, the devil is the master counterfeiter. If he could, he most certainly would bring forth his own son, born of a Jewish maiden, to synthesize what the heavenly Father had done in the virgin birth of Jesus Christ. In what better way could he countermand God's actions and conquer the world for himself than to introduce the world to his own son, possessing his father's power and wicked cunning?

As difficult as it is to accept, it does appear that God allowed the fallen angels to cohabit with women before the Flood, and that, to accomplish His own eternal plan, He will allow the devil to do the same thing with a Jewish virgin in the end times. Arguments to the contrary are weak and seem to be contrived out of a desperate attempt to avoid accepting what is distasteful and impossible in our way of thinking.

As always, we must accept what the Bible reveals God to be actually saying and doing, and not sit in judgment as to whether we believe He can legitimately say or do such a thing. Like it or not, it seems that the Lord will allow the devil to give the world his best shot (including a supernaturally conceived son of his own) only to destroy both him and his evil works in the end. Remember, God's thoughts are not our thoughts, and His ways, not our ways (Isaiah 55:8).

APPENDIX FOUR

The Resurrections of the Bible

The Bible clearly teaches that the dead will be raised back to life again. There are accounts in both testaments of people who had died who were restored to physical life. For example, Elisha raised the Shunammite woman's son back to life after he had been dead for more than a day (2 Kings 4:32–37), and Jesus restored His friend Lazarus to life after he had been dead for four days (John 11:38–44). As amazing as these accounts are, the people who were restored to life were raised only to die again. The resurrection we want to discuss here is the final resurrection of which the Bible speaks: the glorious resurrection into bodies that will never die again.

In the Old Testament, the prophet Daniel made it clear that such a resurrection will occur for all people when he said, *"And many of those who sleep in the dust of the earth shall awake, some to everlasting life, some to shame and everlasting contempt"* (Daniel 12:2). The apostle Paul confirmed that truth before the Roman governor Felix in Acts 24:15 when he said, *"I have hope in God, which they themselves also accept, that there will be a resurrection of the dead, both of the just and the unjust."*

For one who believes the Bible, there is no question as to *whether* there will be a resurrection; the question he faces has to do with *when* it will occur. It is clear that all the dead will not be raised at the same time. We will examine the various resurrections revealed in the Scriptures, and although it seems out of logical order, we will consider first the resurrection of the unjust, and then that of the just.

The Resurrection of the Unjust

The reason we will examine the resurrection of the unjust first is because it is the simplest and easiest to understand. The resurrection of the saints gets much more complicated and more difficult to comprehend. We will deal with the simple first, and leave the complex for later.

The Bible does not speak of any wicked person being raised from the dead prior to the very end of the millennium, just before the destruction of the existing heavens and the earth and the introduction of those that are new. After the devil stages his final rebellion and is defeated and thrown into the lake of fire, the wicked dead will be raised and judged. John puts it this way in Revelation 20:11–15:

> *Then I saw a great white throne and Him who sat on it, from whose face the earth and the heaven fled away. And there was found no place for them. And I saw the dead, small and great, standing before God, and books were opened. And another book was opened, which is the Book of Life. And the dead were judged according to their works, by the things which were written in the books. The sea gave up the dead who were in it, and Death and Hades delivered up the dead who were in them. And they were judged, each one according to his works. Then Death and Hades were cast into the lake of fire. This is the second death. And anyone not found written in the Book of Life was cast into the lake of fire.*

Virtually every Bible scholar on the planet agrees that the wicked dead will all be raised and judged at the same time. However, there is no such agreement concerning the resurrection of the righteous. They all agree there will be at least one, but that's where the agreement ends. Many contend that there will be two, some say three, and a few hold out for four. I tend to agree with the last group; I can see indications of four separate resurrections of God's saints. Let us take a look at each of them.

The Resurrection of the Just

The Resurrection of the Old Testament Saints

The first general resurrection of the righteous dead may have already occurred. There is a passage in Matthew 27:50–53 that causes me to think that the Old Testament saints were raised to life at the time of their Messiah's resurrection. The apostle puts it this way:

> *And Jesus cried out again with a loud voice, and yielded up His spirit. Then, behold, the veil of the temple was torn in two from top to bottom; and the earth quaked, and the rocks were split, and the graves were opened; and many bodies of the saints who had fallen asleep were raised; and coming out the graves after His resurrection, they went into the holy city and appeared to many.*

Many contend that this resurrection was a relatively small matter; a few graves were opened and a few saints were resuscitated (as Lazarus was) and regained their mortal lives for a time, only to die again later. Yet, such an interpretation hardly fits the context.

Those saints were raised right after Christ's resurrection, and in confirmation of it. Our Lord's resurrection was glorious and permanent; why would that of those who accompanied Him be any different? The apostle Paul tells us in 1 Corinthians 15:20, "*But now Christ is risen from the dead, and has become the firstfruits of those who have fallen asleep.*" If the firstfruits experienced a certain type of resurrection, then it stands to reason the rest of the crop that followed after Him would experience the same.

Besides, what occurred in Jerusalem was no minor incident. There was a massive earthquake that ripped the veil in the temple in two, split huge boulders, and doubtlessly caused a great deal of structural damage. Along with all that, God opened all the graves. Why would He go to such lengths if only a few saints were going to be resuscitated? It appears more logical that God was setting the stage for a general resurrection.

However, those who disagree are quick to point out that only *many* of those who had fallen asleep were raised, not *all* of them. They contend that if all the Old Testament saints were raised at that time, then Matthew would certainly have recorded it as *all*. They present an interesting argument, but they have by no means proved their point.

In Scripture, words don't always mean what they first appear to say. On the one hand, the word *all* doesn't always mean *all* in the absolute sense. For example, in Luke 2:1, we read, "*And it came to pass in those days that a decree went out from Caesar Augustus that all the world should be registered.*" Obviously, *all the world* referred only to that portion of the world under the domination of Rome, not all the inhabited earth.

On the other hand, *many* can actually be all-inclusive in certain contexts. There is an interesting passage in Romans 5:18–19 where *all* and *many* are actually used interchangeably. It reads:

Therefore, as through one man's offense judgment came to all men, resulting in condemnation, even so through one Man's righteous act the free gift came to all men, resulting in justification of life. For as by one man's disobedience many were made sinners, so also by one Man's obedience many will be made righteous.

Obviously, the apostle is referring to the same groups of people in both verses, yet he refers to them as *all* in verse eighteen, and only as *many* in the following verse. It is clear that the *many* who were made sinners through Adam's transgression in verse nineteen really includes *all* of mankind. In like fashion, Matthew may well be referring to *all* the Old Testament saints when he says that *many* of the saints who had fallen asleep were raised.

Besides, it doesn't make any sense for God not to raise them at that time. Their bodies had been in the grave for hundreds of years already; why would the Lord leave them there during the next two thousand years of the church age? Their long-awaited Messiah was risen and soon to ascend into glory; why would He not raise His Old Testament saints and take them with Him to spend the following two millennia in heaven with Him in their glorified bodies?

The Resurrection of the Church Age Saints

For those who believe in the rapture of the church, a second resurrection of the righteous is required. Whether scholars see the rapture as taking place before the tribulation begins, at its mid-point, or near the end, they all agree that the saints who have died since Pentecost will be raised at the end of the church age. Most of the scholars concur that 1 Thessalonians 4:14–17 describes the rapture of the church. It reads:

For if we believe that Jesus died and rose again, even so God will bring with Him those who sleep in Jesus. For this we say to you by the word of the Lord, that we who are alive and remain until the coming of the Lord will by no means precede those who are asleep. For the Lord Himself will descend from heaven with a shout, with the voice of an archangel, and with the trumpet of God. And the dead in Christ will rise first. Then we who are alive and remain shall be caught up together with them in the clouds to meet the Lord in the air. And thus we shall always be with the Lord.

I agree with the many scholars who see the rapture as taking place prior to the beginning of the tribulation period. There are many reasons for holding this pre-trib rapture position, and one of them is pointed out in the passage above. Only those saints who *sleep in Jesus* or are *dead in Christ* are raised. As we have seen, the Old Testament saints were raised before the church age began; and, as we shall see, those believers who will die during the tribulation will have their own resurrection. Only those who die during the church age will be raised at the time of the rapture.

The Resurrection of the Tribulation Saints

After the tribulation is over and Christ returns to the earth, yet another resurrection of the saints will occur. Revelation 20:1–3 tells us that at that time, the devil will be bound and cast into the bottomless pit for a thousand years. But before the thousand-year kingdom of Christ begins, John tells of a resurrection of the believers who died during the preceding tribulation period. In verse four, he says:

> *And I saw thrones, and they sat on them, and judgment was committed to them. Then I saw the souls of those who had been beheaded for their witness to Jesus and for the word of God, who had not worshiped the beast or his image, and had not received his mark on their foreheads or on their hands. And they lived and reigned with Christ for a thousand years.*

This especially blessed group does not include any Old Testament saints, or any believers from the church age; it is reserved for those who will faithfully serve the Lord during the reign of the devil's antichrist, and who will be put to death by him because of their witness for Christ and their commitment to the Word of God. They will be the ones raised at the third resurrection of the just.

The Resurrection of the Millennial Saints

Although no resurrection of believers at the end of the millennium is mentioned in Scripture, it stands to reason there will be one. As we saw at the beginning of this appendix, the wicked will be raised after the millennium is over and they will be judged at the great white throne (Revelation 20:11–15). Since the righteous have no part in that resurrection, it is reasonable to assume they will have one of their own. In fact, something like the rapture will have to take place where the dead will be raised and the living translated.

As we saw clearly in the first appendix, during the millennium, the world will be filled with blessed people living in mortal bodies. Although they will live long and healthy lives in a near-perfect environment, sin will still exist, and, as a consequence of it, so will death (Isaiah 65:20). After a thousand years, as a result of accidents and isolated acts of violence, it stands to reason that many believers will have died and their bodies will rest in their graves. They will need to be raised before the eternal state begins.

Not only that, all the living saints will need to be transformed before they can enter into heaven. After the Great White Throne Judgment, in Revelation 21:1, John shares with us, "*Now I saw a new heaven and a new earth, for the first heaven and the first earth had passed away. Also there was no more sea.*" No mortal being could possibly survive the passing away of which John speaks. In his second epistle, the apostle Peter tells us of the coming of that day. In 2 Peter 3:10, he says:

> *But the day of the Lord will come as a thief in the night, in which the heavens will pass away with a great noise, and the elements will melt with fervent heat; both the earth and the works that are in it will be burned up.*

Therefore, at the end of the millennium, the mortal saints will need to be granted their glorified bodies, and the bodies of the righteous dead will have to be resurrected. Otherwise, they would be consumed in the destruction of the heavens and the earth, and they would not be allowed to enter into the glorious heaven God will have prepared for them. Even though the Scripture does not give us this information, such a conclusion is logically inescapable.

Conclusion

This appendix does not cover material of vital importance, and much of it cannot be proved from verses in the Bible. The Scripture clearly does teach us that there will be a resurrection of both the just and the unjust, but we will have to wait until we get to heaven to know exactly how those resurrections will play out. However, having examined the biblical information available, and applied sound reason, I'm convinced we have established solid evidence to form some conclusions.

There will be a single resurrection of the wicked at the end of the millennium, leading to the judgment and condemnation of all unbelievers from all the previous ages. But with the righteous, it appears clear that God will raise them at the end of each age before the next one begins: the Old Testament saints before the church age begins, the Christian believers before the start of the tribulation, the tribulation saints before the beginning of the millennium, and the millennial believers before the creation of the new heavens and earth.

The reason for the difference in the numbers of the resurrections may well rest in the nature of God Himself. God takes no delight in the judgment and destruction of the wicked. Therefore, He waits until the very end and takes care of the necessary, but unpleasant, business all at the same time. But with the righteous, it is not so; God delights in blessing and promoting His own, and doesn't want to wait clear to the end of the ages to do it. Therefore, just as soon as one age is over, He raises His saints who have died in it and takes them to Himself so they can enjoy the fullness of His heaven, and He can enjoy their glorified presence throughout the ages to come.

APPENDIX FIVE

Instantaneous World Travel

In my novels, I have members of God's chosen 144,000 being transported instantly around the world, and many readers have questioned whether or not such a phenomenon has any biblical support, or did I just invent it to facilitate the story I wanted to tell.

I admit I chose that means of transportation to avoid what I considered the hopeless inconsistencies I saw in other end times novels. I grew tired of reading of God's saints, hotly pursued by the antichrist's henchmen, taking off in planes and then flying unmolested to other parts of the world. The antichrist will have control of most of the world at that time, and he certainly will have radar capabilities and plenty of pursuit fighters. It would be a simple thing for him to locate the fleeing faithful and send up an interceptor and shoot them out of the sky, but it never happens. Such absurdities drive me nuts.

Besides that, I didn't have a few saints to move about the globe; I had tens of thousands. There's no way I could book 144,000 young Jewish men on commercial flights to Tel Aviv without attracting more than a little attention. And I felt I had to transport them. Of necessity, the 144,000 must minister for the Lord among His people around the world during the tribulation, but they also must all be present in Jerusalem at the end of it, at the time of His coming. That presented a logistics problem that proved to be insurmountable. Hence, I found the idea of instantaneous world travel, not only to be fascinating, but one of utmost necessity. But that still leaves the question, "Does the Bible support such a concept, or have I totally jumped off the cliff of literary license?"

I am happy to report that, not only does the concept allow me to solve my logistic problem; it has solid support in the Scriptures as well. We will look at instantaneous transportation from three different perspectives: the transportation of heavenly beings, the transportation of the risen Christ, and the transportation of mortal men.

The Transportation of Heavenly Beings

It is obvious that God and His angels don't have to fly wherever they want to go. They're just there . . . and when they're through with their business . . . they're gone.

The being which King Nebuchadnezzar said looked like the Son of God instantly appeared with Shadrach, Meshach, and Abed-Nego in the midst of the fiery furnace, and He instantly vanished before they were taken from it (Daniel 3:25). The sky over Bethlehem was instantly filled with a multitude of angels the night of Jesus' birth, and they departed just as suddenly (Luke 2:13–15). And an angel appeared instantly inside a secure prison where Peter was being held captive, and after he had safely deposited the apostle outside, he vanished instantly from his presence (Acts 12:7–10).

The Transportation of the Risen Christ

After Jesus was raised from the dead, He had a tangible, physical body, but it had some amazing properties. Among those properties was the ability He had to appear and to disappear instantly. And it wasn't just a matter of the disciples' ability or inability to see Him; He actually came and went in an instant of time.

After His resurrection, Jesus walked with two of His disciples on the road to Emmaus, but they did not recognize Him. He consented to dine with them when they had reached their destination, and in the course of the meal, he revealed who He was to them, and then vanished instantly from their sight (Luke 24:30–31).

Later that evening, Jesus appeared to his eleven disciples in Jerusalem. The Scriptures are clear that the doors were securely shut and locked, but the Lord appeared suddenly in their midst (John 20:19). He did not appear in a spiritual form; He invited them to touch His hands and feet, and then He asked them for food and consumed it in their presence (Luke 24:39–43).

The Transportation of Mortal Men

It does not surprise us that heavenly beings, and even the risen Christ, are able to move from one place to another instantly, but the question remains, "Is that also possible for mortal human beings?" I believe the answer to that question is yes, they can.

In the Old Testament, the prophet Ezekiel was taken from his home in Babylon and transported by the Lord to the temple in Jerusalem to see how the Jews had defiled it. He puts it this way in Ezekiel 8:2–3:

> *Then I looked, and there was a likeness, like the appearance of fire—from the appearance of His waist and downward, fire; and from His waist and upward, like the appearance of brightness, like the color of amber. He stretched out the form of a hand, and took me by a lock of my hair; and the Spirit lifted me up between earth and heaven, and brought me in visions of God to Jerusalem, to the door of the north gate of the inner court, where the seat of the image of jealousy was, which provokes to jealousy.*

Some are quick to point out that the word *visions* is used to describe Ezekiel's journey. They say the prophet never actually made the trip to Jerusalem at all; he just saw what God wanted him to see in a vision while he remained physically at home in Babylon. That interpretation is a possibility, but by no means a necessity. The visions might well refer to the things the Lord showed him as He physically took him on a tour of the temple.

The verse clearly states that he was caught up by the hair of his head and transported to Jerusalem. Then, in the verses that follow, Ezekiel is seen busily walking through the temple area, going into separate rooms, and even digging into a wall to discover a secret door that led to hidden abominations (verse eight). These activities are all very physical in nature, and are consistent with things he might have seen and done had he actually been physically transported to the temple.

In the New Testament, the apostle Paul tells of a man (probably himself) who was caught up into heaven itself. He doesn't insist that it was a physical transportation, but he doesn't rule it out either. In 2 Corinthians 12:2, he says, *"I know a man in Christ who fourteen years ago—whether in the body I do not know, or whether out of the body I do not know, God knows—such a one was caught up to the third heaven.* As far as Paul was concerned, that man may very well have made that trip to heaven in the flesh.

So far, the Bible references have only been suggestive, and by no means conclusive, but the next one should remove all doubt for the honest student of the Scriptures. It is found in Acts, chapter eight, where Philip the evangelist had just led the Ethiopian eunuch to faith in Christ and had baptized him in water. In verses 39–40, we read:

> *Now when they came up out of the water, the Spirit of the Lord caught Philip away, so that the eunuch saw him no more; and he went on his way rejoicing. But Philip was found at Azotus. And passing through, he preached in all the cities till he came to Caesarea.*

According to Acts 8:26, Philip was sent to Gaza to join up with the Ethiopian man, and then he rode south with him in his chariot, in the direction of Ethiopia, as he reasoned with him from the Scriptures. By the time they came to the water where the baptism occurred, they could have been a good number of miles south of the city. But the Spirit caught Philip away instantly and placed him in Azotus, which is a city some twenty miles north of Gaza.

What happened to Philip was a clear example of instantaneous travel, and it covered a considerable distance. The evangelist was an ordinary man who was in his mortal body, yet he was whisked away by the Spirit and deposited instantly to another location.

Conclusion

Although the Bible clearly reveals that heavenly beings and the risen Christ moved from place to place instantaneously, the doctrine of instant world travel for mortals is by no means an exact science. It didn't happen often to finite men in the Scriptures, and I know of no recorded incidence of it having taken place among them elsewhere. Yet, it has not been disproved either, and should not be ruled out as a possibility.

Something supernatural definitely happened to Ezekiel and Paul, and something equally supernatural (and solidly physical) happened to Philip. There is no reason God could not choose to do the same thing on a much broader scale with His 144,000 during the tribulation. They will definitely need to travel extensively during that time, and with the world's airways controlled by the antichrist, what better way to move His witnesses about than for God to simply transport them instantly?

Admittedly, I chose to incorporate the unique means of transportation into my novels because of its scintillating effect, and to avoid trying to con my readers into accepting the absurdity of believing so many could travel the world by any other means. But the concept has definite biblical support, and I firmly believe that such a thing falls squarely within the realm of divine possibility. As for me, it will have to do until someone smarter than I am comes up with a better solution.

APPENDIX SIX

The Mysterious Numbers of Daniel Twelve

There are no more mysterious numbers anywhere in the Bible than those which appear at the end of the twelfth chapter of Daniel. The entire chapter is talking about the end times, so the interpretation must be a prophetic one, but just what is that interpretation? Let us look at those last several verses in the chapter where the angel tells the prophet what will come to pass in the last days. Daniel 12:9–13 reads:

> *And he said, "Go your way, Daniel, for the words are closed up and sealed till the time of the end. Many shall be purified, made white, and refined, but the wicked shall do wickedly; and none of the wicked shall understand, but the wise shall understand. And from the time that the daily sacrifice is taken away, and the abomination of desolation is set up, there shall be one thousand two hundred and ninety days. Blessed is he who waits, and comes to the one thousand three hundred and thirty-five days. But you, go your way till the end; for you shall rest, and will arise to your inheritance at the end of the days."*

Daniel is told that God has established exactly 1290 days following the cessation of the daily sacrifice and the setting up of the abomination of desolation, but He doesn't tell us what those numbers actually signify. Then He adds that those who wait until the end of 1335 days will be especially blessed, but again, He doesn't tell us how and why. Those ambiguities have left the door wide open for endless speculation. We will examine three different solutions to the problem that have been submitted by various groups of scholars, then we will look at why I have chosen to ascribe to them the special significance that appeals to me.

The Year-for-a-Day Theory

For generations, scholars have been fascinated with the 1290 and 1335 days of Daniel twelve. Some of them have decided that those days are not to be understood as literal twenty-four hour periods at all, but rather, they are to be understood as *prophetic days*. To them, prophetic days are actually years, so the periods of time should be understood as 1290 and 1335 years respectively.

To justify the year-for-a-day approach, those scholars insist that the Bible supports such a concept. They point out that in Daniel 9:24–27, the prophet foretells a period of seventy weeks before the coming of Israel's Messiah. There is disagreement among Bible scholars as to when the period begins and ends, but virtually everyone agrees that the weeks Daniel has in mind are periods of seven years, not seven days. Hence, the total period is to be understood as 490 years instead of 490 days.

Concluding that since the Bible teaches that a week of seven days can be understood as a week of seven years in Daniel nine, those scholars have made what they consider a logical step in biblical interpretation and have assumed that the number of days in Daniel twelve should be understood as periods of years as well. Based upon that assumption, they have gone about trying to determine when the abomination of desolation took place, and then, after counting forward the proper number of years, they have attempted to set dates for the coming of the Lord and the end of the age.

The Jehovah's Witnesses scholars, along with many others, have thus repeatedly tried to solve that prophetic puzzle, but they have always been frustrated in their efforts to accurately set those dates. The problem has not been in their ability to set starting dates and to count correctly; their problem has been a much more fundamental one.

There is absolutely no justification for arbitrarily deciding that a *year* can be substituted for a *day* in prophetic passages. As a matter of fact, as we learned in the first appendix, every time the Bible introduces days with numerical coefficients, the days are to be understood in a literal sense. And the passage in Daniel nine does not prove otherwise.

It is true that the word *week* in the ninth chapter of Daniel speaks of a period of seven years rather than one of seven days, but there is biblical support for drawing that conclusion. The word *week* only means *seven*, not *seven days*. Whether the seven refers to days, weeks, months, or years depends on the context. There is an excellent example of how the word *week* can be understood as seven years instead of seven days in Genesis, chapter twenty-nine.

Jacob agreed to work for Laban for a period of seven years in order to earn the right to marry his younger daughter Rachel. But later, when he learned that her father Laban had deceived him and given him his older daughter Leah instead, he agreed to work an additional *week* for the hand of Rachel too. Genesis 29:18,26–28 puts it this way:

> *Now Jacob loved Rachel; so he said, "I will serve you seven years for Rachel your younger daughter . . ."*
>
> *And Laban said, "It must not be done so in our country, to give the younger before the firstborn. Fulfill her week, and we will give you this one also for the service which you will serve with me still another seven years."*
>
> *Then Jacob did so and fulfilled her week. So he gave him his daughter Rachel as wife also.*

Based upon that evidence, we can rightly understand the seventy weeks in Daniel nine as seventy periods of seven years, or 490 years total. But no such justification exists for assuming a specific number of days in Scripture can be interpreted as the corresponding number of years instead. Periods of days are always to be understood as literal, twenty-four hour days in Scripture. There are no exceptions.

In Exodus 20:11, the Bible tells us that God created the heavens and the earth in six days, not six long geologic ages. In Revelation 12:6, it tells us that God will protect His people from the wrath of the devil in the wilderness for 1260 days, not a period of 1260 months, or years, or any other unit measuring time.

If those 1260 days, which define the length of the tribulation, are to be understood literally, then how can anyone possibly understand the 1290 and 1335 days of Daniel twelve as being any different?

No, it is not only numerically frustrating trying to establish dates in prophecy by ascribing year-for-a-day values to the numbers in Daniel twelve, there is absolutely no biblical justification for attempting to do such a thing in the first place. The futile quest must be abandoned in light of the principles of good biblical interpretation.

The Spiritual Allegory Theory

Our friends, the amillennialists, have no problem with the mysterious numbers in Daniel twelve. They simply dismiss them as having no literal significance at all. To them, virtually everything in biblical prophecy is to be understood from a spiritual, or allegorical, standpoint. They see no actual significance to the 1260 days of the tribulation, or the 1000 years of the millennium, so why should they bother themselves with the 1290 and 1335 days in an obscure passage in Daniel?

That allegorical approach may get them off the hook in trying to explain difficult passages of Scripture, but it doesn't really solve the issue. As I said above, numbers in Scripture are important, and they are to be understood literally. Just because we cannot always determine their literal significance, it doesn't mean that significance does not exist.

As I concluded in the first appendix, the allegorical approach to biblical interpretation must be abandoned. Otherwise, nothing in Scripture can be understood literally, and all of biblical revelation loses specific relevance.

The Literal, But Uncertain Theories

Many scholars agree that the 1290 and 1335 days in Daniel twelve are to be understood literally, and that they must occur in conjunction with the 1260 days of the great tribulation, but they really don't have a clue as to their true significance. In his commentary on the book of Daniel, Lehman Strauss admits that scholars are at a loss to pin down the meaning of those mysterious numbers. He says:

> Verses 11 and 12 are difficult to interpret. We confess that at this writing we are in search of more truth. Why the difference in time between 1,290 days and 1,335 days, we are not told, nor have we found light upon these two time periods from other Scriptures.
>
> DeHaan believes they are days of grace which the Lord will extend to the nations between the end of the tribulation and His personal appearing to judge the nations.
>
> Ironside suggests that the extra days will be devoted to purging out from the kingdom all things that offend and are evil.

> Talbot says it is the time when the sanctuary is cleansed and the earth purified.
>
> Tregelles believes the extra time will be used to get all the Jews into the land.[146]

Struass' candor is refreshing. He admits that neither he, nor any of his colleagues, knows how to interpret those perplexing numbers in Daniel twelve. One's guess is as good as the other's, and quite frankly, I find none of them very satisfying. I applaud them for accepting the literal value of the numbers as they appear in Scripture, and for assigning them to the tribulation/millennium context, but they still leave the question begging to be answered.

Let me explain why I have chosen in this novel to explain the significance of Daniel's mysterious numbers in the way that I have.

Conclusion

In the first place, let me refer you to my first novel in this trilogy, *A Snowball's Chance,* and to the first appendix, *The Battle of Gog and Magog.* In that appendix, I go to considerable lengths to demonstrate that the famous battle prophesied in Ezekiel, chapters 38–39, will occur after the tribulation is over and before the millennium actually begins. We will not go over all that material again at this time because we're at the end of our discussion, and besides, it would be unnecessarily redundant to do so.

If one accepts my position as to the time of the Battle of Gog and Magog, then the 1290 and 1335 days of Daniel twelve fit in perfectly. Christ returns at the end of the tribulation, 1260 days after the antichrist sets himself up as God in the temple (the abomination of desolation). As I suggest in this novel, during the next thirty days, regathered and redeemed Israel celebrates Rosh Hashanah and Yom Kippur with their Messiah in Jerusalem, and then observes the Feast of Tabernacles with Him, precisely at the end of the 1290 days.

At that time, the nations are told what they must do in preparation for the coming kingdom and are given certain ultimatums. Over the following forty-five days, the righteous flourish as they prepare for the

[146] Lehman Strauss, *The Prophecies of Daniel*, (Neptune, New Jersey: Loizeaux Brothers, 1969), 368.

millennium, but the wicked who have survived the tribulation prepare to follow the Russian Gog as he intends to invade peaceful Israel to destroy and take plunder.

The massive invasion takes place and the wicked are utterly destroyed. The dead bodies are removed, the weapons are gathered for burning, all evidence of man's rebellion against God is removed, and the glorious kingdom begins, exactly at the end of the1335 days. Blessed are all those who have remained faithful till that time and are allowed to enter into the glories God has prepared for His people.

Have I proved my point? Absolutely not! My theories are based on solid biblical investigation, but they contain a good deal of supposition, as does everyone else's. I am certainly subject to human error, and have doubtlessly missed the mark in several places, but I'm convinced my basic understanding of predictive prophecy squares better with biblical revelation than the other theories floating around out there.

But don't take my word for it. Paul tells us in 1 Thessalonians 5:21, "*Test all things; hold fast what is good.*" I encourage you to get out your Bible and my books, and read all fifteen appendices again in light of the Word of God, and make up your own mind. And may our Lord grant you wisdom and understanding as you seek to gain the knowledge of His truth.

To order additional copies of

GOG'S REVENGE

Have your credit card ready and call:

1-877-421-READ (7323)

or please visit our web site at
www.pleasantword.com

Also available at:
www.amazon.com
and
www.barnesandnoble.com

Printed in the United States
202261BV00004B/7/A

9 781414 101507